Resorting to Fraud

Also by Gail Hulnick

The Lion's Share of the Air Time: A Novel

A Bird in the Sand

Resorting to Murder

Resorting to Larceny

Resorting to Fraud

Gail Hulnick

WINDWORD GROUP
PUBLISHING & MEDIA

The WindWord Group Publishing & Media
100 Bull Street, Suite 200
Savannah, Georgia, USA 31401

www.windwordgroup.com

ISBN: 978-1-947527-02-7

Books may also be purchased or the author contacted by emailing the publisher at admin@windwordgroup.com

Cover design by David Stone

Printed in the United States of America

TO DAVID

Always sharing the love and the music

CHAPTER ONE

2019

Santa Cappella, California

The wake-up call came at two that afternoon and it was a shock. Rickey was deep in a dream about a math exam he'd flunked in middle school when the phone beside the bed began buzzing with a frantic sound that made him want to punch it. Sort of the way he felt about the math teacher, Mr. Field, back in eighth grade in 1967.

Not that Rickey was a violent man by nature. Oh no, he was a lover, not a fighter, and he'd proven that on almost every continent of the world. Missed out on Antarctica (although if he were asked for an opinion, he would have suggested it never should have been called a continent. Too weird and under-populated. And—it prevented you from saying "on every continent of the world".)

Maybe it wasn't even called a continent anymore? You have to be cautious. After all, they'd gone and changed Pluto, hadn't they? Back when he was going through the minimal amount of schooling he'd had, there were nine

7

planets. It was different now, thanks to some astronomer or other. Anyway, good thing he didn't have grandchildren to remind him that his formal education was long since outdated.

He rolled over, ignoring the twinge in his left knee. It had nothing to do with his chronological age and everything to do with that brute of a Sinbad he'd ridden at Henry's ranch in Montana last week. Well, maybe not, but it made a better story if his occasional limp or wince had to do with extreme sports rather than extreme age.

Hah! Sixty-five was hardly extreme and he wouldn't win any attention for being able to ride a horse over jumps at his age. Nor for going on stage and doing a half hour rock 'n' roll show, either. Two hours, maybe . . . or four hours. But if he tried that, they'd probably have to wheel him offstage in a chair or a full body cast.

Especially since he hadn't performed in a while. He had been rehearsing, yeah, but that wasn't the same. Good thing he wasn't carrying any extra weight and his fingers still flew over the frets like they'd done since high school.

Rickey squinted at the afternoon light peeking through the gap in the blackout curtains. He rubbed his grizzled chin, skin that would be clean-shaven, sweet-smelling and anointed with the best spa products money could buy, by the time he'd done all his pre-show prep and was ready for his close-up. The phone kept on buzzing and finally he picked up the sucker.

"What?"

"Mr. Rubble?" The voice was professional but intimidated.

"What?" Oh yeah, now he remembered. They were doing the cartoon names thing this time. He was Barney and Booker was Pebbles.

"Mr. Rubble, you asked for a wake-up call at two and this is it." The desk clerk's tone slid from apprehensive to determined. "You said to talk to you, no matter what, you said, until you were fully awake and used the code phrase."

Damn. Okay, this was getting amusing. Did he actually say that to someone at this resort and had they actually noted it down? And decided to act on it?

"What's the code phrase?" Rickey asked.

"No, sir, you have to say it, I can't tell it to you," the young man answered.

Rickey leaned across the bed toward the nightstand, looking for his pack of cigarettes. Nothing there. Damn.

Oh, yeah. Now he remembered. He quit in 1989. "All right, I'll take a guess. Let's rock 'n' roll?"

"Yes!" He could hear the happy smile in the clerk's voice. "That's it, sir!"

"Yeah, well, good, okay. Send up some coffee, would you? And ring Miss Flintstone and let her know I'm awake."

Rickey threw the phone back in the general direction of the nightstand and took a look around the room. Not bad. The furniture was top quality, the square footage substantial. A huge mirror, framed in teak, covered the wall opposite the window. He'd been doing suites most of the time since the seventies and he'd refused to go backward ever since the eighties. Of course, there was a possibility with one of these awards-type show things that they'd try to skimp on the accommodation or the perks but he'd insisted that Booker triple check the rider. The presidential suite, the royal treatment and the green M and M's, right?

He was happy that Booker was here for this occasion with him. He and his manager had been going strong since the sixties, seeing each other through first loves and last calls—too many of those to count.

There was a knock at the door and Rickey pulled himself out of bed to answer it. He was feeling a bit fuzzy this morning—afternoon actually—and it took him a few seconds and a lucky glance in the mirror to realize that he was fully naked. Rickey squinted at his reflection. Not so bad.

He pulled on a pair of jeans and a T-shirt, then opened the door. Two people were waiting outside—Booker and a fifty-something waiter with a tray and a painful grin.

Booker was still a woman you'd pass on any street, in any restaurant or any airport, and she'd blend right in with the doorways and the furniture. A little bit round in the middle. Not tall, not short, not fat, not thin. You wouldn't miss her silver hair though, and the way it hung down her back in a two-foot-long ponytail. You gotta love a woman with long hair. He'd still be wearing his long, if he thought he could get away with it, but the years had messed with him and it was a better idea to keep it short. He still had the soul patch though, plus his pierced ear. And he never went anywhere, day or night, without his shades.

Rickey had the type of build that didn't pack on weight. Good genes. One of the few things he could thank his parents for.

"Mr. Rubble? Here's your coffee. Where in the cave do you want it?"

Okay, a smartass server. But that was better than a starstruck one. Rickey grinned. "Over there by the sabre tooth tiger skin. Hey, Booker, how're we doing?"

"Well, we're running late, as usual. Sound check starts in half an hour."

"Relax, the venue is only five minutes away. Geez, I love a stage with a hotel attached. Or maybe it's the other way around? A resort with a showroom? I forget." Rickey reached toward the cup of coffee the waiter had filled and offered to him, pulling on a pair of oversized sunglasses as he spoke. "Next time, I want a mug not a cup, can you do that for me?"

"I can bring your coffee in a mug, sir. I can bring your meat in on a stick or even live, if you want to club it yourself."

"Hey, this guy is quite a joker," Rickey commented, moving aside as he always did so that Booker could tip the man. Rickey T didn't carry cash. Ever.

The waiter barely noticed the fifty that Booker handed him, stuffing the bill into his uniform pants pocket. He held a notepad out toward Rickey. "Could you sign this for me?"

Rickey sighed, took the pen and scrawled something that vaguely resembled two ovals and a triangle on the piece of paper. Booker opened the door, put her hand behind the waiter's back and gave him a little push out of the room.

"A joker but a fan, too," Booker said as she closed the door. "They're annoying, sometimes, but without the fans, we got nothing."

Rickey made a face. "We still got the music, don't we?"

"Not really," Booker said. "It's wheels within wheels, all connected. We couldn't make the music if we didn't have the money from the fans."

He was bored with the conversation. "Didn't you say we have to get there in five minutes?"

"Twenty-five. But yeah, you better get a move on. I'll check my messages while you get dressed."

Booker stood and looked east out of the window toward the pool and beyond, toward the vineyards and farms that spread out toward the interior of the state.

"Lot of buzzards flying around here," she commented, as half a dozen of the birds wheeled and swooped through the sky.

"That's because of all the fifty-five plus gated golf course communities around here," Rickey commented.

Booker snorted. "That's rude. You're in that age group, you know."

"Ssshhh. Don't tell anybody. Are you ready to go?"

***

Cosmo Lewis rolled over and took a minute to notice the bed. California king-sized, and the best he'd ever been on. Not too soft, not too hard, Huge pillows, outstanding sheets, high thread-count. Oh yeah.

Cosmo had slept in many rougher places, including a cardboard box somewhere in Alabama. Many nicer places, too, including a penthouse in Cannes. But this resort on the

California coast ranked right up there with the best—and the most appreciated.

He was splashing the cash, as the kids would say, because Rickey T was getting a lifetime achievement award for "outstanding contributions to the world of rock & roll music". This justified a little extra spending. He'd been following the guy since the eighties, after all. Not the lazy-ass version of 'following' that social media imposes on all of us these days—looking at pictures and clicking on a heart icon. No, 'following' as in two or three or a dozen concerts a year. Bus tickets, plane tickets and motel rooms. Too many tour T-shirts to count. His apartment in Tampa was almost too small to hold all the shelves of albums, CDs and DVDs, plus the boxes stuffed with swag he'd picked up during all the years in his job as president of Rickey T's International Fan Club.

He looked down at the all-access pass, hanging from a lanyard around his neck. Not a bad photo this time. "Cosmo Lewis". Expert on all things Rickey T.

So, yeah, he was sleeping with it. Call him a king-sized nerd, if you like, but this connection with the world of rock music was the best thing that had ever happened to him. Some men have women, or one special woman, a soul-mate, and some men have men. Cosmo had never found anybody permanent like that, in forty-five years of looking, but he discovered Rickey's songs when he was a teenager and they stayed with him all this time.

Over the years, he'd taken a lot of razzing for pouring so much money and time into being a Rickey T fan. But the older he got, the less he cared about what other people might think. The batteries on his embarrassment meter had completely died.

The California sun sliced through the hotel room blinds and he could tell it was a glorious day outside. Twenty years ago, he might have pulled on a pair of running shoes and gone for a jog along the waterfront but putting on his glasses and taking a book to a nice table poolside was the limit of his ambition now. Besides, he had some work to do before the show this evening. The Fan Club was turning out in major numbers and as president, he would be hosting a meet-and-greet with the man himself before the festivities started. This would be a big deal for the Rickets. The Rickets—man, who ever would have predicted that name would catch on? There were hats, jackets, even boots, and of course, concert T-shirts, worn by people of all shapes, sizes, ages and attitudes. Some of the fans had been with Rickey nearly forty-five years. But none of them had turned their allegiance into a full-time, well-paid job, the way he had.

Cosmo himself would be wearing a vintage shirt from the *Under the Microscope* World Tour. He didn't pay peanuts to some guy online who was purging his closet; he bought it back in the day, at the time and on the scene The shirt had been hanging in his closet—in his various closets—for more than three decades, since he got it in Cannes in the south of France. Man, if that shirt could talk. He was proud of the fact that it still fit, even though he bought it when he was only twenty. Most of his hair was gone now but he could cover that fact with a fedora. The guys who spent their time adding a beer belly, instead of subtracting hair like Cosmo had, couldn't do much to turn back the clock.

Cosmo had worked very hard to promote this show and he was very proud of the numbers of fans who were turning out for it. Rickey T hadn't done a concert in six years and hadn't put out a new album in many more. It was a feat of public relations and music marketing.

He rolled himself out of the sack and headed into what he was sure would be one of the most memorable days of his life. Time to rock.

***

When Rickey and Booker arrived at the hospitality suite, forty-five minutes later, it was crammed with about a hundred people, some Rickey recognized, but most he didn't. Hangers-on were part of the scene, you got used to that in the first half hour. They were spouses, friends, relatives, and employees of the three musicians who were being given Big Name Big Deal Forever Awards at this little shindig—Sugar Kay Scott, James Jesse, and himself. Christ, did anybody say the word 'shindig' anymore? Everybody was dressed up like they were personally responsible for keeping the designers, the hair stylists and the glam squads in business. He cruised the food table and nodded at the massive bowl of candy. All the right colors were present. Tradition. . . tradition! Real rock 'n' roll might be dead as the dinosaurs but every once in a while, you came across a bone or two.

He heard a clicking sound and turned to see a smartphone pointed in his direction. "Can I get a pitcher with you?" The gnome of a woman had already lined herself up at his side, her right hand stretched up into the air with the phone lens pointing at both of them.

He felt his blood pressure rising. You got these people coming at you, night and day. "Just a—" Who knows what he would have said or done if Booker hadn't inserted herself into the situation. Booker the magic fixer, the business genius, the defender of the fans.

"Here you go, I'll take a photo of the two of you," she said, claiming the phone, snapping the photo, then trying to send the fan on her way. "Sorry, we have to rush. Rickey is needed at the sound check."

The woman had a dazed look on her face, as though she'd just been witness to a significant moment in history. She was resisting, her hands covered in silver rings and bangles bracing themselves against the food table, as Booker tried, tactfully, to get her to move on. Please, somebody, save me from the fans, Rickey thought.

That somebody was Booker, always Booker. When they'd started out in the music business together, back in Vermont, they hadn't known they'd end up here. They had determination, yeah, but no certainty. And now here they were, together, lifelong friends celebrating a lifelong success award. Big name, big deal. No irony.

It was the kind of event that left you reminiscing. Rickey knew that he was one of the true survivors in rock 'n' roll. A legend, they called him, and who was he to argue? He had his first number one hit when he was nineteen years old. In those first few years, he brought out a new album every six months. The songs just poured through him like speed through a thoroughbred.

Booker was his best friend in high school. Her real name was Cynthia but no one dared call her that. From day one, she'd had a knack for getting gigs and doing business, and she'd managed to navigate them through the whitewater, past the dangerous wild animals, around the quicksand, and right on up to the front of the stage. Then, he'd take over and put on a show that no one ever forgot. Crap, they oughta make a video game about them!

Instead, the world had rewarded their efforts with the big bucks, and that was even better.

Moments later they were on their way to the showroom, the meet-and-greet thankfully over and done with. Rickey was going to perform three numbers after he was presented with his award. There would be international TV coverage and all the streaming services, with his name and his music multiplied, twenty-first century style. The best of the best studio and stage musicians had been hired for the occasion, and in the final chorus of the last song, the curtains would part, revealing a sixty-voice choir, the singers dressed in blue and gold robes, dancing and singing in unison as though they were born to do this song and no other. It would be a tremendous blast of stage power, not a bad thing since it had been a long time since Rickey T performed. Again, Booker was the brains behind this genius idea.

The resort was built around one of those marquis-style lobbies, where the ceiling was up somewhere so high you couldn't see it. The elevator doors opened, Rickey and

Booker stepped aboard, and he couldn't help but notice the four flight attendants who'd be sharing the glass space on the way down. Gorgeous, every one of them, with their Air France name tags pinned to their lapels. Time was when he would have chatted them up and left the elevator with at least one, maybe more, on his arm and up for a good time. Today, they barely noticed him. It might have to do with his age (and theirs) but somehow, they also seemed to be intimidated by the elevator and the long drop down to the lobby. Booker had to make the joke, of course, that it was funny that people who flew in airplanes for a living would have a fear of heights in an elevator. It was a joke the ladies didn't appreciate.

On the last few floors as they cruised down, Rickey checked out the four bars and lounges, filled with happy campers even at three in the afternoon. Lots of options for after the show. There was some kind of stream built into and running through the lobby that emptied into an outdoor pond with swans, water lilies and little boats providing rides for the guests who wanted a place for some romance and for those with small kids to entertain. Rickey wasn't in the market for either.

The property sat at the end of a half-mile drive through an orange grove and a prize-winning display of roses. Through the glass doors, Rickey could see that the cars parked near the front were all interesting—a Jag, a collectible Porsche, and a Maybach. He walked past the reception desk and toward the hallway leading to the showroom, Booker at his left elbow and on his other side, a burly young man with a sky-blue T-shirt and four inches of architectural beard who joined them the minute they stepped off the elevator. He saw half a dozen people glance at them but they were moving fast enough and the big man was daunting enough that nobody tried to speak to him.

Good.

Through the floor-to-ceiling glass at the west end of the lobby he could see the Pacific, held just out of reach by a wide strand of golden beach. Damn, he loved the water. If he could be there right now, rather than here . . .

"Rickey, they're holding up the sound check and the rehearsal till we get there," Booker said. She was staring at the screen of her phone and he could hear the thing buzzing every couple of seconds.

"Let's go then," Rickey said, breaking into a jog across the lobby. Now, even more people were looking at him, but who cared? If he wanted to get someplace, he'd damn well get there! He wasn't going to stop. He knew his success didn't ride on making time to talk to every single person who wanted to talk to him.

The neon sign above the main entrance to the theater announced the Support-PetFood Auditorium. The rock singer winced, then shrugged. What the hell, it was sponsorship. He could only hope that there weren't cans of "vegan snacks for snakes or Samoyeds" for sale as part of the merch or put out on trays in the green room. Hah. If they pull together a bit more money, maybe next time they'll sponsor the Support-Pet Food Bowl.

Rickey walked toward the middle of the stage. Booker's phone buzzed and she lifted it to her ear, waving at him to go on without her. Two or three roadies were rushing around him, setting up music stands, amplifiers and the piano bench. It was coming together nicely. Rickey would be performing, as usual, with professional musicians hired for the occasion. He had never had a regular, permanent band. He'd always found that exceptional, dedicated players could be hired in any city of the world—but as skilled and talented as these ones probably all were, it would be more likely that things would go smoothly if all of the instruments, the equipment and the tools were as carefully prepared as they could be before the performance.

The performance. Rickey looked out over the empty seats in the auditorium and felt the familiar wave of nausea roll up toward his throat. He walked to the edge of the stage and then paced back toward the center: eight steps, eight paces away from the edge. Eight paces to safety. He took a few deep breaths, then nodded and smiled to acknowledge the musicians who'd arrived to start setting up.

The next minute, he rushed backstage to the small restroom in the wings, slammed the door behind him, and threw up.

He took some time to get back his self-control, rinsing out his mouth and wiping it with a paper towel. For anybody clocking more than forty years in the same business, it would be a milestone, a night like this. For Rickey T, it was vindication. Proof that he'd made the right choices, that he was the winner, not the runner-up, not a loser like they were trying to tell him in high school. To be given a prize, recognition by his peers and appreciation from fans all over the world—Rickey knew he should make sure that he told them repeatedly how humble it all made him feel. Looking into the mirror, he did a little practice on his palms-pressed-together 'thank-you' bow.

The stage fright is a passing thing and you've been dealing with it a long time, Rickey thought. In the grand scheme of things, it's minor. Come on, you know you should be happy to be here and you're a very lucky sunovabitch to be living the life you live. It's all good.

He did the self-coaching for another five minutes, then went back out to the stage, where the backup singers were working on the sound check. The technicians and producers all seemed to know their business, which wasn't always the case. They did the run-through, then Rickey T signed autographs until he was so bored, he could have hung himself. He finally escaped for a bit of solitude before show time. There was some performer—who was it?—who met fans and signed autographs during the intermission of every one of his shows, and for as long after the final encore as anyone cared to stand in line to get one.

Rickey would rather moisturize his knuckles with a cheese grater.

***

The buzz in the crowd was so loud that people had to shout their phony compliments to one another. Cosmo lifted his glass in a toast toward the seven strangers at his table, people he'd never met before and would probably never see again. The multi-purpose room had been set up for this bash like an old-style nightclub, with large tables for ten, covered in white linen and four crystal goblets at each place. The chairs were decorated with white velvet coverings held in place with bows tied at the back. Enormous chandeliers spotted the ceiling at a pace of one per hundred feet or so. The end of the room farthest from the wall of doors that would stand open only until the program was underway was dominated by a massive stage, illuminated with glittery white-blue lights.

Servers in dark blue trousers and crisp white shirts darted among the tables, bringing champagne and plotting the best paths through the room, for the rush that would come when it was time to bring out the first course. Musicians dressed up or dolled up in their finest tuxedos, black jeans, velvet capes and elegant hats filled every seat.

There were two hours to go until Rickey would go onstage to get his lifetime achievement award. As part of the show, he would play three tunes and Cosmo was looking forward to hearing the band that had been assembled for this event; they were all shit-hot players. For backup vocals, Rickey had gone to some of his old companions: Sherri, Roxanne and the epic Bonaire.

Cosmo thought that Bonaire was one of the most beautiful women he'd ever seen. Her dress was a long drink of blue velvet and Spandex, and she was wearing a rope of pearls that stretched to her waist, the exact same length as the numerous braids that made up tonight's hairstyle.

She looked fine and she knew it, Cosmo could tell. He'd been watching performers on thousands of stages for dozens of years and he always got a vibe about the moods they were in. Everyone tonight seemed to have forgotten any of the bumps in the road along the way. Those who hadn't forgotten probably just pitched out their invitations and 'forgot' to watch the show on TV. Those who wanted to be there to celebrate Rickey T, whether as invited guests or purchasers of the few public tickets, dined, drank and waited for the show to start.

On the way in, Cosmo had bumped into a couple of old pals from the Rickets. Anne from Seattle, Bella from New York, and Ethan from L.A. had all put on a few miles, but hadn't everybody? He also spotted quite a few rock journalists in the crowd, working and retired. Dwight Kettle was there, looking like he hadn't darkened the door of a men's clothing store since the nineties.

The show was going to be a blockbuster. It was all fully baked on this stage, with the massive footlights, the twenty-piece backup band, and the audience filled with bold-faced names from rock, from jazz, even from classical music. Cosmo had been rubber-necking for hours now, catching sight of a dozen of his minor heroes. Paul, Bruce, Mick, Eric, Robert, David, John. None was as important to him as Rickey T, though, and none had he met personally, hung out with and worked for, the way he had with Rickey.

And there was not a one who was as big news as Rickey would be, after today.

Cosmo looked around the showroom at the rest of the crowd. Somewhere, his old friend, William, was sitting with his wife, thanks to a pair of comp tickets that Cosmo had had to go right to Booker to get. Cosmo didn't see William anywhere but he did spot Shad Palmetto, the recording company head honcho, presiding over two tables full of mover and shaker guests. Trust the guy to turn up front and center wherever there was credit to be taken.

Another blast from the past there that night was Cosmo's ex-wife, Linda, who sent an email demanding a pair of tickets for herself and her girlfriend, claiming he owed her, after all the lonely nights she'd endured while he was running around, chasing Rickey T.

Two months ago, Booker and Cosmo had decided to set up a contest for Rickey T fans to win a ticket to this jamboree and they'd pumped it up loud, right across the nation. The winners were sitting at the far edges of the room, practically in the kitchen, but Cosmo could see, even at this distance, that they had wide smiles on their faces and no complaints about their seats. He'd had a blast, organizing the Rickets' participation in this very significant occasion. When he got on the plane for the flight west, two days ago, he was about as jazzed as it was possible to be without psychedelics—and he'd given all that up years ago, after that time he imagined a purple elephant swimming across the Gulf toward him.

The show was being televised live and streamed on four different platforms. Cosmo and the rest of the audience sat up when the room suddenly went dark, strobes and lasers raked the air and Rickey ran across the stage. When he raised a fist to punch the air, the crowd saluted back. He stepped back into the shadows, while Bonaire and her two partners, dressed in variations of blue and pearls, shimmied and walked out on stage, with every step, in those tight dresses, a song in its own right. Then the guitar players and the brass section strolled out, picking up their instruments and watching for Rickey's cue.

When the drummer started into the opening beats of the first song, Bonaire, Sherri and Roxanne started to dance. The waves of applause crashed over their heads and surrounded them.

Yeah, this was going to be fun, Cosmo thought.

> *What can I say now*
> *What can I say now*
> *What can I say*

The backing vocals part was simple but as essential as a solid drumbeat. The women's dancing added to the visuals, just as vital as the complex design of the light show that went with the performance. They settled into the song and Cosmo felt the audience anticipation rise like a kid's spirits on Christmas Eve.

Then Bonaire stepped up to the mic, while Sherri and Roxanne stepped back. "All my brothers and sisters, please welcome . . . the one and only . . . Rickey T !!"

The spotlight rained down on the stage where Rickey stood, a teal blue guitar strapped over his shoulder and an arm in a fringed, buckskin sleeve poised to crash downward in the first chords of one of his biggest hits, "This is Me". The crowd had put in three hours for this moment. They'd waited through two other presentations of Big Name Big Deal Awards to other entertainers and they'd waited through two intermissions and countless breaks in the action for TV commercials or technical fixes. They were pumped.

The song was one of the rock legend's best, in Cosmo's opinion. Rickey often said he was sick of playing it but Cosmo never got tired of hearing it, not once in all the years of knowing the singer and helping to solve his problems. Neither did millions of other fans. Many of them had grown up with it, made love to it, played it at their parties, on their road trips and during nights all alone. Quite a few had even tattooed the title, or Rickey's name, somewhere on their bodies, as they turned their skin into canvases for a record of their experiences and their beliefs.

Next, he launched into "Leaving Lorraine". The show producer had asked for three numbers; Booker told Cosmo that the discussion over "which three?" had gone on for months. Rickey wanted something that didn't require much practicing on his part and something that wasn't recent. He argued that that was what the audience would be hoping for, but Booker knew that he didn't give a double F what the audience wanted. He expressed himself, played what he wanted, created what was inside him pushing to get out. Always had. He just didn't like the newer material as much and he remembered the pre-nineties tunes the best.

Laser beams blasted across the stage and up into the upper reaches of the amphitheater. Green, gold and purple rays illuminated the instruments, the players, the singers and the star, the beams dancing around them like some sort of demented Mardi Gras crowd. They were making Cosmo feel a little woozy but he had to concede that they did make the show more exciting.

The third song was "Looking for Someone Looking for Me", one of Cosmo's other favorites. Booker told him once that she thought it was one of Rickey's best, too. She loved Rickey's music, always had, and that made her job a lot easier. Not that she wouldn't have taken the offer and run with it even if she'd hated the music. She'd made it her career ever since they'd connected, back in 1970, she said, but it would have been even harder if she'd had to hold her nose while she listened.

Cosmo didn't believe there was anyone who would want to hold his nose while listening to Rickey's music.

The song came to an end and Rickey took off his guitar, handing it without looking to a roadie who ran forward to take it. It was time for the speech.

"I feel so blessed to be here tonight," the singer began.

Booker said she had commissioned one of the best speechwriters in the business to craft the perfect words for accepting this award. Rickey had wanted to go with "thank you very much" but Booker thought they owed the organizers and the fans a bit more than that. She worked with the speechwriter through five drafts and about a million plunges into the thesaurus.

". . . and I thank you all for coming. Who wants another song?"

Dammit. Booker would be ticked about all the money wasted on that speechwriter and the show's producers would be ticked about the spontaneous addition of a fourth song.

Cosmo squirmed around in his seat, trying to see if he

could catch sight of the producers or Booker anywhere. A buzz among the people around him brought his attention back to the stage. Four men walked out from the wings and Cosmo squinted, trying to focus on them and understand what was going on. The band? But the band was already on stage. He stared at the giant video screens and they confirmed what he thought he'd seen. Every one of these four guys looked like Rickey.

"What the hell is this, now?" The man sitting next to Cosmo wanted to know. Everyone in the surrounding seats and in the entire room was talking, it seemed . . . the buzz was growing from a low hum to steady static.

A stridently amplified guitar chord blasted through the noise and silenced it. What was this, they were going to play? What was going on? Was this some kind of badly timed tribute band? Who needed that when you had the real thing right there?

The four men lined up, each one wearing a microphone and lit by a spot. One was dressed in a broad-shouldered silver satin jacket and dark pants, his hair cut in an eighties mullet and backcombed to the rafters. One was in nineties plaid flannel and jeans. Another wore hipster pants, soft-soled shoes, blond hair streaked with silver and blunt-cut to his chin, a moustache and a short goatee. The fourth looked like Rickey from the cover of his first album, back in the seventies, long hair, moustache, jeans, green T-shirt, boots.

They launched into "This Is Me", each taking a verse, each singing in a voice just like Rickey's, the same cadence, the same intonation, the same way of holding the vowels 'a' and 'e' long on an exhale. They could have been vocal clones but for the guy in the beard who was struggling to hit the notes and sounding like the fifth day of a case of strep throat.

The audience was throbbing. The guy in the seat to Cosmo's left yanked on his sleeve. "What is this?"

"Maybe some kind of cover band?"

The guy shook his head. "Maybe. But why would they

do that, on a night like this, when Rickey is right here?"

"Maybe it's like a gift from Rickey to his fans."

"Doubt it."

"Maybe from his friends to him? Like a portrait or something? A surprise?"

"He does look pretty much surprised."

Cosmo wasn't sure *what* it was he looked. Rickey stood at center stage, staring at the four men surrounding him, and his face was like a carving in marble. Cosmo thought Rickey was amazed, but he might have been angry, or he might have been horrified.

Rickey paced the length of the stage, left to right, stopping in front of each of the singers and staring at the man full on, for a full minute. Just as a spotlight fell on the first Rickey clone and he lifted a microphone to his lips to speak, Rickey laughed, a deep, almost sexy sound, and took the mic away from him.

"Booker?" Rickey said. "Wherever you are? Would you please come up here?"

The shit was about to hit the fan.

The Eighties

CHAPTER TWO

1984

South of France

The pre-show party at the resort on Boulevard de la Croisette in Cannes was five hours old when Rickey finally showed up. Booker watched him strut through the room, acknowledging the fortunate few and hugging the special people. Rickey T was a rock star—and he hated his life. How freakin' unfair was that? He was effortlessly cool and amazingly talented. Everything flowed to him—money, fame, chicks. For free. And yet the guy hated his life.

Rickey was thirty, the same age as she was, but man, he looked like he was eighteen, Booker thought. No sagging middle, no slightly rounded shoulders like many men his age. Hair as blond as a Norse god, back straight and strong in a leather jacket, legs long in jeans cut just right. He was completely not her type, and she'd known him so long he felt like a cousin, or a brother, but she could still notice, completely objectively, that he was easy on the eyes.

This luxury suite in the hotel on the beach, taking up

the entire penthouse floor of the resort and decorated in up-to-date tones of silver and blue, featured a giant mirror ball dominating the dance floor that took up the entire west end. The east side was crammed with tables full of fancy food and expensive drink being inhaled by stylish, gorgeous clotheshorse-folk. The party planners had required each person to submit an 8" by 10" glossy photo a week ago, showing bod, fashion sense, and tan. If approved, they got a call with the location and date for the party.

Booker was not one of those who would have been accepted; she was not tall, not slender and not blessed with a lot of fashion sense. But people did tell her they noticed her hair. Not many women had been growing it long since 1967.

This hotel overlooked one of the most exciting streets in the world, with its lights twinkling against the view of the Baie de Cannes. The French Riviera was the only place to be when it was the first day of summer, Rickey said. He had four favorite places in the world and he tried to be in a different one of them on each of the days that turned the season: Cannes, New York, Whistler, and New Orleans. They were the favorites this year—next year, who knew?

That's the way you do it, that's the way you *can* do it when you're a rock star.

Rickey T was many things to Booker. Her employer, her oldest friend, her favorite musician. Most of all, he was her responsibility.

"Rickey! You look great!" Booker greeted her boss enthusiastically, but with the slightly reserved tone she used whenever they were around other people. Rickey grinned but didn't stop. He seemed to be in quite a hurry to get somewhere.

But she wasn't particularly worried about him these days. Ten years ago, when they were all just starting out, and barely beginning their twenties, he'd done his time with his nose in the coke and with the neck of a liquor bottle almost welded to his right hand. It was a wild time, the seventies, but they'd all survived it. Some of their friends and employees had not, however, and that had been enough of a wake-up call for Rickey.

Le Chateau Riviera had spared no expense in making the rock star and his entourage welcome. A brief mention that he'd stayed there, even for less time than it took to have a drink and to change clothes, would give it publicity rocket fuel for months. That's if he would allow them to mention it—and of course, he would, for a price.

The suite they had given him was presidential, and the view of the Mediterranean was stunning, but Booker saw that Rickey barely glanced at the glittering white lights decorating the palm trees, the hotels and the beachfront restaurants. He really seemed much more interested in the people on the patio. All of the hired musicians had shown up—they knew they wouldn't be welcome to play the next night, if they didn't. The modeling agency had sent over a few dozen beauties, all of them hoping for a spot in Rickey T's first video. A few dozen random strangers lounged around the suite, hoovering up the drinks and the appies. A woman in a leopard-print dress and a glittering necklace that read "Muffy" danced alone beside a speaker that was as tall as she was.

Booker watched Rickey scan the room, his gaze stopping at a young woman sandwiched between the latest disco band millionaire and a fiftyish movie star with a four-carat diamond in his left ear. She was wearing a white blouse, a short kilt, black ankle boots and a side bag almost as big as she was. She looked bored.

Rickey cut a path through the room. "Adrian, are you ready?" he asked, then grabbed her hand, and started to lead her through the crowd toward the bedroom.

She stopped to pick up her massive bag. "Got all my gear and my inks right here."

Booker got a glimpse of a spa bed, lined up alongside the king-sized bed draped in satin sheets, before Rickey slammed the door shut. What was this about? She'd already been asked to make sure Mona Ray, Rickey's latest squeeze, was given a room key for Rickey's suite—she hoped she wasn't going to be expected to get it back now.

When Rickey and Adrian emerged, an hour later, Booker was waiting beside the bedroom door. The rock singer was pulling his T-shirt back on but as he did, Booker caught sight of the familiar tattoo of a green cobra curled up his left side, its tail beginning somewhere near his lower ribcage, with its head and fangs adorning his chest.

"It's my birthday in a few days, and a new tattoo is my gift to myself," Rickey said to Booker. "It had to be special, really something. I brought a sketch." He reached into his jeans pocket and fished out a scrap of paper.

It was a drawing of a woman, a beautiful woman. Her lips were puckered in a kiss. "This is what we're putting on. Just got started."

Booker stared at Rickey as if he'd suddenly started shrieking like a crazy person and banging his head against a wall. Briefly, she felt like doing that herself. His head, or her own. He seemed to break out of his conceited self-absorption for a minute, and noticed Booker's concern.

"Hey, it's okay, man, it's in a place nobody ever sees. Well, hardly nobody." Rickey and Adrian, the tattoo artist, snickered together for a moment and Booker almost reached out to wring the stupid jerk's neck. She wanted to scream at him for about an hour about why it was not okay, listing all the dozens of ways this could screw them up.

People will think you're a criminal, that you've been in prison and got those tattoos there! Do you even know if those needles are clean? People will think you're in a gang and the tattoos are some kind of code for violence or threats or something. Maybe not, but maybe they'll just think you're ugly, that your skin looks disgusting and you won't be the cute, sexy guy all the girls want to dance with. This is 1984, for god's sake—you have to think about your appearance!

Booker grabbed a glass of champagne from the tray held by a passing waiter. It never changes, she thought. Rickey operates like a child a lot of the time. He sees something, he wants it, he takes it, and when it turns out later it was a bad idea, he's completely surprised, and I have to save his ass. Most of us, we grow up, don't we? We realize you gotta wait, you gotta take your turn, you gotta consider the consequences. But not Rickey T. He couldn't find the brake pedal. Ever.

"Rickey." She spoke through gritted teeth. "Shad Palmetto, the new VP for the label, is across the room, right over there . . . underneath that . . . whatever it is." She motioned toward a small, slender man dressed in a suit with a yellow tie and matching suspenders, standing beneath a massive depiction of a yacht, made from tin foil and hanging on the wall behind a white and gold grand piano.

The rock star looked past the business exec and studied the art. "I think it's a sculpture," he said.

"Nah, I'm with you, Booker," a man with an enormous moustache said. "Handicrafts, maybe. Looks like something a kid would make at camp."

Booker didn't want to acknowledge him. Was this Sturgess Mesley guy really a friend of Rickey's? That's what he said, and Rickey hadn't corrected him—at least, not so far. They'd met only last year, when Sturgess, a junior stockbroker at some New York money factory, had sent an unsolicited prospectus on a new luxury boat-building company. Rickey had called him up, an absolutely stunning and ill-advised development, in Booker's opinion. Now, it seemed like she saw Sturgess every time she turned around. Why was he there all the time? Couldn't Rickey see what a dweeb the guy was? Well, people see what they want to see; she'd learned that a long time ago.

Whether he was a friend or a hanger-on, it really didn't matter: Booker knew that no one was more important in Rickey's life than she was, and she didn't need Sturgess or anybody else to acknowledge it. Even Rickey, come to that. She had his back and had done since high school. She had his back—and she had his wallet. She tried to help him watch it as carefully as she did her own. He was terrible at that stuff and that was why he needed her to be his business manager. Booker had been working for Rickey as his manager slash promoter slash producer for more than ten years now, and as far as she was concerned that gave him more history with her than even her own family.

She stood by silently, as she often did, observing Sturgess's way of sucking up as the two of them discussed the suite décor. He wasn't much to look at. Sturgess was trapped somewhere in the seventies, in platform shoes, polyester shirt, gold chain around his throat, and that heavy dark moustache. Guy looked like a poor man's Zorro, Booker laughed to herself.

She tried to relax as Rickey grinned at her in that charismatic way and stared into her eyes—total contact, total attention. "Come on, Book, I told you, let's not do any business at this party. Let's do it after the show."

Somebody turned up the volume on the sound system. Like everything else in this suite, it was top quality. Rickey's latest gorgeous girlfriend, Mona Ray, tailed by a dark-haired kid wearing those old-fashioned glasses like John Lennon used to wear, marched up to Rickey and tucked herself against his side. She was trying to snuggle in under his arm but he wasn't cooperating.

"Hey babe," he said. "Go get me a single malt and water, wouldja?" It was not a question.

Mona Ray sighed, rolled her eyes and glided off toward one of the bars, her red hair hanging down her back past her waist. Everyone watched her go.

Rickey was getting jumpy, like he usually did a few hours before a show. Jumpy and bored. "Hey, Booker, what we gonna do to pass the time? Ya got any ideas?"

In days gone by, that question had been code for a scene that Booker had been happy to see disappear. There had been some raucous parties back then, particularly when they were on tour. Sex, drugs and rock 'n' roll. She remembered one crazy week at the Savoy in London that had become legendary, with hundreds of people coming and going from the suite and a room service bill afterward that compared with the annual budget of a small country. This party today was pretty lively, but nothing to match the old days. They were all reaching thirty years old now, for one thing. The hard partying was something you could do when you were barely in your twenties. Neither Rickey nor most of his friends and associates these days seemed to be as interested in blow or pills as they once were.

"Why don't you go take a break, Rickey? Grab a little rest so you're all set to turn on the power on stage tonight."

He made a face. "Yeah thanks. You're a lot of fun." The nerves were getting to him and he bounced from foot to foot, looking for a distraction of some kind, somewhere. The string bean that Mona Ray had brought in caught his attention. "Who are you, anyway?"

"I'm Cosmo," the kid said.

Mona Ray arrived back at the group and handed Rickey his rocks glass. "He won the radio station contest for an all-access pass and a chance to meet you," she explained. "He's a fan."

"I've been to fifteen of your concerts," Cosmo announced. "All over the world. It's kind of like my hobby."

He had the attention of all five of them now. Booker had heard that there were people like this. They were fans, beyond avid and heading toward rabid, fans who spent too much of their time and money, often money they didn't even have, running up five-figure charge card bills to feed a music habit. But this one was just a child. Fifteen concerts? He didn't look old enough.

"My first one, my mother took me to. I grew up listening to your records, man, and being taken to concerts all over the U.S."

Adrian put a hand adorned with a green and purple butterfly drawing on his shoulder. "How'd you get your ass all the way over here to France for this one?"

Cosmo grinned. They both knew the tattoo artist was looking for tips on how to do that on the limited budget that most young people have, and there was no criticism implied.

"We're a military family," he said. "My dad is stationed over here."

"In France?" Booker asked.

"Germany, technically. It's not far, though. I took a train."

Booker stared at Cosmo. He took a train. Of course. To get to a concert. Had been listening to Rickey's music and watching him perform since the beginning. Was this enthusiasm or was it nuts? Kinda cool, but maybe too much. She decided to keep an eye on this one.

"Hey, did anybody get you something to eat? A soft drink, maybe?" Rickey asked.

Cosmo looked dazzled. "No. But I'm good, I don't need anything."

"What's the radio station deal, you hang out here till the show, then what?" Rickey smiled at Cosmo.

Booker looked at Mona Ray for the answer. "Will you keep him with you until the end of the show?" she asked.

Mona Ray nodded. "Am I leaving after the show with you in the limo?"

"You're going with the band," Rickey said. "Nobody goes in my limo but me. It's in the rider, right, Booker? A limo just for me. Mine. Nobody else in it, unless I want."

"Yes, I know that," Booker agreed. "But we have some business to discuss and I thought I'd go with you this time."

Mona Ray tried the snuggling approach again, seasoned with a bit of flirting. "I could make it worth your while, if you want to put me in the limo, too."

Rickey ignored her. "All right, Booker, you ride with me. But you gotta be ready to roll as soon as we hit the last chord," he said. "I'm coming down those stairs and out to the car in the tunnel and we're going."

"I'll be there," Booker promised.

"And don't bring that suit from the record label along."

CHAPTER THREE

osmo had been to many shows, most of them Rickey T's, but he'd never watched one from backstage. The hallways of the auditorium behind the stage were dark and plain, really stuffy. Nothing at all like the glorious velvet and glittery stuff out front. But it was more glamorous than any place he had ever been before. An all-access backstage pass! He wore it around his neck like a bar of solid gold.

Mona Ray abandoned Cosmo pretty much the minute the tour bus delivered them to the stage door of the venue from the hotel—but Cosmo didn't care. Lots of people don't do what they promise to do. He wandered around for hours, checking out every corner and empty room.

He didn't quite have the nerve to knock on any closed doors and he tried to make himself as invisible as possible. He stopped to stare at a poster or a wall sign when a group of musicians passed by, managing to hold in the urge to talk to some of them. A roadie carrying two microphone stands glanced at him but didn't break stride. One or two giant security guards looked at him with what seemed like suspicious eyes but once they saw the lanyard and the badge, they turned their attention elsewhere and went to look for somebody else to hassle.

Man, Cosmo was looking forward to this concert. The *Under the Microscope* tour. The venue wasn't huge, not like one of those 60,000-seat arenas, and the sound quality would probably be choice. His mother would be so jealous, Cosmo thought, and he was looking forward to telling her all about it later.

Cosmo had a vivid memory of the exact moment he discovered Rickey T's music for himself. One day after school, he'd gone over to his best buddy William's house. They were lying around in the rec room in the basement, listening to vinyl. William bought a CD player when they came out two years ago and he was building a collection of CDs. But he also treasured the shelf of vintage LPs that his dad gave him. Cosmo went over there all the time to listen to the sixties and seventies gold he had there.

Rickey's first album, *Introducing Rickey T*, was in the stack. William pulled it out of the sleeve, put it on the turntable, and put the needle in the groove. Cosmo just drank in those opening notes of "This is Me", already knowing this would be one of the greatest days he'd ever had. After William played the whole album all the way through once, they agreed that it needed hearing again. And again. And again. It was their favorite and they almost wore it out. Cosmo claimed bragging rights for having heard of Rickey first, thanks to his mother's music choices around the house. But William had the record collection.

Cosmo and William went to their first Rickey T concert together at Pier Six Pavilion just before Cosmo's dad moved the whole family from Baltimore to Germany. Cosmo never forgot that August evening. A hot summer night, everyone feeling so good, the music lifting them all. Rickey was at the top of his game that night, owning the stage with his dance moves and his soaring vocals. So much emotion came pouring through! When Rickey strapped on his Gibson and lit into the opening chords of "This is Me", his first Number One hit, Cosmo thought the concert hit its peak.

But most people liked the newer stuff. Rickey T's music had never been so popular, his record sales higher than they'd ever been in the ten years he'd been on the charts. Ten years was a long time for a rock 'n roll musician, Cosmo's dad said, and the window would close, just like it does for a pro athlete. There would come a time when a musician just didn't have the energy and the voice to keep on rocking, he said. But Cosmo was sure that Rickey T would go on forever. It bugged him that he had been born too late for the sixties. But he would hang on to Rickey T and the seventies for as long as he could.

He'd often thought about the reasons that Rickey was his main man. Yeah, it was the songs, the melodies and the lyrics that got him right in his gut and made him feel as though Rickey knew his inner thoughts. It was also the arrangements, the way the piano solos just made him want to dance and the wailing guitar solos made him feel like the sound was reaching inside him, pulling something out.

But the real reason was Rickey's voice. It wasn't the greatest singing voice in the world, but it was special. He'd recognize it anywhere, like Van Morrison's, or Elton John's, or Rod Stewart's or Paul McCartney's. But fantastic as they were, he didn't have those voices embedded in his mind and his soul, the way Rickey T's was.

The show started about an hour late. Didn't bother Cosmo—it was all part of the experience. People passed the time by tossing bean bags around, drinking or inhaling whatever they'd brought in, and lining up for the restrooms. Cosmo didn't do anything—he didn't want any of the concert to go by in a blur. About an hour into the wait, the people who were less chill than he was started stomping and clapping in a rhythm: "We want Rickey! We want Rickey!"

Maybe that was what Rickey was waiting for. Just a few minutes later, he came running on stage. He always did that. Some performers strutted, some walked like they were all by themselves in the mall or something, and some almost pranced, turning to the audience and waving their arms up and down, amping the applause, calling for more. Rickey ran in, strapped on his guitar, and charged right into the first song, leaving the rest of the band to follow him as quickly as they could, get set up on their instruments, and catch up. I guess they do their tuning off-stage, Cosmo thought.

Rickey's 'band' really wasn't that, not in the sense of other long-time bands, like the Beatles or Led Zeppelin or something. Rickey T was a solo act, always had been. He had different guys playing on his records, different guys on stage at different concerts. True fans knew all their names and input, and Cosmo was one of those. He had them memorized, like some other guys did baseball stats.

The next two hours passed in a flash. Song after song, just great, man, just great. And Cosmo met him this afternoon! Hung out with him, met his friends, his girlfriend, for Chrissakes!

Kill me now. I can die happy.

***

Somehow a group of teenaged girls had managed to find their way to the underground tunnel where the car stood waiting to whisk Rickey away from the venue after the concert and back to the hotel. Booker followed close behind as the rock star ran down the ramp. One of the girls tried to stop the singer, waving a pen and pad of paper in his direction.

"Mr. Taggart, please! Could you—"

Oh, no, one of the polite ones, Booker thought. He'll run right over you.

Not quite. Rickey deked to his right and ran around her. The disappointed look on the young girl's face slowed Booker down and she stopped to hand her a business card with the New York office number printed on it. "Call the office, sunshine," she said. "They'll get an autographed photo to you."

"I'm Bella." She grabbed Booker's arm. "Have him

make it out. To Bella. Don't forget. It's important."

Booker could see Rickey a long way ahead of her now, bending down to go through the limo's back door. Tossing the business card to the concrete floor, to distract the hysterical fan and get her to let go, Booker sprinted toward the stretch, then followed Rickey into its protected space.

A line of white lights twinkled in the velvet ceiling of the car and continued down the sides and along the floor. The seats were upholstered in a deep green plush velvet that almost seemed to rise up to meet her as she settled in. A table ran the length of one side of the limo in front of the bench seat, and three crystal decanters, with various levels of amber liquid, were set in specifically designed holders. Sliding doors in the shelving below protected half a dozen different styles of glasses: snifters, rocks, red wine, white wine, champagne tall, champagne shallow. Booker knew that although there was an appearance of hospitality, Rickey had the car stocked with only his post-concert drink of choice these days—Rémy Martin cognac.

When Booker had first started riding this way, she'd felt as though she should be in a prom dress every time, or at the very least in one of the Sunday-best outfits her mother put her in to go to visit her grandparents. She'd long since overcome that, but she still had a constant, low-level feeling that she wasn't quite fancy enough for the car.

The security guard shut the door behind them.

"Let's go, man, let's go, let's go, let's go!" Rickey shouted at the driver and in seconds the limo was rolling out of the tunnel beneath the theater. He leaned against the back seat, closing his eyes, then leaned forward and unearthed his bottle of cognac from the bar. "You gotta reward yourself at the end of a show, Book," he said. "Give yourself something to look forward to. Otherwise, it can be a son of a bitch to get through."

She nodded. "We're going back to the resort," she said. "The after-party is on the roof. But let's cruise around a little first. I have to bring you up to speed on the record company."

Rickey made a face. The business side of it was such a drag to him, it always had been, Booker knew.

"And the video shoot. That's all lined up. We've got a location in a three-hundred-year old apartment near the water in Nice. It's very cool. The director has won awards for features, here in France. The boys are all hyped to play on this thing . . ."

Booker was babbling. She was aware that Rickey wasn't thrilled about doing this video shoot and she was trying to overcome all his objections before he had a chance to mention them.

She didn't quite make it. "I just don't feel like doing it, you know?" Rickey said. "I worked hard tonight and we've got another show in three days in Rome. Why do we have to stick this video thing in now, here? We could do it when we get back to New York next week."

"You scheduled a vacation, remember? The boat, the Mediterranean? It would be a month before we could get to the video shoot and we can't wait around that long. Everybody's doing these and we have to get on top of it. Hell, we have to get *ahead* of it!"

"Booker, relax. It's gonna be fine. All right, I'll behave myself. We'll make this little movie and then we'll get on with our lives." He poured two drinks. "Although I still think it's a colossal waste of time and an insult to anybody who calls himself a musician."

She smiled, and took the snifter that he held out to her. "I think you might even enjoy it, Rickey. It's a performance, like any other. Maybe there will be a bit more starting and stopping, but still. Who else do we know who is going to spend his Sunday afternoon being filmed by an award-winning director for a music video that millions of people all over the world will watch?" She took a long pull on her drink and enjoyed the hot feeling at the back of her throat. "Not Bruiser, not Tiny, not the Kid," she said, naming three of the football team stars from their high school days.

Rickey raised an eyebrow, lifted his chin, then downed half his glass. "No, not one of those losers," he said. "And not Grant, either. Especially not Grant. You're right, I have a better life by far than anybody else—including my stupid brother. Doesn't mean I can't want it to be better, though." Rickey stared into the bottom of his glass. "I might show up and I might not."

Booker didn't even look at him. "Oh, save it," she said. "Save it for somebody who believes your bullshit. I know you'll be there. And so will I."

She tipped her glass to him in a toast and he returned the gesture. They went back a long way.

The limo inched through the traffic. Anywhere in the entire South of France could be a bitch to get through. A couple of years ago, Rickey had seriously floated the idea that they try to get treatment the same as a head of state— police escort, sirens, traffic lights held at green for them to go through every intersection without stopping. The argument was not that they were in that much of a hurry, but that the slow driving breached his privacy. The French were interested in privacy. Rickey would argue that people ran up to the car while they were stuck in gridlock, trying to take his picture or get an autograph. His safety was in question. But Booker convinced him just to request a car with the windows totally smoked and black every time, and that seemed to take care of things.

She mentally checked off the video shoot discussion and moved on to her next item. "Rickey, we need to talk about your obligations to the label."

"My obligations? What about their obligations to me? I've made them a fortune and they know it."

Booker tried another approach. "Yes, they do know it and they're grateful. But we're in business and it has to work for everybody. Shad says—"

"Shad? Who the hell is Shad?"

"Shad Palmetto. The guy in charge of your business at the record label." She could see no sign of recognition on

Rickey's face. "The guy at the party before the show that you wouldn't meet and then wouldn't let ride with us in the limo on the way back."

Rickey's face looked like he'd just had a whiff of ancient blue cheese. "What more do they want from me? I give them two albums a year, almost. We tour constantly, we're doing two, three concerts a week sometimes—what the hell!"

"Shad says they can't do their jobs properly. They need more from us as far as promotion goes," Booker said. "Come on, Rickey. You know we gotta act like grown-ups here."

"What for?"

She shook her head. Was he going to be Peter Pan forever? Where was it written down that musicians had to be so strange? "They can't get the music out there to the people if we don't do our part—"

Rickey stared out at the shining lights across the harbor and at the water he couldn't see. He was silent for so long that Booker thought he'd checked out of the conversation completely, until he said, "You do your part then. My part is writing and playing the music. And in case you haven't noticed, none of you can do your part . . . or get paid . . . unless I do my part." He took a long gulp from his glass. "And in case you haven't noticed, I'm the *only* one who can do my part. Unlike the rest of you."

He had her there, and Booker knew it. Why did he have to be smart when she was trying to get things her way and not-so-smart when he was in a room with tattoo inks or boats for sale?

Rickey noticed her gloomy face and tried to change the mood. "Come on, Book, lighten up! The show's done, it was a good one, let's chill. Whose side are you on?"

"Yours, Rickey, of course. Big time," she said, settling back against the plush upholstery of the car. Where are we going, then?"

"Back to the party, by way of the beach," Rickey said.

"We gotta swim in the Med before we leave. After that, we pick up some French food, go shopping, maybe find some place where we can scream and shout for a while, then look at some French famous places."

"Awesome."

Well, it wasn't really, but what are you gonna do?

CHAPTER FOUR

Cosmo still wasn't quite sure that he wanted to be at this video production shoot in an ancient building in Cannes. "Video killed the radio star", the Buggles sang just a few years ago, but Cosmo agreed with the dudes who said that watching a video was like watching a TV commercial about a band. He really didn't care what the bands looked like or whether they could act; for him, it was all about the music and the sound. He knew that most people his age would disagree; back at home, kids watched MTV every morning and every afternoon, before and after school.

Even though he wasn't a fan of rock videos, though, he didn't want to miss a minute of this experience of watching Rickey T. The concert last night would be a highlight of his life—maybe today's video shoot would be just as amazing. Cosmo looked around. The room was massive, with floor-to-ceiling windows covering two of the four sides and long, brocade curtains pulled to shut out most of the outside light. A few pieces of furniture were scattered around the edges, most of them with a sort of gold, glittery look. The whole place was decorated like something out of a long-ago castle or mansion. Fancy furniture, paintings on the fake walls, a chandelier.

About thirty people seemed to be wandering around, many of them looking busy but quite a few just hanging around. Some of them had tasks that were obvious: people were adjusting lights, moving tripods and cameras, tuning guitars. But a lot of the activity was a mystery to him. A couple of guys were up on ladders, fiddling with something that looked like a cage. A man in a red vest was standing beside a six-foot-tall amplifier, making notes on a clipboard. Another guy was pushing a huge fan toward the smaller of the two stages that had been set up in the middle of the room. On the bigger stage, to the left, right beside the drum kit, a man was adjusting the leaves of what looked like a plastic palm tree.

Nah, Cosmo thought. Couldn't be. Probably some kind of musical equipment he didn't know about.

Cosmo was almost shaking, this was all so cool!

"Hey. Kid." Booker spoke from behind him and he jumped about a mile. "Who let you in?"

"It was part of the radio station prize I won." He thought he should be feeling shy, maybe even scared, but he really wasn't. Somehow, he felt like he was where he was supposed to be. Like he belonged. Like he had a right, maybe, to be there. Rickey's manager had seemed pretty intimidating at the party at the hotel, and again last night at the concert, but the more times Cosmo saw her, the less scary she seemed. Less scary, and even kind of cute, in an older woman, Jane Fonda-sort of way.

Booker stared into his eyes. "All right. What's your name again? Oh, yeah, Cosmo." She looked as though she couldn't decide whether it was cool or weird. "All right. But don't get in the way."

He nodded as energetically and cooperatively as he could, then tried to disappear into the background. Moments later, Rickey showed up, and everything and everyone else faded out of focus.

He strolled in, three other men and two women

surrounding him. Cosmo recognized Mona Ray and Sturgess, the droopy-moustache guy at the pre-concert party who wanted to talk about the casino all the time. He had on a shiny paisley shirt with collar points almost down to mid-chest. Rickey was wearing an excellent white shirt, cut like something James Bond would wear, black slacks, boots, and a dark cape. Geez, a cape! And yet, it didn't look weird. It looked cool, especially with the blue scarf thing he had around his neck.

Mona Ray was rocking thigh-high black leather boots, a mini-skirt and some kind of gauzy blouse on top. Her red hair was combed up high in a ponytail and her bangs were down so low over her eyes, Cosmo wondered how she could see anything. Who cared, she was such a babe. She could stumble around, bump into the wall and she'd still be able to stop a clock. She was carrying two small dogs and a massive purse.

The whole room froze. Everyone stopped what they were doing and turned their attention toward Rickey. Cosmo looked at all of them while they looked at Rickey. What must it be like to live like that? That much attention, that much money, that much fame?

Rickey swept the cape off his shoulders and dropped it on the floor. "Okay, so I'm here. Let's do this stupid thing."

This stupid thing? Rickey must think like I do, that it should be all about the music, Cosmo thought. We didn't need to see the artists doing little movies of their songs.

"Oh, but just before we start," Rickey said, putting an arm around Booker's shoulders and starting to walk her away from the group. "I want to talk to you about the schedule. It's New York next, then Vancouver and Whistler, then Toronto for a festival, right? And somewhere else, I forget."

"Boston," Booker replied. "By the Charles. Another outdoor venue."

The two walked off and huddled a few dozen feet away for about ten minutes, everyone else on hold till they walked back. Cosmo thought the video director looked annoyed but he couldn't be sure. Most of his own experience with 'annoyed' had to do with his mother and father, who tended to speak sarcastically all the time, and with his former girlfriend, who mostly gave lectures like his teachers did. He'd never been in a working situation like this, and he hadn't seen many French men. Maybe that pained, pissed-off look wasn't 'annoyed'; maybe it was the way they looked all the time.

Mona Ray dropped herself into a chair near the stage, the dogs on her lap, and reached into her bag. She brought out two doggie bowls, one labeled Shaw and the other Zulleezay, and a handful of treats that she tossed into the dishes. The little dogs started to go nuts and she let them jump down to the floor.

Booker and Rickey re-emerged from the shadows at the edges of the massive room. "We've got a storyboard set up over here," Booker said. "Gaspard did the whole song with stand-ins and took photographs so that you could see in advance what he's going for."

"All right, let's look at it," Rickey said.

"By the way, what's he doing here?" Booker asked, motioning toward Sturgess.

Rickey made a face. "I didn't ask him. But I guess we can't avoid him now."

"What do you mean?" Booker's voice was low but Cosmo could hear every word.

"Didn't you hear? He told me that he's been talking with Staten Island Records for a while and they just gave him a job as that suit's assistant."

"Shad's? Shad's assistant?" Booker's eyes were like headlights on high beam in a fog.

A tiny man, about the size of a jockey, bustled up to the two of them. It was the annoyed guy. "Hello, Rickey. Yes, here it is, the storyboard. You can see here, we open with a shot of a parade on a sunny day—"

Rickey concentrated on the piece of cardboard taped to

the wall and waved the others away. Booker and Gaspard stood back, giving Rickey his space while he stared at the lines of thirty photographs or so that covered the storyboard.

"This . . ." They all held their breath while they waited for Rickey's comment. He made them wait about ten seconds, then ". . . is crap!" Rickey's voice was low but his face looked as though his brain was shouting. Cosmo could tell by the looks on the musicians and the backup singers' faces that he wasn't the only one who wondered whether Rickey would hang in until the shoot was done or go storming off to wherever it was that he went when he was pitching a fit.

Rickey stood, hands on hips, staring at the storyboard and the two-foot by two-foot color photo of the director mounted just above it.

"It's insane!" Rickey shouted. His voice had caught up with his brain. "Who is this guy anyway?"

"He comes very highly recommended," Booker tried to sooth him. "He's done a dozen of these things and he's won awards."

"That just means there are other people as idiotic as he is!"

Gaspard glided toward him. "Monsieur Rickey, let's discuss the problem," he murmured. He put a hand on Rickey's arm and that seemed to be enough to make the rock star explode.

"The problem . . .is you! The problem is this stupid video. What the hell? Pigeons? Hawaiian shirts? Hiking boots? French freakin' berets, for God's sake?"

Gaspard looked offended. "The concept is travel. He is running, running away, and he doesn't know where he wants to go, and he goes to the tropics, then the Alps, then France . . ."

"And who are these women?!" Rickey pointed toward a trio in matching Moulin Rouge ruffles, black thigh-high stockings and chokers, standing around microphones on the small stage. Cosmo had no idea who they were but he hoped that Gaspard would come up with a good reason for keeping them on the set.

"These are her friends . . . and this is Lorraine," Gaspard said. "He is leaving Lorraine."

"That's not Lorraine!" Rickey yelled. "Don't you even say her name!" Rickey spun around, searching the room. "Booker!"

Booker stepped in between the two of them, obviously with the same worry that Cosmo had: Rickey looked as if he were seconds away from taking a swing at the video director. Cosmo wasn't much of a judge of fight scenarios—he'd only ever seen two in his life, one on a high school football field (after school, not during a game) and one in the stands at a hockey game between fans. Both times, though, the impression that one guy was about to have his fist make contact with another guy's flesh and bone was about as strong as it was in here. The tension was intense.

"I'll take care of it, Rickey," Booker said soothingly. She seemed to spend a lot of time telling other people to 'chill out' and that she would take care of things, Cosmo thought. "Gaspard, the song is very personal to Rickey."

"It's Mr. Taggart, to him," Rickey shouted.

". . . and Lorraine is a real person. We have to be sensitive."

"I am sensitive!" This seemed to have caught Gaspard below the belt. "And I am creative! This video will express the emotion behind the lyrics and will use visual aids to help those with a less developed imagination to understand the meaning—"

"What a load of bullshit!" Rickey shouted as he headed for the door.

Gaspard stepped forward and right into Rickey's path. "Give it a chance, Monsieur Rickey! You will see! Let us finish, play the song, get a few takes and you will see, it will work!" He reached for Rickey's arm, then clutched his sleeve.

Rickey looked down at Gaspard's hand. "Yeah, make my day."

Gaspard let go of Rickey's shirt, but didn't move.

It might have turned even rougher if it weren't for one of the props guys, sitting up on a ladder by the cage full of birds. He was watching everything going on below with so much interest that he didn't notice that he'd let his balance get wonky. He leaned too far out, the ladder shifted, and he reached out to get steady. The cage was right there—the door, actually—and he grabbed it with both hands. It swung wide.

Two seconds later, the ceiling of the warehouse was filled with pigeons, trying to escape. Pigeons, man. Fifteen seconds later, they found their way downward, zipping back and forth like … well, like caged wild birds set free in an enclosed space. Scared, loud, wild . . .and that was just the input from Buttercup and Brandy and Angie or whoever they were. All three ladies were screaming while the pigeons flew and dove overhead. The roadies and props guys were screaming with laughter while the session guitar player, who'd been tuning up, launched into a Lynyrd Skynyrd tune.

Rickey glanced up at the ceiling. "I'll be back at the resort, Booker. Call me when you've got rid of this guy."

And he was gone. Gaspard looked as if something had just happened that he couldn't quite understand, something that had left him reeling. He shook his head a few times like a boxer who'd been hit in the jaw and Cosmo wondered whether he was going to stagger and go down to the mat.

"Mademoiselle Buchanan?" Gaspard tried to get the attention of Booker, who was staring at the door Rickey had just nearly taken off its hinges. "I think we will take a break now, let's say until tomorrow. We shall begin again then."

Booker dragged her focus back to the video director. "No, I don't think so, Gaspard. Rickey doesn't want you and so I think we're done here."

"Done? But that can't be," Gaspard said. "We have a contract."

"Don't worry, you'll get paid," Booker said.

"It's not only that," Gaspard replied, his nose screwed up even higher, as if he'd inhaled a really big stink. "I know I will get paid; my attorney will see to that. But what about the reputation? I can't have it getting around that I started a production and it wasn't finished. Especially with someone like Rickey T!"

Booker stared at him for a few moments. "I see the issue," she eventually said. "Let me think about it. We'll work something out." She put a hand behind Gaspard's back and began propelling him toward the door. "Give me a week."

She heaved a sigh as soon as the director was gone, then seemed to become aware that Mona Ray, Sturgess, "Lorraine", her two sidekicks, and Cosmo were all staring at her. The session musicians were packing up their instruments. "Hey, come on, don't worry, you'll all get paid," she said. "And I'll call you as soon as we have a new director and a new shooting schedule set up. Not you," she added, looking at Mona Ray. "That's up to Rickey, I don't know about you."

Mona Ray nodded and started to pack up the big bag she'd brought along, stuffing things she'd unpacked back in.

"What's all that?" Booker asked. "Are those knitting needles?"

"I gotta pass the time," Mona Ray said, as she stuffed three big balls of red wool into the depths of the bag, following them with two paperbacks.

"You knit?" Booker was astonished.

Mona Ray pulled herself up to a height she didn't really have. High-heeled boots could be very handy. "I do whatever I want," she said. "You seem to be living with a lot of stereotyping. Sign of a lazy mind. I knit for my family and for my friends. All the time." And she swept out.

Cosmo thought she looked sensational.

Booker was back to fuming. "Just freakin' unprofessional," she muttered. Cosmo couldn't tell whether she was referring to the video director or to Rickey—or maybe to Mona Ray? "Man, I gotta get outa here, too. All of you, we're done for the day here. I'll be in touch, let you know what's happening next, and when," she announced to the people still in the room. "Singers, musicians, crew, we'll still need you all to get this video made."

"Booker, when is this likely to happen?" The drummer interrupted and came around to the front of the bigger stage. "I got a few other commitments."

"I'm going to aim for tomorrow, find a space, new director." She noticed a commotion near the door. "Oh, crap, he's back."

Gaspard had come marching back in, forceful but seeming calmer. "Mademoiselle Buchanan, I cannot leave without payment. The risk to my reputation is bad enough but if I also don't have a check . . . well, I am sure you can see my concern."

Booker squared her shoulders, looked way, way down at Gaspard, and seemed ready to have the shouting start. "Why would that be my problem?"

"There is a lot of money to be made on the fringes, you know," Gaspard seemed to be speaking in a very friendly tone but the words weren't very friendly. "I have photos, stories to tell. People to quote."

Booker said nothing for such a long time that Cosmo started a silent count. *Was she ever going to say anything?*

"All right then, sport," Booker said. "I don't have checks on me, but I'll make a call to the accountant. She's here in town. Kid, pass me that backpack over there."

Cosmo could hardly believe he wasn't invisible. He practically ran over to the table that Booker pointed out and brought back the bulky canvas carrying bag. She reached into it and pulled out a beige object that looked like an oversized telephone receiver.

"You seen one of these?" Booker seemed quite distracted, and quite proud. "It's a cellular telephone, I can call anybody from right here."

"Why don't you just call him from that phone on the wall, right over there?" Gaspard asked suspiciously. "It is not complicated. You call them, tell them I will be over to pick up my check in half an hour. I have a taxi waiting outside."

"I could use the phone on the wall, sure, but what if there were no phone on the wall? These things are the wave of the future," Booker said, as she punched at the buttons on it. "Four thousand bucks."

"Ah, so that's why you wanted to be sure I knew about it," Gaspard said. "Yes, I can see that you are all so successful, so confident, so rich and famous. Yes, I am impressed, we are all so impressed with you and your Mr. Rickey T. That doesn't mean I am so fortunate to know him and to spend time with him that I will overlook the money he owes me!"

Gaspard would have been quite formidable if it weren't for the way he had to duck every few seconds to avoid the pigeons still zooming around the warehouse.

"Yeah, yeah, I'm on it," Booker said, then finished putting in the phone number. She spoke briefly into the mobile phone then put it down, pulled a pen and notepad from her jeans pocket and wrote down an address. "She's expecting you."

Gaspard looked really smug as he left and even Cosmo found himself wanting to punch him. Booker sighed as if she were suddenly very tired, then looked very surprised when she turned around and realized a lot of people were still in the room.

"Hey, I think we're all done here," Booker said. "We'll fulfill on everybody."

As the musicians and crew packed up and left the building, her new phone rang. "Yeah?" she said. "Yeah, he's gone, but listen, he's on his way over to you. At the hotel. We have to give the guy a check, he'll smear us all over town if we don't. You've got a copy of the contract, pay him the full amount. Yeah, I know it's hefty but I've got no alternative . . .what do you mean, give you a couple of days to cover it? What are you talking about? What's missing?"

Booker seemed to wake up and realize that half a dozen people were still nearby, listening to her. She stepped away, into a darker, quieter corner of the room, swatting at a pigeon or two as she went. After talking for a few minutes, she came walking back, waving her arms around, her voice now about ten decibels louder and half an octave higher. "Look, just transfer the funds over from one of the special purpose accounts, the savings accounts, yeah. We got plenty to cover it, just need to get it into the right place. Yeah, you do that. I'll be in tomorrow to go over a few things with you."

Booker punched a button on the cellular phone that must have been the button that disconnected the line, interrupted the transmission, or changed the frequency or whatever it was it did. She laid it on a table, her hand still curled around its edges, sat herself down in a chair beside it and slumped like she had the weight of nine planets on her shoulders.

Then, she pulled her hand back and screeched. A bird had pooped on the phone.

CHAPTER FIVE

Germany

Double-checking his jeans jacket pocket to make sure his InterRail pass was still in there, Cosmo exhaled in relief. If he lost it, he might not be able to get home. He had just enough money to eat, but no money for a hostel. He would sleep on the train back home to Mannheim.

If he slept at all. Even though it had been a long day, he was still so hyper and so pumped about all his experiences in Cannes that he doubted he'd be able to sleep until he was twenty-one! He'd grabbed some paper at Rickey's resort hotel and he was going to use it to write William a letter that would blow his mind.

After the video shoot disaster, the band, the singers, Mona Ray, Sturgess and Booker had scattered. Cosmo wandered out of the building, scanning the streets to see whether he could spot a taxi or a train station. A tubby, badly dressed guy, about thirty years old, approached him and asked if he'd been part of the Rickey T video shoot.

"No, I wasn't in it," Cosmo said.

"But you were in the building." The man rummaged in

a pocket in his lumpy tweed jacket, then pulled out a business card. "I'm Dwight Kettle, ABD Radio. Doing a piece on Rickey T. Do you work here? Live here?"

Cosmo shook his head. "Neither. I was just watching them make the video."

"So, there *is* a video." Dwight groped around in his other pocket, producing a small notebook and a pen. "Which song did they do?"

That was a hard one to answer. "I don't really know," Cosmo said.

Dwight stared into his eyes. His right hand scribbled notes on the page of the palm-sized, spiral-coiled notebook in his left, but his gaze never left Cosmo's face. "Who are you, exactly?"

"I won a radio contest for concert tickets and they invited me to watch them do this video," Cosmo said.

"Name?" Dwight barked at him in a take-charge kind of way that reminded Cosmo of his father and all of his military friends.

"Cosmo Lewis."

"How long were you inside, Cosmo, and what did you see?"

"Not long. I saw them setting up for a video, instruments, costumes. You know."

"What was the video about?"

Something told Cosmo that the reporter was leading him down a road that he'd rather not follow. "What was your name again? What's this for?"

"Dwight Kettle. I'm a music journalist. Not sure where it will be published or even if it will be. I'm just gathering background." Dwight lifted his chin slightly and seemed to be waiting for Cosmo to fill the silence.

After a few seconds, Cosmo made a move to break Dwight's gaze. "Yeah, well, I don't know what the video was going to be about, I only saw them getting started. Something about traveling, I think," he said, hiking his backpack up over one shoulder. "Look, man, I've got a train to catch."

"Just a few more quick questions," Dwight didn't move. "Traveling where? And you mentioned, costumes, what kind of costumes? Was Rickey T there?"

Cosmo took a step back. "Yeah, he was. I don't know, French costumes. Like I said, Mr. Kettle, I don't want to miss my train. I'm not the person you want to talk to."

Dwight stopped writing and closed his notebook. "All right, kid, thanks anyway."

As Cosmo walked toward the main drag, he wondered whether he should have told Dwight Kettle a few more details about the video shoot. It might be cool to have his name in a magazine or on the radio, talking about Rickey T. But his second thoughts didn't slide into third or fourth ones, and all in all, he felt good about closing off the conversation when he did.

He hitchhiked from Cannes to the train station in Nice, catching a ride with a couple who put him in the back seat of a Renault between their eight-year-old twins. When the family heard he was American they filled the half hour drive with questions about the movies and TV shows they'd seen. They used a mix of English and French, and everybody got a good workout for their foreign language skills. How do you say *Blade Runner* in French? How do you explain the rules of a TV show like *Des Chiffres et des Lettres* in English? The miles went by quickly.

The train station, Gare de Nice-Ville, was full of people Cosmo's age and he thought some of the chicks were really cute. Another time, another place, he'd have been mixing, meeting, collecting names and phone numbers. But he just couldn't get into the 'now'. His head was full of the images of the past few days: meeting Rickey at the hotel, the concert, the video shoot. He felt like he'd been to the moon and back.

He barely noticed boarding or finding a seat. Somewhere near Stuttgart, Cosmo began to have a feeling that his conversation with the radio reporter had been a bad idea. It was nothing in particular that either one of them had said—he just had an uneasy feeling about it.

Cosmo zipped open the side pocket on his backpack and pulled out the crumpled white card. *Dwight Kettle, Freelance Journalist*, it read, with an address in New Jersey. Cosmo had no idea what the cost of a phone call to area code 201 might be, but Dwight wasn't in the States right now, anyway. It would have to be a letter. He would write to the guy as soon as he got home, ask him not to print anything that Cosmo had said and to leave out his name.

When Cosmo opened the door to the house, the smell of spanakopita in the oven greeted him. Man, he loved his mother's cooking! And he was starving—he could eat an entire pan of it himself.

"Hey, when's it ready?"

His mother was in the kitchen—she was always in the kitchen. "Right now, Cosmo. Wash your hands. How was your trip?"

"Excellent. The concert was super, the people were nice."

He brought her a plate from the cupboard and she lifted four big squares onto it. Two hunks of bread and a scoop of hummus, keftedes and a little tzatziki. That would do for a starter.

Cosmo's mother beamed, as she always did when she watched him eat. "You are so lucky you have the system to burn off all those calories. I only wish."

He gave her a hug. "Yeah, I know. Hey, pop."

His father liked to show up as soon as Cosmo got back from wherever he was and quiz him as if he were applying to work for him or something. "Hello, Cosmo. How was your trip?"

"I was just telling Mom, they treated me really nice. The show was rad, the music was terrific."

"Rad?" His father asked. "That must be a word from another language you've been smart enough to learn, Cosmo. But never mind, I can figure it out." He took a plate about half full of food from my mother and sat down at the table.

"And Rickey? He is as good as ever?" Mom still loved Rickey's music. I think she would have gone with me, if she could, Cosmo thought.

"It was his second-to-last concert in Europe. He goes to Rome next." Cosmo filled his mouth with the delicious spinach pie. The cheese and pastry were just awesome. "He did the States just a few months ago . . . although, not all of them and there is talk there will be a new album next month, so maybe he'll be touring again."

"Then maybe you will have your chance to see him perform again," my father said. "When he's back on stage in the U.S., I mean."

There was silence all around for a few minutes. Some things just need to sink in. But somebody had to move us along, and, as usual, it was his mother. "We are going back?"

My father forked up the last of his meal. "We are."

A new school. For twelfth grade. Ten schools in eleven years for Cosmo.

"Baltimore?" he asked. He liked Baltimore, and he was still in touch with William.

His father shook his head.

Not Texas, Cosmo thought. Please, don't let it be Texas. He didn't meet a single person in Texas that he liked, and quite a few who didn't like him. It was one of the places where Rickey's music was the only thing that got him through.

"California."

California. Beaches, movie stars, Pacific Ocean. Someplace completely new.

***

Rickey had had it with France and he was looking forward to getting to Rome, finishing off this tour. He pulled his suitcase out of the closet and got to work on getting his clothes ready to go. Booker had offered many times to hire somebody to do the packing or suggested he let somebody from the hotel do it, but it was one of the things he kept for himself. It defused the stress, somehow. Maybe it was the repetition or even the rhythm: off the hanger, onto the bed, fold, fold, smooth out the wrinkles, fold, lay it down in the bag.

He had a message to phone his friend Henry back but he'd take care of that later. He had just a few hours before he had to be on the Lear, heading for Rome and the last show on this tour. Man, he was looking forward to it, and to the vacation on the Med, afterward. Mona Ray had hinted around for an invitation but he'd ignored her.

A knock at the door interrupted his wrinkle-smoothing rhythm.

"Yeah? Who is it?" Rickey called, expecting to hear the word "housekeeping".

"Shad Palmetto."

Now that was an answer he had not been expecting. Rickey marched to the door and opened it. Over the shoulder of the record label VP, Rickey could see the rest of the suite, with all the debris from last night's get-together scattered over the couches, the piano and the bar counters. Too bad it wasn't housekeeping.

"Shad. Hello." Rickey kept his voice as flat as he could and avoided eye contact with the man. It wasn't hard to do, since he had about six inches in height over him.

"Hello, Rickey. I hope I'm not disturbing you," Shad said smoothly as he began forward motion through the door.

What the hell? Rickey was in the awkward instant of deciding whether to physically block Shad's entry. Something about the guy's confidence, despite his pint-sized presence, compelled Rickey to step back and let him in.

"What can I do for you?" Rickey asked, trying to recover control.

"We missed connections the other night, after the concert. I thought we'd get a chance to talk during the ride back to the resort but after I got through the crowd, I couldn't find the limo. I guess we got our wires crossed." Shad's smile only went halfway up his face. His eyes were hard and Rickey thought he read a threat in them.

"Yeah, we got our wires crossed," Rickey said, not moving. He'd let the guy in but he was damned if he was going to relax for a second or make him welcome. "What's up?"

Shad sighed. "I was hoping we could do this conversation in a friendlier way—"

"Friendlier?" Rickey said. "What's not friendly about my bedroom, Shad?"

Shad didn't smile back. "Let me just cut to the chase, Rickey. I know you don't have a lot of time before the plane leaves for Rome. I'm getting heat from the label about picking up the speed of things. They want you to bring out the records a little faster and they want to start planning next year's tour now. Booker can get better terms by making arrangements as far ahead as possible."

Rickey leaned toward the door, trying to use his body language to get Shad to leave. "Is that so? Well, I'm sure that's something that you and Booker can go over and work out. I don't have any time left before I have to be on my way to the next gig, so—" *There's the door, buddy.*

Shad planted his feet and refused to take the step backward that Rickey was urging on him. "Come on, Rickey, we both know that it comes down to you. Booker doesn't write or record the songs or go on stage, you do. And if you're suggesting that I'm not supposed to talk to you directly, that I have to go through your employee to get a message to you . . . well, that's just not happening."

That was exactly what Rickey was suggesting. But apparently, suggesting wasn't working. It was time to be direct. "What I'm saying, Shad, is that if you want more records and more touring, you need to keep me happy. And you showing up at my hotel suite, threatening me, is not a way to keep me happy."

"Threatening you? I didn't threaten you! But I will now. Get this straight, Mr. Rickey T Taggart, if you don't buckle down and grow some ambition, we'll cut you loose."

Well, now, that took a little thinking about. Rickey had no appetite for shopping for a new label at this point in his career and he had zero interest in starting his own. He wanted to streamline the business part and reduce the amount of stuff he had to do other than make music. If Staten Island Records kicked him out, he'd be going in the opposite direction.

Shad wasn't finished. "Or maybe we won't cut you loose. Maybe we'll keep you around, locked down by that ten-year contract you signed, and we'll hold you to every tiny letter and semi-colon in it. I can make life very easy for you, Taggart, or I can make it hell. You pick."

Now that he was good and ready, Shad stepped back from the bedroom doorway. Rickey slammed it shut, then, ten seconds later, heard Shad's footsteps moving through the outer part of the suite toward the hallway door.

He grabbed the phone to call Booker, then let it drop before he even punched in the number. Man, he was just so tired. Of this, of everything, of all of it.

CHAPTER SIX

Barcelona

You get yourself on a boat and you block out all the crap that's bothering you. Rickey let out the jib and watched the wind fill the sail, his lungs and his heart filling along with it. Yeah, of course, there were crew on board who could do this, and most of the time, manual labor would be his last choice, but the boat was the exception. He loved doing this, almost as much as he loved making music and writing songs.

He had insisted on this vacation break, even though he knew Booker wasn't happy about it and the record label wasn't happy. But without these brief pauses, he'd go completely crazy. Some days—most days—he could only see two ways to go. Quit the whole friggin' rock star nightmare or just medicate himself enough and take vacations as often as he could, until he croaked.

He squinted to cut the glare from the bright sunshine and to bring Barcelona into focus. He could barely see the hotel in the distance and the marina where he'd chartered this pretty little thing. Where the hell were his sunglasses? He almost shouted for Mona Ray to find them and then he remembered that she wasn't there. He'd decided to let her go in Cannes, after that godawful video shoot, when she sided with that toad of a director. She'd told him she thought he was being narrow-minded about the whole video production idea. That was bad enough, but when he found out that she'd slipped her brother in to watch, without asking his permission, or even Booker's—! The guy had been hanging around with a clipboard, wearing a vest she said she knit for him. Rickey had made fun of the guy's clothes and Mona Ray got really worked up about that. She was very insulted that Rickey wasn't impressed with her knitting. Knitting, for god's sake! He made himself scarce in Rome and got Sturgess to pass a message to Mona Ray. A good-bye letter and a first-class ticket to the States. She was on the next plane home.

He wasn't missing her—not her in particular, and not female companionship in general. He had no doubt that day would come but for now, he had everything he needed and wanted. When you were on a beautiful boat like this *Sassy Thérèse*, you could just let everything else go, you know?

Rickey made the line fast on the cleat and gave a thumb's up to the skipper. The big man behind the wheel was smiling ear to ear, his massive hands resting lightly on the dark, polished wood. If his beard looked a little shaggy and his clothes a bit faded, so what? It was the first time he'd hired this guy, Captain Maxime, and he would use him again. Captain Maxime just oozed competence at the helm and you felt you could count on him to get you through any storm. But at the same time, Max was able to put across his confidence in Rickey's abilities as a sailor. He seemed to have a sixth sense for knowing when Rickey wanted to take over, when he wanted to crew, and when he wanted to kick back in a deck chair and not lift a finger.

Like now. Rickey dropped his butt into his favorite spot, on the port side, midships, and groped around for his sunglasses. There they were. See, he didn't need Mona Ray after all. Maybe that was a bit cold, but you have to have a sense of humor about these things. Otherwise, you'd go nuts.

The shrink he'd recently begun seeing, back in New York, would probably tell him that there was significance in the fact that he was even thinking about her. But he wasn't thinking about her! Not in an "on my mind" kind of way; her name had just popped into his head because there was something that needed finding. Briefly.

That reminded him that he needed to make an appointment to see his guy when he got back to the city. He knew that Booker had a "to-do" list a mile long, waiting for him. He thought that this vacation would relax him enough that he would be ready to return to his job but whenever he thought of performing, meeting people, just being himself—it made him want to scream. The stage fright was getting worse, too.

Rickey looked around and, like magic, the steward was there with a tall, frosty one in his hand. He held it out to Rickey, grinned at him, then pointed toward Captain Maxime at the wheel. The skipper grinned back and gave them both a thumbs-up. Yeah, the guy knew just what he needed and the exact moment he needed it.

Rickey downed half the beer in a couple of gulps. He was feeling mellow, yeah, but he'd be even better if he could shake Mona Ray out of his head. Maybe there was a song in it, something about the woman and something about the sea. Or the boat. Or Barcelona. Rickey pulled one of the small notebooks he always kept around out of his shorts pocket, wiggled the short pencil out of the wire coil and started to write.

Or, try to write, was more like it. Nothing was coming, not a word. Rickey sighed, then lubricated his dry spell with a few more gulps of beer. He hadn't been able to settle down to write for weeks. It was just one interruption or distraction after another. The concert in Cannes, that horrible video shoot, Mona Ray, the prospect of going back to New York, of going back out on tour, of doing the next album, of doing media, of seeing the fans . . . the prospect of his whole, effing life. How could he be expected to write under these conditions?

He liked to reach for the best possible song he could make, always. It took him a long time, unlike some others, who said they could sit down and have a song pour out in about fifteen minutes. Rickey had to work at it, slave over each line and phrase. His goal always was to find the right combination of notes and words to give people some particular experience, some particular feeling. With lyrics, he thought, it was easier. With music, it was too easy to veer into the obvious or the clichéd. Crashing chords, soft melodies, haunting, minor progressions—sure, but everybody knew all that. You had to go beyond, find the musical phrase that gave the listener that epiphany, that "yeah, that's how I feel!" moment. And it had to be unique.

He put the notebook aside and reached for the football he carried with him wherever he went. Somehow it soothed him, just to toss it up in the air, either going for a nice, regular rhythm or heaving it higher with each throw.

"Hey, Captain Max!" Rickey shouted as he raised his left arm and began to pitch the football aft. "Go long!" He saw the boat boss laugh, then shake his head as the ball soared out toward the shore. Yeah, well, you'd have to be very surprised if he actually made any move to run for it. Or swim for it. Surprised, but entertained, yeah? Rickey shrugged in the captain's direction, then made a note to tell Booker to order a few more footballs for him.

As the afternoon wore on, Rickey watched Captain Maxime steer the *Sassy Thérèse* back toward Barcelona and Port Vell. He had plans to spend an evening exploring La Rambla and it occurred to him that the sailor might be an enjoyable companion. There really was no one else that he wanted to plan to have dinner with, although he had a Rolodex jammed full and he knew he could come up with a name and number or two. He could call Booker and ask her to set something up, for that matter—he'd done that a few times before—although he and Booker seemed to be rowing in opposite directions right now.

Maxime handed off the helm to one of the crew and came over to where Rickey was sprawled on a deck chair. "You're going ashore, Mr. Taggart? I can arrange a car, if you'd like."

"I would like, Maxime. Yeah, much as I've enjoyed the food on board over the past few nights, I want to see some people tonight, you know?"

The captain grinned. "Perfectly. I'll call the car."

"Would you join me?"

If the sailor was surprised, he didn't show it. "Yes, sir, I can do that. Just give me a few minutes to change."

When he reappeared above decks ten minutes later, Max had ditched the charter company uniform and was dressed more casually. That worked for Rickey because whenever he went out, he preferred not to draw attention and he usually dressed down as much as possible, even going incognito sometimes. He'd wear a wig, with dark, sloppy hair, glasses, even a little plaster to give himself a bigger nose, some fake hair for a moustache. It could take a lot of work and a lot of equipment to look natural and just like everybody else. Nothing wrecked his night faster than being recognized and made the center of attention by people he didn't want to meet. He and Booker had talked this over once, her saying she didn't get why a guy whose whole life and success were based on public recognition wanted to hide out and him saying she didn't get it because she'd never experienced it.

He lost all control in those situations. The music industry—the machinery—had tried to turn him into a product, putting him on a conveyor belt, to go around and around. If he cooperated with that, it would just get worse, he told Booker, and eventually, he would lose any humanity he had left, as well as any ability to write songs with any depth or substance.

So, he had to stay in charge, had to control the public's

and the industry's access to his time. Yeah, he had to make appearances and he realized there was more to the business than just writing and recording albums, but that didn't mean that he was for sale and that he had to jump every time the assholes said jump. He did have a private life and he did have some private time. Tonight was one of those times.

He met Maxime on the dock, his hair tucked under a hat and a pair of dark glasses shielding his eyes. He wore a checked shirt, a pair of jeans, cowboy boots and a big belt; he thought that if anyone were to try to place him, on being told that he was a singer, they would go for the country and western names.

The bodega they chose looked like nothing special, but the service was fast and the faces of the other diners were happy. The restaurant was tucked away on a little side street only a few hundred yards from a cathedral. A dozen chairs surrounded round, wrought-iron tables on a patio in front of a whitewashed building decorated with flower pots cut in half and anchored in the wall. Beyond the heavy wooden door that opened onto the sidewalk, a dimly lit interior sheltered about ten tables, each one tucked into an alcove made cozy with suspended wine racks and an occasional bookshelf. When Rickey and Maxime walked in, a server in white and black with a half apron over his pants looked up from the table where he was taking an order and waved them toward an empty spot. On his way to the kitchen the server (or perhaps he was the owner) stopped by their table and with a friendly 'hola', dropped the menus beside the blue-checked napkins.

Rickey had his own face tucked behind a menu when he heard his name called. Oh shit.

"Rickey! Rickey T! Ohmigod, way out here in Spain, I don't believe it!"

He braced himself and tried to crawl farther into the fold of the menu as the owner of the screechy voice approached. "Can I get an autograph?"

He got ready to paste on his phony smile and ask her if

she had a pen, which often shot the autograph request dead in the water when the demander didn't have one. Then he realized that she was passing his table and not stopping. Rickey pulled his hat a little lower and turned in his seat. Over by the dark wall, about midway between a rack of bottles of wine and the door to the toilets, was a thin, young guy with blond hair, wearing a faded denim shirt and jeans, tucked in by himself at a small table for two, his long legs stretched out and crossed at the ankles. He looked up at the woman, looked her over, and then nodded. Slowly.

Rickey was mesmerized. Who was this kid . . .? And would he get away with it? She shoved a notepad and a pen at him, almost hopping from one foot to another while she waited. He took the pen, put the notebook down on the table, then scribbled on it. She was babbling, something about a concert in Rome, but the young guy didn't say a word. The waiter came over, took the woman by the elbow, and ushered her away.

Well. That was interesting. Rickey had heard of people calling themselves "Doctor" in order to get a little more respect and a reservation at a restaurant that was fully booked, but never of somebody agreeing to give an autograph as somebody they'd been mistaken for.

It seemed it wasn't over yet, either, but about to be even more entertaining. The imposter raised a hand toward the waiter and beckoned him over. Rickey tried to read their lips but it was too dim in the restaurant. Moments later, after a short conversation between the two, the bogus Rickey stood up, the waiter picked up his drink, and the two strolled over to what was undoubtedly the best table in the restaurant, near the edge of the sidewalk with a primo view of the street but just enough distance that his famous self wasn't hung out in the middle of traffic. A buzz was starting in the little restaurant as people recognized the rock singer—or thought they did—and a few were brave enough to go over to ask for autographs. He met them all with a smile.

Rickey gave a few thoughts to blowing the whistle on

the guy but after a second Scotch and a whole lotta laughs with Maxime, he really didn't care enough. You go whichever way the wind is blowing, right? This guy, this kid grew up looking like a famous rock 'n' roll singer, why not make the most of it? Rickey actually thought it was pretty ballsy of the guy—ballsy and inspirational. He stared at the youngster, then ordered his third Scotch. This kid might just be the solution to his problems.

Rickey lay awake that night in his stateroom on board the *Sassy Thérèse*, trying to decide what to do. Did he have the nerve? Was it even possible? To con the fans, con the critics, the hangers-on? Best of all, it would put one over— a big one—on the industry itself. Shad Palmetto, all those other suits, those know-it-all record executives, the business managers, the producers . . . shit, the critics, the journalists, even some of the DJs. He could fool 'em all.

Mostly, it would be an escape, though. He'd reached his limit; it just wasn't worth it. They weren't paying him enough to put up with so much crap. Sure, he'd made millions but it still wasn't enough. He'd given them his music and his time, but they seemed to think he owed them his soul. Well, he didn't, and he wasn't going to go along with it any longer. It was time to bail; you only have to give so much before it's time to think about yourself and do something to protect yourself.

But could it be done? Rickey dwelt on that point for about a minute before he convinced himself that of course, it could. By him. Somebody else would probably screw it up, but he could make it work.

So, what should he do? You could say he was just . . . taking a walk. Taking a little break. He'd done it before, in a way, very briefly, when he'd put on a disguise and dressed up as someone else. This was the same thing, except that it would be someone else dressing up as him. It would be just 'reverse-disguise'.

And it wouldn't be for anything or any time fundamental. Not for the song-writing, or the recording, or the performing. Just for the public appearances, for a time when having a stand-in wouldn't matter much. It wouldn't matter to the public and it would allow him to hang on to his sanity and his mental health. Man, it was just the same as an actor using a stunt double. Nobody minded that, and nobody would mind this either.

It was possible, he knew it was. He could keep the show going and keep the Rickey T mystique alive but once in a while, off-load the tasks that were killing him. He could take back the control. Puppet master, rather than puppet.

By sunrise, Rickey had decided to go walkabout for a while, travel around, think things over and polish the details of his plan. He already knew though that when he got back, Booker was the first person he'd have to get on board. He wouldn't con her; he probably couldn't, she was so alert. He'd long since given up waiting for her to zone out, occasionally. When it came to him, and to the business, she was always wide awake.

But this was a good thing. He needed her to make it work with the suits, and he needed somebody to make it work with the fans. And he needed somebody like this guy tonight to be the stand-in. But Booker was the key part. Would she go along with it? Would she want to be part of it? Only one way to find out.

CHAPTER SEVEN

New York

New York City was every bit as beautiful, in its own way, as the places they'd seen in Europe. In these past weeks, Booker had been flooded with a feeling of good vibes about being back in the good old U.S. of A. Travel was awesome, but getting back home, that was even better.

She was the only one who thought so, apparently. Rickey had taken off and seemed to be sailing his way around the Mediterranean with plans to carry on travelling through every country anybody ever heard of and quite a few that nobody ever had. Maybe easier to be anonymous in places like Moldova or Liechtenstein. Whatever his reasons, he hadn't communicated with Booker, Shad at the record label, his friends, or his family. Booker had even checked with Mona Ray; the woman had just laughed at her.

Booker hadn't been able to talk to her boss, in person and alone, since they'd parted company at the video shoot in Cannes. He wouldn't come back for a second day, even though she'd booked a different director. Everyone had flown off to Rome for the final stop on the tour and Rickey had closed himself off at the front of the Lear, with Mona Ray and Sturgess on either side of him. No one else was allowed.

After the date in Rome, Rickey had disappeared into a limo and pulled up at some boat dock on the Spanish coast. She had had only three phone calls from him since, a very unusual situation. In the first call, she'd tried to take the opportunity to communicate with him about the financial situation. He was furious. The second call was short and to the point: he was on vacation now and he'd call her when he was ready. Things were very cold. The third call was no better.

But while one part of her was hurt, one part was shaking it off. The silent treatment was childish and painful, but she refused to let him get to her. As she puttered around her condo in the West Village, she left the phone out on the kitchen table, within reach so that she wouldn't miss a call. No matter what he did, she'd be there, that was their deal. No matter what he did. And maybe he would reciprocate. She liked to look at it that way.

Who knew if he returned the loyalty that she'd decided she owed him? It didn't matter. She was confident he would turn up in New York like he was supposed to. If affection for her wasn't in the picture, and their history meant squat, surely professionalism would round him up and bring him in. There were things to do, people to see, places to go. Rehearsal for recording in three weeks, a tour shortly after that.

In that first phone call, she'd tried to convince him that it was time to be practical about the money. Things weren't desperate, and at least Booker had never had to worry about Rickey developing a taste for smack, as had so many of the others in his situation. But things weren't ideal, either. She wanted everyone to cut back a bit, but when she tried to express that to Rickey, the rock star went off the deep end.

"What are you talking about, cut expenses?" Rickey's voice at the other end of the phone line was as hoarse as if he just done three screamer vocal solos in a row. "We're making money, piles of it! It's roaring in here like a river! We sold out every show in twenty cities in twelve countries! We just finished a sold-right-out tour of the U.S. before that!"

"Yeah, we're bringing in money, but we're not hanging on to it, Rickey," Booker said. "Expenses are monumental, you have no idea. Next time we get together, let's sit down with the books and I'll show you—"

"I don't want to have any idea!" Rickey shouted. "I'll make the money, you manage it. That was our deal from the beginning." There were a few seconds of silence, then she could hear him gulping something. "Man, I am getting so tired of this crap."

"So am I, dude, so am I."

"No, Booker, you're not hearing me. I am totally tired of being who I am. And I'm starting to hate the music, too, this corporate pop, eighties crap."

"Yeah, Rick, but what else can we do?"

The question was rhetorical in her mind, but not in his. Turned out he had some very definite ideas about what they could do, all of them unreasonable, unrealistic and implausible.

They talked some more, he hung up, and then she didn't get the second phone call until a week later. "I'm on vacation, I'll call you when I'm ready," he said, and then he was gone.

The third call, another week later, was a bit more rational.

"How are you? Feeling better? I'm glad you're taking a break and I'm glad Rome was the last show," Booker said.

"So am I," Rickey replied. "It would have been a drag to have to cancel anything."

Cancel? Whoa, Rickey must be skating closer to the edge than Booker realized.

"Let's just leave everything rest for now," he went on. "Do we need to worry about the money right this minute?

No, we don't. Let's just coast along for a bit. I'll call you when I'm back in the States. Cool?"

Cool? Of course, cool. When had she ever crossed him? They were a team. They'd made many plans over the years and designed albums, tours, launches, and campaigns together. She still laughed when she remembered the PR event they'd orchestrated when the *Pavilions of India* record dropped. Who knew you could find an elephant for rent in New York City? She loved that kind of flashy stuff.

So, yeah, she'd let him coast for a bit. She wasn't coasting, though. She was here, back in New York City, getting on with it. They were expected in the recording studio very soon and new material had to be ready. She'd been reviewing tapes from songwriters, just in case Rickey discovered himself to be uninspired or distracted while he was away. She'd also been interviewing session players, reconnecting with reliable musicians they'd used in the past and meeting new ones they could call on, either for the recording sessions or the upcoming gigs.

And upcoming gigs there were. They had a swing through Canada planned, with a festival on Ambleside Beach in the west and a concert in Toronto scheduled soon after the Vancouver concert was done. Booker wasn't exactly sure when it was, she'd have to look it up, but it all felt like everything was coming up very soon, like a massive freight train rolling straight at her heart. It reminded her of that feeling of facing a major exam back in high school, one of those tests that had your parents glaring at you over the breakfast table as if they were wondering why your science textbook wasn't glued to your hands.

They also had an appearance booked at a small venue in Whistler, about eighty miles from Vancouver. Just a hole-in-the-wall club where the audience would probably be hikers, mountain bikers, and summer vacationers just looking for a little diversion in the evening, an audience that would be absolutely shocked and thrilled to discover they'd stumbled in on Rickey T performing. Six months ago, when she set it up, she thought it was exactly the sort of space that would be a good place for Rickey to try out the new songs. The Rolling Stones had done the same sort of thing in Toronto and people were still talking about it, years later.

But now she'd come to the conclusion that this would be exactly the wrong sort of gig. Too much risk, given the importance of these next few months. The prospects for the next tour, the quality of the next record . . . too much riding on it to have him appear even in a small venue where perhaps there might be big press.

She picked up her cellular telephone. "Wayne? Listen, it's Booker Buchanan, calling about the Rickey T show in a few weeks. . . Yeah, we were real excited about it too, man, but I'm calling because we have to cancel."

Somewhere out on the street two drivers got into a horn-honking discussion about some traffic dispute. Booker moved away from the condo window. "Yeah, I'm sure you are but it can't be helped. . . .Oh, no, he's ready, he's always ready. It's just that—no, not a scheduling conflict. . . it wouldn't help to reschedule. We've just decided it's a bad idea. Too hard to control, the word would get out and the crowds would be crazy. You don't want the security hassles do you, small place like yours? Probably don't want the liability, either? I know I wouldn't.

"Well, okay, yeah, I suppose a kill fee is appropriate. . . yeah, I get that you've tied up the date for us for months. . . What are you thinking?" Booker sighed, and rolled her eyes up to the ceiling. "Yeah, all right, send us an invoice, would you? Thanks, Wayne."

Booker shut down the phone and put it back in the case. Geez. No wonder they were bleeding cash.

As the afternoon wore on, Booker couldn't keep her mind on anything she picked up. She even gave up for a while and opened up the ledger, but after an hour of staring at the numbers she was in an even worse mood. She wandered over to the couch but she was too restless to sit down. A walk would be good.

The sun went down and she grabbed a deli sandwich for dinner, then carried on with her walking and thinking. The miles of New York pavement were working their magic and she was feeling much better. She decided to distract herself with a bit of a tour through New York's underground music scene. She'd been meaning to do that one of these times when she got home but until now the trips back usually lasted just long enough to do laundry and re-pack the suitcase.

Out in front of her building, Booker raised an arm to hail a cab. She could have used a guide, she supposed, but she'd thought of that too late, and so she decided to just follow her nose. She had the taxi drop her at CBGB's and stayed a while, then later, she caught another one to the Bottom Line. It was always refreshing to hear music played in a club, not on a stage in an arena or in a public park with neighbors all around, many of them complaining about the 'noise'.

The eighties club scene in New York was still pretty wild, although not nearly as insane as the seventies. The whole city was being cleaned up, and now you didn't have to live in terror of muggings or attacks every time you stepped out of your hotel room, the way it had been, when she'd first arrived from Vermont.

She got bored after a while and went looking for a third spot, the Mudd Club. She'd heard it had closed a year ago but she was hoping that her information was wrong. But there it was, looking deserted and miserable. This former hangout for the Ramones and the Talking Heads was yesterday's news before she'd even managed to get her butt over there even once.

The back pack she had slung over her shoulder began to ring insistently and she looked around for a few minutes, as did some of the people passing her on the street, before she realized she was the one making the noise. She pulled out the phone and held it to her ear.

"Yeah?"

"Hey Pebbles, it's Bam Bam." The sound was garbled and there was static but it certainly sounded like his voice. "I'm back from Europe and staying in New York for a while."

"Hey, Mr. Rubble, nice to hear from you," Booker said. "Glad you're here. We're rehearsing the band, starting tomorrow. "

"I'm sure Earl is on top of things."

Earl Russo was one of the best band leaders in the business. "He is. And he'll be with us when we go out to Vancouver to record the new album." Where would they be if they didn't have Earl to count on when it came to everything to do with the musicians? "We've had a few other changes."

"Lay it on me."

"Rehearsal in a different place here in the city than last time."

"Yeah."

"Four new backup singers to audition for the two open spots."

"I got somebody I want to try out, too," Rickey said. "Where's rehearsal?"

"West 18th, in Chelsea. Who's this new girl?"

"It's a guy. You'll meet him tomorrow. What other changes?"

"Going into the Vancouver studio to record in three weeks."

"Uh huh. That's a little sooner than I thought." Rickey paused and Booker waited him out. "Okay."

"Good to hear from you, buddy. I was starting to worry," she said.

The static went on for about fifteen seconds and then Booker thought she heard "… Whistler first."

"Nah, Whistler's off the table."

"We wanted to get there, Book. It's a good place for me to write."

"Don't be such a diva," Booker said. "You just had a

vacation, didn't you? And you can write anywhere, whenever the feeling moves you, remember? You're the one who told me that. That's when you know you're writing a hit."

She heard a sigh, like something coming from a very old man. "Do you know that the Beatles once had the top five songs on the Billboard Hot 100? One, two, three, four, five, all the Beatles. It was 1964, and they're the only act ever to do that. And they've had more No.1's than anybody. I'm never gonna do that, Book. I can't write that fast. Nobody will hit those numbers, ever. We might as well all give up."

"But, Rickey, what are you writing and recording for? To set records? To please the largest number of people? I mean, it's good to set your sights high and try to compete with superstars like the Beatles but really, it was a specific moment in time and space for four specific people. It's not you, Rickey, not your life. Don't go diving down into some cave of depression because you're so busy comparing yourself."

"I won't, Book, you know I don't have time for stuff like that."

"Do I?"

"Yes, you know it. It's just that I'm not sure what I want to do right now, and I feel like I deserve some space to figure it out. I did my time, I paid my dues with all that disco crap in the seventies, and now I'm making my own choices about how I spend my time. I want to go to Whistler to write."

Booker held her opinion back for as long as she could and then she exploded. "Grow up, Rickey! We've got obligations, bills to pay, fans to feed. We're doing the Vancouver show, then right on to Toronto."

Booker couldn't tell whether the silence had to do with the bad reception of the cell phone or Rickey's reaction to her explosion or both.

"All right," the rock star finally said. "I hear you."

"Are you coming to rehearsal tomorrow?"

"What time?"

"Tomorrow at noon."

"Yeah, I'll be there. And I want to talk to you. Privately."

Booker waited. There seemed to be more coming.

"You gotta have an open mind, Rickey said."

"I always have an open mind," she protested.

There was no response. He'd hung up.

She stared at the piece of hardware in her hand, then stuffed it back into its case. She felt a bit guilty that she'd blown up at Rickey that way, but what he didn't know was that she was just passing along some of the crap that Shad Palmetto had laid on her earlier in the week.

Pulling the pack over her shoulder, she headed off down the street. There was always something to see in New York, something to take her mind off her own problems. These days, she saw fewer drug deals going down and fewer creeps who compelled her to make sure that she was alert. She was starting to love the place. It's always good, if you can love the place where you live. Saves you the time, making plans for your next move.

She was liking the city, more and more, but she couldn't deny that it made her feel lonely. Millions of people, but not one of them belonging to her. Or knowing where she was or when she'd get back. Maybe she should get a cat.

Three tourist couples who looked as though they had just stumbled out of Times Square filled the sidewalk in front of her. Why did out-of-towners walk so slow? Booker tried to work her way around them, then her portable phone rang again. Geez, would she ever get used to this thing? Was it worth the aggravation?

"Yeah." Booker said. "Who is it? . . . oh. Yeah. Yeah, we're on. Yeah. Meet me at rehearsal tomorrow at noon . . . no, make that 11:30. In the morning, yeah, of course, in the morning."

She thought she should wander on home but she still felt restless. Yeah, here she was, she had made it there and she could make it anywhere. She had invited the city to be her lover, and New York had accepted. So, why did she feel so damn lonely?

"Hello, Booker Buchanan."

The woman's voice, coming from behind her, was familiar but Booker couldn't quite place it. As soon as she turned and saw the long red hair though, and the thigh-high boots, she wondered why she hadn't identified her right away.

"Mona Ray. Guess you got yourself back here. Is this home?"

"Actually, I'm from L.A. but I'm thinking of moving." Mona Ray carried one of her giant purses and she was staring into the depths of it, fishing for something. "You got any cigarettes?"

"Quit last year," Booker said. "So many places with rules now, I just gave up."

Mona Ray nodded. "I know what you mean. But sometime nothing takes the place." She found her pack and pulled one out. "You want to bum one?"

"Thanks, but no," Booker watched her light up with a gold lighter. "For now."

Mona Ray grinned, then inhaled. "Aaah. Good." She zipped her bag, then looked up to make eye contact for the first time since she'd spoken. "So, are you all back now?"

"By 'you all', do you mean Rickey?" Booker started to scan the passing traffic for a cab. "But I would have thought you'd know about that."

Mona Ray took a drag. "No, we're done. He made that clear in Europe. Too bad, 'cause I think I coulda been good for him. But . . . " She shrugged.

"He needs somebody," Booker agreed. "But it would have to be a very unusual lady. Someone willing to put up with his shit."

"Which I am not." Mona Ray seemed eager to be understood. "I draw the line, you know? I mean, yeah, he's famous, he's gorgeous, he's one of the geniuses of our time. But that doesn't give him permission to act like a total asshole, right? At least, not with me." She finished her cigarette, stamped it out under her heel, and got ready to light another one. "No, I don't care whether he's here or not. In fact, I'm on my way to meet up with someone else, right now. For drinks, at a place right near here."

Booker raised her arm to call a cab, proud of herself for not giving in to her nicotine craving. She didn't think she had another ten minutes in her, though, so it was time to go, even though Miss Mona Ray looked like she could go on talking forever. "Oh, I don't think Rickey is an asshole, Mona Ray. You didn't really know him all that well. But it's best that you've gone your separate ways. Good for you." A taxi swerved from the middle lane over to the sidewalk where Booker stood. She pulled open the back door. "Have a nice night," she said to Mona Ray and hopped in.

Booker leaned back against the seat and gave the driver her home address. As she glanced out the window, she saw a man approach Mona Ray and greet her with a hug.

It was that Sturgess Mesley guy.

CHAPTER EIGHT

Cosmo was so bored he was ready to chew off an arm. Sitting just a few miles away from Times Square in the City That Never Sleeps—you'd think he would be thrilled. New York! the Big Apple! But the whole experience had been a big letdown.

The days in Germany last month had gone by like a Volkswagen Beetle driven by an eighty-year-old. He knew his parents had to focus on getting the family moved, and he didn't really want their attention anyway. After his adventure in Cannes, life in Mannheim was almost unbearable. But he put up a calendar on his wall and marked off the days until he could get back to the States.

For most of those days, Cosmo hung out in his room. His mother was worried about that, he could tell. She often knocked at the door and stood there a long time even after he shouted at her to go away. But his room was his haven and his special place. He had to have somewhere he could go to be alone.

She didn't seem to get that he was all right, that he wasn't in there plotting anarchy or (at a minimum) rebellion. He was just there, breathing, living, loving his music and waiting for his real life to begin.

Cosmo had big dreams, but she didn't know that. Nobody knew that. Sometimes, he lay on the floor with his head underneath the turntable and played Rickey's albums while he imagined myself running the biggest hotel in the world. Massive lobby with chandeliers, a kickass bar, a restaurant with amazing food that he could drop in and sample any time he wanted. People in uniforms, running to him, asking questions, asking for decisions. A huge suite of his own, like the one he'd seen at Rickey's party in Cannes. Balcony the size of a football stadium, with a view of water. Three televisions, including one in the bathroom. His girlfriend would live there with him and they'd have room service all day and all night, just part of his pay, as the hotel manager. That is how it works, isn't it?

Cosmo watched the magazines and listened to the radio, wondering whether there would be any news about Rickey's European concerts or a new music video. He believed that he knew more than most, about Rickey's high standards and his desire to be classy about everything he did. He'd seen it for himself, in action, that afternoon at the video shoot and he was sure that Rickey would hate for anyone to know anything that he didn't want them to know. Cosmo hadn't been asked for his allegiance but he was ready to deliver, if anyone ever did. He knew, too, that he'd rather die than be a source of unwelcome and unfavorable press attention.

Just before they left Germany, Cosmo got a letter back from Dwight Kettle, the rock writer, promising not to publish anything about the conversation they'd had outside Rickey T's video shoot. It was great that Dwight had turned out to be a good guy. Cosmo could relax now and stop worrying about getting into trouble. Maybe he could even turn Dwight into a very valuable new contact—maybe he knew somebody in the hotel business who could help Cosmo out?

Eventually, the days passed and Cosmo's family was on the transport back to the States. He hoped to be able to connect with William for a quick visit but nobody seemed to care about finding ways he might get from New York down the road to Baltimore. Well, yeah, of course, he knew how to get there but he had to have the bread first, and neither of his parents was inclined to help him out. They talked on the phone but William couldn't get to New York either, so there it was.

They were supposed to stay a week, before going on to the new place outside L.A., but Cosmo was ready to leave pretty much immediately. Everybody said New York was so exciting, bright lights, big city and all that, but he thought the bottom line was you had to have the big bucks to enjoy yourself there. His mother was totally paranoid about the subway and wouldn't ride it (or let Cosmo ride it either). She wouldn't spend money on taxis so there they were, pretty much limited to the geography they could walk around the hotel. That wouldn't have been too bad, he could walk a long way, but she didn't want to let him out of her sight.

Cosmo was counting the days again, just wanting to get to that Pacific beach.

***

The rehearsal space in Chelsea was once a dance studio, a place where Broadway dreamers cut their teeth. What was that word Madonna had coined? Wannabes. Somehow, it wasn't quite as sweet as the word 'dreamer'. Booker took off her coat and took over a power chair, right beside the producer. She'd taken to looking at fashion magazines lately, trying to figure out what to wear. Her jeans just didn't seem to get her the respect she was looking for. She had on one of the latest jackets, with the padded shoulders and the big check pattern. Very executive. She felt like she could raise her voice at Rickey now, even if he were in a mood to dominate the hell out of her.

The players and the backup singers had shown up on time, professionals all. Rickey was actually on time, too, strolling into the space with a guitar case in hand. Booker realized she was almost holding her breath. This was going to be a big day.

"We're gonna rehearse half a dozen of the golden oldies, then Rickey will take over with the new material," she explained.

Rickey had been very mysterious about this rehearsal. Booker was used to a certain level of diva behavior around the early stages of a new album. She got it, that Rickey was sensitive to criticism and wanted to bring out these creations of his brain, heart and soul in a way that would leave him wanting to do more, rather than wanting to jump off a bridge and end it all.

But this one had a whole new level of tension. The session musicians seemed on edge, and there were a lot of sour notes and missed cues. The backup singers seemed off, too. Booker stared at them for a while, trying to figure out what it was. Two of them, the two women, Bonaire and Dorothy, were old friends, but the guy, Jake, was new. His voice was excellent and his look was fine, but there was something that bothered her, something tickling at the edges of her awareness.

Then, she got it. He looked like Rickey. A lot like Rickey. What the hell?

They ran through the new songs half a dozen times each, then took a break.

Booker took her opportunity to confront Rickey. She marched up to the bandstand, and after Rickey sent the musicians off for a break, signaled him with a beckoning finger, and led the way to a quiet, dark place behind the drum kit and the speakers.

"What is going on?" she asked, trying to keep her voice to a whisper.

"What do you mean?"

"Let me tell you what I see. I see you barely phoning it in. I see a Rickey T double, hanging out in the backup section, singing his heart out. What's going on?"

"I was going to tell you after rehearsal was over, take you out someplace nice and roll it out for you."

"I don't need someplace nice! What do you think I am, a date?" Booker plunged her hands into her jeans pockets and tried to make as intense eye contact as was possible in the dim light. "What is going on, Rickey?"

"All right." He took her elbow and drew her back even farther into the shadows. "I have a plan, an idea for the next phase of Rickey T world."

What was he talking about?

"You know I've been suffering from the pressures of the job," he said.

Suffering? He was being a childish douchebag, a millionaire childish douchebag, turning into a whiny drama-queen.

"I have to find a new way to handle this, Book. I gotta find some peace of mind. This is killing me."

Booker held herself as still as she possibly could. Did he have any idea how many tens of thousands of singers, songwriters, musicians, and performers would give any essential body part to spend even one week, living his life?

"But. I get it, I have to continue. I'm Rickey T, it's who I am, I can't just stop being that. And I need the bread."

Thank God, he hadn't completely lost his mind. Of course, he is Rickey T and he has to continue. And we *all* need the bread.

"So, I've come up with a plan."

Booker inhaled, and counted, to keep herself calm. Geez. "I'm listening."

"The fans come to hear the songs. We can continue to give them the songs, the old songs, the classics, and lots of new songs, which I will write. But they don't really see the performer. They're busy singing along, dancing, running their lighters, screaming out requests, or just screaming . . . they don't really know if it's a person up there, or not.

"So, what I'm thinking is . . . we hire a stand-in. Somebody who looks like me, sings like me . . . let the crowd scream at him. Maybe not for every show, just once or twice. Just for a break. Just for the ones I don't want to do."

Booker stared at him. "Isn't that all of them, these days?"

Rickey laughed. "You got that right. I'm just sick of it, Booker. It's not even like making music any more . . . well, all right, yes, it is, but I just don't want to do it anymore. The performance part, that is. I still want to write—"

"And you still want to collect the paychecks. And be the star." She didn't have to look into his eyes to know that the ambition was still there.

"Yes, I do. The royalties come in for the writing and the concert bucks come in for the show. I created Rickey T and that's what they're coming to see. So, yes, I will still collect the checks. But we'll pay the performer the same way we pay the musicians. Better! Maybe even give him a percentage."

"Won't the people who know you well spot the difference?"

"Not if we do it right. Get a guy who is not only able to sing my songs but is a good actor, too. Come on, Book, don't you see the beauty of it? Admit you do. You have no idea how hard it is, to do that rock star thing all the time. I want to be you! I want to be behind the scenes, doing my job, making my money, without all the performing, the traveling, the celebrity crap. The bullshit."

Booker nodded. "I see the appeal, I do. A lot of people wouldn't, and most—hell, all of your fellow rock stars wouldn't. They get off on the fame. A lot of them would be very worried if the fans *stopped* bothering them. But I hear you, Rick, I really do. But you can't pull it off, no way." She started to pace.

"Yes, way. And like I said, it wouldn't be every concert or every appearance. I'll be back, frequently. It won't really be that much different than some of those times that we've dressed up a guy and sent him out ahead of me after a show to make a diversion on the way to the limo and the getaway."

Booker shook her head. "This is different. What you're talking about here is fraud."

"No, it's not. Rickey T is a name, a face, some songs. They'll be getting that. Maybe we could put some fine print on the tickets or something." Rickey's voice was tense. "I have to get away from it, Book. Do you want me to quit, or die or something?"

"No, of course not, but do we have to resort to lying to the fans?"

"The fans come to a concert because they want to see Rickey T, singing mostly the songs they know and maybe a few new ones. That's what they'll get. What's underhanded about that? Nothing."

Booker thought it over for a while. For once, Rickey didn't seem in a hurry to break off their conversation. He waited patiently until she spoke.

"Yeah, all right, I can see it. I can see it working . . . . if you get the right guy. If he's good enough to fool all the musicians you work with, the backup singers. If the people in your personal life . . . . " Booker tripped on that thought. "But—who is there, really?"

"Nobody." The idea didn't seem to bother Rickey.

"What about people like Mona Ray? Or Shad or some of the other executives from the record label?"

"Those meetings, I'll continue to take. Mona Ray is history, anyway, and there won't be any new ones that I'll spend that much time with. The stand-in guy will have to understand that he can't breathe a word about this to any girlfriends or wives either."

"How long do you expect this person to go along with this?"

"Well, we'll see, won't we?"

Booker waited, and he got from her expression that it wasn't a good-enough answer. "I don't know, I'm thinking I'll just try it. Once or twice." Rickey put an arm around her shoulder." It'll be a lot easier for you, and a lot less stress for me, if you can get Fake Jake to do that video you've been wanting me to do."

"What if the stand-in runs right off and sells the story to Dwight Kettle, or one of the other rock journalists? Or to one of those tabloid rags, for God's sake?"

"I don't know how workable any of this is, but I can't answer any of those questions until we give it a try."

"And what's the payoff?" Booker asked. "Why do we do this rather than keep on the way we have been? We've been doing very well, Rickey."

"We can't keep on the way we have been, Book. We won't. So. We make this little change and the payoff is that the Rickey T legend goes on for a while longer. If we don't hire this stand-in, then we'll be calling a press conference to announce Rickey T's retirement. Full stop."

"It's that bad?"

"It's that bad."

***

Rickey called the musicians back, and as they rehearsed, he smiled his way all the way through some of the saddest, love-lost songs he'd ever written. You had to admit, that had gone well. He did consider the possibility that Booker's head would explode and she would reject any thought of doing something like this, but that hadn't happened. She seemed to be more concerned with the how-to's and the details, rather than the overview issues of honesty and accuracy. Just proved, once again, you never can tell about people. Even those you've known for a million years.

The door to the street opened and a shaft of sunlight pierced the intimate atmosphere in the room. Rickey looked over to see Sturgess walking in. He stopped playing and motioned to the others to take a break, then walked over to the doorway.

"It's a closed session," Rickey said.

"I figured," Sturgess replied. "But I thought you might

not mind, since it's me. Shad wanted me to drop by and just see how things are going."

Rickey's mood dropped a few notches. "Shad, huh. Shad. Who's that, now?"

Sturgess laughed. "Come on, Rickey, you know exactly who he is. Listen, it's just business, all right? The label has a lot riding on this next album, and on the one after that, and the one after that. There's going to be some interest in watching it come together, and we thought it would be better if you had a friend here, doing that job."

"A friend, huh."

"A friend."

"Rather than Shad."

"Rather than Shad."

Rickey turned around and headed back toward the instruments. "Screw off, Sturgess," he called as he went. "And don't let the door bump you in the ass on your way out."

Sturgess stood his ground for a few minutes, staring at the musicians and singers lined up and watching him. He tried a silent appeal to Booker, but she just shook her head, and finally, he left. Good riddance.

During the next few songs, Rickey focused on the backup singers and observed the guy, Jake, very closely. He definitely had the physical resemblance and some of the copycat moves. He seemed to be a natural performer and his voice was top quality. They'd find out later whether he would be able to imitate Rickey's sound convincingly.

Rickey had seen Jake a few years back at a tiny club in Atlantic City and he'd been impressed by their resemblance to one another even then. Height, weight, hair, playing style, even the song choices. When he started making his exit plan, he remembered Jake Meisenstern and it hadn't taken the private detective that Rickey hired much effort to track him down. Jake had quit the music business and was making a living teaching in a small town upstate. When Rickey had called him and asked him to come to the city for an audition it had only taken Jake ten seconds to agree.

As soon as he walked in, Rickey knew he was on the right track. Their looks matched and Jake had enough comfort with his body that it wouldn't be much of a stretch for him to move like Rickey. Those were important points, Rickey thought, but not nearly as important as a potential stand-in's personality—his priorities, his interest in being part of a scheme like this and his ability to go the distance.

Another important part, of course, was whether Jake's discretion could be trusted. Rickey knew that you had to find ways to ensure somebody's loyalty, but first he had to get to know Jake. Did he respond to money? They could certainly funnel lots of it in his direction. If he responded to threats, they could make sure he stayed permanently scared of the consequences if he didn't hold up his end of the bargain. If there were lovers, or a girlfriend, they could find out who it was and get that person onboard—although it would definitely be less complicated if Jake were a loner, with a long list of honeys and a new one in every port. If there was a wife, Rickey probably would have to forget about Jake and find another possibility for a stand-in.

Vices, generally . . . that would be another lever they might use. It would not be blackmail exactly: just making sure he knew that it would be in his best interests to keep their secret, either because of the money he'd make, to fund those vices, or because of the losses he'd incur, financial and personal, if it turned out that he had a big mouth.

Rickey had a clear understanding of how risky this would be. Letting another person in on a secret immediately raised the odds that it wouldn't be kept. But geez, he needed this. He was down to believing that he had only two choices left: find a stand-in like this one—or quit for good. He couldn't stand it anymore. Strangers, thinking they knew every detail about the 'real' Rickey T. Business jerks, trying to tell him where to hang out, how to live and what to write or sing. Some days he wasn't sure that he could keep a lid on it for one more hour and that he would explode, doing or saying something he couldn't take back, just the way he'd done in high school. Fake Jake was going to be his savior.

Next step was to get Jake to audition for the gig. He'd get Booker to set that up for tomorrow.

***

The next day, staring at the microphone hanging from the rehearsal hall ceiling, Jake listened to the last notes of the tune fade away, then let himself have a few seconds to gloat. Yeah! He'd nailed it. And he could tell by the looks on the faces of the backup singers and the session musicians that they thought so, too.

Man, I gotta pinch myself every goddam second! Here I am. Me. Freakin' Jacob Meisenstern, standing in front of a band, singing Rickey T hits and getting every ounce of respect and attention he ever got! This has got to be the best gig I've ever had—the best gig anybody's ever had!

When they first approached me to audition to cover his songs, I was a bit freaked out, I gotta tell ya. I mean, I can do one or two, and I used to do that, as part of my set when I sang with The Pirates, but they wanted me to do forty-five minutes! Nothing but Rickey T! But— I pulled an almost all-nighter last night, running down the song book, and it seems like they think I'm doing not so bad.

Maybe it's not a cover band. Maybe not a tribute band, either. It's kinda weird. Maybe it's one of those Broadway shows—Nah, but if it were, I think they'd have said so, and there would be a lot more guys here auditioning, and there would be union rules and shit.

Nah, I think it's some kind of special gig, with me standing in for him. Maybe for his birthday or something"? Nah, but there he is, right over there, watching me, so it's not gonna be any surprise for him.

Jake caught sight of himself in the mirror that ran the length of the wall and retied his scarf. Looking fine.

***

Booker sipped her tea and watched every move this Jake made. Not bad, not bad. He could certainly be mistaken for Rickey, if the lighting was right and you'd had a drink or a toke or two. Maybe this would work out, if it were just for a few months, until Rickey sorted himself out and changed his mind. She had a feeling that as soon as he saw some other guy up on stage, dressed in his clothes and pretending to be him, he'd get jealous and reclaim his spotlight and his life, anyway.

She heard the hallway door open and saw a sliver of light slice through the darkened rehearsal space. Mona Ray stood silhouetted in the doorway, mini-skirt and thigh-high boots, with spike heels that looked as though they could stab an alligator. She looked, to Booker, uncomfortable as hell. Did the woman ever relax in a pair of jeans?

Mona Ray closed the door, then made her way over to Rickey, who was watching Jake sing from a private spot behind a speaker. They whispered for a few minutes, but it didn't look intimate, or even friendly. More like an argument, but with hissing instead of shouting.

Suddenly, Mona Ray was stomping (as much as any woman can stomp in seven-inch stilettoes) toward the hallway door. Booker tilted her head and stared at Rickey, to see whether he would pursue her. Nope, not going in that direction. He had his attention fixed on the stage, and on Jake. Mona Ray's exit went almost completely unnoticed.

Booker's new phone rang and she went out into the hallway to take the call. Very convenient, this, to have anyone able to reach you without having to be tied to your desk, waiting for phone calls.

Unless it was your mother.

"Mom, hi," she said. "What's up?"

"Just calling to say hello, Cynthia. You've been back from Europe for quite a while and I haven't heard from you."

"It's been really busy here, Mom."

"I rather think that nobody ever gets so busy that they can't call their own mother, Cynthia."

"Yes, they do, Mom."

Booker sighed. She loved her mother, she was a nice mother, but she had no sense of business hours, and keeping personal things to personal hours. Of course, Mom would probably say that since Booker's business hours went pretty much eighteen out of every twenty-four, it was rather difficult to pinpoint a time to call that wasn't "calling during work hours". And that since the other six, those 'personal time' hours, tended to fall between four a.m. and ten, and to be spent sleeping, it was quite impossible.

Her mother liked to use 'rather' and 'quite'. Booker wasn't sure where that came from, since there weren't many other people who used them, in Vermont, but her mother had spent quite a bit of time in England in the war years; maybe that was why?

Booker tried to tune back in to her mother's words. Something about Dad and a fishing trip, something about Grandma and a letter from a cousin in London . . . Booker could hear the sound coming from the rehearsal studio but she had no idea what was going on, and it was driving her nuts.

"Mom, I gotta go. We're right in the middle of working on some new material and doing some interviews and I just have to get back to work."

"Cynthia, it might be none of my business, but I have to say. I think you work too hard and too much."

"It's not a union job, Mom. I don't punch a time clock. I have to work when there is work to be done."

"You should take some time off."

There was no arguing with her. "I'll try, Mom. But right now, I gotta go."

Booker felt the need for some fresh air before going back into the studio. She walked through the front door of the building and almost bumped into a tall, dark-haired kid wearing a concert tour T-shirt. She took a closer look and realized it was the shirt from the Rickey T tour that had just ended. Then she took another closer look and realized the kid was familiar, too.

"Miss Buchanan?"

As soon as he spoke, she put it together. "Cosmo, of course. From the radio station contest and the concert in France. Call me Booker, all right?"

"All right!"

He seemed quite thrilled to see her but at a loss for anything to say. Booker waited a few seconds, but she didn't have many to spare. There was a lot of work to do, back inside that building.

An older man and woman who had walked a few feet past the building had turned back and seemed to be coming over to Cosmo.

"Well, listen, nice bumping into you. Keep in touch." Booker grabbed the door handle, yanked it open, and got herself back inside.

Rickey was standing four feet from the band stand, when Booker arrived back in the rehearsal room. He was watching Jake pour his heart into one of the first hits, "Sedona Circle". The dude was a total double for Rickey, and not just the looks. He had the voice, the tone, the husky quality and even Rickey's growl of "help me" down so accurately that it was just on the verge of parody. Booker hoped that Rickey wasn't going to take this the wrong way, wasn't going to think that Jake was making fun of him, or trying to show how easy it would be to impersonate him. But after the last note faded away, Rickey started applauding.

"Freakin' awesome, man, freakin' awesome."

Rickey didn't have much experience at managing people, and absolutely none when it came to guiding somebody who was going to be a stand-in, but somehow, he knew that appreciation would work wonders with Jake. Booker had rarely seen Rickey applaud for anybody but at least now, at these early moments, he seemed to be willing to give the guy some approval. Once they had his signature on a contract, it wouldn't matter.

Booker arrived at Rickey's elbow. "That imitation was so good, I honestly thought it was you when I first walked in." Catching sight of the beginning of a sour look on Rickey's face, she scrambled to rephrase. "I mean, I didn't really think it *was* you, nobody is as good as you. At being you, I mean. You are you, nobody else is, he's just copying, but he did it well, that's all I'm saying."

Rickey relaxed. "I asked him to sing lead for a few numbers, said I needed to take a break to go make a phone call."

He motioned her over toward a quiet corner at the back of the room. He wasn't sure it was necessary, since Fake Jake and the session musicians seemed to be absorbed in tuning for the next number, but you couldn't be too careful.

Booker was still trying to play peace-maker. "Geez, Rickey, lighten up. Don't get ticked. I only said the guy can do some of your moves. Isn't this the point of what we're doing here? Don't we want him to be believable, as you?"

"Yeah, you're right. I guess I'm still getting my head around it."

"Do you still think it's a good idea? Because we haven't gone that far down the road. We could reconsider."

"Nah, this is something I gotta do, Book. Did you know I've been going to therapy for six months now? My shrink says I'm under too much stress, I gotta choose, my career or my life." Rickey grinned to take the edge off the words. "Course, I think he's over-dramatic but it got me thinking about ways I could have both, and this works. I'm tired and I just want to be on my boat for a while."

"But if that's it, we could just schedule more time off, Rickey. Do we have to do something so extreme?"

"Yeah, I do. I'm sick and tired of always having to be in the spotlight, always having to perform, always having to prove something. I been doing it since high school, you know that . . ."

Of course, Booker knew that. She'd been there, when they were both growing up, and had seen the way his parents favored his big brother, the football star. They'd dumped on Rickey, constantly, when he found rock 'n' roll and let his marks drop a little bit. They cut him off, when he started skipping classes and then dropped out. Rickey had never stopped appreciating that Booker stuck by him, no matter what.

"We're going to do this stand-in thing," Rickey said. "You talk to him."

She made a face that said "Well . . . okay" and turned to go. She was holding back but she was starting to come around.

"You talk to him privately, of course," Rickey said. "Make sure he understands the importance of discretion, here."

"Are we going to tell anybody else?"

"Not for right now, and maybe never. I'm still working out the kinks but I wanna get started."

"Because, you know, there's about a million details. How far do we go, in letting him use your name? What do we do if somebody calls bullshit? How do we make sure he stays in the tent?"

"Yeah, yeah, I know. I'm working on it, and we'll talk."

"And you know, Rickey, you've been all over the map about what this guy is actually going to do. Are you planning to have him stand in for you just a couple of times? Or for good?"

Rickey waved a hand. "No, no, not forever. But I want to have him on stand-by."

"All the time?"

"Yeah, all the time. Ha, the stand-in on stand-by. I think we'll only put him out there occasionally, but I want him ready for anything. For now, just hire him and tell him he's got some rehearsing to do. And he has to learn the whole catalogue as soon as he can."

"I think it's going to take a whole lotta money."

Rickey grinned. "We've got a whole lotta money. And we're gonna make much, much more."

When they knocked off for a lunch break, Rickey and Booker didn't get far. He was eyeing the buffet table, particularly the scallops wrapped in bacon, which he loved, when the door opened and Shad Palmetto came walking in.

Damn! They needed to do something about that receptionist. Maybe get a security guard, instead.

"Hey, Shad, how are you? You're just in time for some lunch, will you join us?" Rickey waved his glass in the direction of the well-stocked table.

"Thanks, I ate earlier," Shad said. "Rickey, I can't stay long, but I just wanted to let you know that Sturgess brought me up to speed on his visit over here yesterday."

"Yeah, yeah, he was here," Rickey agreed.

Shad waited for a few moments, seeming to expect something more. After he realized that he wasn't going to get it, he plunged in. "I just want to make it clear, maybe clearer than he did, Rickey, that we're looking for more product from you. A faster pace. The people want to see you. The fans have an *appetite* to see you and we want to capitalize on that, don't we?"

What's with the "we", you jerk?, Rickey thought.

He put a hand on Shad's shoulder. "Absolutely, Shad. Faster pace. More product. Hungry fans. I hear you. Come over this way, Shad. Since you're here, you should meet some of my musicians. This is Earl, this is Shorty, and this is Bonaire. Everybody, this is Shad, our main man at the record label. Oh, and Shad, I'd like you to meet Jake."

Rickey felt a few seconds of actual glee, even though he knew he was the only one (besides Booker) was witnessing this passing of a torch.

CHAPTER NINE

Vancouver

Booker looked out of her hotel window at Stanley Park and the harbor. She could see a floatplane, coming in for a landing on the water. If the soundproofed walls weren't in the way and if she could hear the hum of the plane's engine, the panorama through these floor-to-ceiling windows would have her feeling as if she were outdoors, in more ways than just the visual.

It was a phenomenal scene—Vancouver was one of her favorite places, with its mountain view and ocean view, all in one. Booker had every intention of coming here for a vacation one day. Not that a vacation was high on her list of priorities, not while she had her hands so full trying to make this mad scheme of Rickey's work out. She was spending most of every day stuck in the hotel room making calls or pacing the hallway outside the rehearsal studio they'd rented.

They'd been working at Little Mountain Sound, recording the new album, *Music for Medicating*, for two weeks, night and day. Booker had Jake stashed back at the hotel, rehearsing and memorizing Rickey's entire list, and then bringing him over to the studio, late at night, to listen to the tracks that Rickey had cut that day.

She was ninety-nine per cent sure of Jake's commitment to this project, but it wouldn't hurt to have a little insurance and Booker was on the lookout for information about Jake and his motivation. Rock 'n' roll life was packed with stories of people who'd zoomed off the track once they got a little money and a lot of love. Booker remembered the story of the bass player from Macon who suddenly started to want to bring his pet iguanas, all twelve of them, on stage with him every night. Then there was the drummer in an English band who smuggled priceless Egyptian artifacts in his kit on the way home from a tour. Scariest of all, the trio of backup singers for one of the biggest acts in Spain had disappeared the night of a huge, international fund-raising concert and held up the whole show for hours while their boss (who was also sleeping with two of them) insisted on waiting for them. Turned out they'd gone out looking for new shoes.

Professionalism could never be taken for granted, Booker had told Rickey many times. She was grateful for it every time she saw it. She had to find out what Jake's story was, in that department.

Booker still didn't quite have a clear picture of what jobs Rickey was going to have Fake Jake do. Some days he was talking as though it wouldn't be much, but then, the next, he was saying that he wanted Jake on stand-by all the time. He'd supervised Jake's preparation over these weeks, with intense guitar practice being the biggest focus. Jake already had the vocals and the appearance part down pat. After stumbling around in the first few rehearsals, he seemed to get the hang of what it was they were wanting him to do— he caught the ball and started to run with it. It was just like an actor getting into character, if the magazine articles Booker read were giving accurate descriptions of the experience.

Jake's confidence grew with every passing week—hell, with every passing rehearsal, every set, every song he sang.

He wore clothes like Rickey's, he watched old concert footage and copied Rickey's moves and vocal style, he adopted Rickey's way of speaking and choice of words. Booker watched Jake pretend to be Rickey every waking minute. Well, of course, it couldn't be *every* minute. There had to be some down time, when the guy was alone, that he reverted back to his real self. But Booker was with him many hours for many days. She was seeing Jacob Meisenstern disappear and Rickey T take hold.

At the studio yesterday, Rickey told her he was seeing it, too. "Yeah, I'm impressed. He can play the opening riff on "Seen Better Days" and that sealed the deal, for me."

"Yeah, he's worked really hard, learning all the songs, and getting into your skin," Booker said. "Trying to, anyway."

"Only 'trying to', right. There will never be anyone quite like me, right, Book? He smiled, but it was a demand, too.

"Nobody like you, Rickey. Nowhere." She smiled back. "But we're working on getting this right. He's committed."

"Well, that's great! Well done, Book. I want him to step in for me at the Vancouver concert."

Booker was stunned. A concert? This soon? It had only been a few weeks and Jake had only done his act in front of Rickey and Booker. He hadn't had to fool anybody for real yet, and Rickey wanted to put him out on stage in front of sixty thousand people?

"I don't know, Rick." Booker felt that she could be telling him only what he wanted to hear, and maybe she should, but their relationship had been built on the honesty that they often couldn't offer to anyone else. She wasn't about to change their terms now. "Maybe Jake should get some exposure beforehand, I think. I do think he's ready to play the tunes. He's a musician, he's a mimic and he's got a lot of charisma. But it will be a whole different thing, to go out on a stage not as Jake but as Rickey T, and feel sixty thousand people coming at you. You know what I mean?"

"That I do." Rickey's face looked a bit grim. "How

about this? Put him on for the first time somewhere that's a bit lower stakes, you know what I mean? Smaller venue, smaller crowd, even no press, if that's possible."

"Yeah, that's a great idea! Remember, we started out just planning to have him do the occasional small thing, once in a while, whenever you didn't feel you could. Or wanted to. Not something big, like a whole concert."

"There is nothing small, Book, when it comes to my stuff. Press interview one-to-one, private party at a club, arena concert . . . what's the difference, when you really think about it?"

Booker *was* thinking. "There is that Whistler club that we stiffed last year."

"We didn't actually stiff them, Book. There was no money involved. We just canceled. We gave them notice."

Sometimes Rickey's assessment of things could be a bit loose. "Well, they were expecting you and they weren't happy when you didn't show up. Maybe we can make it right by having you show up now."

This was going over well with the rock star. "Yeah, yeah, that'll work. Put Fake Jake out there as me in an intimate club setting, let him get used to the treatment before and after, prep him for the big one. Can you set it up?"

"I could, yeah. But do you think it might be more likely he'd get spotted as a stand-in when it's a tiny place like that?"

"If he does, we'll just laugh it off, then look for somebody else." There was a stubborn tone in his voice.

"All right, Rickey, I'll set it up."

***

Jake paced the length of his hotel room, stopping from time to time to gaze through the windows at the North Shore mountains. He missed New York. This was a pretty place, sure, but it felt like there were hardly any people living here.

105

But, enough complaining. There was nobody to listen to him, and he wasn't here to socialize, anyway; he was here to work. He caught sight of himself in the mirror and locked on his own eyes. The high collar of his polyester shirt was annoying and he didn't like the hair style they were insisting on, but otherwise he thought he looked very fly.

I am so freakin' ready for this show that I almost can't sleep. The messed-up schedule doesn't help either. I can't figure out whether it's a good or a bad thing with these people, if I take a break in the daytime to catch a nap. Nobody says anything. But none of them seem to be sleeping much at night either. The parties go on till four every night, for some people, for god's sake. They must be having some kind of chemical help.

But they work just as hard as they party. I've had to know every one of the songs inside and out, practice the moves—lucky for me Rickey doesn't do a whole lot of dancing on stage. But he does do his share of strutting around and he holds the guitar a certain way. I have to get it right.

Now, they've got me lined up to do this little gig at a club in Whistler, the ski resort up the road. Probably a good idea, before doing the stadium. Not that I've got stage fright or anything. But I do want to make sure that I can pass for him, even up close.

Booker asked me the other day whether I am sticking to my part of the bargain, as far as the secrecy part goes. She was kind of joking when she said they might ask me to take a lie detector test, but I told her they could, but they wouldn't need anything like that. I am making SO much money, I'm not going to do anything to screw it up.

It's just the best gig ever. I look like the guy, I can impersonate the guy—and he doesn't object! In fact, it was his idea and he's paying me to do it!

I have no doubt whatsoever that we can get away with it. And I'll do whatever I can, to make it work. I tell nobody, nobody at all. I broke up with Wendy, I'm staying away from my buddies . . . and I'm not missing any of them, either. I don't wanna discuss any of this with anybody. Nobody would get it, except for Booker and Rickey himself. It's worth it and it's bigger than anything else, to me.

And, as my Dad used to say, "if you ain't cheatin', you ain't tryin' ".

***

Cosmo watched the sweep of the Fraser River from his window seat, as the pilot lowered the landing gear and headed toward the runway at Vancouver International. He could see the lights on Grouse Mountain twinkling through the gathering dusk and the rest of the Vancouver sparklers, outlining bridges, streets and high-rise towers. This was his first visit to Vancouver but it wasn't the city itself that he was coming to see. Rickey T had a show scheduled in the huge, new stadium there and Cosmo would be there for every note, thanks to a healthy hit in the wallet from his old man.

Since his father had moved the family to California, he'd lightened up on Cosmo quite a bit. Was it possible that he was feeling guilty about uprooting him yet again? It was hard to tell what he was thinking, he was so random. Lately, his dad had been hinting that it was time for Cosmo to start saving up for a place of his own and be ready to move out next summer, after graduation.

He'd been scanning around for a part-time job. It wasn't an easy thing to figure out. He didn't want to be in a mall and he didn't want to be in a fast-food joint. He didn't want to be outdoors with a shovel. Something in music would be good or maybe hotels. The old man had been hinting around about him joining up, pointing out (over and over again) that he could get college paid for, if he did, but Cosmo wasn't interested in college or the military.

Cosmo knew he didn't have unlimited time to think things over. The friction at home was getting to be too much and he needed to come up with a firm answer for his father. He was just inches away from agreeing to sign up, but this week in Vancouver was just a little gift he was going to allow himself before letting them put him into harness.

The plane touched down and he felt that hundreds-of-miles-an-hour speed drop off, as the jet gradually coasted to a slow taxi toward the terminal. Cosmo shuffled along behind all the other passengers and then looked for the place to get the bus downtown. He was there for the BC Place concert but first, he wanted to pick up a connection to the bus to Whistler. There was a rumor that Rickey would be trying out new songs in one of the clubs up in the mountains.

Cosmo was so excited by the thought that he almost couldn't sit still. He had no idea whether the rumor was true, but Whistler sounded like a cool place to see, anyway.

The bus pulled out of the station and zipped along Georgia Street toward the bridge. The mountains he'd seen from the airplane were now looming up into view at the north end of the Lion's Gate. The bus took a long curve, then straightened itself out on Marine Drive to make the right turn onto Taylor Way and then north to the highway toward Whistler. Cosmo stared through the window and wondered about the people who lived on these streets, drove these cars and looked at these views. Did they have any idea that Rickey T was nearby?

It was about ninety minutes before the bus pulled off the highway and into Whistler village. It was a tiny place with just a few roads, grouped around a square with restaurants, shops and apartments. Condos, he supposed, was the right term for them these days. The streets had a vaguely European look and the place reminded Cosmo of some of the ski towns he'd seen on family trips to the Alps. But it all seemed newer, somehow. Newer and younger. Maybe that had to do with the people he was seeing around town—dozens in his age bracket.

The sun was starting to set and Cosmo had only a couple of hours to wait until the show at the Bulldog.

He found his way to a coffee shop across from the grocery store and ordered the cheapest thing on the menu. He didn't have much cash and it had to stretch until the end of the weekend, when he'd head back to Los Angeles.

The brunette sitting at the next table was eager to talk. "Hi."

"Hi," Cosmo said, looking at her and liking what he saw. "I'm Cosmo."

"Linda. Had a good day on the mountain?"

"Didn't hike today. Came up for a concert. Well, a show, actually . . ." He kicked himself for mentioning it. The guy at the record store in California who'd told him about this gig had also told him that it was being kept very hush-hush. Not a secret, exactly, but it was a small club and if the whole world found out, it might be difficult to get a seat. Cosmo gulped at his coffee, wishing he'd though this through before he said anything. Damn.

Maybe she would be the type who didn't listen, he thought.

"Really? What show?"

Nope.

Cosmo looked around and over each of his shoulders to make sure there was nobody else in earshot. "Okay, I'll tell you, but you have to keep it quiet, all right?"

Her eyes sparkled and Cosmo suddenly had a feeling that he had become much more interesting. "Absolutely. What's going on?"

"It's Rickey T. He's doing a small show here, just to try out some new material and to warm up for the Vancouver concert in a few days." Cosmo stared into her brown eyes, trying to get his point across as solidly as he could. "Don't tell anybody, okay? They haven't advertised it and they don't want a thousand people there."

Linda smiled. "No, I won't tell anybody."

"Would you like to go with me?" Cosmo asked.

"I'm already going," Linda said. "It's why I'm here."

It took a few seconds for Cosmo to take this in. "It's why you're here?"

"Yeah. I have tickets for the Vancouver concert but a chance to see Rickey T twice in one week? Who would say no to that?"

"Yeah, who?" Cosmo said. "Do you think a lot of people like you know about it?"

Linda shook her head. "We all would like to see him perform in a small place. Nobody is spreading it around too much. I'm here with a few girlfriends from the fan club."

"The fan club?"

"The fan club. Seattle chapter."

A fan club. Of course, there was a fan club. Cosmo had never joined one, but as he looked at Linda, he started to think it was a very appealing idea.

"It was Maria who heard about it and got us all organized."

"Is she the fan club president?"

"Yeah. And she's my boss at the hotel."

"Where do you work?"

"Ocean Shores Resort."

"Are they hiring?"

Linda shrugged and laughed. "I have no idea, but you can ask her."

Cosmo felt his hold on the situation slipping. "It's only a few hours till the show starts. Why don't we walk over and check it out?"

Linda shrugged again, but she stood up and pulled on her jacket. "Let's go."

When they turned the last corner toward the Bulldog, Cosmo stopped short. Hundreds of people—no, make that thousands!—were standing outside the doors and a large man with biceps the size of hubcaps was trying to get them organized.

"All right, everybody!" He shouted. "The Bulldog is not open! Not open! And it won't be until six. Go away! Go home! You can't get in!" He was waving his arms and trying to resist the pressure of the crowd, trying to push him backward toward the glass doors.

"We'll wait!"

"No point!" The guy shouted back. "Our capacity is

seventy-five and we will only let in the first seventy-five. Look at those people." He pointed toward a line of people in an orderly line beside the building and stretching around a corner. "They've been here four, five hours already."

Cosmo heard silence for a few seconds as the people in the crowd took this in, then another roar, as they rejected it. "We'll wait!"

"How are we going to get in?" Linda asked Cosmo. Apparently, this was going to be one of those test-the-guy situations.

Cosmo shook his head. "All I can think of is we get in the line. Maybe some of them will give up and we'll get closer to the front."

The afternoon would have been a drag, any other time, but Cosmo was captured by Linda's smile and her conversation (not to mention the special way her jacket and pants fit). They talked nonstop while the hours passed. It started to rain around four o'clock and that killed the mood for a few minutes, but a husky guy in a football jersey, about a dozen people farther up in the line, brought out a portable cassette player and filled the air with Rickey's tunes. Cosmo hummed along with the first few, then let his natural shyness fall away and belted out the words to "Seen Better Days" along with everybody else.

Cosmo always was impressed at how much Rickey's lyrics grabbled you. The guy just totally got how you'd feel when you were stressed about people pressing in on you, with everybody wanting a piece of you. Like your dad insisting you had to get ready to get a job and move out. So bogus.

Around five o'clock, the crowd started to grow. In a substantial way—not just growing but exploding. Thousands of kids poured into the plaza, looking for a place to wait for the show. The muscular bouncer who'd been guarding the door all afternoon gave a thumbs-up in relief when four others joined him. About half an hour later, two police officers joined the group guarding the door.

Cosmo stood behind Linda and braced himself against the pressure coming from the back of the line. The crowd was lining up behind the people who'd been there since morning, but they were running out of space and starting to push forward, trying to fill up every inch of room.

"This is getting nuts!" Linda turned her head to say over her shoulder. "Do you think they might open the door soon and start letting people in?"

Cosmo shook his head. "Hard to say what they're going to do."

A large black Cadillac limousine rolled across the plaza from the opposite direction. It pulled up in the lane beside the Bulldog, coming to a stop at the barrier that blocked the lane from the plaza. The chauffeur got out, then opened the back door for a woman in jeans who jumped out and stomped around to the door of the club. Cosmo's jaw dropped. He thought he recognized the woman—she looked a lot like Booker Buchanan, Rickey T's manager, the one he'd met at that amazing concert in Cannes early in the summer and on a street in New York City just a few weeks ago.

Booker stopped to look over the crowd that surged behind the wall of security guards and police men. After just a few seconds, she plunged back to the car, grabbed the door handle before the chauffeur could get to it, and jumped back in, slamming the door shut.

Was Rickey T in that limo?

The rest of the crowd had the same thought at the same time as Cosmo. The fans rushed toward the car and the driver gunned the engine as he started to back up the car. In less than a minute, it was gone.

Pandemonium broke out in front of the Bulldog.

"Where's he going? Was that him? When does the show start?" The people shouting the questions seemed to expect answers, an attitude that Cosmo just didn't get.

The guards and police said nothing, just stood their ground. For long minutes that then ran on into hours, the fans waited, until well past the time the show was supposed to start. Finally, the last of the fans accepted the fact that they were not going to see Rickey T and they might as well leave. The bar never did open, a result that probably left the owners a bit annoyed, and low on revenue for the week, Cosmo thought.

He hung around until almost ten, but Linda didn't want to stay and keep him company. She was jumpy about finding her friend, Maria, and catching her ride back to Vancouver and she politely declined Cosmo's invitation to stay on a few hours longer (*or days? How about the rest of your life?*) to see some Vancouver sights and maybe go to the concert with him. He didn't feel brushed off in the least, though; she was interested, he could tell.

And so was he. Both in Linda, and in this Rickey T fan club. A tiny idea was starting to brew, way back in his brain. What about . . . a World Wide Rickey T Fan Club, with activities and experiences far beyond anything offered by any other fan club? And stuff, lots of stuff! It would be the best fan club on the globe, and the only place to be, if you had any feeling for the man's music at all. Period.

"Hey, call me if you ever get to Washington," Linda said, and Cosmo invited her to do the same in California.

She said she doubted she'd be coming to California any time soon, but that didn't matter to Cosmo. If it was meant to be, it would be.

CHAPTER TEN

Booker paced the halls backstage at BC Place Stadium, hoping that Jake would arrive soon and be ready to justify all the money they'd spent on him so far. Every once in a while, she took a step back, mentally, and took a look at this situation. She and Rickey had decided to do something so far out there, so insane, that she still couldn't quite believe it, some days.

But it was real and Jake Meisenstern was proof. He swore up and down that he believed in what they were doing and that he wanted the income bad enough that he would do whatever it took to make it work, and she had to believe him. He certainly seemed as though he wanted to be a performer at Rickey's level. He'd been very disappointed the day before yesterday when she had to cancel the appearance at the little club in Whistler. But man, what a zoo! There was no way she was having him get out of that car and go into a place that only had one seat for every two hundred people waiting outside.

The doors to the underground driveway opened and Jake strolled in, his two bodyguards close behind.

"Booker! Great. Here you are, here I am—let's put on a show!"

He was wearing a well-cut dark blue suit with a bright white shirt and open collar, cowboy boots and Rickey T's signature scarf. The three of them had debated the look for hours the day before the show, just after Rickey had informed them both that his decision was that Jake take the stage tonight. The look was exactly the same as he was wearing on the cover of the latest album. He'd called Jake and Booker the night before and dictated the set list to them over the phone. He'd let Earl go, writing him a hefty severance check that Earl protested for about five seconds and then accepted. From now on, they would use freelance local band leaders, just for one or two performances at a time. Jake was comfortable with that, but wanted to argue in favor of a slightly different set list, including a couple of numbers and leaving out a couple of others. He also wanted to wear something more glam than the suit.

The whole discussion left Booker with a bit of a bad taste in her mouth about Jake. He'd been aggressive and even occasionally half-hysterical during the discussion on the phone. It was as if he felt he had to hold his own, in an argument with Rickey, rather than just take direction, which was what Booker expected (and what she suspected Rickey would demand, eventually). Just something to watch.

Booker smiled at him. "Let's put on a show!" she agreed. "Your dressing room is over this way."

She led him along the corridor to the private space they'd set aside for him. Rickey had insisted that the treatment Jake got was as good as the arrangements that were made for him, for the times, he said, that he was going to step in and do the show Geez, Booker thought. As if it weren't complicated enough already, Rickey wants to "drop in" once in a while? Well, they'd cross that bridge when they came to it. In the meantime, it wasn't difficult just to keep on using the same contract they'd always used, with the same riders and the same preparations. She didn't know whether Jake was particularly observant or experienced, but if he was, he'd know that he was getting the five-star treatment.

The dressing room was stocked with enough food and beverages to satisfy a hundred people or more. Rickey had always wanted to be left alone before a concert, particularly in the last couple of years, and afterward he was out of the venue while the last chords of the last song were fading. But Jake had already sent out signals, to the musicians, the singers, the roadies, and pretty much anybody else he'd met in the past week, that his room was to be party central.

Booker sprawled out on the couch. "How ya doin', Jake, you good to go? You look ready."

"Oh, I am, for sure. What have we got, about an hour? I am *so* ready." He slipped off his jacket and sat down across a side chair, his arms over the back of it.

"What are you thinking about, an hour before going on stage as a rock star?" Booker found that she was actually curious.

Jake shrugged. "Not much. I'm just ready to kill it, you know? Want to get loosened up and get ready to enjoy myself."

"Got any worries at all?"

Jake grinned. "Naw, none. Why, did Rickey sweat it before a show? Little bit of stage fright, maybe?"

"No, he didn't have any performance nerves at all. A natural, just like you. He loved going out there, under the lights." Such a whopper of a lie. Booker looked around for a beer cooler and went over to help herself to one. Jake reached for one, too, but she shook her head. "Better you don't till after the show, wouldn't you think?"

Jake shook his head. "Are you kidding me?" I'm a rock star, right? I party before, during, and after." He popped open a can of beer. "Did Rickey have any worries about anything?"

"I wouldn't call them worries," Booker said. "He had the fear that a lot of successful musicians and bands have—what if the songs dry up? What if I can't write anything new?"

"Then you keep on promoting the old stuff and living off that," Jake said. "Don't you?"

"I think Rickey thinks of himself as a songwriter first, and so he's paranoid about that evaporating on him," she said. "I don't think he could be happy, just doing the old stuff."

"But he's so unhappy about doing a lot of it that he's not even here," Jake pointed out. "That reminds me, there was something I wanted to ask about. With the new stuff, the new album we're touring on right now, whatever might be coming next . . . how are we handling the ownership part of it?"

"The ownership part? What do you mean?"

"Well, you know, half a dozen songs from the new album are on the setlist for tonight. I know Rickey wrote them, but I'm the one singing them, and interpreting them, you know what I mean? If I add my own shading, maybe emphasize a phrase a certain way, maybe change a word or two, or a line, wouldn't that make me a co-writer?"

Booker stared at him, her eyes colder than the cubes of ice surrounding the brews in the cooler. "No."

If Jake was intimidated by her tone, he wasn't letting on. "What if I had a few ideas off stage, not in the moment, you know what I mean, and I ran them by Rickey before I made the changes?"

Booker gulped her beer, then put it down, stood up and walked across the room to Jake's chair. She squatted down so that she was at eye level with him and drilled him with her gaze. "No. Rickey is the writer. The songs are his. The sole writing credit is his. The copyright is his. He won't share that, not with you or anybody. And you shouldn't ask. He'll incinerate you."

Again, Jake wasn't backing down. "But you just said a minute ago that his biggest fear is that the songs will dry up. This way, he has backup. It's insurance. If he goes into a creative dry spell, he has me, ready to irrigate." He beamed proudly, and Booker fervently hoped that wasn't a sign of his writing style.

Not that it mattered. "Jake, we hired you to sing. To sing, to perform, and to pretend to be Rickey T, onstage and at promotional events. And to keep your mouth shut about the arrangement. That's what we hired you to do and what we're paying you millions to do. That's all. You got it?" Again, she stared into Jake's eyes with what she hoped was enough determination and communication that he'd get the message—and the threat.

Jake raised his hands as if he were at gunpoint. "All right, all right! I hear you. Forget I ever said anything about it. Crap, I had no idea it was such a touchy subject. I thought Rickey might be cool with it."

Booker stood up and walked out of the room. If Jake thought that, he hadn't been paying much attention.

***

Cosmo's seats were in the nosebleed section but he didn't care. He was so friggin' happy to be there, he thought he might blast off, right out of this folding seat in the next-to-last row and up to the air-supported roof. More than fifty thousand other fans were sharing this experience with him and he could tell that they were all just as pumped as he was.

Throughout the sixty-minute wait for the show to start, Cosmo was flooded with more ideas for his International Rickey T Fan Club. The thing about fans is that some are more committed than others. Some just buy an occasional album, some buy every album, maybe two or three copies, and some buy them as gifts for every one of their friends. Some just go to a concert every few years, some see every show that comes to their town, and some travel to see every show, everywhere. Some just buy a T-shirt or a poster, and some have every inch of the walls in their room covered— or even an entire apartment! Outer circles and inner circles, or maybe warm water and boiling water—this fan club would have room for both.

He would get somebody to design a cool logo and maybe they could get it put on hats or shirts or jackets or something. There would be a package of great stuff that would go out to anybody who joined, and they'd get a newsletter about Rickey's concerts and new albums. A *regular* newsletter. He would have contests to win hats or shirts or jackets or photos or something. Maybe Rickey would donate some stuff!

Cosmo raised a hand toward the short guy with curly hair and glasses who was out in the aisle, carrying a tray of boxes of popcorn and soft drinks. His five-dollar bill passed handed to hand down the row to the food vendor and then his box of popcorn passed back. He sat and munched on what had turned out to be his dinner, as contented as if he were sitting down to eat one of his mother's twelve-dish feasts at Christmas. Now, he had to think about how he would get the word out, about this gigantic new fan club.

The lights suddenly went down and a drum roll, amplified to reach every row and section of a football stadium, crashed in on his planning. It sounded familiar— yes! Those were the opening beats from "Smugglers Notch". Cosmo couldn't help himself. A massive smile spread across his face. He settled down into the seat for a few moments, then when the laser lights came on and the new video screens lit up with the close-up view of the stage, he jumped to his feet, along with tens of thousands of others. He roared, they screamed, the drum pounded, and they all got ready for Rickey T.

And suddenly, there he was, running across the stage. Afterward, when Cosmo replayed the concert in his mind's eye, he asked himself whether that was an anticlimax, but it really wasn't. Rickey ran out into the spotlight, his musicians half a dozen steps behind him, and everything was still in crescendo. Those video screens were absolutely dope—he could see Rickey's every move. It would be a bit better if they'd zoom in closer on his face, but that was a minor point. The whole thing was rad! Cosmo was on his feet for the entire two hours, pumping his fist in the air, clapping till his hands were raw, and closing his eyes to wring every feeling out of the moment on his favorite songs.

He could see on the video that Rickey was enjoying the show as much as his fans. He was striding up and down the stage, from right to left, and up to the very front, where thousands of people were dancing and shrieking, hoping to be noticed. Inner circle, Cosmo thought. One day, he'd have enough money to buy a floor ticket and get himself right up at the front like that.

Rickey reached out to take a towel that someone in the audience handed him, mopped his face and then handed it back. The crowd went nuts.

Rickey was fantastic, everything that Cosmo had expected, and more. He did three encores, and even after that, people were still stomping their feet, clapping their hands, and shouting "Ri . . . kee", Ri . . .kee", over and over. That went on for close to five minutes, and then he came running back out from the wings, acoustic guitar in hand. He stood alone, under a huge spotlight, centerstage, and gave them "Leaving Lorraine". It was an encore in another sense of the word, because he'd done that song earlier in the show, with the full band and the backup singers doing their part, but somehow it sounded like a completely different song this way. Cosmo felt every word of the lyrics and he remembered the day he'd first heard it. He'd probably listened to it about ninety million times since. Yet every time he heard it, he was thrown right back to the first time, that day he'd been torn from his home by his father's job, leaving everything familiar behind and being forced to say good-byes on somebody else's timing. But hey. Whatever doesn't kill you makes you stronger, right?

Rickey ran off the stage and the house lights went up. Cosmo's eyes were blinking, trying to adjust after the deep darkness of the previous three hours, and his ears were ringing. Even with the lingering effects of this banquet for the senses, he was aware of a hollow feeling in the arena, as if a presence that had been there had suddenly vanished. He was still dancing a little bit, even though the music had stopped. Just as his bouncing and grooving slowed down, the stadium speakers began pumping out some kind of muzak, strings and pianos playing some kind of soothing, waltz-like sounds that finished the job. He was calm again.

Cosmo became aware that people to his left had turned toward the aisle, and were standing behind him, expecting him to join the file and let them follow him out. He shuffled along with the crowd, barely aware that he was moving, his head still back in Rickey's world. He walked up the last few steps to the top tier, down the tunnel to the concourse, and out past the concession stand. In the shadows to one side of the hot dog counter, he spotted a familiar face.

"Hey! It's Booker, isn't it?"

"Hello." She squinted at him and didn't seem to be upset at being noticed. "Oh, now I know. You're the kid from the radio station contest in France."

"Yeah, that's me," Cosmo said. "Great show."

"Was it?" She seemed to really want to know.

"Yeah, it really was. What are you doing out here?" Cosmo couldn't believe that she'd watched it from any of the cheap seats near where he'd been sitting.

"I like to roam around during a show, see it from a bunch of angles. How was your seat?"

Cosmo made a face, then grinned. "It's what I can afford. But with those video screens—what a great idea!"

"You don't feel like you're watching TV instead of a show? I've heard some people say that."

"Nah. It was fine. And the music fills every part of the place. There are no bad seats when it comes to sound."

"You're right, there," Booker agreed. "Well—"

She seemed ready to move on, and Cosmo suddenly found himself intent on keeping her there, even if only for a little while longer. "Have you got a minute? I'd like to tell you about this terrific idea I've got. For a fan club for Rickey."

"There already is a Rickey T fan club. It doesn't do much and he doesn't like it much."

"This would be something completely different. And he'd like it, I guarantee it!"

She was amused. "Guarantee. Really. What would be so different about it?"

"Well, for one thing, it would be international." Cosmo was grabbing for ideas, he knew it, but so far, she hadn't cut off the conversation. "And it would bring fans together in a way nobody has ever seen before."

"I'm still not hearing much detail."

"That's because I don't want to say too much right now. But trust me, you haven't seen anything like this yet. Can I get in touch with you when I'm ready?"

Booker laughed, then fished a business card out of her pocket. "All right, there you go. Somehow, I get the sense that you were born ready, Chris."

"It's Cosmo."

"Cosmo." She smiled. "Greek?"

He nodded and stroked the business card between thumb and forefinger. He heard a ringing, buzzing sound somewhere. Booker groped inside the huge black shoulder bag she carried, then pulled out a cell phone.

"Hello? Yeah, I'm still here, just walking around." She waited a minute or two. Cosmo could hear a man's voice, muffled against her ear. "Yeah, it was really good, everybody's pleased. Yeah. Yeah. Absolutely, you were. Yeah, I'm not surprised they're saying that. No, nobody else could have. Yeah, of course, you should. Yeah, listen, I'm on my way, I'll be there in five."

She poked at a button, then stowed the thing back in her purse. "I gotta go, but it's been nice talking to you, Cosmo. Send me your stuff."

You bet he would.

***

"Rickey, are you there? The reception's not great, I can hardly hear you, where are you?"

Booker wasn't surprised that he wanted to talk almost immediately after the show. He was as tense as she was about Jake's ability to pull this off. They had a contingency plan, what they'd say if somebody saw through the deception, but they both had their fingers crossed that they wouldn't need it: Rickey, because he really wanted it to work, so that he could get out of the fame spotlight once in a while, and Booker, because she really didn't want to get caught.

"Yeah, we'll be back at the hotel shortly and I'll bring him up on the service elevator. He's babbling something about wanting to party but I'll talk him out of that. No, I can't put him on the phone, I'm in another part of the venue. Took a walk around to get a different perspective. And guess who I ran into? That kid from the concert in Cannes. No, not Otto, Cosmo. Yeah. He's got some big ideas about starting an international fan club. More than a fan club, sort of a cliquey, us-versus-them kind of thing. Ambitious kid, sounds like. Yeah, interesting idea. Anyway, I gotta get back to the after-party, before Jake does anything stupid. Nah, I just meant about blowing our cover. I don't really know how he'll be with a few drinks or whatever in him. But he should stay cool, we're paying him enough. He's got a lot to lose."

Rickey asked a question, and Booker tucked in behind a post to make sure she had full privacy. "I think it's going to work out as long as his head doesn't grow to twice its normal size, you get me? I think it's just that he's on a natural high because of the performance but I'll keep an eye on him."

She listened for a few minutes, then laughed. "Yeah, it would be better if we could see each other while we have these phone calls and it is about time somebody invented something. Yeah, Dick Tracy could do it, way back in the fifties, on his wrist, so . . . Still, yeah, it's best you didn't come here, we don't want anybody spotting two Rickey Ts in two different places at the same time . . . Okay, we'll talk tomorrow and I'll let you know how the party goes tonight and how Jake is handling everything. I'll keep a lid on him, right. Yeah, I do have a way of being in touch with this Cosmo kid. You want in on the fan club idea? Yeah, I suppose we really should be. Yeah, it could be useful, you're right. Yeah, everything's set up for the tour."

She listened for a few more minutes while he listed the rest of her tasks, then he was gone. It was the way they did things; Rickey was always the one to end the call. Booker stowed the phone back in its bag and drew a deep breath. Were they really going to get through this without anybody noticing?

CHAPTER ELEVEN

1985

New York

One year later

After the Vancouver show, Rickey went back to work for a while. Booker suspected he got a bit jealous when he read the reviews and heard about the surge of requests for interviews and personal appearances. This was just nuts because the attention was all about the songs he wrote, the voice that Jake was imitating and the performances that he could do, anytime he wanted. In a weird way, he was being jealous of himself.

Whatever the reason, he went back out on the road for quite a few dates in the southern U.S. through that fall and winter, after he'd sent Jake off on a vacation to a luxury resort in Fiji. Every few weeks, he sent his double an envelope with a copy of his non-disclosure agreement in it.

By spring he was tired of it and he wanted Jake to come back to work.

"For just one concert?" Booker asked, as they both

kicked back in the hotel rooftop bar with glasses of Rémy Martin.

"I don't know, Book, can't say."

"I thought the original idea was that you just needed to do this last year, because you were burnt out," Booker said. "Are you burnt out again?"

Rickey grinned. "Sure, call it that if you want. Look, it's just that I tried it once and it was good. I thought I just wanted to satisfy my curiosity, do something different, but lately I've been thinking a lot about it and I don't see why I shouldn't try it again."

"You know what you sound like, don't you?" Booker asked.

Rickey waved her off. "You worry too much. It works for everybody and we're going to do it."

"Do what exactly?"

"Have Jake do the summer tour."

"The entire tour? That's not what you said when we first started talking!"

"Yeah, well, I've had a little more time to think about it. We're doing a show a week, practically, and if there's too much switching back and forth between us, it might make it easier for someone to notice any differences."

Booker had to think this one over. "True. But it just feels like you're getting ready to step farther and farther back."

"Book, I've been ready to step back for months! Years, really. I've been here most of last year and through all the beginning of this one. I'm going out there night after night, heaving my guts out beforehand, putting up with strangers wanting a piece of me everywhere it go—I want Jake to step in now and I want to go backstage. I don't know how to make it any plainer."

Booker put her hands up in surrender. "All right. I'll get him ready to roll. He'll need to brush up on a few things and I'll make sure he's still solid on the need to be discreet. We'll go out on the road in a few months. You'll be in touch?"

"Oh yeah. I'll be watching every move."

***

Montréal
The landscape beneath the plane as it landed was spectacular—islands in the river, the mountain overlooking the city lights, the downtown. After it touched down, the musicians raced from the airplane to the limos to the hotel and then out to the venue, where thousands of crazy fans cheered, chanted and sang along. Jake played every song that they'd come to hear.

Then he ran off stage, down the steps to the backstage corridor, out to the tunnel, into the limo, and off into the night and toward the airport.

Boston
A summer heat wave had the state and all its people in a sweaty grip that only added to the sexy vibe that this tour was taking on. Jake kept to himself during sound check and ducked the invitations to go out after the show to party.

Booker let him know she was impressed with his new level of maturity and discretion, slipping him a few extra thousand during a hug and a handshake when they boarded the plane the next morning.

Philadelphia
The grown-up act didn't last long. Booker had to conclude that it was only the weather (and possibly, a desire to play a temporary game of 'hard-to-get') that had Jake avoiding the invitations to party in Boston. Jake took full advantage of the fun in Philadelphia.

It was beginning to feel like it would be an epic summer.

Baltimore

The after-parties were living up to Jake's expectations now. The onstage hours had been mind-blowing from the beginning. Now, the food, the booze, the poppers and the groupies were improving at every stop and so was his mood. The kids lined up at the arena doors, at the concession stands and at the merchandise counters, and the money changed hands faster than cards dealt at the professionals' table in Vegas.

In Baltimore, they were dancing in the streets, and everybody knew they had a hit record on their hands. Not just a single, but the whole friggin' album.

New York
Killed it in New York.

Nashville
The southern leg of the tour. Had them on their feet in the aisles. Jake was ecstatic about the reception and his confidence was growing by the minute. Even Booker's tense reaction to Shad Palmetto's arrival on the scene hadn't thrown him. He greeted the record label executive at the after-party and accepted his compliments on the show the way any rock star would. He told Shad what he wanted to hear about plans for new albums and tours, and he assured Booker that she was imagining things when she said she thought Shad was suspicious.

Memphis
Jake had never been to the South, but he didn't get to see much of it, when he was just running from stage to limo to airplane to stage. But he'd get back one day, when he wasn't working. And in the meantime, the money was flowing into his bank account like the Mississippi through the Delta.

Rickey phoned every night, got Booker's enthusiastic report, and then slept the deep, complete-surrender sleep of an exhausted toddler.

Los Angeles

On a steamy, classic Saturday night at the Hollywood Bowl, Jake did a note-perfect rendition of the Rickey T concert he'd been polishing all summer. Fans saluted him with tens of thousands of cigarette lighters waved high over their heads. They called him back for five encores and he treated every one like his first time on stage.

Then he went backstage and consumed a fifth of Jack Daniels in less than an hour.

***

Dwight Kettle wrote a rave review for his national rock ' n' roll magazine.

"The *Music for Medicating* Tour caught fire in Montréal, that slice of Europe-in-North-America, and then carried on into Boston, Philadelphia, Baltimore and New York, before heading south for a swing through Nashville, Memphis, and Austin. The tour will finish in the west, in Portland and in Seattle. The album is setting sales records and people are starting to talk Grammys.

"In my time I've seen about a thousand summer festival shows and this one ranks in the top half. But I couldn't put it in my Top Ten. I'm not a perfectionist but I've got a short attention span for false starts and meandering endings. The Rickey T show has plenty of those, with Rickey as the cause, but maybe he's on automatic pilot for some reason, this summer."

Cosmo looked up from reading the new issue of *Melodies Coast to Coast* that he'd tucked inside the guest ledger at the reception desk. A family, probably from somewhere in the Midwest, wanted to check in and find out how to get to Disneyland. He loved the excitement these newcomers brought along with them—he'd brought it himself, when he first came to L.A. Now, after almost a year, he felt he'd been here forever and that he owned the place.

This part-time job at the resort helped. He'd dragged

his feet when his dad first set it up with his friend from the golf club but it turned out to be not so bad. It had cute girls working in the restaurant, a pool that he was allowed to use certain hours of the week and a regular paycheck. No more cutting grass, delivering flyers or leaning on his mother for a few extra bucks.

Plus, he had access to the office fax machine! This was probably the best perk of all. That machine was magic, man, the way you could get a piece of paper into somebody hands instantly. Cosmo was using it to build the Rickey T Fan Club and, bit by bit, the numbers were growing. A first-time, in-person gathering of the Fan Club was planned for Seattle this year. Rickets rule, man!

He went back to his reading. This guy, Dwight Kettle, was pretty good, although he had the name of Rickey's 1979 tour wrong. Cosmo still had a soft spot for him, though.

Jerry, his manager, stopped by and dropped a handful of fax pages in front of him.

"How's our in-house wheeler-dealer?" he asked. "Fan club's really taking off, I see."

"We're singing their song, I guess," Cosmo said.

"I read your latest newsletter. You planning to go to this big meeting in Seattle?"

"Have to, it's my baby." Cosmo glanced over the sheets. "That's assuming I can get the time off."

He could tell from Jerry's grin that it wouldn't be a problem.

At the end of the summer, he opened his miserable savings account and pulled out what he had. Just enough for a bus ticket to Washington and a ticket to the Rickey T concert. His father said that borrowing the car for a long weekend to go north was out of the question and his mother worried that he'd lose his job if he took a few days off. He'd tried contacting Booker Buchanan about getting some sort of stake, to help him get to Seattle, writing her a long, powerful (he thought) essay about the future of the Rickey T Superfan Club, the passion of the Rickets and the prospects for increased wealth and prosperity for all of them, if she would only get Rickey to endorse and fund the club. But he hadn't heard a word back, even though he'd written twice more to ask if she'd received his letter, sent it again by fax and telephoned long-distance once, after midnight and before 6:00 a.m., when the rates were low and it was only 8:30 in the East. He couldn't get her on the phone, but he wasn't going to give up.

***

Seattle

Booker was lost in the halls of the Seattle Center Coliseum. She wanted to get to Jake's dressing room and have a few motivational minutes with him before the show started, but she was running out of time, as she turned corner after corner.

Her mood wasn't getting any better either.

Her cell phone rang and she unzipped her bag to fish it out. She'd gone from making sure she checked every voice mail within an hour, six months ago, to trying to pick it up on the first ring, always. It was a tool—and it was a ball-and-chain.

"Hello? Booker Buchanan," she said.

"Booker! Well . . . wow. I was *not* ready for this."

"Who is this?"

"Booker, this is Cosmo Lewis. We met in France last year and again at Rickey's show in Vancouver a while back."

Oh, yeah, that kid. "What is it?"

"I've been trying to get in touch with you about our fan club. Rickey's fan club. Your fan club," he said. "It's really taken off, *really* taken off, and I think there are some ways you could get involved. Rickey could get involved. For everybody's benefit." He finished in an apologetic tone, and it was pretty lame.

She was impatient. "How so?" When he didn't answer right away, she asked the one question she was curious about. "How many members do you have so far, anyway?"

"One hundred twenty thousand."

Okay, he had her attention now. Who knew that that many people would bother with any rock star?

"And I'm going for eighty million."

She couldn't speak. Who could?

"Booker? Miss Buchanan? Are you still there?"

"I'm still here, Cosmo, I'm still here. Okay." She cleared her throat. "What do you have in mind?"

"Well, I'm having some trouble keeping up with the traffic, as I'm sure you can imagine. I've got the membership fee high enough that it covers a lot of the costs, but not all. I need some financial help and I need somebody to bounce ideas off of," he said. "I think if we played it right, it could be huge."

It already is, she thought. "I'm interested, Cosmo, I'm definitely interested. I'll need to talk to Rickey, but I think he's going to see it my way, too. When can you meet? Do we need to come to L.A.? Is that where you live?"

"I'm in Seattle for the concert," Cosmo said.

"Better and better," Booker said. "Tomorrow morning. The Electric in Pike Place Market."

She stowed her phone and went back to hunting for Jake. She was just chewing over that eighty million fan club members figure when she heard the sounds of music and carousing squeezing out from under a closed door. She opened it on a scene of drinking, snorting and toking. Jake, dressed in his stage clothes, was in the middle of everything.

"Rickey!" She hissed at him. "I need to talk to you. Right now!"

He gave her his best rock-star attitude. "I've got a show to do in half an hour, Booker. I need some space."

She looked around the room with her best 'I-call-bullshit' attitude. "Really?"

He backed down. "All right. We can go in here to talk."

The alcove in one corner of the dressing room had a small couch, a makeup table and mirror, a beer cooler and a chair. Booker looked it over, then took her chances on the chair and sat down. No one in the crowd in the main area of the dressing room took any notice. "Jake, we need you to slow down a bit, fly under the radar for a while."

"I don't think so. If anything, I think Rickey T should be going for every bit of noise he can get. As a matter of fact, I've had an interview request from Dwight Kettle. They're thinking of doing a cover story on me."

"Who is?"

"Well, he writes for *Melodies Coast to Coast.*"

"Sometimes. He also writes for lots of other people. Did he say this interview was for *Melodies Coast to Coast?*"

"Well, not exactly, but . . . "

"Jake, I don't think it's wise for you to do too much press. We're taking a fairly risky road these days as it is."

Jake reached into the cooler to get a drink. "I disagree. I think I've shown that I can carry it off, from a distance and up close. We've fooled them all and I've made you a lot of money."

"It's the Rickey T name and music that makes the money."

Jake shook his head, his mouth screwed up into an unpleasant and unattractive line. "It's me. I've taken what he started and added a whole lot more."

Booker stared at him. "You're turning into an asshole, Jake. Are you going to be a problem?"

Jake shot back. "Are you?" He walked toward the main part of the room, slowing down only to toss over his shoulder, "Let's not forget who's doing all the work."

Booker was steaming when she left the dressing room and by the time the first chords of the concert rang out through the arena, she was at a full boil. Watching from the wings, her mind was a million miles away, considering all the possibilities. Was Jake going to ruin it for everybody? Should she be doing something about that now, rather than waiting for a crisis?

When Rickey phoned to hear about the concert, as he

did after every show now, he had an opinion. As she'd expected.

"Cut him loose."

"Are you ready to come back? That's good news."

"I'm not saying that. I'm just saying we can't afford to keep some diva on the payroll, especially one who could capsize us in any one of a dozen ways. Talk too much. Spend too much money. Get drunk or wasted too much. Screw it up on stage."

"Demand copyright royalties," Booker added.

"What??!!"

"Yeah, he's hinting in that direction," she said. "But I still don't think we can cut ties with him. He's too volatile to dump."

"He's too volatile to keep. Don't worry about it. We'll offer him so much money he won't want to ever make a move that might piss me off."

"And what do we do next? Announce Rickey T's retirement?"

"Absolutely not. We're having the best year ever. The album's a huge hit, the tour has been selling out. Nothing but horizon, baby."

"Have you got some new songs?"

Long silence. "I'm working on it. Don't worry."

But Booker still had questions. "Even if you keep writing and recording, what about the other stuff? Are we going to announce Rickey's retirement from performing?"

"No, we just hire somebody else. Cut this Jake asshole loose, and get somebody else."

"Rickey, this was only supposed to be a temporary thing, an occasional thing, because you were fed up with the fame."

"Who said it was going to be temporary? I didn't say it was going to be temporary."

Booker fought down her urge to scream at him. "But every new person who knows is one more potential hole in the wall that will let the whole tide come roaring in to drown us."

"I'm not saying we have to do something right away," Rickey said. "And you know, every new person can be controlled, just like the old one. It's a good plan and it's been working for over a year. We'll get a new guy, a better guy, and build up Rickey T's popularity to a pitch where it just can't be questioned."

"I have a new idea about that, by the way," Booker said. "You remember Cosmo Lewis, that kid we first met in France a while ago? He's building a superfan club and has it up to a hundred twenty thousand members. Says he's going to eighty million, worldwide."

"Eighty million!"

"Yeah, right? He's very keen to be on the inside with us and I think we should find a way to make that happen. Piggy back on what he's done so far with this club and let him grow it."

"Why don't we just take it over?"

"I don't want to run a fan club; do you want to run a fan club? Nah, let's just bring him in the tent and let him do his thing."

"All right. And in the meantime, keep an eye on Fake Jake." And he hung up, leaving Booker, once again, with the feeling that her Must-Do list was about forty lines too long.

She wandered out into the middle of the stage, where the roadies were rushing around, getting the equipment ready to be loaded into the trucks. The lights were on full force and the clanking noises from metal boxes being moved and chairs being dismantled filled the space that had held magical darkness and evocative music just a short while ago.

Booker found her way to the stage door and slipped out past the waiting crowd of autograph-seekers. She wanted to get some air for a while and waved the drivers to go on without her. She'd find her own way back to the hotel in a taxi later.

"Booker! Hey, wait up. I want to talk to you." The voice

had an authoritative tone, as if the owner had no doubt that she'd stop.

She turned. Damn. It was Shad.

"Booker, let's take a few minutes. Here, we can sit here," he said as he guided her toward a bench. "I want to talk to you about some rumors I've been hearing about Rickey."

She looked around: nobody within earshot. Good. "What rumors, Shad?"

"That he's partying like a mad fool," Shad said. "Drinking, drugs, women."

Booker shrugged. "That's rock 'n' roll, Shad. You've been in the business long enough to have seen a lot of that."

"I've seen a lot of people burn out, yeah, and we've got too much invested in Rickey T to stand by and let him self-destruct," Shad said.

Booker stared off toward the Space Needle in the distance. "What do you want me to do about it?"

"Set up a meeting with him for me. Make it clear to him that he can't dodge it—he's been doing that to me for a few weeks now."

"If he won't meet you and won't take your calls, I guess that means he doesn't want to talk to you, Shad," Booker said.

"Well, he has to. That's all. He just has to," Shad replied. "I want to sit him down, straighten him out. Make him face facts."

Booker sat in silence for a few minutes. It was not so much that she had to think over her response, but that she wanted Shad to think she was seriously considering his plan. She was not.

"That might work, Shad, it might. I'm concerned about him, too. I wouldn't say that to too many people, but I'll let you in on it, yeah. I'm concerned about him, too." She slid sideways to turn on the bench so that she could give Shad her full attention. "I'll talk to him. That's the best way."

Shad crossed his arms over his chest. "Can you make it

clear to him that he's on thin ice here? The label expects a certain kind of productivity from him, and I know damn well he can't write and record and perform the way he needs to if he's hanging around, snorting $35,000 lines of coke up his nose!"

"I know, I know, Shad." Booker tried to sound soothing. "I can make it clear to him, yes. I'll sit him down when we're in Miami next week and make it clear."

"Good." Shad stood up. "Because somebody has to straighten him out."

"That'll be me, Shad, don't worry," Booker said.

"If it's not you, it'll be me," Shad said. "Very soon. I can go to where the hell he is and get in in his face in a way he won't believe. I will be watching that sucker's every move from now on, believe me. There is no reason we can't turn his career and his records into an unstoppable success. I can make him a mega-star and I can keep him up there the rest of his life, but he has to cooperate. He has to understand that when it comes to the business side he has to get out of my way. And he has to stay clean!"

After he marched off toward the waiting line of limos, with no inquiry about where Booker was going next or offer to drop her somewhere, she sat on the bench for another half hour. Somehow, she was going to have to make Rickey understand that, with Shad breathing down their necks, this would be the worst possible time to cut Jake loose and try to find a new stand-in.

CHAPTER TWELVE

1989

Toronto

Four years later

Taking one last look at herself in her hotel room mirror, Booker decided she looked okay and headed for the elevator. She had a meeting in half an hour with Cosmo about the fan club, and Rickey had decided to join them. He'd taken to going out in public quite a bit, in the past few years, always in disguise and always taking delight in the risk of being caught.

It made Booker crazy. Weren't the risks steep enough, without him thumbing his nose at the possibility that they'd have to start explaining to people what they were up to? But he'd been the piper in this little parade of theirs, as he had been their whole lives. He was in charge, and if he wanted to take a meeting occasionally, or sneak out of his lair and scope out something personally, who was she to say no?

After they'd decided they had to give Fake Jake another chance and make sure they all flew under Shad Palmetto's radar, the whole plan had worked perfectly for almost five years. A lot of the results (Booker wouldn't say 'all' because she thought she deserved some credit for the success) had to do with decisions Rickey made.

For example, the decision not to have Jake go back out on the road in the winter of '87. There was a lot of pressure after they won four Grammys for the *Music for Medicating* album. Booker thought it was Rickey's best yet, and the sales showed that the fans agreed with her opinion. So did the music industry, as the voters lined up to give the awards to Rickey T and ensure that the rest of his year was very, very nice.

Well, not that nice, actually. Almost the day after the event, Shad was on Rickey's case to start touring again. They'd just finished traveling most of the summer and fall, with Booker holding her breath the whole time that Jake wouldn't screw things up. Now they had the stand-in tucked away in a luxury villa in northern Africa, enjoying whatever it was he enjoyed, and with his promise that he understood that his huge paycheck depended on his discretion and his fear of the confidentiality contract he'd signed.

The last thing any of them wanted was another tour. She spent several days in meetings in L.A. .and then flew back to New York for more meetings. Shad was demanding to see his star but she held him off by mentioning Rickey's reclusiveness and his fear of being mobbed by fans if he went out in the daytime hours. That was semi-true, anyway.

Thankfully, the record continued to sell and to pick up momentum. Rickey T didn't need to tour—that was her story and she was sticking to it.

Throughout the winter of '87, she managed to string them along. It was nearly two full years since Rickey T (or Jake) had been seen on a concert stage, but that didn't hamper his success in any way—if anything, it added to his mystique. The label released a *Greatest Hits* compilation that included half a dozen of the Medicating tunes, and it was his biggest seller yet. Then, they lay low for a while, and it wasn't easy. Booker became a master at dodging phone calls, making excuses, and coming up with creative explanations for Rickey's alleged decisions and activities. With a combination of bull shit and bad manners, she got them to put off the next tour until the summer of 1987.

Meanwhile, this little booster club of Cosmo Lewis's had taken off like a Concorde supersonic jet. Booker had to tip her business-woman hat to the guy. He'd grown the numbers, in just four years, to hundreds of thousands, all of them eager, even ecstatic to pay extra—for early access to tickets, for merchandise, for supposedly "insider" information. The Rickets had become the most profitable Rickey T revenue stream, after album sales. Cosmo was a dream of a partner—cooperative, creative, ambitious—and he was completely satisfied with their deal. Fifty-fifty, everything split right down the middle, with him running the Rickets and Rickey (and Jake) staying out of his hair.

Once or twice, during telephone discussions they'd had about upcoming shows, Booker had been almost sure that Cosmo had figured out the Rickey stand-in story. She mentioned it to Rickey on the phone and he pointed out that she'd been sure, at various times, that Sturgess had noticed something, that Jeannie the accountant was suspicious, and that Dwight Kettle, the writer, was hinting that he had a whistle to blow. None of her disaster scenarios came true and he convinced her that Cosmo had no idea that his idol had a double.

By the time the Chicago concert opened in 1987, the fans, the record label execs, and Jake Meisenstern were more than ready to have Rickey T back on stage. Demand had been pent up so long it was practically enough to flood Nevada, and the tickets sold out in seven minutes. Jake had stayed in training the entire two years, and despite the fact that his personality had shrunk into a mean, self-centered, petulant crumb of a thing, his ability to carry off a show had sustained. If anything, it had grown.

And that made him even more of an egomaniac.

Rickey was there, watching that show, wearing a disguise, and had declared himself, in the post-concert debrief telephone call, even more satisfied with his doppelganger's job performance. Rickey insisted that Booker pass his comments along to Fake Jake, and then, as she told Rickey later, the stand-in's head became even fatter than his wallet.

The next year was a repeat of '87, with "Rickey" staying out of the public eye and real Rickey living on his boat, loving the privacy and pouring out new songs like a waterfall. Booker met with him once or twice in '88, and each time he showed up in a different costume, complete with a mask or makeup that made him unrecognizable. Quite a few of his contemporaries were changing their looks and reinventing themselves every few months, and Rickey said he saw the potential for their situation. He insisted to Booker that if rock star Rickey T were to start wearing full makeup on stage, or even to cover his face entirely, it would make the stand-in scheme much easier to pull off, especially in the coming years, when he and Jake Meisenstern might age differently.

Booker said she'd think about it and get back to him.

Meanwhile, 1989 had rolled around and they were in Toronto, ready for a big show at the CNE Stadium. Booker hopped into a taxi outside the hotel and gave the driver the address of the BamBoo, her second-favorite place in Toronto, after the El Mocambo. She liked to suggest it as a spot for a business meeting when the people she was joining were sure to be surprised by the surroundings.

That wasn't the case with Rickey, who'd been there dozens of times. She suspected, though, that it would be just Cosmo's kind of place. When she met him at the door, Cosmo was grinning at the sight of the moon mosaic on the floor.

"Cool place, Booker, thanks for suggesting it."

"Food's good, too," she said, as she led the way through to the stairs leading to the Treetop Lounge.

They were barely settled with their drinks when a thin man in a long, black cape, black shirt and black jeans came over to their table. Thick black hair, heavy bangs brushing his eyelashes, and pasty white skin gave him a sort of Count Dracula look, Cosmo thought.

"Hey, Rickey," Booker said.

Cosmo almost spit out his mouthful of Molson Canadian beer. The man stuck his hand out. "Nice to see you, Cosmo."

This was the second time Cosmo had met Rickey T and even though he was five years older, the impact was still as massive. Cosmo wouldn't have recognized him—even the voice was slightly different—but he would have been blown away by Rickey's charisma, even if he thought he was sitting down with a total stranger.

Cosmo shook his hand. "Nice to see you too, Mr. Taggart." Couldn't help it. More than two decades of being raised by a military man.

Rickey made a face. "Please. And don't you dare call me 'sir'. I'll punch you."

Cosmo smiled. *This was going to be fun.* "Are you drinking?"

"I am." He turned to the server who had appeared at his elbow. "I'll have a glass of cognac. You have Rémy Martin?"

After the server disappeared, Rickey leaned back in his chair. Not too far back, because the thing looked a little delicate. Just enough to look cool. He always looked cool. "I'm hearing great things about this fan club you're building."

Cosmo couldn't help it, he felt as though someone had just handed him a Grammy. The way he imagined it would feel, anyway.

"Booker's been telling me about your efforts, how much time you're putting into it. I know we've been helping out a little, financially, over the past four years. And with supplying you with swag and so forth. "

Cosmo nodded and sipped at his beer.

"We'd like to get fully on board with you," Rickey said. "And we hope you want to get on board with us."

Cosmo could hardly breathe. "Absolutely, Rickey. Anything you say."

"We can smooth the path for you in a lot of ways," Rickey continued. "Plus, I think you should be making a lot more money." He looked up at the server who'd arrived with his drink, took the glass and downed it in one gulp. In the next second, he was standing. "Booker will work out all the details with you, is that cool?" He looked at her very directly. "All the details."

"Is that wise?" she asked.

"Completely." Rickey answered. "We need to have the fans on our side and any questions under control. He digs me, big time . . . don't you, Cosmo? He should be on the crew."

"Crew could be getting too big," Booker said.

"I know what I'm doing," Rickey said as he stuck out his hand once more. "Cosmo, I gotta split but Booker will take you over to the concert and hang out for a while before the show starts."

After he was gone, they finished their drinks in almost complete silence. Booker seemed to have something on her mind. She asked the waiter to call a taxi and they were on their way. By the time they pulled up to the CNE Stadium back door, the vibe was definitely anxious.

"What's the problem?" Cosmo asked.

"We're running a bit late," she said. "But it's not terminal. We'll be okay."

She led the way past security, snagged a couple of passes and lanyards, and headed off down the corridor. "We'll just check in on Rickey."

Check on Rickey? We just saw him ten minutes ago.

They arrived at a closed door and she knocked. No answer. She knocked again, the expression on her face changing from a little ticked to royally pissed off, then she opened the door. It was a standard backstage dressing room, mirrors, makeup table, clothes on a rack, food, beverages and who knew what else on a side table. No one was inside.

Booker pulled her cell phone out of her purse and punched in a number. "Where the hell are you?"

That was a bit rough.

"Yeah, well, that doesn't cut it. I'm sending the limo over. You be ready for it."

Cosmo gave her his best look of 'ready to help', but she didn't notice. "Listen, Cosmo, I have some work to do, so I'll have to split, okay? You can find your way around, yeah? With your pass, you can hang out anywhere back here and when the show starts, you can watch from the wings with me. I'll meet you about ten to eight."

"Cool," he said as she hustled him out of Rickey's room. He heard the lock click when she shut the door.

Cosmo roamed around for about half an hour, but the truth was, it wasn't nearly as glamorous back here as it was the first time. Kind of dull, really. There was a brief flurry of action when a group of dancers went by, but other than that, there was nothing much to do but look at the music posters, about a dozen times.

Eight o'clock approached and Booker appeared from somewhere. She was more than a little upset about something, pacing up and down the hallway. A few minutes later, the musicians arrived and everyone milled around in the wings. Out front, they could hear the audience starting to mutter.

"What do we do, Book?" A short man with thick glasses and a binder under his arm asked.

"Give it five minutes, then send the boys out," Booker said. "Five more minutes, and if we need to, we'll send out the backup singers to do a number. I'll go and give them a heads-up."

She was only gone a few minutes when Rickey shattered the quiet, shouting as he strutted in from the tunnel. "I'm here, let's get this show on the road!" He looked like his normal self again; the black wig, makeup and cape were gone. He did a dance step or two, then pirouetted.

Booker materialized and planted herself in his path. "You're an hour late!"

"I was delayed. It's cool, let it go."

She didn't move. "It's unprofessional."

His big smile faded and the movement stopped. All his energy focused into one still, pinpoint of calm. "What did you say, lady?"

Booker became just as still. "What did you call me?"

They stared each other down, and Rickey was the first one to blink. "Hey, Booker, lighten up. I'm a little off my timing, that's all."

She made a face and rolled her eyes. "Are you warmed up? Can you go on now? Listen!" Booker grabbed his arm. "The band's started."

"The show doesn't start until I get out there. They can play all night, I don't give a shit, it won't start until I'm ready to go on."

Booker lost it. "You can be replaced!" She yelled at Rickey. "Your demands have been outrageous for a long time, and if you're going to start being late, and unprofessional—"

"Yeah, well, I quit!" Rickey screamed, storming back out toward the limo.

What was she talking about? Rickey T couldn't be replaced, it was his show. But Booker was swinging into action; there was no way this show wasn't going on. She stormed out of the green room and down the hall to the backup singers' dressing room.

"Bonaire!" She pounded on the door. "Are you here?"

The door opened and the six-foot-tall Nordic blonde dressed in a sequined minidress and stiletto heels walked out. Her smile was megawatt.

"I'm here, Booker, ready to go. The other girls are right behind me."

"We need you stage front tonight. Rickey's got some

issues and for now, we'll do the set list but you're singing lead. You know them all?"

Bonaire didn't miss a beat. "Like I know my own name." And she was off down the corridor, running in those incredible shoes. Cosmo had no idea how she did it.

Well, this would be interesting, a woman singing Rickey's lyrics.

Two other singers, wearing matching outfits, followed Bonaire out of the dressing room and toward the stage. By this time, the band had played the opening bars of the first song about a dozen times and had moved on to an instrumental version of the song. Then, I heard the crowd roar and Bonaire's amplified voice blast out.

"Hello Toronto!!"

The audience roared back its approval—Cosmo thought they were impressed by the shoes, too—and Bonaire launched into the opening verse of "Seen Better Days".

"Well, if this had to happen, at least it's not happening in New York or L.A.," Booker muttered.

Cosmo walked over to the edge of the stage and then out behind the gargantuan speaker, as far as he dared without risking being seen. Bonaire was out in front, microphone clutched between five long fingers with purple talons, swaggering and sashaying up and down the stage like she'd been doing it every night for years. Maybe she had, in her imagination, during all those years she'd been twenty feet from stardom.

Her voice was powerful and the song took on a whole different meaning with a female voice carrying it. Cosmo started to dance along to the beat. He could tell that the musicians were into the groove with it, too—this was turning into a fine time.

Cosmo felt the air stir and something brush past him. It was Rickey, running toward the spotlight, carrying a guitar. He put himself shoulder to shoulder with Bonaire, then began to sing along with her. He reached to take the mic, but she hesitated, then stood her ground.

This was unlike anything Cosmo had ever seen at a rock concert. They were almost in a tug-of-war over it. Rickey put up his other hand to grab the mic and his guitar swung from its strap. Everything seemed to go into slow-motion, and then Cosmo saw his guitar whirl around and hit her. She was slightly off-balance anyway, in those monster-truck shoes, and when that guitar hit her, she went down.

The musicians all stopped playing, some because of anger and protectiveness, and some because of shock. The audience fell silent, as everyone tried to comprehend what had just happened. Matt, the saxophone player, stood up and came around to the front of the stage, reached a hand down to Bonaire and pulled her to her feet. The audience let loose with a huge round of applause, as he held out an elbow to her and escorted her, grandly and courteously, into the wings. The other backing vocalists followed, and then, one by one, the musicians left the stage. Their disgust was obvious in the way they were shaking their heads and ignoring the singer. The keyboard man stood up from his piano, gathered his sheet music and walked off behind them, also refusing to look Rickey's way.

Rickey stood there, and Cosmo could see that he was about as angry as it was possible to be. Then he drew a deep breath, pulled the electric guitar off over his head and set it down. An acoustic guitar was on a stand near the drum kit and he pulled it down, strapped it on and stepped up to a floor mic. He strummed the opening chords to one of his seventies hits and started to sing.

The audience wasn't having it. Even though the house lights were still down, Cosmo could see shapes standing up, moving around, and shuffling toward the aisles. Rickey tried to keep going but they just ignored him. Finally, mid-chorus on "Leaving Lorraine", he said 'the hell with it', and walked off.

The house lights came up. Thousands of people were heading for the exits. A lot of them were probably on their way to the box office to demand their money back.

Rickey brushed past Cosmo and he looked so red he might burst. By the time he reached the far side of backstage, he was running. Cosmo wasn't sure why, but he decided to follow. When Rickey got to the stairway that led down to the tunnel, he slowed down a bit and turned around to look back. Maybe it was all the drama, but Cosmo felt something was off, somehow.

Rickey looked at Cosmo but he seemed to look right through him.

Following Rickey down the stairs, Cosmo saw him pull open the back door on the limo.

"Let's go!" Rickey screamed at the driver, who was standing a few feet down the tunnel, having a smoke. The rock star jumped into the back of the car and slammed the door. Stubbing out his cigarette, the driver/bodyguard headed toward the car just as Booker Buchanan walked up.

"I've driven a lot of celebrities but this guy is a piece of work. Man . . ." The driver seemed really upset. "And I even like his music! Even so ..." He stared at Booker, as if he were looking for any answer or something.

"I know, Greg, I know," she tried to soothe him. "He can be a bit intense."

The driver shrugged and opened his door. Rickey's voice could be heard all over the subterranean floor of the stadium. "Get in the bloody car and drive it, you moron!"

Booker reached forward and opened the backseat door. "You're fired," she announced.

Cosmo was stunned. Fired? How could that be done?

"Yeah, well, I quit! And you—" he bellowed at Greg, "Drive the bloody car, I said!"

Greg seemed to be stumped. Cosmo wondered about it, too—Did the driver still work for Rickey, then, if the rock star said he'd quit?

"Uh, man, am I gonna get paid?"

"Just drive," Rickey snarled. "Drive, goddammit!"

"Can't, man," Greg said. Rickey jumped out of the limo,

screaming a stream of curses.

"Calm down," Booker said. "There's no reason to get so upset. It's just business. You were late, the fans were waiting, we started without you. You lost your shit, we fired you, you're history. End of story."

She looked over at Cosmo. "Hey, you need a ride? Let's go." She slid into the back seat of the limo and he followed. This amazing night was getting more amazing by the minute, Cosmo thought.

Greg started the engine and the big machine prowled out of the stadium basement. They rode in silence for a few minutes, and Booker checked to make sure the soundproof privacy screen was shut tight. Then she said, "You know this afternoon, when Rickey referred to telling you all the details? Well, here comes the biggest one, the one he was referring to. That guy you just saw, screaming at me? That was not Rickey."

"That guy? The one who was just on stage? Yes, it was."

"No, it wasn't." Booker reached into the bar, then pulled out a bottle and two glasses. "We use a stand-in from time to time."

Cosmo felt like he'd been hit by a wrecking ball. "From time to time?" he repeated. "From what time to what time?"

"Well, a lot of the time," she said, pouring herself a drink.

He shook his head, like a boxer trying to bring the ring back into focus. "This kind of explains a lot," he said.

And it did. Why didn't Rickey T agree to do very many interviews? Why was he so reclusive and so mysterious about where he lived, what he did between concerts, and so on? Why didn't you ever see photos of him out on the town? Why didn't he have an entourage? Cosmo had discussed this with friends and with his brother and they all seemed to think it was because Rickey wasn't as big a deal as Cosmo thought he was. But they were just busting his chops. And trying to stop a conversation they thought was boring.

"But . . . . why? Why has somebody else been

impersonating Rickey?"

"Rickey doesn't want to do it anymore. Doesn't want to do the concerts and the touring. He's still writing and recording, and he figures somebody should do the performing, but he'd rather delegate that."

"When did all this start?"

"Oh, I don't know, a few years ago. It started gradually, because he got fed up with the hard parts of living with fame. At first, he just hired a guy to double him once for a public appearance he had to do that he was just freaking out about. Then, one other time, he had a broken foot but rather than call off a whole concert we had Rickey sing off-stage while this guy went out front and did his moves."

Cosmo stared out at the passing traffic and tried to get his head around this.

"Where did this stand-in guy come from?"

She seemed to want to be vague about that, but he asked her a few times, and finally got what seemed like it might be a full story. Her answers sounded like a lot of bullshit at first, but the more she talked, the more Cosmo started to see it. The fans expected fresh material, regularly, and they expected to be able to go to see their idol, in person. This was the next-best thing.

"We keep it very quiet," she was saying. "Only a handful of people know . . . only three, really. And we're committed to keeping it that way."

"Why are you telling me?"

"We want you in the handful," she said, smiling at him and looking him straight in the eye.

"Why?"

"We think you could help us. And you could help yourself, with this. We've talked it over many times, Rickey and I, and we realize the fans are the most important variable in this whole equation. You guys are who we do all this for: the fans, the crowds, the audiences, you're the ones who make him what he is. Nobody can come along and just declare himself a rock star. Well, I suppose he could," she grinned. "But people would just laugh. Unless they have the numbers to prove it. And you're the at the front of that whole parade, Cosmo, you're their leader. You could keep the momentum going, you could supply Rickey's fans with what they need. You could be their main information source, with a whole lot of help from us. You could help us grow the Rickey T legend, help keep the excitement building, help keep the history special. You—and we—send all that to them, and they send back to us their dedication, their intensity, their . . ."

"Their dollars?" he said.

Booker laughed. "Yeah, Cosmo, that, too. But that's not the only thing, I hope you believe me about that. If you don't, then this conversation is probably at an end. But if you do, if you agree with me, that it's important to keep Rickey T onstage, in some way, then you'll be ready to join the team. The real team."

"Who's on the team?"

"It will be the three of us, basically. Rickey, you, me. That's it. Oh, we have to include a few others, from time to time, to get something specific done."

"And the Rickey stand-in guy."

"Oh, yeah, him. We'll have to hire a new one, but we'll be a little more careful this time. Try to find somebody who won't grow into an egomaniac."

"What do you do about the one who just left, what's his name?"

"Fake Jake? He responds to money, and there will be plenty. The new guy, probably the same. Don't worry about it, Cosmo. The bottom line is that it will be the three of us. He shines the light, you bring the people to see the light, and I make sure everything stays plugged in. Basically," she grinned and poured another drink for each of them.

"What would I have to do?"

"Besides being one of Rickey's best friends and living your life up close to a star? Just keep on running the fan club, Cosmo, build it up into this super-thing you've been telling us about, work toward your vision, while helping us keep Rickey T on the stage."

"And he'll still be the one writing the songs and recording them?"

"He will."

"I'll get paid?"

"You'll be a partner, Cosmo. That's what I'm trying to tell you. Beyond your wildest imagination, man."

"I'm in," Cosmo said, having no real idea of what he was saying or what she was talking about.

The Nineties

CHAPTER THIRTEEN

1991

Palm Springs

Two years later

Booker slid as far down into her pool lounger as she could. She tipped the brim of her sun hat down over her eyes, then took a long pull on her iced tea. She'd been looking forward to this little vacation for months and she was reveling in every moment of it. March, at home in New York, was an obstacle course of slushy gutters, stalled vehicles, and people muffled up in woolen scarves. The California desert, on the other hand, was an oasis of green grass, turquoise swimming pools, and people in bathing suits. No contest.

Of course, it wasn't really a vacation. She didn't take vacations, not really. She was just like most of the people she knew; pretty much everyone who had come through the eighties worked hard. Twenty-four seven, as the new saying went. Who said that first? Whoever it was, he made up a good one.

Almost everybody in the eighties had discovered ambition and perpetual striving; now, in the nineties, they were supposed to be reaping the benefits. Maybe it was all the new knowledge everybody in America now had about the habits of the Japanese. Maybe it was living through a time of borrowing rates that were in the mid twenty percents—whatever it was, it left everybody rushing to keep up, all the time.

Very different from the laidback seventies. And the sixties! Well, as that saying went, if you remembered the sixties, you weren't there.

Today, after she toasted herself for a while, she would be meeting Rickey's old friend, Henry Ryland, for a round of golf. Henry had moved from the humid South to the Montana prairie in the seventies and then to the dry desert, for the sake of his allergies, just a few years ago, and Booker took every chance she could to do an in-person meeting with him. He had the mostly honorary title of creative director in their organization. She was operations director, Cosmo was about to become public relations director, and Rickey was artistic director. But of course, when it came right down to it, it was a one-man team and Rickey ran them all.

"Booker, you look like a dream! It's great to see you!" Henry wrapped her in a bear hug—their hand-shaking days were long past.

"You, too!" She hugged him back.

He was wearing a polo shirt, slacks and white shoes, and somehow still managed to look as if he were on his way to a meeting at a bank. He shouldered his bag of clubs and strode off toward the first tee, clearly expecting her to carry her own. Another reason she liked him, in addition to the positive aspects he brought out in Rickey: sometimes Henry treated her with chivalry and deference, and sometimes he treated her like one of the boys. He always knew which to do when.

They played three holes before they got down to some

serious discussion. Booker was the one to strike up the band.

"Henry, I know Rickey has told you he's been ducking some of the concerts and using a stand-in."

Henry walked over to the tee and lined up for his drive. "Some of the concerts? I understood that he hasn't been on stage in six years."

"Yeah, that's about right. Why does it feel better to me to say he's just been ducking some of the concerts?"

"Because somehow you think there's something wrong with this. That he's cheating people somehow, or fooling people in the wrong way."

"Isn't he?"

"I don't think so. No." Henry watched his ball fly through the air and land just a foot short of the green. "He's hardly the first rock star to make something up or to try to fool the journalists or the public. He's doing it on a broader scale, perhaps, but it's just part of the show. The show people want to see."

Booker considered this as she chose her club and hit off the tee. Not the ladies' tee either, another detail that pleased her. It would never occur to Henry to suggest that she play shorter yards because she was female. She was going to lose, she knew that, but she didn't want any favors to try to help her win.

"What if somebody finds out?" she asked as they walked toward their balls.

"If anybody does, he'll just stop doing what he's doing, and come back to the stage. What are you doing to keep a lid on it, by the way?"

"Well, we have non-disclosure agreements signed by everybody who works on the tours or the shows in any way. Whether they see anything interesting or not, they just can't talk to anybody about anything Rickey T or we'll sue their asses all the way to Hong Kong."

Henry nodded. "Jake, in particular?"

"Jake, in particular. Plus, he's getting freaking millions

to keep his mouth shut. He made millions with us when he was performing and he's getting even more now, to stay off the stage and just to keep quiet," she said. "He was ticked when we let him go, obviously, but the guy was just out of control and it had to be done."

"He couldn't handle the fame?"

"Oh, he loved it," Booker said as she watched Henry selecting his iron. "That was a big part of the problem. He sucked up every bit of attention he could get and he lived out the 'sex, drugs, and rock 'n' roll' scene every single day. He started to believe the drivel that was written about Rickey T and his ego swelled up like you wouldn't believe. By the end, I don't think he really knew where he left off and Rickey T started."

Henry put it up on the green within just a foot of the cup. "So, you fired him. And you're sure he won't embarrass you?"

"I think Rickey scared him a little bit. I remember there was some talk about goons and broken kneecaps."

Henry joined in with her laughter. "Well, he can spend a bunch of this money he's getting for not working on the security personnel he's going to need now."

"I'm sure he will."

"Is Rickey coming back?"

Booker took a good swing at her ball and managed to get it to the edge of the green. "He doesn't want to."

"That surprised you?"

"It did. I thought this was just him taking a break, playing a joke on the music writers and some of the fans. But it turns out he doesn't ever want to perform any more, or go out in public or be recognized. He wears disguises all the time now, some of them really strange. Full-face masks of super-heroes. Animals! Can you imagine, last week he traveled from the airport to the dock where was boarding his boat, wearing a leopard head!"

Booker stomped off along the fairway. "He won't do videos, he wouldn't do any more appearances after the

Grammys a few years back, and now he's saying he doesn't want to go into studio and record. He wants the new stand-in, whoever he is, to be able to fool everybody in the studio too!"

She was getting upset and she knew that Henry could see it. He bent over his putt for a long time.

"Don't get too upset, Booker. Anything is do-able. It could work, in the studio, if you just have each of the musicians come in on his own to lay the tracks for his part, couldn't it? You've been managing details for years on this, keeping Rickey out of sight, so that he could live his life the way he wanted, haven't you?"

As she stood waiting for Henry to line up his putt, Booker remembered the first time Rickey introduced them. It was the late seventies, just after all the fame and success hit, and it looked as though Rickey might be going off the rails. While crossing a trestle. Over a gorge as deep as the Grand Canyon. In a railway car that had no handles on the inside of the doors.

Henry had shown up at a party, one of the constant parties with a steady stream of people heading to the bathroom and emerging minutes later in a noticeably better mood. She and Rickey were in their mid-twenties, Henry in his mid-thirties—not that much of an age difference but somehow Henry seemed calmer and more Zen than anybody else they knew. An old soul, Rickey liked to say. He was related to Henry somehow (some third or fifth cousin or something) and Henry lived in whatever town it was they were playing that night.

When he walked up to them at the party, Booker almost laughed. The burly man was wearing a suit and tie, and looked as though he'd got lost on his way to a meeting at the bank.

"Who let this guy in?" she snickered. "Maybe he's a narc."

"He's not a narc, he's my cousin. Sort of," Rickey said, over his shoulder as he stepped forward to greet him. "I told you he'd be coming tonight. I've been looking forward to it for weeks."

Henry's hair was as wild as his clothing was conservative. Booker was mesmerized by the curly, black strands that seemed to stand out at right angles to his scalp, each one doing some kind of frizzy, frenzied dance. When he reached out to shake her hand, a move that wasn't that common with women in those days, she smelled a faint woodsy, outdoorsy cologne. Most of the men she saw every day and night smelled like cheap red wine or pungent body spray, and this was a nice change.

"Booker, this is Henry Ryland. He's . . . well, he's a friend. A good friend," Rickey said. "Kind of like a mentor to me."

Henry looked neither flattered nor cornered by that description. "I do talk with him once in a while," he said in a sort of relaxed cadence that put Booker at ease right away.

"Are you in the music business?" she asked.

Henry smiled. "Right now, I'm in the ranching business. In Montana. But I used to play a little, write a little."

Having Henry at the party seemed to put Rickey on better behavior than he'd shown in a few months. The two of them set up in two armchairs near a window and dropped into a deep discussion that had them both leaning forward and talking, nose to nose. Somehow, nobody dared to interrupt or disturb them, not even the big-haired supermodel twins who'd come to the party, each on one of Rickey's arms.

After that, Henry showed up every few weeks at a concert, always arriving on a Lear jet that Rickey had sent for his transportation. Over the years, Booker learned that Henry wasn't really related to Rickey; that was probably an example of Rickey's wishful thinking. Henry came from an old wealthy Southern family, one that he'd parted ways with over opinions about the war in Vietnam (and about the one they probably called the War of Northern Aggression, Booker suspected). He loved horses, music, and creative people, and he'd put his money to work behind all three. He'd staked Rickey in the very early days, writing him checks and making a point of going to meet the singer backstage frequently after shows in crummy, little dives in upstate New York.

Henry knew that Rickey was desperately unhappy almost before Rickey did. He watched the drug use and abuse getting crazy, but that wasn't his only clue, he told Booker. Sometimes, after all, a party is just a party. But in Rickey's case, the music was starting to suffer, Henry thought. Through the early eighties, particularly as Rickey's twenty-seventh birthday approached, Henry stayed close to the scene. Granted, it was ten years after Janis, Jimi Hendrix, and Jim Morrison had died, but superstition pervaded music almost as much as it did sports. Henry offered his companionship, hanging out with the boy as often as he could, and Rickey never brushed him off. Henry was one of the few people who knew about Rickey's extreme stage fright.

When the rock star told Booker, about a year after Fake Jake had been hired, that Henry knew about the deception, Booker was not surprised.

"When he first told me about it, he talked about a five-year plan," Booker said. "But he's already extended it by a year, even more, and now he wants a new five-year plan. He wants to be a hermit!"

"All he wants to do is write, Henry said.

Booker ran through the implications in her mind while she played her ball. She was rattled, and she hit too hard three times in a row. She was starting to feel that she'd rather kick the damn ball into the hole than hit it one more time, when she finally sank her putt.

"Whoever is doing the job will have to be a lot more discrete than Fake Jake," she said. "If the stand-in is in the studio, people will spend more time with him, will have a chance to watch him up close.

"And women, what about women? Jake had a steady

girlfriend who was just as thrilled about being rich as he was and who didn't ask a lot of questions about where he was when he went away and where the money came from. What if the next one plays the field more? What if he has a lot of friends that he lets in on it? Jake had no friends, so that wasn't an issue. What if this new one isn't a dead ringer for Rickey, visually? What about the tattoos?" Booker was starting to feel a bit hysterical. "Jake used those fake, paste on ones, but up close, that won't be any good. This new stand-in will have to be willing to get the tattoos. Where are we going to find somebody like that?"

"For several million bucks?" Henry asked. "Probably in a lot of different places. Booker, I think you're spending too much time, thinking about the 'what ifs."

"It'll have to be somebody who can handle the fame better than Jake did," she said.

Henry picked up his bag and they walked off toward the next tee. "Being a famous person is a separate skill, a whole other thing in addition to being a singer or a musician or a writer. It's beyond a lot of people, acquiring that skill, and they get ruined by it. If this new stand-in is going to live even more of the Rickey T life than just performing, I think you should make sure there is some help with that."

Booker nodded. "Good advice. I'll talk to Rickey."

"Be upfront at the auditions. Tell them it's an audition for a Rickey T tribute band, not for backup singers. I think you'll get a different crowd, and maybe somebody more likely to be a good fit.

"You might also mention to Rickey that this new guy will need to spend a lot of time with him off-hours, to learn to copy his style and his ways. It's one thing to watch video and concert tapes to imitate somebody but a whole other thing to act like him in private life."

Booker nodded at a couple who walked by, wearing matching outfits, right down to the identical ivory leather golf glove. Who were these people, who identified with one another so strongly that they wanted to wear the exact same clothes? She couldn't even find a man who was willing to pick the same movie to go to. Most of the time, Booker was too busy with work to give any thought to her lack of a private life, but every once in a while, she got lonesome, just like everybody else.

Henry noticed her noticing. "Which one picks out the outfit in the morning?"

Booker laughed. "It boggles the mind."

When they finished the round, Booker invited Henry to come to L.A. for the auditions but he declined, mentioning some family business that needed attention. When he drove away in his rented Jeep, heading for the airport, she wished she were going along.

CHAPTER FOURTEEN

Los Angeles

The one-way glass covered the entire wall of the immaculate studio. Booker could watch the singers and the band but all they saw was a mirror. She leaned forward in her chair, while the technician handled the sliders and played with the EQ. Even before the production help, the guy sounded very good, and now, she was ready to seal the deal without hearing either of the other two.

But she was always thorough. She'd auditioned a dozen men that morning, each one of whom was thrilled with the idea of fronting a Rickey T tribute band, and she had it down to a shortlist of three. This tall drink of water was definitely the most promising, visually, but she owed it to Rickey, to herself, and to the fans to listen to the other two. Who knew, there might be a surprise coming.

Not from this second guy. He was good, as expected, but something about the shape of his mouth and the way he leaned toward the microphone just weren't Rickey. Booker reached behind her head to take the diet soda her assistant was holding out. One more to go, then a decision, an offer, and a meeting with Rickey at Spago.

The third and final guy walked up to the microphone and leaned in. What was his name? Booker looked at her clipboard. Oliver Dash. The singer waved an arm at the backup band . . . was he going to sing acapella? He was. He did his entire rendition of "Seen You a Thousand Times" without any musical accompaniment, and as the last note echoed away, Booker had her answer. This was the guy.

She sent the other two on their way, thanked the freelance recording technicians and producers she'd hired for the day, and got Oliver into the back of the car.

"Spago on Sunset," she said to the driver. "West Hollywood."

The man made a face . . . or at least, she imagined he did. All she could see was the back of his head, but his tone told his reaction. "I know where it is."

Booker pushed the button to roll up the partition. "Oliver, thanks so much for auditioning today. I think you've probably figured out that you're our pick. I'm taking you out for dinner now. We're going to meet Rickey."

"Rickey T?"

Oh, no. A dumb one. But maybe not. Maybe just temporarily overcome with the excitement of getting the job——although you wouldn't think somebody thirty-seven years old would be overcome by anything much, anymore.

"Yes, Rickey T. He leaves it to me to get to this point, but he'll have the final say in hiring you."

"To front a tribute band for him."

Booker shook her head, then pushed the button to uncover the bottles and glasses in the limo bar. "Not exactly. The job is a little different than what we led you to believe."

Oliver accepted the glass of wine she poured. He looked a little wary. "How so?"

"It will pay more than a tribute band, for one thing."

The suspicious look changed to one of greed. "How much more?"

Booker turned on the limo sound system, and started

blasting *Thriller.* She reached under the seat and pulled out a file folder. "Sign this first," she said, shoving the non-disclosure agreement under his nose. She watched as he scribbled his name on the dotted line, then carefully put the folder away.

"Look, Oliver, here's the deal. Rickey T, the real one, the rock star, Richard Taggart, doesn't want to be Rickey T on stage anymore. He's finding the performances a real grind. The fans, the travel, the fame. . . . how do you think you'd be with fame?"

"Just fine." Oliver took another swallow of his wine but never took his gaze off her face.

"Good. Here's the job. You would stand in for Rickey T at concerts, public appearances, video shoots, maybe a few other things. Not all of them, but quite a few. We'll let you know the schedule. Rickey will still do the writing, the recording, etc. For this, you would be paid extremely well."

To his credit, he didn't ask 'how much' again. He probably knew he could get pretty much whatever he asked. Booker was pleased that she wasn't faced with his question right now, because her answer would be 'how much do you want?' Always better to get that information first. The negotiation would come later, once she'd gotten to know him a little better.

"Was he wanting to quit, when he did the Toronto concert in '89?"

Aah, he'd done his homework. And he thought the real Rickey was still on the stage two years ago. Booker allowed herself a moment of celebration and made a mental note to remind herself to pass this on to Rickey. Many people (Most people? Everybody?) had no idea that Fake Jake had been standing in for Rickey.

Oh yeah, it was working. The whole, crazy scheme had worked. Now, it was just a matter of hiring the right guy, so that it could go on working.

There was no reason to tell Oliver that he wasn't going to be the first Rickey stand-in. "Yeah, he was wanting to quit then. He's wearing out, on the performances, and on the video shoots. You think you could handle the music videos?"

"Yeah, sure. But there must be a million people who've met Rickey T. How are you going to keep this quiet?"

"Are you an actor, Oliver?"

Oliver seemed almost pathetically eager to please, yet it was good to see that he could still maintain his cool vibe. "I was an actor before I was a singer. Well, not technically. At the beginning, I was a singer. And a songwriter. But then I came to Hollywood, and became an actor." He was started to stumble over his words, maybe seeing the light at the end of a twenty-year tunnel. "I can do both. I can do either, I mean. Whatever you need." He gulped the last of his wine. "How much are we talking?"

A-ha. "How much would you think we should be talking?"

Oliver looked crafty, for a second. "Hundreds of thousands?"

This would be so easy. "Millions," Booker said, and poured Oliver another drink.

***

Rickey was eager to meet this new guy. He'd seen the audition videos and heard all about him from Booker, and now he was on his way, from the studio on Melrose to Spago to meet the guy and have dinner. Rickey drove by, then circled back toward the restaurant. He was always impressed by how little L.A. actually resembled its reputation—at least, its reputation in music world. Maybe 'impressed' was the wrong word. 'Amused' was a better one. You have this idea that L.A. is the promised land, the Shangri-la, all glamorous and golden, and then you get there and you see that it's miles and miles of suburbia, parking lots, malls, and low-rise apartment buildings, all kind of dusty and dry, and sometimes baking in a strange, orangeish glow, depending on the time of year and the thickness of the polluted air.

Rickey was in complete costume, one of his favorites for keeping appointments in L.A.: a gray-haired wig; a suit with a boxy jacket, a wide tie, and a pastel shirt; and a walking stick. Something that would have fit right in on the TV show *L.A. Law* (except for the walking stick—that was only intended as a distraction). He would have preferred one of his silk scarves to the tie but he left that at home when he went out. It was better that the stand-in be the only one seen wearing a scarf or a cape, out in public.

Rickey parked his Maserati a block away on Sunset, much as he preferred valet parking most of the time. He didn't want to draw any kind of attention or speculation. The restaurant was one of those where people went to be seen, and it impressed anybody who hadn't been there before. That was one of the things he wanted to do, with this new stand-in. Impress him with the upside and impress him with the consequences of blowing the deal.

Rickey had a lot riding on this new guy. He really needed to get out of the spotlight for a while and go somewhere to get his balance back.

He walked around the corner, tipped an imaginary hat at Tower Records, and saw two Rolls-Royces, idling in front of the less-than-imposing front door on Horn Avenue. The valet guys seemed rushed off their feet and a little backed up, and he was pleased with himself for choosing not to drive right up to the door. When he walked in and gave the maître d' the name for the reservation—Buchanan—he didn't note even a flicker of recognition or interest. Even after six years of sending out the Rickey-fake in his place and walking around like an anonymous everyman himself, he was still getting used to that. Man, he loved it.

The maître d' led Rickey to a table with great sightlines throughout the room. Rickey settled into his chair, enjoying the view. Nobody famous, that he could see, and nobody was looking at him. Perfect.

His cell phone rang and he answered it, just for the pleasure of seeing the cranky looks from the other diners nearby. "Yeah?"

"Rickey? It's Cosmo."

"Cosmo, hey, how are ya."

"Good, Rickey, how are you?" Cosmo still was freaked out at the idea that he had Rickey T's number and could call it, Rickey could tell.

"I'm good, Cosmo. I'm in. L.A. Where are you?"

"So am I. Working at the resort. Leaving for a new one in Whistler next month, though."

"Whistler, I love Whistler. Love to write there."

"I heard they got a new recording studio. Way up on a mountain, you have to get there in a helicopter."

"Rad," Rickey said. "What you calling about?"

Cosmo switched gears, quickly. "The Rickets. The Fan Club. We're thinking of doing a big event, like a fan convention, connect it with your concert in '93."

"What's the projected revenue?"

He could hear Cosmo grin. "Sixty mil."

"What do you need me to do?"

"Help with the promo, the merchandise, do some meet-and-greets that we could advertise heavily, ahead of time. And it would be outstanding if you would do an appearance."

Booker was so smart to get this guy on board. "It might be me and it might be the stand-in. Not sure right now, but it'll be covered."

"So, yes?"

"Yeah."

***

Booker jumped out of the limo without waiting for an opening or assistance from either the driver or Oliver Dash. Rickey waited inside, and she was eager to get to him to show him her latest discovery.

As she was walking toward the maître d', her path was blocked by a music journalist she vaguely remembered meeting in some hotel suite or green room. He bumped right into her.

"Ms. Buchanan! Oh, god, sorry, I really should wear my glasses." He stuck out a hand. "Dwight Kettle, *Melodies Coast to Coast*."

"*Coast to Coast*, really? Or *Coast to Coast*, once upon a time, for some one-off assignment, and now you're dropping their name for every lame-ass idea you have?"

Dwight grinned, while still fumbling for his tape recorder. "You know the game, Miss Buchanan. Are we on the record?"

"We are not. Not ever," she said. "Get out of our way. We have a dinner appointment."

"Who are you having dinner with? Is it Rickey?" Dwight asked her new hire, holding out the tape recorder microphone. Geez, he thought Oliver was Rickey. Hot damn. This was working already.

"I really can't tell you that," Oliver said. "If I told you, I'd have to kill you." He smiled and winked at Dwight. Yeah, Oliver was charismatic, there was no denying. But was he believable, as Rickey?

Dwight relaxed, and put his microphone away. Totally, working already.

"Hey, could we do a short interview later? When you've had your dinner with whoever? And before you kill me?"

Booker held out her hand for his card. "Give me your number. Maybe he can call."

She led Oliver over to Rickey's table. They ordered the caviar pizza, Rickey staring at the new guy and taking his measure every minute. Booker could feel Rickey relax, underneath that ridiculous gray wig, and she knew they had it built. The three of them chatted, during drinks, the pizza, and the dessert, and she could see that both men were comfortable with each other. The mood wasn't even disturbed when she leaned over, during the brandies, and told Rickey that she had lined up a telephone interview for him.

"What, now? Geez, Book."

"It will only take five minutes and it will throw this guy off the scent. This music "journalist"," she said, sarcastically. "And it will give Oliver a chance to see how it's done."

With a grumpy look on his extremely made-up face, Rickey took the phone from Booker. "Yeah, man, this is Rickey Taggart. What's up?

He listened, then winced, probably at the inane questions. "Yeah, I'm back in the recording studio. Got an album's worth of new songs, yeah. No, no concerts right now, maybe in a year or so. I think we're organizing a new tour, I'm not quite sure, you'll have to talk to management about the details. Anything else? You sure you don't want to know what my favorite color is? What I had for breakfast?"

Rickey snorted and handed the phone back to Booker. Oliver watched, wide-eyed. When Rickey looked across the restaurant and saw Dwight at a table, putting away a phone with what he imagined was a look of supreme disappointment, he was delighted enough to order another round of fifty-year old brandy.

"I'm not doing any more of those interviews, Booker," Rickey said. "That will be your job," he said to Oliver, who nodded as eagerly as a ten-year-old kid being given his first lawn mowing assignment. "No more interviews, no more meeting fans, no more awards shows, no more videos. I will still be the writer, though," he said solemnly. "That's the only good part."

"That and the money," Booker added.

"That and the money," Rickey agreed.

Oliver just looked from one to the other, and grinned.

CHAPTER FIFTEEN

Whistler

Whistler had changed a lot since Booker had been there last. It was a different season this time, too—winter, instead of summer. There was a crisp bite in the air and snowfall was expected any minute, to add to the four inches that already lay on the ground in the village and the fifteen inches of fresh powder expected on the hill.

For non-skiers, this could be miserable weather. But this new Rickey stand-in hadn't uttered a word of complaint since he'd arrived. Oliver seemed to be able to adapt to whatever was going on. He was cool, stylish, just as ego-focused as any rock star Booker had ever met, of course, but there was an earnestness to him, too. It made him much easier to take. The previous guy—what was his name again?—would have been whining like a disco queen at a hootenanny but this guy, Oliver, seemed to be much, much less of a diva.

He also seemed to be much smarter than the previous one.

Pretend Rickey 2, was the way that Booker thought of

him. He looked just like Rickey, in the right clothes and the right light but with an added dose of sexiness that was going to drive the ladies wild, out on tour.

First things, first—new songs. Rickey had sent along three new tunes that he'd written while on his boat near the Maldives, and he'd flown in to Whistler to record them. Oliver was going to sit in the control room of the studio, get a little more observation time, before he started in on the biggest performance of his life . . . the concert coming up in Miami.

Oliver sat between Booker and Mark, the sound engineer with the gray fedora and the hands like a basketball player's. They were looking through the glass panel that separated the control room from the studio where Rickey stood in front of the mic, getting ready for the third take on this new song. Oliver could see his own reflection, too—the dark, mullet haircut wig, the shades, the three days of beard stubble, the turtleneck sweater. He looked like hell but he'd understood the necessity for the disguise right away when Booker mentioned it. Only one Rickey T on the premises at a time.

Booker watched him stare at himself in the glass, and wondered what he was thinking.

You know I've spent half my life around stages and music, and I thought I had an idea of how it might be. I had NO idea. They treat you like a freakin' king, man. Like a rock star, I guess. Everything is first-class all the way. And it's all the psychology, you know? I don't sing any better or play or move any better than I ever did when I was just copying Rickey T. but now that they think that I am him? Suddenly I'm great.

I don't get it but I don't need to.

I don't know what it was that made Rickey decide that he needed to take a break . . . such a major break! . . . away from an incredible scene like this. In the world of lucky guys, he is THE lucky guy. Big time.

Yeah, I don't get it but I don't need to. I'm just here, now, playing the part of Rickey T for a little while.

For a lot of money. And a chance to write music.

Rickey (and Booker) don't know about that part yet. That I can write. It's what the business guys call 'value-added' these days. I've got a folder full of songs I've written, and some of them are pretty damn good, if I do say so myself, as my grandma used to say. Of course, these ones we're hearing today are Rickey T songs, and they're fantastic, but I've got a few, too. The rock star might think he's going to have it all his way just because he's a rich bugger, but I think he'll realize he's not holding all the cards here. I've got a few.

Writing is my thing, now that I've finally given up on the painting thing. Ramona says I'll never be a success at singing if I don't start thinking of it as 'my thing', and give up on these 'childish dreams', she calls them. Ha. Little does she know. I'm a success right now, if she measures it by money. She thinks I'm in Canada for a small gig and then going to Miami for another small one. If she ever would agree to come with me to any of my shows, maybe she'd know. But she hasn't been willing to lower herself in ten years. Just go to work, and bring home the money, she says. We need a new couch or we need an ice-making refrigerator. Makes it very easy to keep Rickey's secret.

The training for Oliver had gone much more smoothly than for Fake Jake in 1984. Booker believed he was what the athletes call 'coachable'. He took direction, he did what he was told and he knew who was the boss. She had seen him in rehearsal two dozen times since they'd hired him in L.A., and each time he impressed her with his resemblance to Rickey and his improvement over the last time. Every day that went by, she was more impressed with the guy's dedication and professionalism. Why hadn't he ever become a star under his own name? Who knew? Maybe some missing ingredient, maybe just the wrong style or fashion for that point in time . . . or maybe just no luck, good or bad.

She leaned back in her very comfortable chair in front of the mixing console. They were working on the album *H8GNSLO*. Shad, their "go-to guy" at the record label, made no secret of his lack of enthusiasm for the album title. He kept on calling it a "working title", and he kept on calling himself "your go-to guy", over and over, until Booker wanted to smack him.

She could understand his interest, of course. This was Rickey T's first real album in more than two years. There had been yet another 'greatest hits' compilation and a Christmas album, but no new songs since 1989. What happened in this studio was crucial. Shad was phoning every couple of hours and she made a point of taking his calls, putting him on speaker-phone so that he could feel that he was speaking to everyone, especially Rickey, and not just to the manager. It was better to have him on the phone than risk having him show up in person. She didn't know why it was that bumbling, offensive, unlikeable, incompetent losers seemed to pop up at every record company she'd ever been involved with. It was either useless jerks or bullies. Shad was a little of both, but as long as he kept his distance, she could deal.

It was her private goal that this new album ship gold. The key to that was advance sales . . . and the key to that, Booker was convinced, wouldn't have anything to do with Shad Palmetto. But it might have everything to do with the man she was going to meet once this sky-high session was done.

"Thanks for calling in, Shad," she shouted in the direction of the speaker-phone. "We're wrapping up now."

"All right, Booker, I'll go. But I might—"

Mark had correctly interpreted her chopping-across-the-throat gesture, and cut off the power to the telephone line or turned down the volume or did whatever technical thing it was he had to do. She didn't want to hear what Shad might be thinking of doing, especially if it had to do with him showing up at the studio. It was doubtful that he would trek all the way to Whistler unless he absolutely had to, though. Most of those L.A. and New York types thought of Canada in general as being off in the middle of nowhere.

Whistler was an hour and a half drive from the nearest big city, Vancouver, and the studio itself was halfway up a mountain, a helicopter ride from the village. Booker felt safe from Shad's interference.

Lord knows how they got this equipment up here, not to mention the grand piano and the drum kits in the studio.

She had been a little green around the edges after the helicopter ride up to the top. The pilot insisted on telling them all, several times, that they weren't actually at the summit, only at a meadow about halfway up, but it looked high enough to Booker. There was supposedly some kind of cachet in using this studio, because it was so remote and because it was equipped with the latest toys, but Booker, not being a producer or a rock star, didn't really care. She'd be very glad when the recording was finished and they could all get on to the next project.

"Mark? Are we almost done?" Booker asked the sound engineer.

"I've got everything I need, if Rickey's satisfied," Mark said. He waved at Rickey, got a thumbs-up and they all watched as Rickey pulled off the headphones.

Rickey was pumped, after doing the recording, as he always was, and he greeted Booker with a big hug. She gave him a warning look, in case he said something revealing while they were still within Mark's earshot. After agreeing that the helicopter pilot would take the three of them down to the village then come back for the sound engineer when he was finished working, Booker, Rickey and Oliver climbed aboard. Booker held her breath and closed her eyes as the helicopter swooped down toward the valley.

"Hey, I'll see you later at the Chateau," Booker said. "I have to take a meeting."

The wind blew across Lost Lake and Booker pulled her coat tighter. Who knew it got this cold in March? But it was the mountains, after all. She was on her way to the High Sky Resort that Cosmo was managing these days. As far as she knew, everything was going well with the Rickets Fan Club, but she'd had a request from him for a meeting.

She had an agenda item of her own. She wanted Cosmo to keep an eye on Oliver at the fan events and put out any fires of suspicion that might start to smolder.

The High Sky Resort was one of the mid-size ones in Whistler. The building was designed and decorated in a French Alps style and Booker took a moment to enjoy the atmosphere. If Cosmo was managing this place, he must be doing well in hotel world.

"Booker!" His smile was as sweet and open as it had been when he was twenty, when she first met him. He looked more like a grown-up now, particularly in his manager suit.

She gave him a hug. "Cosmo! Great to see you. What are we doing, drinks?"

"I'm ready for something to eat, if you don't mind. Why don't we try the restaurant?"

He led the way to the resort dining room, its white table linens continuing the motif of the snow drifts outside. A huge, candle-inspired chandelier dominated the ceiling and windows framed a cobblestone alleyway, lit by gaslight-inspired streetlamps. It was probably very charming, after dark.

Cosmo looked around the room and frowned. "Just a second, Booker, I'll be right back. Have to take care of something."

"What is it?" She was interested.

"I'm not liking the distribution of the diners through the room," he said. "We've got all those empty tables over there and over here, we've got people practically sitting on top of each other. I think we're seating people for the convenience of the servers rather than the quality of the dining experience. I'll just go make sure they fix that, with the next group coming in."

He went over to speak to the maître d'. Booker admired his air of confidence and decisiveness. She had never regretted her decision to bring him in, and whenever they discussed it, Rickey felt the same.

Booker looked around the room and nearly fell off her chair when she spotted a familiar face. Was that Mona Ray . . . what was her last name? The one from France and then from New York? She'd stayed in touch, sending Booker the occasional card or fax, but their paths hadn't crossed in seven years. You'd think that she'd have changed, at least a little bit, but she hadn't. Same long red hair in the same style, same 'it's my world' manner.

"How are things going with the album?" Cosmo had returned to the table and was sliding into the chair beside her.

"Well, Pretend Rickey 2 is soaking everything up like a sponge and Real Rickey is just killing it on the recordings," she said.

"That's great," Cosmo said, as he signaled the waiter. "The Caesar salads are terrific here, why don't I get us a couple?"

Booker nodded, while she kept an eye on Mona Ray. Her instinct was right; the woman was coming over to say hello.

Booker could tell in an instant that Cosmo remembered Mona Ray, and vice versa. He didn't take her eyes off her as she walked across the restaurant. Booker made a mental note to copy the 'black T-shirt with white jeans' outfit that Mona Ray was wearing.

"Hi, Booker, it's nice to see you."

"Hi, Mona Ray, nice to see you. Way up north here in Whistler. You remember Cosmo Lewis?"

Cosmo had jumped to his feet when Mona Ray got to the table. Wow, where had he picked up his polish? "I certainly remember you, Mona Ray. Welcome to our hotel. Would you like to join us for a few minutes?" He motioned toward the chair he'd just vacated but Mona Ray shook her head.

"No, I'm sorry but I can't stay." She glanced back toward her table, and Booker followed her gaze. The server had returned and was putting large plates with what looked like steaks in front of each of the three place settings. Two men sat there, watching. Was that Sturgess Mesley?

The silence was just long enough to become uncomfortable and Cosmo rushed in to fill it. "What have you been doing since I saw you in Cannes?"

Mona Ray smiled. "I live in L.A. now. West coast office for Staten Island Records."

"You work for our record label?"

"I scout new talent," Mona Ray said, glancing back again toward her table.

I'll bet you do, Booker thought.

Mona Ray turned back to look at her table. "My guests look a little lonely over there, I'd better get back." She grinned at Cosmo and stuck out a hand. "Nice to see you again, Cosmo. Congratulations on your job, and your club . . . and on growing up pretty good, I guess."

"Thanks, Mona Ray," Cosmo said. Booker could tell he was glad they'd had this coincidental meeting. She was not so sure.

"Small world, yeah?" Cosmo said, as he tucked into the bread basket. "So she stays in touch with you?"

"I'm not sure why." Booker said. "She was one of the . . . . *liveliest*, for want of a better word . . . of the female fans around Rickey in the seventies and then she managed to get his exclusive attention for a while there in the eighties."

"Who does Rickey see now?" Cosmo asked.

"Absolutely nobody, he tells me. Says he doesn't need anybody and really likes to be alone."

Cosmo nodded to the server who had arrived with the coffee pot. "That brings me to the reason I asked you to come over to see me today."

"What's up, Cosmo?"

"I know he really likes to be alone and the point of having Oliver on the job is that Rickey is protected from all of the hassles of being famous," Cosmo said. "He doesn't meet fans any more, but I wonder whether he might make an exception for this big Fan Convention we're planning in two years. I know Oliver can handle it, and we will stage-manage it so that there is zero chance he'll get busted. And nobody will know but me, that it's Oliver and not Rickey. Rickey told me a while ago in L.A. that I'd have his support for the convention but he wouldn't commit to making an appearance. But if there is *any* possibility that Rickey would be there, that would mean a lot to me. Just to know that he values the Fan Club enough to show up, you know?"

Booker did know. She promised Cosmo that she would run it by Rickey and as they left the restaurant after lunch, she promised again. Walking through the village, she enjoyed the fresh air and the gorgeous views of the mountain peaks. The people passing by were equipped with every kind of outdoor gear she could imagine: backpacks, walking sticks, hiking boots, and a few with skis, mountain bikes or climbing ropes. The clothing ranged from plaid to denim to ski suits, with a few upscale, downtown dresses in the mix. It was a terrific place for people watching, almost as good as New York.

A display of miniature hockey player figures playing the game against a team of Mounties stopped Booker in front of a Canadian souvenir store called The Melodious Moose. In the reflection in the window, she could see the stores across the road, the sidewalk in front of them filled with people and dogs. One figure caught and held her attention. Was that Rickey?

He was not wearing a disguise at all and looked as if he were thoroughly enjoying the day. Booker thought she noticed one or two passersby pause and do a double-take. *Was* that Rickey T? Here? In Whistler, of all places? He was walking along at a brisk pace, and by the time his presence registered, he was half a block gone.

Booker decided to go over and say hello. She caught up with him in front of the jewelry store. He slowed down to look at an arrangement of jade and amber rings.

"Hi, Rickey." She spoke in a quiet voice, planning to help him keep his low profile, if that's what he wanted.

He didn't turn. "Guess again," he muttered.

Oliver. He pulled his jacket collar up around his ears and crossed the road, heading off toward the village square. Booker shook her head, grinned and walked off in the opposite direction. It was funny, but it was a little scary, too.

Booker reached the end of the Village Stroll a few hundred yards on, and then turned back to head toward her hotel. Through the crowd she saw two more people she recognized. Shad and Mona Ray were walking toward her, about a block away. Oliver was only about a half block in front of her, on the other side of the street. She saw Shad notice Oliver, then half-raise an arm to wave. He came to a stop and stared across the road, his head cocked to one side. Booker had to do something.

"Shad! Mona Ray! Well, how about this. Small world!" Booker closed the gap between them as quickly as she could.

Mona Ray looked as if she'd just been asked to wear last year's party dress style. "I just saw you at lunch," she reminded Booker.

"How's it going, Shad?" Booker forged ahead. "Are you enjoying Whistler?"

Shad was still gazing across the road, but the man he'd noticed had now disappeared in a crowd of walkers and window-shoppers. "Was that Rickey over there?"

"Over where? No, I don't think so, I didn't see him," Booker said. "He's been hunkered down in the studio and in his room for days, writing, recording. Working on new material."

"I know, I've tried to see him a few times while we're here, as you know. I thought that was him, but—" Shad was still looking over at the crowd across the street.

"Might have been, might have been," Booker fumbled for the right thing to say. "Maybe he was taking a short walk, clearing his head or something."

"No, no, it wasn't him. Looked a lot like him, but there was just something . . . not right, I don't know." Shad seemed to reel his own focus back in and turn it to Booker. "Anyway, I'm glad to hear that he's working so hard and that we're going to get a new album soon. You tell him I said hello. We're leaving for Vancouver in about half an hour, and then back to L.A. tonight. I'll catch up to him some other time."

CHAPTER SIXTEEN

1993

Miami

Two years later

Cosmo shifted from one foot to another, side to side and up and down, trying to see around the long line of fans waiting at the Will Call window. Of course, he probably could have asked Booker to leave his comps at the hotel or even just showed up at the stage door; he knew most of the security guards. But he liked to have the same experience that his customers and his Fan Club members had when they were buying tickets or seeing a show. It gave him all sorts of valuable information.

This was the first appearance by 'Rickey T' in two years, and everyone was pumped. Miami was one of the key stops on any rock 'n' roll tour. The potential audience reach was all over the South, and many musicians lived and worked in Miami in the winter and spring months. Booker told him that she had blasted out invitations and various kinds of gifts to a long list of glamorous potential attendees, for the added benefit there would be if the paparazzi saw that Madonna or Steven Tyler or the latest boy band was on the guest list.

Cosmo was out in front of the main doors now, but two hours ago he had been backstage. He even had a few minutes in the dressing room with "Rickey", watching him make up for the show. Cosmo always thought of him as "Rickey" with the air quotes; if he started thinking of him as Oliver, he was at risk of saying that name out loud, by mistake. Although there were many, many ways the secret could be blown wide open, Cosmo didn't want any dynamite to be traced back to him.

Oliver had seemed to be pretty confident. He was looking in his dressing room mirror, adding another layer of eyeliner. He had on a silver-colored satin jacket with dark pants; his hair was cut into a modified shag. He was a little too put together for Cosmo's taste, but he was happy to see that Oliver was barefoot, inside his Italian loafers.

After a few compliments, Cosmo left him alone and went looking for the green room, the food and the ticket holders who had won the 'Meet Rickey in Miami' contest that the Rickets club had run throughout the months leading up to the concert. "Enter the draw to win a chance to mingle with Rickey T after the show" . . . but you could only enter if you were holding a floor seat ticket and you could only have one of those if you came up with $500 for it.

Pricey ticket, and yet the fans pushed and shoved to get it. Booker always said she was surprised anybody would pay that kind of money to see a concert but Cosmo wasn't. People want what they want.

There was that much demand for the nose-bleed seats, too. People had camped out, the night before the Rickey T concert tickets went on sale, another supply-and-demand feature that Booker claimed left her puzzled as shit. Cosmo doubted that she really had any trouble comprehending the Rickey T fan's obsession. Regardless, whether she had any trouble understanding it, she had no trouble appreciating it. The fans, and Cosmo, their Pied Piper, were as essential to her as satisfied guests to a five-star hotel.

After shaking a few hands, making sure the VIPs had lots to drink, and giving his promises (again) that Rickey would drop by to meet them after the show, Cosmo gathered up his Rickets gear and headed for the box office. As he walked along the corridor, he saw that Oliver's dressing room door was open a crack. Cosmo could hear his voice as he did his vocal warm-up. Yeah, the guy was smooth. Cosmo squinted through the door, wanting to watch but not wanting to interrupt. Oliver had talked with him earlier but Cosmo wasn't sure how welcome he would be, this close to show time.

Oliver was in front of the mirror in his dressing room, singing scales, a pot of what was probably warm honey within reach on the table in front of him. After the C major, he stopped to mutter, "Really, how can you be disappointed about anything about this gig? It's the best it's ever been, Dash, and you know it. So, they won't put any of your songs on the setlist, so what? You get to sing some of the greatest songs ever written."

This was interesting, and Cosmo couldn't stop myself from wading in. He pushed open the door. "You want to do your own songs, Oliver?"

His eyes were startled for just a minute and then the mask went on. "Shut up, Cosmo, Geez. No names, right? Come in, close the door. Geez."

Cosmo followed orders and then flopped down on the couch. "Sorry, man, but there's nobody around out there. It's like a tomb. That's why I heard what you were saying so easily."

"You're sure it wasn't because you were leaning up against the door, trying to spy on me? Why are you back here, anyway?" The words were aggressive but Pretend Rickey 2 grinned when he said them. The guy seemed so confident—Cosmo could see that nothing would faze him.

For some reason, Cosmo felt the urge to rattle him. Maybe it was that he didn't want anyone to be able to step into Rickey's life too easily.

"They won't ever let you do your own songs, you know," Cosmo said. "Rickey is the writer."

Cosmo could see that Oliver wasn't happy with this opinion, but as he pulled on the blond wig, he seemed to have decided to let it go. Cosmo was just trying to figure out how to make a graceful, grown-up exit when he heard a voice behind him say, "This makes no sense whatsoever."

It took Cosmo a few seconds to place the man standing in the doorway, but slowly, after he looked at the photo ID and the name on the backstage all-access pass, it sunk in. It was that guy from Cannes all those years ago. Sturgess Mesley. The one who talked about gambling all the time. Hadn't he turned up a few years later, working for Shad Palmetto at Staten Island Records? He'd changed a lot in nine years—the bushy moustache was gone and so were the platform shoes. He had his hair spiked up and a headband around his forehead. A white T-shirt, a plaid shirt tied around his waist, jeans and sneakers, and a color-blocked windbreaker added up to his outfit . . . and that's how it came across, like an 'outfit' he had thought out and put together, his 'outfit' for going to a concert on a Saturday night.

Oliver seemed frozen and freaked out, so Cosmo took over. "Not at all. Sturgess, isn't it? I think we met in Europe a while back on one of the tours. I'm another friend of Rickey's, aren't I, Rickey?" Oliver nodded, like a 'stupido', as Cosmo's mother would call it.

"Rickey always speaks of himself in the third person when he's talking about writing, and he's got me doing the same," Cosmo explained. "The Rickey who writes is a different guy from the Rickey who performs, at least in the sense that there are several Rickeys, you know? Different sensibilities, different auras, different *personas*, you know? All within the same skin, this armor, this structure that houses the real Rickey, the *true* Rickey."

Sturgess looked at Cosmo as if he'd lost his mind, which he probably had. "Why did you call him Oliver?"

"It's a nickname, a pseudonym, a label we use, he and I, just to keep it straight, who is speaking in any given conversation." *Geez, any "given" conversation??*

Sturgess turned to look behind him, down the corridor, probably to see whether there was anyone who might come to his rescue if this turned totally weird. "And who are you, exactly?"

Cosmo surged forward, in his most authoritative, in-charge manner, something he'd learned from watching some of the movers and shakers he'd seen on vacation at the resort. "Cosmo Lewis. I am president of Rickey's international fan club."

"Oh yeah, I've heard of that," Sturgess conceded. He was already started to relax and his eyes didn't look quite so suspicious. He glanced past Cosmo. "Lots of buzz about this fan club, Rickey. They say you got millions of members now."

"Tens of millions," Oliver said, ignoring them both as he stared into the mirror and started to put on more eyeliner.

Sturgess watched him for a few more minutes, then made a move to leave. "Well, hey, you're busy. I just dropped by to say 'have a good show'."

"Thanks."

"You wanna hang out after? It's been a long time. We could catch up."

"I've got plans, but thanks, man."

"Is there an after-party?" Sturgess interrupted his backward lean, out into the hallway, and leaned forward. "Like the old days? We could connect there."

"Nah, there's no after-party, those days are gone. I need my beauty sleep, you know? But thanks for stopping by, yeah?"

They watched as Sturgess backed out of the door, as if he were leaving the presence of a queen or a cobra, then pulled it closed behind him. Both listened for the sound of his footsteps disappearing down the hallway.

About thirty seconds later, after the shock wore off, they both started laughing. 'Is there an after-party?' Cosmo asked, about a dozen times. 'I heard you got millions in your fan club', Oliver said, over and over. Then, the two had a long talk about the implications. What if Sturgess decided he had to share his suspicions with somebody?

"I don't think Sturgess has any suspicions," Oliver said. "I'm the best freakin' actor around and Sturgess thinks he just spent a little quality time with Rickey T. That's what he wants to believe and that's what he wants to tell people."

Cosmo wanted to believe him.

"Yeah, it's a bit terrifying to get challenged like that," Oliver said. "But don't worry, man. Everything's under control."

"You don't think he's running off to blow the whistle on us?"

Oliver shook his head. "Not a chance. He believes he saw Rickey. *I* believe he believes he saw Rickey. And that's crucial. In any acting job, you have to believe you *are* the character. If I don't believe it, nobody else will."

It was a fantastic bonding experience for Oliver and Cosmo—until Oliver got bored and wanted to be alone. Cosmo could feel it in the dressing room; it was almost as if a cold front moved in. Maybe it wasn't boredom, maybe it was pre-show jitters. Whatever, all of a sudden, Cosmo wasn't welcome and Oliver let him know it.

As Cosmo was leaving, he saw the singer pick up his guitar and sit down on a stool in the corner. Was he going to rehearse some more, with just half an hour until the concert? Or was he writing something?

As Cosmo walked off down the hall, heading for his seat for the show, he wondered whether he, Booker and Rickey were suddenly at a lot more risk. If Sturgess took what he'd seen, grew a few new brain cells and started to ask questions, someone would have to move fast to make sure he didn't capitalize on all that. And if Oliver ever decided to use what he knew, to get more money or to get his way on the writing thing, someone would have to pay up.

Maybe even fold, although Cosmo couldn't imagine Rickey tossing in his hand unless he absolutely had to. Booker, now, she might be the type to cut losses, but Rickey would stay in the game until somebody pushed him out.

The concert was a triumph, start to finish. Cosmo was sitting in the second row, He had probably looked at about a million photos of Rickey in his time, and yet he would never have noticed any differences between the real Rickey and Oliver, the copy, if he hadn't been looking for them. This guy, Oliver, was really earning his money—and Cosmo knew, from conversations with Booker, that the amount was significant.

He wondered whether it would be enough to keep Oliver happy, though. When they were talking before the show, Oliver told Cosmo all about his conversations about song choice with Rickey, about the tunes on *H8GNSLO* and about the specific titles they planned to put in the set list for the shows coming up this year. Rickey had introduced each one to Oliver, explaining the germ of the idea, the development of the concept, and the polish. They sat together in the booth in the Whistler recording studio and Rickey shared his feelings about each and every song. Oliver had done his best to show Rickey that he got it, that he had enough emotion of his own to be the perfect stage channel for Rickey's songwriting genius. He was just another tool, just like an amp, a turntable, or a radio—a channel for Rickey's originality and sound.

Oliver told Cosmo that he did tell Rickey that day about his own songwriting aspirations. He tried to show, through the words he used and in the same songs he played for Rickey, that he was a colleague, not a fan. Oliver then took a deep breath and presented his dream: could he play, as Rickey, one of his own compositions?

Rickey sat as still as a panther in the jungle, crouching and ready to pounce, before he said "No." That was all, just "no".

But, Oliver said, that was all right. He knew he'd been hired for his looks, his voice and his playing, not his writing.

From the sound of the crowd in this stadium in Miami Gardens, the looks, the voice and the playing were all right. Cosmo looked around at the fifty thousand people, lighters flicked and lit, hands clapping, feet stomping for an encore, and he knew he was in a good place. His happy place.

The after-party wasn't quite at the same level. They were all at a club on Ocean Drive in South Beach where a private room had been set aside for Rickey. The crew wasn't as big as at some of the other concerts he'd been to, but that made it better. Cosmo don't know if he was getting old or what, but he was starting to feel done with the really wild scenes. He didn't like looking around and not recognizing eighty per cent of the people in the room anymore. For him, the highlight of the weekend was the concert and the live music, with the Fan Convention, coming up on Sunday, as a close second. The partying? He could take it or leave it.

Every table, chair and couch in the VIP room was taken when Cosmo got there so he joined the standing-room crowd near the bar. Pretend Rickey 2 wasn't there yet; after they finished the meet-and-greet with the fan club people he still had about twelve dollars' worth of stage makeup to take off and another twelve dollars' worth of street makeup that would give the camouflage he needed to slide through this little get-together. Cosmo had listened to Oliver and Booker discuss his appearance at these things a while back. Booker was all for him showing up, as long as he could cover off any differences any of the partiers might notice. Oliver was confident that he could, and so far, he was right. Some of these people had seen Rickey numerous times over the years, on stage, on the bus or the plane, and at the hotels, but none of them ever said anything, at least as far as Cosmo knew.

The Fan Club meet-and-greet had gone really well—the guy really was a hell of an actor. Not one of those fans saw anything missing or different about this Rickey. Booker had mentioned that this was one of Oliver's biggest assets, his ability to schmooze the fans and the journalists, because it was one of the parts that Rickey hated the most. Rickey hated it but meanwhile, Oliver reveled in it. When Cosmo had asked him once about the novelty wearing off, he just said he felt nothing but grateful every day.

Cosmo was convinced that if this house of fraud came falling down, it wouldn't be that Oliver was the one to knock over the cards. The buzz in the room started to ramp up and when he looked toward the door, there was Pretend Rickey 2 coming into the room, escorted by a club manager intent on sucking up, two supermodels wearing the latest crop tops, and a tall redhead in boots that seemed to go right up her thighs to her armpits.

Mona Ray. How did she fit into this picture?

She was chatting comfortably with Rickey and nothing seemed out of whack. Cosmo couldn't help it, though; it was his style to anticipate disaster. If she was talking with Rickey, or even someone pretending to be Rickey, fireworks might be next on the agenda.

"Aw, Cosmo, are you forecasting doom again?" Booker was at his elbow, holding out a beer.

Cosmo took it and gulped half of it. "I just think the day may come when one of these people who knew the real Rickey . . . knows the real Rickey—"

She poked him in the ribs to shut him up, then guided him over to the far, less crowded end of the bar. "Anybody who knows the real Rickey is concerned about his well-being and would understand what we're doing and why we're doing it. For his sanity, for his future. And he's been such a hermit the last ten years, there's hardly anybody around who might claim to be a friend, never mind an old friend. Stop worrying, Cosmo."

"Can't help it, it's genetic," Cosmo said, laughing. "But what about her?" He pointed with his beer bottle in Mona Ray's direction.

Booker shrugged. "Maybe she just wanted to get out to see a concert. Or, maybe she's scouting the opening act."

Cosmo doubted it, but Booker was right. He probably did worry too much. And what did it help?

Cosmo signaled the bartender. Time for another beer. "You want anything, Booker?"

"Hmm?" Her mind was obviously elsewhere.

"A drink, you want something to drink?"

"No, thanks, not now."

"I think I ought to go over there and talk to Mona Ray for a while. Make sure she's convinced that Oliver is the real deal."

"If you think so," Booker said, distractedly.

"What is it, Booker? What are you thinking about?"

"I want us to have a phone call later. You, me, Rickey . . . and Oliver, too, this time."

"Sure, I'll set it up. What's on your mind?"

If she'd asked him to guess, he never would have predicted her answer in a million years. "Tattoos."

***

Later, when Cosmo got on the phone with the other three, Booker showed where she was going with this. She wanted Oliver to get the same tattoos as Rickey had—including the one on his inner thigh of a woman's face.

Oliver balked like a Clydesdale draught horse being urged to go over a three-foot hurdle and then across a ten-foot water pit.

"No way, man, that's just over the top! I've done everything you've asked me up to now—stayed undercover, dodged questions from my family, put my own career on the shelf—but this is asking too much!"

Cosmo could definitely see it his way. If it had been him, he would have been howling, too. He was a coward when it comes to physical pain.

"Hold on, there, son," Rickey said. His voice sounded soothing, and Cosmo relaxed. He was concerned that Rickey would start shouting, to back up Booker, and he didn't want to handle any more stress this afternoon. Linda had told him last night that she didn't want them to be exclusive any more, and he'd barely been able to think of anything else since.

"Rickey, he's pretty much the same age you are." Booker had a dry, amused tone in her voice.

"Well, yeah, you got me," Rickey said. The two of them were going to come up on each side of Oliver like two bouncers with a drunk in a classy place, slide up alongside him smooth as silk and just glide-walk him into the place they wanted him to be.

Nobody said anything for a few minutes, and then Oliver stepped back in. "So,   . . . we're cool, then? No tattoos?"

"Yes, tattoos! Geez, Oliver, don't you get this? You work for us! You get paid a monumental sum to act like you're someone else, once in a while, in exotic places, living the five-star life. Come on." Booker sounded exasperated, and Cosmo could picture her going for a drink, pulling the wine bottle and a glass out of the cupboard.

"Put what career of yours on the shelf, exactly?" Rickey asked. "If you had a lot goin' on, you wouldn't be willing to do this job, wouldn't you say?"

"I'm doing this job in the short-term, Rickey." Oliver was starting to sound like he wanted to punch somebody. "We talked about this before. I'm a performer, yes, but primarily, I'm a songwriter."

"Primarily. Oh . . . *primarily*, you're a songwriter." Rickey jeered. "Tell me, Junior, which radio station would I tune in to hear one of your hits?"

"Rickey, he's told you he prefers to be called Oliver," Booker pointed out. "Don't diss his songwriting career and don't mangle his name."

"Me!" Rickey hooted. "I'm not the one asking him to sit for needles and ink that he doesn't want!"

The silence hung for a few minutes and then, Cosmo plunged back in. "Booker, could I ask why you want Oliver to do this?"

"Sure. I decided at the after-party the other night. Where Oliver did a fine job, I might say, of keeping people from looking at his wig or his face too closely and of walking, talking, and acting like Rickey. But I saw this woman there, someone from ten years ago, and I realized that there are some things about Rickey that some people are going to remember."

"Not a lot of people, Book," Rickey said. "I wasn't quite the sleaze you thought I might become. In fact, I can't even remember whether Miss Mona Ray spent any time with me at all after that last tattoo went on. No, I'm pretty sure, I didn't have my pants off in her presence at all after that French concert. And most of the tattoo went on in the weeks after that, after she was long gone, on the plane and heading back to the States."

"And you tell me you've been pretty solitary since then," Booker said. "But I ask you. Is that a long-term solution? Are you going to stay celibate for the next ten years? Only have sex under a pseudonym? Laugh, when they tell you that you look like Rickey T, the rock star?"

Booker was getting herself worked up. "You remember, this was *not* my idea, Rick. But you insisted. You made me get on board, you made me bring Cosmo on board, and now you've got Oliver, sidelining his own life for you.

"And if it gets into print somewhere that the real Rickey T has this woman's face tattooed on his thigh and then some young thing—or Mona Ray, perhaps?—happens to see the white skin of Oliver's thigh, no stamp in sight, how's he . . . how are *we* going to talk our way out of that one?"

"There's nobody going to be seeing the skin of my thighs," Oliver muttered. "And a new tattoo would create more problems than these imaginary ones it's supposed to solve. I have a girl-friend, and Ramona's not going to like it if I suddenly have a huge, gross image of some other woman on my leg!"

"Tell her it's the inspiration for a new song. Or maybe you did it because of your devotion to Rickey!"

"She'd never buy it. *I* wouldn't buy it, if I were her. Look, it just isn't necessary. I'm not going to get naked with anybody who might also have been naked with Rickey, once upon a time."

"People talk," Booker said. "Quite a few people know he has the tattoo. The tattoo artist, remember her?"

"Yeah, yeah, I do," Rickey replied.

Cosmo remembered her, too. Adrian with the little plaid skirt and the big bag of inks.

"So, I'll just make sure nobody sees my leg," Oliver said.

"You promise?" Booker asked, with the smirk on her face coming through in her voice, loud and clear.

"Really?" Oliver demanded.

"Promise?" Rickey backed her up.

"Why don't you get yours taken off?!" Oliver was getting really worked up.

The silence that met his suggestion reminded all of them who the real star was. Rickey would not be doing anything about his tattoos unless he decided to.

Oliver got into line. "All right. I'll put an image of a woman on my thigh, to match the one Rickey has. But not a tattoo! Markers, or makeup, maybe, but no tattoo. And no complications because of my love life."

It had to be one of the weirdest conversations Cosmo was ever in. Too bad he would never able to tell anybody about it; it would have made a perfect after-dinner story. But discretion was one of his best qualities, he'd been told, and he worked at keeping it in prime condition.

***

The main hall of the Miami Convention Center was packed, shoulder to shoulder, with Rickey T rock 'n' roll fans. Cosmo had been working so hard, so long to organize this Fan Fair that he almost couldn't believe it was actually underway. Most of the people who were there were members of the Rickets and had attended the concert earlier in the weekend. It was a high point of the year, for some of them, and of their whole lives, for others.

Cosmo walked the length of the Convention floor, stopping at every booth to enjoy the energy and the creativity. He saw displays dedicated to Rickey T's early years, to each of his albums, and even a few to individual songs. In one room, videos of Rickey T concerts played continuously; in another, attendees could lounge in beanbag chairs, wear noise-canceling headphones, and listen to Rickey T albums for hours.

It was going to be a great end to a great weekend; the only crappy part, for Cosmo, was that Linda had only come along because he pressured her. After weeks of discussion, she'd finally agreed to attend, but she was determined not to have a good time.

The silver lining in the cloud was that Booker had held true to her promise to ask Rickey to show up in person and not send Oliver in his place. Rickey had agreed. Cosmo was still not sure why or how, but Rickey was going to be there; that was all that mattered.

Cosmo was there when Rickey arrived. The fans who'd won the contest to attend the meet-and-greet were thrilled and Cosmo thought he even saw a hint of enjoyment for Rickey in the whole scene (a thought that Booker told him was inaccurate, when he asked her about it later). Well, whether Rickey had a good time or not, Cosmo still felt it

196

was worth it, asking him to make a personal appearance. He'd seen Jake and he'd seen Oliver do their act for the fans and both were very good, but there was nothing like the real thing.

Cosmo saw it as a favor that Rickey had done for him, and for all the Rickey T fans who were there that day. It was a favor, and he was ready to have it called in, any time, just as he was for the favor Dwight Kettle, the reporter, had done for him, back in France when he hadn't published the answers that a naïve Cosmo had given him that day after the video shoot in Cannes.

Cosmo waved goodbye to Rickey as he took off in his limo, then made his way to the concession stand to get a hot dog and some onion fries. As he sat there at the little table, enjoying the mustard dribbling down the bun, he saw Linda coming down the concourse. Once upon a time, he might have been happy to see her and might have thought it was reasonable to expect that she'd be happy to see him. From the look on her face, it wasn't this time.

From the look on her face, it might take a long time for her to get past her resentment over being made to attend this party and for him to make it up to her.

CHAPTER SEVENTEEN

1995

Boston

Two years later

Despite the problems with Linda, Cosmo wasn't into that 'deeply unhappy' zone he'd experienced when he'd gone through other breakups. Maybe it was because he was getting enough ego strokes just being the president of the International Fan Club, or maybe because they kept giving him promotions at his hotel job—for whatever reason, the world still seemed like a very good place. The pothole he'd hit with Linda was just a temporary problem, Cosmo was sure of it. She was as much of a Rickey T fan as he was and she didn't mind a bit that when they moved from Whistler to the apartment in Orange County, the U-Haul they'd pulled was more than half full of Rickey vinyl, posters and swag. They went to three or four Rickey T concerts a year together, but Cosmo went to many more on his own, and the position as head of the Fan Club gave him constant reason to schedule a trip to see the show, even if he'd been to one just the week before.

It didn't bother him at all that he was watching a stand-in perform. The songs were still the same, the whole scene still stirred him up the same as it always had, and if anything, there was an added pleasure in knowing that he was only one of a handful of people in on the game.

Each time they had a fight he managed to convince Linda that breaking up was a bad idea and as the months went by, his resistance to the idea of marriage started to crumble. She suggested it numerous times, and one night, he just gave in: Why not? It never occurred to him that starting out married life while sitting on top of a pile of secrets wasn't the best approach. Cosmo assumed that she also had friends that he didn't know, interests and hobbies that fell outside the slice of world they shared, and he didn't see how or why he would go at things any differently. The secret he kept for Rickey and for Booker was his business, not Linda's.

They got married in June, because that's what everybody does. Their rough spots, including the Fan Club Convention fiasco in Miami, were a distant memory. His parents, particularly his mother, loved Linda, and taught her how to make a really good spanakopita.

The travel and the time away from work for the Fan Club were turning into a problem, though. Unfortunately, his bosses at the resort weren't as understanding about his frequent absences as Linda was, and after the grumbling went on for weeks, one day they pulled the plug on him.

He moped around for about two months and Linda started to run out of patience with him. Having to look at a guy who wore sweatpants day and night wouldn't be any woman's idea of an ideal newlywed year.

It would have been a nightmare except that Cosmo had much more important, and happier things to think about. Summer festival season was right around the corner.

A summer music festival was a rite of passage, a

glorious moment frozen in time, and a memory in the making. Cosmo had made it a point to attend at least one every year since 1979 . . . and that meant he was closing in on fifteen of the suckers.

He had his strategy—every summer music festival fan did. He got his tickets about two months before the event, and thanks to this new interweb he could do some research on how the tickets were selling and whether this would feel like a happening or a funeral. He'd been to a few that just crashed, because of bad weather, headliner no-shows, heavy police presence—and he'd been to a few that surpassed their billing.

This one in Boston felt like it would be an awesome event. A warm, sunny day by the Charles, six of the hottest bands of the moment, and Rickey T as the final performance, just as the sun was going down and the vibes were the deepest. It would be awesome and it would be memorable.

Cosmo had asked Linda to go with him but she said no. She was wrapped up in her new job at the resort, back in Newport Beach . . . ambitious girl, that one. Lately, she'd been talking about trying to get a transfer to Florida. Cosmo understood her commitment to her job but still, he wished that she were willing to drop the reins a little more often, leave the tasks to someone else, come and be with him. But yeah, he understood. A hotel wouldn't run itself and she had a career to think about, too. She couldn't let her whole life be about following Cosmo around.

He had turned his whole life into following Rickey around but that was different. This was his passion and maybe even his career now. After Cosmo had been out of work for a while, unsuccessfully searching for another hotel manager job, Booker had offered him a full-time paid gig as Executive Director of the Rickey T International Fan Club, when the woman who had been doing the job decided to leave to go to work for a Fort Lauderdale public relations firm. Cosmo was grateful to Booker, although he still had aspirations of making his mark in hotel world, maybe even owning and running a small boutique spot of his own one day. But in the meantime, the rent had to be paid, the groceries bought and the wife kept onside.

And if you had to have a day job, this was one that was exceptional. Lots of daily admin, yeah, but all aimed at those events, those concerts, and that music. At least, that's how it looked on paper. So why did he still feel so crappy?

It might have to do with what he thought of as 'the Rickey lookalike angle'. One part of Cosmo just wasn't happy with the fact that each concert he saw featured Oliver Dash. Walking like Rickey, singing like Rickey, playing like Rickey, yeah. Nobody in the crowd knew the difference and everybody was getting their money's worth, as Rickey often pointed out in their regular phone calls. But Cosmo knew the difference.

He'd asked Rickey once why he didn't just pull out, if he was that disenchanted. Announce his retirement, a farewell tour, and then ride off into the sunset. Organize a really good tribute band, if he felt so strongly about keeping his name alive and in the spotlight. Really good, the best tribute band ever, Cosmo said. But as Rickey quite accurately pointed out, people want the real thing.

He missed the irony completely.

It was complicated though. It would have been easy just to be angry at him and critical because he was dodging so many of the responsibilities of being who he was. But was that fair? He wanted to write songs; the fans wanted to hear and love his songs. Cosmo knew that Rickey and Booker would each have their own ideas about how it evolved. His take on it was that the whole deception had started out so slowly, so innocently. At first, Rickey just didn't want to do stupid videos, so he started to use a double. Then, meeting the fans became a tedious, and sometimes dangerous chore, so he raised the ante with the next impersonator. The concerts were a nightmare for Rickey, and no one could really hear the music there anyway, so he delegated that piece of the picture, too.

Just bit by bit, it had ended up where it was now. Oliver was the one on stage, with twenty thousand people believing they were watching their rock god. Booker said, if none of them could tell the difference and they felt as though they'd had their money's worth, who cared? She was right, Rickey was right, yeah.

But—it just felt bogus.

But those pay checks every week weren't bogus and Cosmo needed them. Linda appreciated them, too, and they kept her from complaining too much when the travel pulled him away from home, week after week. This summer they had five festivals on the schedule: Boston, Burlington, Portland, Albany, and the Garden State Arts Center.

Cosmo watched the Oak Glade Court Clan for half an hour, admiring the way the lead singer was putting it all out there. He was dressed in something that looked like a mash-up of the most extreme clothes of the fifties, sixties and seventies and he was dancing as if this were his last chance to dance. All the kids in the crowd were into it, too.

The next group up, Cape Coral, chose to showcase songs from their new album, unfortunately. The crowd had come to hear their hits, and they had about a dozen of them, but for some dumb reason, artistic integrity perhaps, they chose to go with the new material. People were restless, then bored, then heading for the exits.

Fortunately, the show producer was a decisive sort. Suddenly, Cape Coral was wrapping up its set, the MC was out on stage making an announcement, and Rickey T was taking over.

The flow away from the stage reversed itself and people re-camped. The mood changed in a few moments, and everyone was happy once again. Oliver/Rickey launched into a medley of the top hits from the early days, and then settled into an extended, well-rehearsed, very tight version of "Dance Your Brains Out".

Cosmo was always aware that he just didn't get how this

deception could go on, and on, over years, but no one in the crowd ever seemed suspicious and there was never a mutter or a hiss of 'that's not Rickey T!' At the beginning, he'd had nightmares that that would happen, and that somehow, they'd know he was partly responsible. The crowd would turn on him, screaming and demanding his head on a pike. But it never happened. That had to do with what outstanding actors both Fake Jake and Oliver Dash were, of course, but Cosmo thought that it also had to do with the audience's own psyche. They expected to see Rickey T and that's what they believed they saw. Hide in plain sight.

After the show, during the drive back to the hotel, Cosmo complimented Oliver on how well it had gone. He wasn't interested.

"Same old, same old," he muttered.

"What!" Cosmo thought maybe a joking approach would be the best here. "How can you say that about the music of our idol, Rickey T? Come on, man, it was a great show! Twenty thousand happy fans, what's old about that?"

Cosmo clapped Oliver on the shoulder but he pulled away. "You know what I mean, man. I can do those songs in my sleep."

Cosmo knew exactly what he wanted to hear and what it was that Oliver wanted attention for. It was pure ego but Oliver had to hear the reassurance or he might decide to quit, and that would leave all of them in a mess.

"I know you can do them in your sleep. But what is it you want, Oliver? Tell me exactly."

"I've said it before and here it is again. I want to write my own songs."

"What's stopping you, buddy? You can write all the songs you want."

"And have them be part of the set. Make them part of the show."

Cosmo took a pause, as if this were really something to consider, as if he'd never heard it before. "And what, have them announced as yours, using your real name?"

Oliver shook his head. "No, I don't need to go that far. They can go un-announced completely, as far as I'm concerned. Just have them rehearsed and played on stage, let people hear them. Let me know they're being performed, hear them out there, see how the crowd responds, that's what I want."

"And have them published under your name?"

"Or under a pseudonym that flows to me, I don't care. But yeah, I want the publishing."

"What, they don't pay you enough money? You could talk to Booker about a raise."

"That's not it!" Cosmo could see how frustrated he was. "I want songs out there that I created, not just songs that I channeled. Does that clarify it?"

Not by much. It seemed to Cosmo as if Oliver was insisting on returning the biggest gift anybody could be given. Geez, if Cosmo could sing or dance or looked the least bit like Rickey and was offered a job like Oliver had, he'd think he'd died and gone to heaven.

"Do you want me to speak to them for you?" Cosmo asked.

Oliver's face was as hard and closed as a granite statue. "Don't think it would do much good. That asshole isn't going to make room for anybody else."

Aahh. Oliver was not a Rickey T fan anymore.

If he ever was one.

Cosmo promised to speak to Booker and Rickey on Oliver's behalf, but he didn't think it would do much good. It turned out that he was right. Rickey sent a message back to Oliver, that it was his job to make Rickey's songs sound as good as he possibly could. If he had any energy left over after that, for writing and performing his own songs, then he wasn't doing his job properly and he should give back his pay check. Rickey also threatened him with various physical challenges if he tried to keep on going down the songwriter road and if he revealed any of this to anybody.

Cosmo knew fear when he heard it.

When they got to Burlington for the Maple Creemee Festival, Oliver was on the edge. Every little thing seemed to drive him up the wall, Booker said, and the one thing she was grateful for these days was that, unlike Fake Jake, Oliver had not developed any sort of taste for coke, vodka, or any other substance that could be consumed to ease the pain of being a rock star. Ease the pain, stifle the inhibitions and loosen the tongue. But since he had no escape, Oliver just roared around his self-built, imaginary cage, pounding the walls and driving everybody to the point of wanting to quit. Many of them did.

That summer of '95 was a hot one, and in addition to the 'fun' that Oliver's ambition was putting them all through, Cosmo had the pleasure of listening to everybody griping about the weather. Linda flew out to watch the Vermont show and all he heard about were the L.A. things she was missing—the beach, the fantastic burgers at two o'clock in the morning, the high-end shopping, the Pacific Coast Highway. Yeah, well how about the smog and the traffic jams? They weren't on the same page at all and that made Cosmo sad. Sad and mad, all at once.

Aside from her, and the weather, and Oliver, this whole summer of festivals was letting him down. But—there was one thing saving it, and it was the same thing it always was. Rickey T and his music. Cosmo still had it playing all day and half of some of the lonely nights—"Leaving Lorraine" was on replay a lot these days. *H8GNSLO* was Cosmo's new favorite of the albums—he liked it even better than the early stuff from the seventies. It was helping him rise above the Linda hassle and his feelings about Oliver—well, not just about Oliver himself but about the entire situation. Oliver, Jake, Booker, Rickey—Cosmo couldn't help it, the entire idea still bugged him, and although he could see the joy that they were bringing the fans, by the millions, he still couldn't quite grasp the necessity of it, you know? Wouldn't they pour their feelings into someone or something else, if Rickey T weren't around?

But Rickey kept on insisting that the whole story was necessary, that it was all part of an intricate whole where every piece depended on every other piece, and that for each and every one of those fans there was only one Rickey T, unique and irreplaceable. Nobody else would do—not Mick, not Elton, not Rod, not Michael, not Paul, not Bruce, not Bob—and their allegiance would never be transferred to a different performer.

More irony, that his reason for being on board with using a Rickey T stand-in had to do with his dedication to the fans, who believed him to be unique. This also made it all quite inconsistent, which made him quite uncomfortable, which made him stop thinking about it. Much easier to dwell on Linda, and how much they weren't getting along.

In Portland, Maine, at the back of a grassy amphitheater, Rickey, real Rickey, sat dressed up like a local, listening to the bands and munching on a sub sandwich. He'd only intended to wander through the crowd for a few minutes then watch the show from the VIP area backstage. But the organizers hadn't really given much (or any) thought, to the privacy needs of mega-stars traveling incognito and when Booker went to speak to them about a separate room or space of some kind for Rickey, they'd just said 'no'. He'd pitched a quiet fit, she told Cosmo later, then announced he'd sit with the crowd and wandered off, bodyguards surrounding him and twitching, like stressed-out wild cats. They almost lost it completely when Sturgess arrived, walking right up to Rickey, towering over him, then dropping to the grass beside him and throwing an arm around his shoulders.

Cosmo did have a clue that the guy was on his way in. Sturgess sent him a fax a few days ago, saying that Shad had asked him to "drop by and say hello". The only place he could work into his schedule was Albany, Sturgess said. So, what was he doing here in Maine? Booker said that the guards said Rickey didn't seem surprised to see Sturgess and told them to back off, when they tried to do their jobs. The two of them, Rickey and Sturgess, sat on the grass together and chatted for a while, then Rickey told him it was time to head backstage, got up and left with the bodyguards.

If he'd stayed ten more minutes, Sturgess would have seen Oliver on stage pretending to be Rickey, while he was sitting right there beside the real thing.

Booker agreed with Cosmo that that would have raised a few questions, even from a slug like Sturgess, but she didn't share his concern that one of these days Rickey was going to shave it just a bit too fine.

"Cosmo, you're just not enough of a risk-taker," she said.

You're all freakin' nuts, he almost said to her.

Booker was a tough one to figure out. Obviously, Rickey was her 'reason to be' and she didn't seem to have anything else going on in her life. No husband, no exes, no friends, that Cosmo had ever heard her mention. Of course, she might have plenty, just kept well out of sight of this crazy part of her life.

If she had a private life, it was well-hidden. Her only passion seemed to be for Rickey—and not even for Rickey, but for his shows and his music. Most of the time, she was cool and soft-spoken but if she thought something was happening that was to Rickey's detriment, she was right there, in your face, like a mad, wet hen.

It was at the show in Albany that Booker took issue with the way a female DJ who was handling the MC duties introduced Rickey. It was not even really Rickey, but, as she told Cosmo later, everybody *thought* it was Rickey and so the insult was to him, not to Oliver. The woman barely seemed to know who Rickey T was and she cracked a few jokes about having trouble telling all those classic rock stars apart.

Even worse, though, the DJ started to riff on Rickey's appearance and what age did or didn't do to rockers in their forties. Cosmo realized that intense attention to Rickey's appearance was the last thing that Booker wanted, and that's why she did what she did next.

Booker stomped onto the stage and took the mic away from this radio chick who looked as frightened as if a serial killer had locked her in a car with no door handles. Next, Booker spoke to the crowd, corrected a mistake about one of Rickey's albums, gave the DJ a shove and then threw the mic on the stage. When she came down the steps at the side, half a dozen of the festival honchos were waiting, with security, to escort her off the premises. The whole show lurched to a halt, in total chaos. Oliver went back to his dressing room to wait things out.

The festival people wanted to throw Booker out and ban her from the rest of the performances. Rickey got on the phone to them and made them understand that if Booker were thrown out, he wouldn't perform. Not good, for their PR and for their bank account, if the crowd started to demand refunds. Not a hill they wanted to die on. They backed down, Booker was allowed to stay and Oliver's set went like clockwork.

Last stop of the festival season for Rickey T was the Garden State Arts Center. Seventeen thousand rock 'n' roll fans, give or take a few, got the show of their lives. Oliver was just awesome and even Rickey was blown away. Cosmo, Booker, Oliver and Rickey got together in Rickey's suite for a few drinks afterward and each one of them was deep into his or her own little cocoon of satisfaction. Good show, good season.

"Nice work, Oliver," Rickey said, his smile as wide as the oceans he was fond of sailing.

"Thanks, man," Oliver took a long pull on the vodka bottle. "All I'm doing is putting the cherry on top. You built the whole thing."

Rickey stared at him. "There's an edge there, man. What are you saying?"

"Same thing I've been saying for years now. I want to put in something of my own, not just copy you."

Rickey looked like he was getting ready to explode and Booker rushed in to cool things off. "Oliver, it's not the time or place to discuss that. We just finished a show, we can talk about this later."

"You've said that before," Oliver said. "And. We. Never. Do."

"Of all the ungrateful, egocentric, selfish . . ." Rickey looked ready to take a swing at somebody and Cosmo was desperate to find a way to defuse the tension. He didn't know why he thought this was his job, or why he thought the subject of the lifetime achievement awards list was a good distraction, but that was the drivel he suddenly found coming out of his mouth.

"Hey, did you guys see that the Big Name Big Deal awards list came out?"

"What?" Rickey looked at Cosmo as if he'd lost his mind. And maybe he had.

"What?" Booker was right behind him, but she looked as though Cosmo was throwing her a lifeline while she was out in the middle of an ocean somewhere, drowning. "What awards list?"

"Well, it's kind of like a Hall of Fame, like in sports. It's an award they're giving to musicians who've been stars for at least thirty years."

"Might be kind of a small field," Booker said, trying to make a joke. It was weak but it was a way out of the tension in the room.

Rickey was rigid, staring at his look-alike, and then suddenly, he let it go. He broke the eye contact, took a swig of his drink, and laughed. "I guess I have a while to wait."

Cosmo joined in the phony laughter that they all shared but he didn't think any one of them was giving so much as a second thought to the Big Name Big Deal awards or to Rickey's many years as a rock legend. He could see that Rickey felt that the subject was closed.

Oliver did not.

CHAPTER EIGHTEEEN

1998

New York

Three years later

During the past few years, they all managed to stay away from the clash that Cosmo felt had to be coming. Rickey disappeared into boat world, Booker was working in New York on keeping the Rickey T legend alive while Cosmo did his part at the Fan Club headquarters in Tampa. They had parked Oliver at a glorious resort in Thailand and they heard from him very rarely. Booker thought that no news was good news, but Cosmo felt the silence was ominous.

That fall, the buzz around the latest Rickey T album *Cut and Run* had been building, and when it finally dropped, the day after Labor Day, the stampede to the record stores was almost audible. Cosmo loved every song on it, and almost wore out the CD, if such a thing could happen. It was on the Billboard chart right from the beginning and as the weeks went by, climbed up through the Hot 100, to number four.

It had gone platinum by Christmas time, and Booker called Cosmo early in the New Year, to tell him about the European tour that was to follow that spring.

"Can you come along, Cosmo?" she asked.

How could he say no? He knew that Linda might have a dozen answers to that question, but maybe this time she would want to come with him. There had been a lot less travel over the past three years, since Rickey wasn't touring and Cosmo spent his working time on Fan Club business, in a small office in a strip mall not far from the hotel where Linda worked now.

"Of course," Cosmo said. "Somebody has to smooth the way for all those European fans wanting face time with our Rickey."

"Yeah." He could hear Booker scowling. "Some logistics to be worked out there. Oh, well, if we get close to any trouble, we'll just put it all down to the language barrier. Do you remember '84?"

He did, for sure. And he was more than ready to see Europe, and a rock 'n' roll tour again, but this time as a grown-up.

"How's Oliver doing?" Cosmo asked.

"He's turning into as much of a pain in the ass as Fake Jake ever was," Booker said. "What is it with these guys, that their egos just grow out of control?"

"Uh, I don't know, could it be because they're adored by millions?" Cosmo watched Linda walk into the room, without looking his way even once. She disappeared into the bedroom and he picked up his end of the conversation again. "What's he doing?"

"Same old, same old. Wants to put some of his own songs on the set list."

"Have you heard any of them? Are they good enough to perform?"

"Yeah." She sounded like she was stifling a laugh. "They're shit."

"Is there any thought from him about giving the guy a break and letting him have his moment with just one song, maybe? After all these years?" Cosmo was trying to make sure that he didn't say anything that could be understood by any third-party listeners but it wasn't easy. He was very sure that Linda had no interest in eavesdropping on his conversations, but 'very' wasn't 'completely'.

"Not for a second."

"Could be a long tour," Cosmo said.

"Nah, come on, Cosmo," Booker said. "You know it's gonna be nonstop fun."

The more Cosmo thought about it, the more he thought it would be. It hadn't been easy, once he'd made up his mind to go, to get Linda to agree to his going, but Rickey came up with the brilliant idea that Cosmo would be on the crew as the public relations director, handling media in every city they visited.

They hadn't even made it out of New York before Cosmo was hit with his first PR challenge. Dwight Kettle turned up, asking for an interview with Rickey T on the 25th anniversary of his arrival on the rock 'n' roll scene. It was not just to be any interview, either; Dwight wanted three days with Rickey, following him around, watching his life.

Rickey pitched a fit, as Cosmo had known he would. When he went back to Dwight to deliver the bad news, Dwight didn't take it easily, pointing out to Cosmo that Cosmo "owed him one".

It took Cosmo an hour on the phone to make Dwight understand that he couldn't call in his favor this time, this way. He only got him off the phone by agreeing that he did still owe him a favor, a huge one now, and when the time came, Dwight would be there, looking for the right answer.

While Cosmo was running interference in New York, Rickey was sailing near Greece and trying to figure out how he felt about Booker's hints that he should be ready to take over, just in case their expectations about Oliver just weren't met on the international stage. He even went so far as to try to learn something about aversion therapy, on his own, and to think about how he might conquer his stage fright that way. He had long since given up on traditional solutions—talk therapy, hypnosis, stress relievers of various kinds—he did things on his own, and he believed they turned out better that way.

He sat on the deck one balmy evening, enjoying the breeze and reading a biography of Marco Polo. When the call came in from Booker, he was tempted to let it go to voice mail, but his curiosity won out.

"Hey Booker, what's up. You're just calling to chat, right?"

"Something like that," Booker said. "Chat about Shad Palmetto and Staten Island Records."

"What is it?"

"He's pushing for more disclosure on our records. Something about expense accounts, apparently—"

"Crap, I've got another call. It's this new thing, this call waiting, I can see—oh, crap, it's Sturgess," Rickey said.

"You should take it," Booker said. "He might give you some insight into what Shad's up to. I'll wait."

Rickey put her on hold. "Hey, Sturgess. How's it going?"

"Good, Rickey, good, how're you?" Sturgess sounded very tense. "Look, I won't take up too much of your time, I know you're busy. Truth is, I'm not that good. I've run into a bit of trouble with some gambling debts and I'm looking for a way to improve my cash flow fairly quickly. I thought of you . . . and I wondered whether you could help me out for a few weeks."

Rickey looked out at the lights onshore and thought this over. He'd been asked for handouts many times over the years; people always ask famous people for financial support for everything from worthwhile charities to their nephews' college funds. "Could be, Sturgess, I guess so . . ."

Sturgess could hear Rickey's lack of enthusiasm. "I will pay you back right away, you'll barely notice the money's gone before it's back," he promised. "And I'm sure I can return the favor any time you need it."

"With money?" Rickey laughed. "Naw, don't need that. But I do have an idea, Sturgess. I'll tell you what you *could* do for me. You're still at Staten Island Records, right?"

CHAPTER NINETEEN

1999

Ireland

One year later

The exterior of this hotel was exceptional. Even Rickey, who had seen thousands of hotels, let his jaw go to the table as he stepped out of the helicopter onto the pad behind the main building. You'd think you were in ancient Rome, not twentieth-century Ireland, looking at this bright white sweep of an architectural brush stroke that was just a masterpiece.

Rickey's tail was dragging quite a bit, he had to admit. Amazing how quickly his cache of saved-up relaxation had been spent. He left the boat in the Med just last Tuesday, spent a couple of days shopping and meeting with Booker in London, took in a Rickey T performance from backstage at Wembley, then wandered around Dublin incognito. He was already feeling fed up with the whole scene and anxious to get back to peace and quiet.

First, he had to show up for this last concert on the

European leg, though. Booker said it would be good for morale, although Rickey didn't see how that meant anything, since he and Booker were the only two who mattered, and they weren't in need of having their morale boosted, like kids. But now that the travel was done and he was here, in Powerscourt, he was glad he'd made the trip. Something in the air at that last concert in England had given him a sense that his presence would be important here.

He had had a lot of time to himself, over the fifteen years of this . . . *project*, as he liked to think of it. What was it, exactly? A con? Certainly, a long one. Was it a fraud? No, he didn't think so. A caper? Yeah, that was it! What did you call it, when something went on for decades or centuries or generations? A saga! It was a caper saga.

Rickey strolled around the grounds of the resort and let his eyes feast for a while. His bodyguards were discreetly hanging back a few dozen feet, walking with the hotel manager who'd greeted them at the helicopter pad. After a few close calls, he and Oliver had worked out a good system of arrivals and departures, whenever he wanted to come into the public eye, from time to time. Basically, the system was that if Rickey wanted to do anything, Oliver was to stay out of the way, so that they'd never be confronted by the problem of two Rickey T's stirring up suspicion.

The classic lines of the building were a perfect contrast to the abundant curves of the vegetation surrounding them. Rickey loved the dozens of shades of green that layered the Irish landscape, although he knew he'd never be one to put up with the numerous days and nights of rain that made the color palette possible. He came upon a half-life-sized chess set, a game partly finished, and wondered whether he could get away with playing some chess with Booker, out in public. It didn't seem like there was anybody much around to bother him. Too bad they couldn't find more places like this to stay during a tour. It was only about a few miles from Dublin where the band would do the show and a helicopter would bring Oliver back to the resort before most of the audience had left the building.

"Hey! Rickey!"

Aw, man, was that Sturgess? What was he doing there? Rickey stared at a bishop for a second and wondered whether he could get away with making a run for it toward his room, pretending he hadn't heard. Not likely.

"Hey. Sturgess. How's it going?" He contemplated the chessboard without turning around and hoped that Sturgess would get the message that he wanted to be left alone.

"Well, it's going great, guy, thanks for asking! I got these terrific tickets for your show at the last minute. Not a hotel room to be had in Dublin, though, so booked in here, just picked the name of the place out of a hat, and here you all are! Don't supposed I could catch a ride to the show with you, do ya?"

"I don't know, Sturgess. Booker always has us leaving really early, getting there hours ahead."

"I don't mind, I'll find something to do backstage." Sturgess followed Rickey's gaze toward the chess pieces. "Hey, you wanna play a game?"

"Well, I guess I'm stuck," Rickey said. "Not much else I could do."

"You could always cut and run, haw, haw, haw." Sturgess was obviously delighted with his little joke, working in the name of Rickey's latest record. He got busy moving all the pieces back to their opening places.

"Yeah, right," Rickey said. He watched Sturgess for a few minutes, then decided he would do exactly that.

"You know, Sturgess, I don't have a lot of time before we leave for the show. I think I need a little downtime on my own."

Sturgess stopped what he was doing, straightened up and walked over to face Rickey. "I think you need a little one-on-one time with me, don't you think? Making sure I'm a happy camper? Just in case I'm not, and was in a mood to go looking for someone else to talk to? Someone writing for a major newspaper or magazine, let's say?"

Rickey hardened his gaze and stared straight back into Sturgess's eyes. "You have to be kidding. After the last conversation we had? After the money I loaned you? That you haven't paid back yet?! After the hints you gave me that you'd be able to get me special treatment at the label? Let's say someone did that, Sturgess. Someone might find he didn't have many other people left who'd talk to him."

Sturgess played eye-chicken for a few more seconds then pulled off the road. "Yeah, and someone might not be that sure about what he was saying, you know what I mean?" He made an attempt at a grin.

Rickey didn't join in. "Nobody should ever say anything about anything unless he's absolutely sure he's got it right. Now, you have to excuse me, Sturgess. I've got a show to psyche up for."

As he walked toward the main building, Rickey tried to get a feel for what just happened. Did Sturgess really know, or think he knew, something about the long con Rickey and Booker were pulling on the fans? Or was it something else entirely? Did he think a rock journalist would be drooling at the idea of any kind of insider dope about life in the Rickey T entourage? Did he think of himself as an insider?

He had to find time to dissect all of this with Booker later.

***

Oliver had been on call to work as 'Rickey T' for six years now. When he'd been performing a lot, a few years back, he stayed in character all the time. That was the way he thought of it, "in character". It was a part, a role in a play. A very lucrative, demanding play. He'd had some time off and had been laying low, but now it was time to shine again.

He was in the basement bar of this very luxurious resort just outside Dublin, polishing off his fifth beer. Rickey had decided to show up at this stop on the tour, and because of that, it was also Oliver's job to stay in the shadows and help make sure nobody spotted the two of them in the same place at the same time.

He was a bit cranky about that. This was his first time in Ireland and he would have liked to have had a chance to look around. But really, the traveling musician's life usually wasn't much about sightseeing anyway. It was usually more about going from the stage to the bus to the hotel and onto a plane . . . or maybe another bus. Being anonymous and invisible when he was offstage just added another layer to the routine. Oliver had his own stash of hats, wigs, sunglasses, and even a few stick-on moustaches and beards, so that he could change up his look if he needed to.

His room in the hotel was spectacular. Floor-to-ceiling windows covered the entire wall that looked out over the gardens, with curtains that were remote-controlled. The soaker tub in the bathroom was huge, and he'd taken advantage of it, for a long stretch, while watching an episode of *The Simpsons* on a TV screen set into the bathroom mirror. If he had to be hiding out and pretending to be nonexistent, this was a good place to do it. But even a deluxe suite starts to feel like a cage after a while, and Oliver had ventured out. Not far, just to the pub that was in the basement.

He stared at his reflection in the glass behind the bar.

I'm not wild about the idea of always having to do things on Rickey's timetable, always playing things the way he wants them. But what can you do? The one who pays the piper calls the tune, somebody said once. And the money he's paying me will set me up for life. It hasn't been easy and I've earned every penny, I think—even with the big chunks of time off. Keeping his secret, doing all those damn videos, schmoozing the fans. The hardest part is playing his bloody songs on stage over and over. Not that they're bad songs, they're good songs, but I've got a few good ones, too. That nobody's ever heard. Because he won't let me bring them out, not even one. The guy's ego is enormous.

***

That night on stage, Rickey's impersonator blew the audience's mind. Oliver was good all the time, and Cosmo had seen him do exceptional performances several times, but this was at a whole new level. He ran out from the wings, roared "Hello, Dublin!", let the roadie help strap on his guitar and then launched into the stratosphere. Song after song, he seemed to mean every word and pull every last ounce of tone out of every lick. Cosmo was just as ecstatic as all of the other fans.

Oliver seemed to really be Rickey tonight. Maybe it was the scarves, the hats, the clothes, all sorts of things that added up to a disguise, really, now that Cosmo thought about it. It certainly was the walk, the (very little) talk, the gestures like waving to the upper rows and clapping his hands over his head during the acapella part of "I Won't Ever Be the One to Say Good-bye", and the rituals, like yelling out the name of the city at the beginning and bowing deeply from the waist before running off-stage at the end.

But it was more than just that. It was the songs themselves. When Oliver sang those lyrics, it felt as if he was living and re-living them, just like when Cosmo sang the words alone in the shower or driving with the CD player at full blast. The songs had a life of their own and they turned the singer into Rickey, just for a few minutes.

After twenty minutes Oliver gave the crowd a breather and the musicians a chance to set up for the next tune. He pulled the electric guitar off over his head and replaced it with an acoustic.

"This next one is for my mother," he said. "It's not about her but I wrote it for her."

His mother?! Cosmo thought. Does Oliver know anything at all about Rickey's mother? Most of us avid fans know only that he never mentions her. What was Oliver going to say?

"She's not with us now . . . but she actually is." He strummed the first few notes. "It's called 'Unseen'."

Crap, this was getting weird.

But as Oliver strummed the first few notes, Cosmo looked around and saw that no one else was disturbed by this. The eager smiles and joyful expressions were still there, on all those faces of all those people who go to live concerts to celebrate life and their enjoyment of a musician. And, after all, like the lyrics of so many songs, those words "she's not with us now, but she actually is" could be interpreted to mean anything from 'she's dead but I keep her ashes in the piano bench' to 'she had to go to Bakersfield for a dental appointment but I talked to her on the phone an hour ago' to 'she's refused to speak to me for years so I used her name for my bodyguard's K-9'.

Cosmo listened as hard as he could but he didn't recognize the opening riff on this song. After a few more seconds, Rickey's stand-in slid into a gentle ballad about the one who was gone. It was a lovely, soulful lament for a love that just shriveled up and died—nobody's fault, everybody's trouble—and Cosmo could see that the crowd was digging it.

He liked it immediately, too, and it was kind of cool to hear a new Rickey T song, to know that he was among the privileged thousands at Croke Park to be the first to hear it. The glow lasted all the way through the next two hours of the show.

But it shattered as soon as Cosmo was invited into the limo with Booker and Rickey for the drive back to the resort. Oliver was being picked up and delivered by helicopter. The doors of the limo were barely closed, and the soundproof privacy screen behind the driver snapped shut, when Rickey started fuming.

"What the hell was he doing! What the hell was that!" Rickey was practically foaming as he fumbled with a bottle.

Booker took it out of his hands and pulled out the stopper. "Here, let me. Where's the glass?" She poured slowly and almost ceremonially handed it to Rickey. "Now. What's going on?"

"Oliver wrote a song!"

He shouted it as if he were announcing that Oliver killed the world's only talking kangaroo.

"I think Oliver's written quite a few songs," Booker said.

"Wrote and performed! For his mother!"

Aah. Cosmo saw the problem. "Unseen" was not Rickey's new brainchild. It was Oliver's song—and perhaps, a description of his own reality. Cosmo picked up a glass and held it out to Booker. She nodded and poured them each a stiff one. This could be a tense half hour, coming up.

"He knows the boundaries!" Rickey wasn't pacing furiously, but he might as well have been, with his right knee bouncing with stress. "He's been whining for years that he wants to perform his own material and we've been saying 'no' for years! I write the songs, nobody else!"

"Maybe he thought just this one time, after six years of coloring inside the lines, it might be okay?" Cosmo said.

Rickey would have incinerated him, right there on the leather bench, if he'd had a flamethrower handy. "Are you on his side? Are you making excuses for him?"

"No, man, I—"

"I don't want him to write songs! I want him to do the stupid videos, talk to the stupid journalists, meet with—" They watched him mentally catch himself, take a breath and then go on. "We need him to perform and to do the things that make me crazy, the things that get in the way of the writing. Nothing more, nothing less. Why doesn't he get that? God knows, I've said it to him three thousand times!"

"So, you have to say it three thousand and one." Booker's voice was soothing.

"No," Rickey shook his head violently. "No, that's one time too many. It's completely different now. He didn't ask, he went right over the line and did it. That's completely different."

"And so, what now, Rickey?"

"So, he's fired!"

"And you'll do what? Hire another one? Ask me to find another one?"

"They're all over the place! Look at the tribute bands, the impersonators! It won't be that hard to do!"

"Maybe Fake Jake would come back?" The second Cosmo made the suggestion, he regretted it. They both glared at him.

"I had a fax from him just this morning," Booker said. "It's not bad enough that I have to write checks to him every month, but I have to get messages from him, too."

"What did he say?" Cosmo asked.

She answered him, but her eyes were on Rickey. "He's got a new gig coming up. In Australia. Under his own name, but he's got a line in the press release where he says that he's covered music by some of the biggest names in the world and that he even "took the stage as Rickey T, a few times, back in the eighties". He says tribute bands are very accepted in Australia—it's seen as a compliment, not an attempt to hijack the real thing or steal from him. Or her. Apparently, it goes back to the days when it was difficult to get to Australia and a lot of performers just didn't want to go there.

"He's asking us if it's okay if he leaves that sentence in, will it fit within the language in the contract he signed to get the regular monthly pay checks?"

Rickey looked nauseated. "What do you think, Book?"

"I have no idea what the attorneys would say, but I'd be worried that letting him say that publicly would be a step in a bad direction, even if it's a tiny one. This time, he might be willing to say "took the stage a few times" but what if next month, he's claiming to have done all your singing for ten years?"

"And not just 'claiming', " Cosmo added.

Not a good comment. Rickey glared at him.

Cosmo backtracked. "I mean, he could be insisting, or getting people believing his crap."

"So, what are we going to do?" Booker asked.

"Sue his ass." Rickey was pouring himself another shot of cognac.

"I think we should go for the carrot rather than the stick," Booker said. "Too easy to lose control, in the legal scenario, or end up giving a fortune to the lawyers."

"What do you suggest, then?"

"More money," Booker answered. "I think that's what he's after anyway."

"All he did was some performances," Rickey had long since written this script. "He acted in a few videos, shook a few fans' hands, did a few shows. Didn't write the songs, didn't make the recordings. Those are all me. As we've said a thousand times, this is no different than stunt doubles in the movies. In an action movie, the actors don't make every move in every scene. They don't crash the motorcycle into a wall, or jump through a plate-glass window."

"Tom Cruise does," Cosmo said.

"All right, except Tom Cruise," Booker said.

Rickey went on. "The rest use stand-ins and stunt doubles but the star carries the film," she said. "He's the name the people are paying to see. His face, his body, his voice. They also want a story, some action, a few car chases, you know, and they don't really care whether the actor is driving that car that smashes up, or diving out of that third-floor window."

"Just as long as there are a few good close-ups," Booker put in.

"Exactly. And I'm the close-up. I write the songs, I record them, I'm the deal. But if I have some other guy stand in for me, here and there, what the hell?"

Cosmo had to admit, this was all making sense to him these days, this stunt double rationalization. The audience doesn't care about stunt doubles, doesn't know their names, doesn't choose to see a movie because of them—and Oliver was just Rickey's stunt double.

Soon to be "ex-stunt double". They pulled into the resort driveway and Rickey stomped off toward the back of the hotel, where he expected the helicopter to land soon. The lawns and gardens were lit somewhat but not enough to prevent him from stumbling into one of the metal sculptures dotted around the grounds. Rickey cursed and kicked at the thing, but missed—good news for both the piece and for his foot.

The sound of the beating of the rotors filled the air before the copter moved in above them, stirring up the branches of the trees on the edge of the property. Cosmo's hair blew around his face and Rickey's scarf looked as though it might take flight itself, any minute. As soon as it was safe, Rickey ran toward the machine and yanked open the door. The half hour they'd waited and the cognac he'd drunk hadn't calmed him down any.

Booker was right behind him. She waved frantically at him, trying to mime a "zip it!" command and stop him from shouting something that would let the pilot know what was going on. He got the point, and held back while Oliver jumped from the copter, ducked under the blades and walked along the lawn. They all watched as the helicopter took off, then Rickey turned on Oliver.

"You asshole!" he shouted at Oliver. "Where do you get off, dedicating songs to my mother? You don't know my mother! Have you ever met my mother? Have you ever heard me mention her, ever?"

"I wasn't talking about your mother; I was singing about *my* mother!" Oliver yanked his arm out of Rickey's grasp. "Back off, man!"

"And what song was that anyway? You know our agreement. It's a Rickey T show. You've asked me about playing other people's songs, and I've said no."

"Not 'other people's songs'! Mine!"

"Nobody's!" There wasn't room to insert a piece of paper between Rickey and Oliver's noses. "You're fired!"

"No, I'm not!" Oliver shouted. "I quit."

He walked off toward the hotel, but only went about ten feet before he came back. "Let's cool off, Rickey. I can't do this to you."

Rickey looked ready to hit him, but Booker still had her head together. "Do what?" she asked.

"Leave you up in the air like this," Oliver said. "What would you do, if I quit? Nobody else can do what I do."

Rickey snorted. "I can get a dozen more just like you. Tomorrow!"

Booker stepped in. "I don't think we're going to resolve this tonight. Everyone is just too upset. Oliver, get some sleep and we'll talk about it in the morning, on the plane. Rickey, I just need to talk to you about one more thing before we say goodnight."

Oliver disappeared into the darkness in the direction of the hotel.

Booker had an arm around Rickey's shoulders. "Relax, buddy, we'll sort it out. You need to get into your suite, before anyone sees the both of you here."

"He's fired."

"Yes, of course, he is. Details tomorrow. But yes, he's fired. I'm not sure what we'll do next, but it's clear he has to go."

Rickey's shoulders were slumped and he looked exhausted. "Sometimes it just seems like storms coming from every direction, Book, you know?"

"Yeah, I know. But don't worry about it, Rick. I've got your back. I always have, haven't I? Ever since we barely knew how to wipe our noses, ever since your evil parents and your football jock brother made your life hell. Don't worry, I'll be here. You're my responsibility, right?" She gave his shoulders a squeeze.

He pushed her away. "Just put together a plan, Book."

The three of them walked in silence along the path beside the lawn for a few minutes, and then Rickey spoke. "I'll come back to work. Full time."

"Do you mean it?" Booker stopped. "What do you mean, exactly?"

"I mean I'll suck it up and do everything. For a while,"

he said. "I'll do the shows, do the interviews, meet the fans. I've had a good long break. The album is just out, the videos are done. I can handle it."

"Are you sure it's been a long enough break?" Booker asked.

Rickey came back with what might have been a laugh, although there didn't seem to be much amusement in it. "I guess we'll see, won't we? I might hate it just as much but it might be all right. And it'll be a relief not to have to deal with either of those guys or the whole situation, really."

"And it will be good to tell the whole truth for a while," Cosmo contributed.

Rickey glared at him.

"Well, it wouldn't hurt my feelings to be done with it, either," Booker said.

Rickey nodded and pulled his scarf in tight, against the wind. "For a while. I won't pretend that I'll like it all that much, but it has to be done."

Rickey walked along for a few more minutes, then stopped. "No, I can't do it. Booker, you'll have to get another stand-in."

"Aw, geez, Rick, really? You're going to change your mind again?" Booker looked like she was ready to lose it. "It's not going to be easy."

"Well, I know, but I just can't go back to that. How hard can it be? Couldn't you just hire somebody from one of those rip-off groups?"

Cosmo could feel the annoyance building in Booker. "I'll try, Rickey, but like I said, it's not going to be easy. Why did you say you'd go back to work when you didn't mean it?"

"Why does anybody say anything? It sounded right in the moment, but it didn't feel right. Besides, I think we've got a lot of people knowing about this. Too many people." He looked off toward the resort entrance. "Where's that driver gone? I want to get out of here for a while, think about things. Maybe I *will* take everything on again. I'll be back, Book, I'm just going to get him to drive me around for a while. You'll take care of that other matter we discussed, too, right?"

After he spotted the car, sprinted off to the door that the driver had opened, and jumped in, Cosmo looked at Booker. "Want to lay bets he'll change it again tomorrow morning?"

"Yeah, who knows what he'll do?" Booker seemed preoccupied. "Listen, Cosmo, there's something I have to talk to you about. As you heard, things are in motion and we don't know what's coming next. There's so much stress, so many moving parts—"

"And it's so ironic because the reason he wanted to do this in the first place was to get rid of the pain!" Cosmo said.

"Rickey and I want to cancel your arrangement," Booker said.

For a few seconds, the only thing Cosmo could hear was the rumble of trucks on a distant motorway. The air was completely still around him and he had to concentrate to inhale. "But why, Booker? And what does that mean?"

"It's just getting so complicated and like Rickey just said, there's a lot of people who know about our story over the past fifteen years. Too many people, maybe. I don't know what will happen next, but I do agree with him that it's a good idea to try to draw the circle tighter now. We'll take care of you, of course, and there will be ongoing support for you and for the work you're doing with the Fan Club. There will be an NDA and we'd expect the same discretion from you that we have getting from Jake Meisenstern and we will be getting from Oliver Dash."

He started to shiver a little. Ireland could be cold in the evenings. "Of course, you can count on my discretion, just as much as on Jake's or Oliver's. And I completely respect your thoughts about this."

Probably the thing that was bothering him the most about this conversation was how frequently she used the word 'we'. He wanted to get at her feelings specifically. But something told him she had lined up with Rickey on this and there was no space between them for him to find a place.

The Thousands

CHAPTER TWENTY

2000

London

One year later

'London in summer' was probably one of her favorite phrases. Booker could even put up with the traffic at Heathrow, where her driver was circling endlessly, looking for a parking spot. They were there to pick up Shad and Mona Ray, from the record label. It was just one of those diplomatic things that had to be done. Booker would rather be almost anywhere else.

Shad would deny it, but he was here to check up on Rickey. Even after Rickey had done well over the past year, even after Booker had reassured the business guys at the label, repeatedly, that everything was under control—Shad was there to check up on Rickey. Booker wasn't quite sure why Mona Ray was along for the ride: did they think that her (ancient) history with Rickey made her more likely to be able to manage him?

Booker gave herself a shake. Maybe she was getting

paranoid. Maybe it was nothing more than that this was a part of Mona Ray's job. Maybe she and Shad had a relationship; stranger things had happened. None of that involved her or was relevant to Rickey's career. The only thing that mattered was that these two not be allowed to bother him or interfere with his writing.

She was also determined that they not be allowed to raise the tension level for everyone—including her. Last year, when Rickey went back to work, she had a lot less stress. He'd made his appearances, done his videos, met his fans, answered the journalists' questions and done the shows; so far, he seemed content to continue. She believed they weren't hurting anybody, with the occasional use of substitutes in the past years. But doing all the doing that had to be done to keep it going was tiring, and she was glad it was over. She had less control, in Rickey's life, but she had more over her own.

Sometimes Booker was quite skeptical about the possibility of getting away permanently with what they'd done. Somebody was bound to catch on or find some evidence. The only question was: who would it be? One of the pensioned-off fake Rickeys? One of the short-term musicians? A backup singer? A journalist? Some days it seemed amazing to Booker that it hadn't happened by now.

But it hadn't. Maybe the real mystery was when would that day of revelation come? And who would be the announcer?

***

Cosmo didn't understand why Linda had come all the way over here if she didn't want to spend any time with him. From the moment he'd picked up her from the airport three days ago, she'd done nothing but avoid his eyes. He called her on it almost right away but at first, she insisted it was just jet lag. It was past time for that excuse, though, and she'd given up trying to cover up. She'd just given up on everything, Cosmo thought.

They were having drinks in the hotel lobby bar, getting ready to go to dinner at a restaurant he'd researched himself. Well, he'd asked the concierge for a recommendation, and that was practically the same thing, wasn't it? Cosmo was having trouble getting her to say anything, and after ten minutes of trying, he blew up.

"What the hell is going on? You've barely spoken to me since you arrived, Linda, what is it? What's wrong?"

She sighed and spoke to the ice cubes melting at the bottom of her glass. "It's the same thing it's always been, Cosmo."

"What? What?" He demanded. "You were fine for the first half hour after you got here but ever since you've been . . . I don't even know what to call it!"

"Don't you remember what you said to me, after that first half hour? You don't, do you." She gulped down another couple of ounces of her drink. "It's always the same."

"What, Linda? What did I say? Or do?"

"I asked you what you wanted us to do, here in London, and the first thing you could think of to talk about was Rickey T! That's all it ever is!"

"Well, duh! We're here for a Rickey T Fan Club meeting, that's why I said that's what I wanted us to do." He stared at the top of her head. "Isn't it? Isn't that why we're here?"

"I'm sick to death of Rickey T," she muttered. "I thought you might say you wanted us to explore the city, or go for a ride on the river, or visit galleries and museums, or go shopping. Or make love."

Cosmo felt like he was playing dodgeball. "Yeah. Well, yeah. All those things. But we're here for a Rickey T Fan Club meeting. We can come to London any time."

"But we never do," she pointed out. "And I'm sick to death of your obsession with Rickey T, Cosmo. We're done. I'm going home."

She stood up and grabbed her bag. As Cosmo watched her walk through the half-empty bar, he had a sudden feeling of certainty that she meant it.

Maybe, though, the feeling was actually one of wanting her to mean it.

***

Rickey was in the midst of the writer's nightmare—what if the songs dry up? He'd come to this hole-in-a-wall flat near Tower Bridge to try to find the way to turn the tap on again. Over all the years, thirty of them since he'd scribbled his first lines of lyrics in a school notebook, he'd never had so much trouble coming up with a phrase, a hook or an idea.

Ironic. He'd gone toe-to-toe with that idiot, Oliver, when the guy wanted to hijack the song writing and take over everything. Rickey had discussed all this with Booker last year and she'd insisted that he was overreacting, but he didn't think so. You have to know what is at the core of what you do and not let anyone too close to it. He had no problem with Oliver singing his songs, copying his moves, answering questions on his behalf, or posing for photos. But he drew the line, deep and solid, at writing the songs. Rickey put up a barricade around his territory.

But now here he was, with nothing to protect. It had been three months since a single new idea had crossed his mind. Rickey hadn't yet confessed to Booker that he didn't have a pile of new songs, ready to go, ready to come together on an album to meet or exceed the success of *H8GNSLO*. He knew she wouldn't hesitate to point out the lunacy of firing the guy who *wanted* to write songs and perhaps could have led them out of this maze.

Oliver Dash wasn't fired for writing songs, though, Rickey reminded himself. He was fired for being so completely unreliable as to stand up at a Rickey T concert, centerstage and in the spotlight, and sing a tune that wasn't on the approved setlist, wasn't in Rickey's repertoire, and wasn't good enough to be, either. Oliver was history, whether or not it was ironic, and whether or not he'd gone quietly into Rickey-retirement.

Rickey stood up from the piano and walked across the living room to the window looking out over the Thames. This neighborhood had once been a maze of laneways and smelly streets, home and marketplace for some of the poorest of London's residents. Somehow, in these hours and days of finding his mind a complete blank, as if it had been erased by a bomb set by the creativity gods, Rickey felt like it was appropriate he was looking out on such an uninspiring view. He deserved nothing better, no prospect of a beautiful panorama or a water horizon.

He had to do something to shake this black dog. Two hours of pacing, and Rickey arrived at his solution. *The block had come when he went back to work as a performer*. The answer was easy: he had to stop performing. Also—stop meeting the fans, stop doing the videos, stop attending the awards shows, stop doing the press and PR. Then, his songs would return.

Rickey was so excited about solving the problem that he couldn't wait to tell Booker about it. He reached for his phone; he had no doubt she'd be just as thrilled with his breakthrough as he was.

She was not.

"Rickey, that's bullshit!" Her voice was low but it sounded dangerous. "We need you at work!"

"I'm trying to work, my most important work! But I can't write songs as long as I'm doing all this other stuff. Come on, Book, you know it makes sense. And you know we have to hire another stand-in for me."

"Where am I going to get another person?" Booker demanded. "It's not like it's been easy, you know!"

"I know, I know it hasn't," he said soothingly. "But let's pull it together once more, okay? For me? For my sanity?"

***

Whatever argument it was that worked, Rickey was grateful that he'd stumbled on it. Three weeks later Booker emailed him to say she had a possibility of a guy, and Rickey should meet them at a neighborhood pub near his flat. Grateful was putting it mildly, really; he was downright ecstatic! Man, he'd hated being back in the show, these past years. It was almost as bad as it had been in 1979 when the success first started really happening. Dreading that open stage all day, throwing up in the can every night . . . and nothing he'd done to try to conquer his stage fright since then had made any difference.

By then, back then, he'd had five years on the road, and it really had come to own him. Drugs weren't his problem and neither was sex. He didn't have an addictive personality, no gaps to fill. He'd been able to see the trouble coming and avoid it. But he couldn't outrun the anger, somehow.

He remembered his first time on a big stage. It was 1974, he was twenty. Twenty years old, and his dream had come true. Rickey thought of some of the twenty-year-olds he knew now. Millennials. Almost every one of them was still such a long way away from being the grown-up he was, at twenty. Of course, he had to admit, that he wasn't anywhere near the grown-up that his father was, at twenty, flying bombers over Germany in World War II—a family fact that his father never tired of reminding him of. His father and his brother. So, yeah, he was young, at twenty, to have the success, the fame, and the money he had, but he wasn't taking it away from anybody. He was just living his own dream.

That first night, when he heard the crowd roar his name and sing along with lines he'd written while sitting on the floor of his crappy bedroom in Middlebury, he knew he should be lighting up like a floodlight. And he did, for a while. But then he strummed the opening chords of a song and some jerk near the front started yelling at him to sing a different song. He asked for quiet a few times and didn't get it. He saw guys staring at the chicks dancing nearby, rather than at the stage. He heard women screaming his name and he could barely hear his own voice, singing his poetry.

From that very first concert, Rickey was aware of the negative side of a performance. He had no control, really, but instead of that making him humble, it made him angry. Then, as the months went by and he learned about the rest of the dream—the crazy fans, the sleepless nights in hotels, the crappy tour bus food, the show after show after show, having to perform no matter what his mood—he realized that he wanted the dream to be over and he hated his life.

For a while there, he'd found a way to live it while not living it. Then Moron Oliver had messed things up, and Fake Jake before him, and Rickey had had to return to playing rock star again. Those days were almost gone again.

The door swung open and Booker strolled in with a tall, middle-aged man with gray hair and a goatee. Flinch was his name—or nickname—Rickey didn't quite get that straight. But all of the boxes had been ticked and it seemed like this guy would fit the bill. Mid-forties, just like Rickey, and mellowing a bit, like he was. Not as likely to go off on a rant, like those first two.

Fake number three's full name was Flinch Warren. Who knew where the first name came from, whether it was a nickname or whether it really was the name his mother had given him, as a way of remembering childbirth.

Anyway, Rickey was happy enough with the guy Booker picked, particularly when she showed him some of the songs Flinch had written. While Rickey's main reason for wanting to stop the performing was to get the songs flowing again, one small part of his brain was whispering, "What if that isn't really the problem? What if the songs don't come back anyway?"

It was no answer to point to the hundreds of songs he'd already written and recorded, and suggest to Booker and to Shad, that they promote those and build the concerts around them. There had to be new material: there always had to be new material, and hiring Flinch was to be Rickey's insurance.

Rickey motioned to the chairs across the small round table; Booker and Flinch sat down. It was a typical corner pub, with black-and-white-checkered linoleum floor, hunter-green walls and signs everywhere, warning people that thieves would be after their bags and backpacks if they didn't watch them. Rickey flagged down the server as she bustled past, carrying a huge round tray full of full pints.

"When you get a minute, we need menus."

"Be right back, sir," she said.

Rickey turned to Flinch. "Tell me a little something about yourself."

Flinch glanced at Booker, then tipped his head to one side. "What do you want to know?"

Backatcha. Right.

Rickey leaned back in his chair and crossed his arms. "Why would you want a gig like this one?"

"Well, it's the right time of my life for it," Flinch said. "I don't kid myself anymore that my big break is right around the corner. My name isn't going to be up in lights thirty feet high and my albums aren't going to sell in the tens of millions. I've made a comfortable living, playing gigs all over the UK but I wouldn't mind the chance to see a little more of the world. I'd like to make more money and think about putting some away for the day when all I want to do is watch telly and talk about my ailments. And I like putting on a show, I can't deny it."

"It's not that you're a huge fan of my music and you'd love the chance to sing my songs for a living?"

Booker nodded enthusiastically but Flinch just sniffed. "Naw."

The waitress zoomed past their table, slowing down just long enough to drop three menus. Rickey opened his, saw the list of standard pub lunch items, and closed it. Flinch didn't even glance at his.

"You've seen my tapes," Flinch continued. "I think you know I can do the job. I can guarantee you won't have to worry about me going off on a bender or putting all the profits up my nose or into my arm."

"What about shooting off your mouth?" Rickey asked. "The price of the world travel, the retirement savings and the chance to show off for the crowds is going to be complete discretion. Absolute confidentiality. If you breathe so much as a word about our deal to *anybody*, I'll have to cut your heart out with a rusty knife. As they say."

"As they say," Booker repeated, with a smile to cut the tension.

Rickey didn't want the tension cut. "Do we have a deal?"

Flinch nodded. That would have to be good enough (and of course, Booker would have the thing papered with a contract that was like the threads that the little people used to tie Gulliver to the ground). Rickey lifted a hand to call the waitress back.

***

Rickey didn't stop trying to compose, even though he now had Flinch for a backup. But he hadn't expected that his writer's block would turn into paralysis.

It started slowly, the trouble. Just silence, in his head, in the spaces where the melodies and the words were supposed to be. It had been a long time since he'd been ready to play anything new for Booker. She called him about twenty times and he brushed her off as often as he could before he finally had to give in. He invited her to a well-hidden rehearsal spot, a bench in a park beside the Thames, and sat down to play her his new song.

It was called "Under the Palms" and the tempo was slow, with just a touch of a suggestion of calypso running in the spaces between the rock beats. Rickey kind of liked it, some days, and some days he thought it was crap. This was nothing new; all his life he'd had phases where he hated his own work and didn't believe anyone who insisted that a new song was good. Usually, though, with a little time passing and some work on the details, he came around to being proud of it. He'd been giving this one some time for months now and it still came across lame.

He waited as long as he could for Booker to say something, then—"Look, I can't stand it anymore! Do you like it or not?"

You could tell that Booker was going to choose her words carefully. "It's got potential, Rickey, it does—"

"It's a yes or no question," Rickey said.

"Then, no. It's not quite there yet. Maybe if you give it another pass or two?"

"I've been going over it for months," Rickey said. "I'm sick of it. I thought I just needed to write something else, but I couldn't get started on anything."

He went silent and they just stared at each other for a few minutes. "Well, Rick, what do you expect from me?" Booker asked. "I don't know what to tell you. That the skill or the talent or whatever will come back? I don't know. That we can go forward without new songs? I don't know, would that satisfy the fans? Would it satisfy you?"

Rickey made a face. "I think I'd be fine with it. It's not like I have songs inside me, bursting to be heard."

"Unlike Oliver, who we fired last year."

"I had that phase, I'm on to other things now." Rickey said. "But let's not put out anything that's not up to standard. We'll just take me out of the songwriting part of it."

Booker nodded slowly. "Okay, we can do that. Nashville is full of songwriters; we'll get in the stream and start listening to some stuff."

Rickey shook his head. "That doesn't feel right. Rickey T has always put out his own stuff, except once in a while, doing a duet or a feature."

Booker looked very frustrated. "Well, what do you suggest?"

He let so much time go by that Booker might have been thinking he'd forgotten the question. He was getting older, but not that old. "I suggest we lean on Flinch there, and make him start earning his money."

Booker stared at him. "We've already got him planning on doing the concerts, the videos, the PR."

"His big money," Rickey said. "We pay the guy, what, five million for half a year's work? A lot of it spent just waiting for a call? I'd say there's still room for us to assign a few more duties."

"You want him to write the songs, then," Booker said. "What else, do the recordings?"

"No, I'll do that. It'll be my way of staying hands-on, adding my own stamp to things. You know, it's a lot easier to edit somebody else's draft than come up with one of your own, from the blank page," Rickey said. "Go. Call him and tell him. Tell him we need something for the first of the month."

***

Songwriting had never been Flinch's forte, although he had been known to come up with a tune or two. But hell, this writing on demand, the way Booker and Rickey had it set up, was just killing him. He took another long pull on the wine bottle at his elbow—the second of the day.

When Booker hired him, she'd said nothing about songwriting being a significant slice of the deal. In fact, it was his understanding that Rickey was a brilliant songwriter, had been for close to thirty years, and that the only thing that was needed was someone to stand in for him at the concerts and a few other places. Anybody does that many years of concerts, they'd probably be sick of it, too. All those places, tens of thousands of people, all that noise. Flinch had been watching a video done live at a Rickey T concert five years ago and thought he saw the rock star shaking his head and pointing to his ear. Poor guy had probably done some permanent damage to his hearing by now.

Maybe that was part of his writer's block. Whatever it was, Flinch was standing by, ready to pitch in, eager to please. Really, he was. That's what he was known for, being always ready to help out. But he hadn't expected this level of pressure.

Wouldn't hurt if they'd thrown in a bit more money. One thing you found out when you started to get some was that it didn't go nearly as far as you might expect. He saw dozens of items on TV, and in the magazines online, that he still wanted. The Aston Martin, the house in Spain, the private plane—all of those were still beyond his reach.

And he wanted them. He'd done without for so many years, lost two greedy wives due to his inability to deliver on their demands, and he was convinced that this was his shot. His resemblance, in middle age, to one of the biggest stars in the world, and his own musicality meant that he might actually be able to pull it together. Then, when he had it all, would he return to Barbara? Or even going further back, to Sharon? Lay it all out in front of her and say "I told you so. I told you I'd make it." Hell, no, they could just rot away in Brighton or Edinburgh or wherever they'd ended up. He'd keep his mouth shut, as he'd promised, for as long as Rickey wanted him to do this job. Then, he'd take the big payoff promised at the end of the gig, when Rickey didn't need him any longer and he'd played along through every month and every show of the whole damn con. He would take the money and run as fast as he could toward a new, better woman.

But first, he had to solve this songwriting sucker. First of the month, Rickey said. Flinch picked up the rhyming dictionary he'd bought at a bookstore and opened it at random. "Kentucky, lucky." Hell, he could do something with that.

***

Booker leaned back against the wall in the local, examining her pint and trying to make a decision about changing apartments once she got back home to New York. The neighborhood was changing and she wasn't that comfortable with the gentrification direction it was taking.

The waitress approached the table with a refill on her Guinness. "You got a phone call, dearie," she said, then jerked her head toward a public phone mounted on the wall in the passageway between the back of the bar and the restrooms. Loo, as the Brits would say.

"Me?" How did anybody know she was there?

Rickey's voice was at the other end of the line. When she asked him, he said "Well, I know where you're staying, don't I?"

He got straight to the point. "Look, I'm getting freaked out about Sturgess and Staten Island Records."

Booker waited.

"He called me from L.A., just to schmooze for a while, he said, and then he made a few comments about noticing changes in my stage style over the past few years. Says it's different than last year, which was when it was me, of course, and five years ago, different still. I told him the years are going by, for all of us, including him, but he still seemed . . . thoughtful, you know?"

"What do you think we should do?"

"I don't know, Book, I really don't. I just think we should be aware. On guard, with this guy. I did him a favor a while back, but that may not go far enough. Maybe you need to do a few more things to bring him into the tent."

"You want me to make nice with a guy I don't know very well—or like—because he's made some comments about your stage style?"

Rickey sighed loudly enough to be heard all the way to Yorkshire. "You know as well as I do, Book, how delicate this all is. We've been lucky enough to keep this going fifteen years—"

"Hasn't been luck, it's been a lot of good decisions, on my part," Booker said.

"So, make another one."

Rickey sounded sincerely freaked out about all this and so, Booker relented. "All right, I'll think about it."

"And I'll get ready for the most amazing recording session you've ever heard. Once Flinch gets those new songs to us."

***

St. Croix, USVI

Flinch picked up his guitar for the forty-fifth time that morning, heaved a heavy sigh and tried, once again, to coax something melodic and original from the strings. He was sitting on a rattan couch that had pink and green cushions to blend in with the rest of the Caribbean décor. A green rug picked up the leafy pattern on the couch and the chairs, while pink dominated all the accessories in the room: frames on the artwork, placemats on the table in the dining room and tropical fish in the aquarium.

The suite was just the right size—large enough to feel important and yet not so large that he was aware that he was alone. His privacy was complete; although he knew there were other guests in other suites around him, he wasn't aware of any of them at all. The resort clung to a cliff that towered over the two-lane road below and a tropical breeze wafted through the patio doors from the private pool. In the distance, he had a view of Buck Island. It had been distracting him pretty well all morning. He stood up and walked over to a glass-fronted cabinet in the dining room. His reflection looked grim.

I know I shouldn't have jumped on the plane to get down here to the Caribbean but it just seemed a like a rock star kind of thing to do, you know? I HAVE to come up with a song (or twelve!) by the end of the month. And I have no doubt that Rickey will show me the door if I don't. I'm completely dispensable. Just the way I have been everywhere, my whole life.

So, I'm holed up in this villa, three days now, and I don't have anything to show for it, except a wastebasket full of mistakes.

I had a hell of a time getting here. Tiny airport, everybody chill they say, and I'm walking out to the rental car window and suddenly some dude is taking my picture. 'It's Rickey T!' he says to his wife and she starts squealing and before you know it, I've got a dozen people around me, pointing cameras at me, digging in their handbags, shoving pieces of paper and pens at me for autographs.

I didn't mind meeting the fans and signing the autographs, although I was feeling kind of bagged and I wanted to get to my place, kick off my shoes and relax. But after about ten minutes, a guy with professional-level camera gear showed up and a woman standing beside him, wearing a bright yellow dress and a big hat, started asking me questions about what I thought of St. Croix and whether it was my first visit. Ironic as shit—I was not the famous one, not really, and yet I was getting all the hassle.

I needed a drink. Preferably with rum.

***

That night, Flinch found himself in a funky little café, listening to some local guy sing and watching some tourist teenagers try to pick each other up. The place was open on three sides, with the warm tropical air bathing the whole scene, inside and out, in an atmosphere like something out of a movie. A dozen gleaming white sailboats were tied up at the marina outside and several happy couples, hand in hand, strolled up and down the docks, looking at the boats and fantasizing.

A tall, slender server dressed completely in white arrived with Flinch's fish tacos displayed on a wooden plate, a colorful salad and a pot of guacamole finishing off the meal. The man barely looked at Flinch as he put down the plate and nodded absent-mindedly at Flinch's 'thank you'. It looked as though the incident at the airport was just a one-off and that he'd be able to wander around St. Croix without being bothered every step of the day. Just to be on the safe side though, he had taken to not shaving, wearing a ball cap on backwards and putting on a Southern accent, dropping his 'g's' and going for the lilt at the end of a sentence.

At last, Flinch was in a place that felt right. No one would bother him here and he wouldn't be the least bit tempted or distracted.

Booker was bugged by the fact that he'd gone so far away and was off on his own. But, hell, everybody was connected nowadays; if she wanted to get in touch with him, it wouldn't be hard. And Flinch had managed to convince her that he would be plunging into the songwriting work and would come out of it with twelve brilliant songs, any one of them a hit, any one of them number one with a bullet. Shit, he'd managed to convince himself.

A few days later, Flinch had a creative rebirth. He got to work, filling up a dozen pads of yellow paper. He did throw a lot of pages away, too, but it was all part of the process.

He had a nice little routine going: getting up every day about eleven, writing until three, eating something healthy, writing some more, going for a long walk on the beach and then ending up at David's Café for a brew or a rum-something. Flinch was not talking to anybody and he found he wasn't missing that, either. He was starting to see what it was that Rickey saw in the hermit life.

***

The phone rang in Booker's New York condo. She recognized the number and picked up. "Hey, Flinch, what's up?"

"Checking in, Booker. Everything cool?"

"All good. Everybody's very happy with the new songs."

Flinch broke into a whistle, a habit of his that she'd had to coach him to keep under control. Rickey wasn't known for whistling, and once a session musician who'd worked with him in the past commented on it. She'd told him it was something new that Rickey had picked up in his middle-age and they'd both laughed. Better that than underage girls or anything else that might put him on the front pages for the wrong reasons. But she'd made a point of telling Flinch to cut it out, or pick up a harmonica or something.

She listened to him whistle for a few more seconds, then broke in. "And how do you like St. Croix? What's it like?"

"Oh, man, it's paradise! Just like they say in the commercials. The water is turquoise, the sun shines all the time, the weather is so warm."

"What did you do? Any swimming? Snorkeling? Diving?"

She could hear Flinch planning his response. "Nah, I didn't have time for any of that. I was just—writing. Getting it done. Laying down the pages." He made it sound like pipe in a ditch, or something.

A few days later, Booker found that the tune that Flinch had been whistling was running through her memory. It was one of those music bits that you just can't get out of your mind. Sometimes it seemed vaguely familiar, others it was just catchy, and before long she found herself humming it. She resisted for about an hour, then had to call him.

"Flinch, that tune you were whistling when we spoke on the phone last time."

"Yeah?"

"Are there words to go with that?"

"There are. You like it?"

"You know, I hate to say it, because too much enthusiasm is the sign of the amateur, but I have to say yeah, I like it. I might even love it." Booker waited a few seconds and delivered her message as clearly and with as much conviction as she could. "I think the rest of the world is going to love it, too."

"You do?"

"I do, Flinch. Go have a rum punch on me. I think you wrote a hit."

The song was called "He was Long Gone Before I Moved Out" and once Booker finally got her hands on a tape of Flinch singing the whole thing, beginning to end, she was sure of it. Well, how about that Flinch Warren? His stress about being asked to contribute songs as well as do concerts was no big deal after all. He'd stepped up, big time.

She made arrangements for a bonus check for him.

CHAPTER TWENTY-ONE

New York

Flinch came back from the Caribbean with twelve songs ready to go for the next album. Booker finished listening to the tapes he'd made and then wandered into her vast barn of a kitchen to make some tea. These rainy Sundays always brought her down. She didn't really know what to do with herself when she had free time like this. Pretty weird, to get to age forty-six without a single hobby. But that was the way she liked it—she worked to live and she lived to work. Anytime they weren't touring, she always felt adrift. Over the years, she'd taken a few vacations, but she'd never had a good time.

So, it turned out that Flinch hadn't gone down to the Caribbean for a good time, either, or just to sun his lazy ass on a sandy beach. He hadn't really taken a vacation at all. He'd worked hard. She was surprised, and everybody was pleased with the material they got from him for this new album.

Rickey had actually managed to come up with two tunes as well, during those six months, and had insisted they go on the disc. If Booker were forced to be honest, she'd have to say she thought they weren't up to the standard of Flinch's effort, but nobody asked her a direct question and she was always tactful.

Tactful, and loyal. Ever since the earliest days, in the seventies, once she'd fallen in love with Rickey's music and his career, she hadn't looked back or questioned. Why would she? Second-guessing yourself like that is a one-way ticket to misery, she believed. Her devotion was to Rickey and that was that.

Did she love the guy? Maybe, in a way . . . . no, she'd have to say no, not really. She'd just made a decision once and was sticking to it.

That meant many things. She saw herself as someone who smoothed the path for Rickey—and, over these past sixteen years, for his stand-ins. She was someone who made excuses for him and ran interference with the Shad Palmettos and the —what was the name of that fan who was becoming a nuisance? The one she'd had to sic Cosmo on to get her to go away and stop trying to phone Rickey all the time? Booker took a few long sips on her tea and came up with the name. Bella, that was it. Persistent and arrogant, she also remembered that, too.

Flinch had come up with eleven other fantastic tunes for the album and they called it *Island Afternoon*. It wasn't as big a hit as *H8GNSLO* in its first few months, but it was doing pretty well. The DJs were pushing it, especially in the frozen northern states where they needed some better weather and a chance to think about clothes that weren't parkas. Rickey was invited to several of the big TV talk shows; he took those appearances for himself but left the small-town meet-and-greets to Flinch. The two of them were like twins and somehow it all worked out. The video for the title track featured Flinch strolling sandy beaches, playing guitar in a local dive bar, and then watching some tourists stomping along the Boardwalk wearing snorkels, masks and flippers. Flinch told Booker he'd drawn the line when the director wanted him to be the one wearing the mask. "For humor". Booker thanked whoever God was, once again, that Flinch was there, to do the videos. Rickey would have had a conniption.

It was a snowy New York afternoon, two days before Valentine's Day, when Booker heard raised voices in the outer office and went out to see what the commotion was. Her assistant, Jennifer, raised her hands helplessly. "I told him he couldn't go in to see you."

"Don't need to go in now," the man in the brown suit said. "You've been served, ma'am."

At first, Booker didn't know whether she was more bothered by the "ma'am" than the law suit, but it didn't take long for her to figure it out. Richard Taggart aka Rickey T was being sued for copyright infringement for most of *Island Afternoon*—Rickey, his production company, his management company, his publishing company and his holding company. Booker read through the document, line by line, then sat back in her chair. Her personal phone started ringing and she hesitated over whether to answer it. Jennifer was screening all the calls to the main number but if someone had Booker's private number and was using it, it might be someone she should talk to. She took a look at the call display and winced. Shad Palmetto. Just what she needed right now, a schmoozey phone conversation with an executive from the record label.

Not so schmoozey, as it turned out.

"Booker, do you know what's just been delivered to our L.A. office? A lawsuit. A plagiarism law suit!" Shad was screaming. "They're saying Rickey copied at least part of the melody in almost every one of the songs on this latest album! Some guy says he has proof up the wazoo—a CD he recorded and put out five years ago—and he says he met Rickey and played it for him at some bar in the Caribbean. What the hell, Booker! Can that be true? Has Rickey even been to the Caribbean?"

She spent half an hour, calming Shad down and getting him off the phone, before she had time to answer the question for herself. Could it be true? She hated to think that Flinch was putting one over on them, after all they'd done for him. But she and Rickey weren't exactly shining examples of unfailing honesty, a comparison that Flinch pointed out to her when she finally got him on the phone.

"Look, you had me under so much pressure to deliver new songs within a very short time frame, and I really didn't think this guy would surface," Flinch said.

"He had a CD! The songs had already been recorded! Come on, Flinch, clearly that's a case of stealing material! If you liked it so much, why didn't you just introduce me to the guy. Maybe Rickey T could have covered some of his material."

"That wasn't the assignment, Booker, as I understood it. I was supposed to be writing new songs, songs that would have Rickey T's name on them as songwriter, isn't that right? Rickey T doesn't cover other writers' material, he's the writer, right?" His voice had a sarcastic tone that Booker really couldn't hold against him. He was right.

"So, I paid him for the songs outright. A big old whack of bread. But I guess it wasn't enough for him, once he started to see the way *Island Afternoon* was going up the charts."

"No, I guess it wasn't," Booker said. "No use trying to explain to him that a lot of that success had to do with the arrangements, the other musicians, the packaging, the promotion—"

"You sound like Mr. Palmetto," Flinch said. "And no, no use."

Booker stared out of her office window at the snow drifting down. The trip home after work would be tough. Maybe it was time she took off for some island, somewhere.

"But we do have a defense, I think," Flinch said. "The songs are similar, yeah, but I only used them as a foundation. I changed each one up a little, made the bridge a little longer, repeated the chorus here and there, you know. And of course, the lyrics are all mine. We'll have the lawyers talk about musical influences, how Rickey was just absorbing the island culture, the calypso, the reggae, the soca. Then, some of it—okay, a lot of it, seeped into his consciousness and into his music." Booker could hear Flinch's enthusiasm growing with each sentence; he was seeing a gap in the bars of this cage he felt trapping him.

"You're right," Booker said. "Those are the sorts of things the lawyers will be saying, once the thing gets to court, eventually, five, six, seven years from now maybe, and once the record has made a lot more money and there's a lot more at stake. It may not even get to court. We're certainly going to make Mr. Whoever he is an offer to settle."

"Ah. Good." Flinch seemed to be exhaling as he imagined himself to be home-free.

"The thing is, Flinch, we can't leave things as they are, while we wait for the legal system to do its slow, frustrating thing. There is going to be a lot of bad press over this, and a lot of controversy over whether Rickey T wrote these songs, legit, or copied them. Where does 'influence' start and stop? What about intention? Did he intend to copy them? Did he know he was copying them? If not, why did he pay the guy any money? Did you give him cash, by the way?"

A long pause. "A check."

"Geez. Ah. Well. So, we've got a PR nightmare brewing here. We've also got the record company mad as mud. I just got off the phone with Shad Palmetto and he's freaking out. After I finish this call, I have to phone Rickey and discuss it with him. That's something I'm really looking forward to. It's just a gong show, Flinch, and you caused it. I'm sorry, I hope you've figured this out by now, but we're parting ways."

"What do you mean?"

"I mean, you're fired. You screwed up and you're fired."

There was a long silence, as she'd guessed there would be, while he tried to choose the best thing to say. "I don't think you want to do that. I know a lot of stuff, Booker."

Not that.

Booker took a long breath, then took aim and let go. "If you threaten me, Flinch, I will make your life a living hell. You have no idea what I can do, but believe me, I will make you so sorry you started this conversation——! I will chase you all over this world, if I have to, and I will make you pay, if you try to ignore all those confidentiality agreements you signed.

"Or, you can be reasonable, you can see the reason I'm doing this, put yourself in my shoes. I think I can contain the damage, but I'm not totally sure. But I do know that I can't do it if you're around and I'm stressing the whole time about whether the rest of this story comes out. Not to mention, trying to guide Rickey through this whole mess."

"But what are you going to do? You've got a tour coming up. You need me."

"We have options, Flinch. The tour isn't fully booked, we're still in discussions on most of the stops. And we have Rickey, after all."

"But Rickey doesn't want to perform, that's what the whole thing has been about! He won't change his mind now! You need me."

"Nobody's indispensable, Flinch, not even greedy, blackmailing singers who impersonate actual stars. There's the door. If you walk through it, gracefully, and keep your information to yourself for ever after, you'll go with enough money to last you a lifetime. If not, watch out."

Booker stared through her window at the snow piling up on the tree branches and the sidewalk below, waiting while he made up his mind.

"All right," Flinch said. "I see your point."

"I'll have a contract and a non-disclosure agreement drawn up and sent over to you," Booker said. "Thanks,

Flinch. Thanks for letting me wrap it up, and for all you've done, for Rickey and for all of us, these last few years."

"Yeah." Flinch said. He didn't sound like it was an experience he planned on remembering fondly.

CHAPTER TWENTY-TWO

2004

Glasgow

Four years later

The first time Booker went to Scotland, she watched pipers at the Edinburgh Festival and drank Scotch at a famous distillery at ten in the morning. This time, she had spent every minute of her five days there so far in the hotel, on the phone or in meetings. When had life become such nonstop work? Why had she allowed it to happen?

She looked around the dark, cozy bar and thanked her stars for small mercies. Just like the people in so many countries, the Scots knew how to set up a spot with dim lighting, good food, drink and the right music. Perhaps it was just that Booker avidly sought out these places wherever she went. I've become an expert, a connoisseur, she thought.

She knew, deep down, why she worked so hard. Rickey was her responsibility. She'd brought him into this rock music world and it was up to her to guide him through it.

Rickey didn't make it easy for her to do this, but that was just part of the challenge. She didn't expect him to see that he was her responsibility, a duty that would never end. He thought *he* was in charge, and had been since about 1976 or so. There would have been no way to make him understand that he wasn't, not unless he ever took on the same sort of bond with another person. She doubted he ever would.

Why was he so much her responsibility? Sometimes, she understood it in karmic terms. It was a connection that couldn't be severed because she'd saved his life, in a way, when she showed him, as a teenager, that he was worth much more than his horrible, dysfunctional family would let him believe. His condescending parents and their miserable favoritism for his quarterback brother—it will infuriated her whenever she thought of it. She'd shown Rickey how to find the door and just walk through it. So, in a way, he owed her his success and she owed him lifelong vigilance and her best advice.

In the four years since the Flinch fiasco, Booker had worked so hard to recover from the embarrassment and the financial damage that she'd barely had time to think about anything else. Once the truth about its true writer and composer came out, the *Island Afternoon* record sold very few copies, despite the optimistic sarcasm of Sturgess, who thought it might sell a million because it would be a rare thing, an album from Rickey T but not *really* from Rickey T. Shad poured marketing and PR muscle into it in a sort of frenzy, as if he were determined to prove that the music wasn't really what sold records. It didn't work.

The law suit rambled its way through the courts, one judgement, then an appeal, then another judgement, another appeal. Finally, the result was out and was clear: it was plagiarism and they owed the Caribbean composer all the royalties from the record and some big bucks for damages. Rickey bitched that they'd given the guy so much international press and raised the recognition factor for his name so much, he should be thanking them, not collecting from them. He didn't get much sympathy for his point of view.

In the end, the lawyers got most of the money and Rickey T was left with a reputation as someone who was either too easily influenced by other musicians, best case, or caught in the grip of terminal writer's block, worst case. He didn't do anything to address either opinion, over the four years—didn't release any new songs, didn't record anything, didn't put on any concerts, and didn't do any press. He barely talked to Booker on the phone, when she called him every month or so.

Cosmo was gone, too, and the fan club fire had gone out without him there to stoke it. Booker had lost a lot of sleep over that decision, letting Cosmo go, but Rickey still believed it was the best choice. He'd been trying to tighten the circle of people who were allowed to have an opinion about anything he did. Too late to tighten the circle of those who knew about the past, but he wanted to have more control over the future.

And he ran this metaphorical railroad. Even though he'd been missing in action for most of the past few years, he still ran everything. The trains were sputtering, the tracks were old and in need of repair, and the employees were like ghosts, but Rickey was still the one in charge.

Booker had a feeling he was ready to make some changes, though. She'd let him know that this European promoter had invited her to a meeting before their show in Glasgow to discuss a short tour and she knew she heard definite interest on Rickey's side of the conversation. This Glasgow show was a one-off and the only one she'd been able to arrange for all of 2004, so far.

Their money situation was turning really dark. At first, the strategy was 'no tours, no public appearances, intriguing mystery', and it had worked for a while. But bit by bit, even Rickey's rabid fans found somewhere else to be. The new record was crap and everybody who wanted one owned one of the old ones. Booker had been asking Rickey to consider a change in strategy for the better part of a year and it finally felt like he was coming around.

She wasn't looking forward to telling him that they would have to front a large percentage of the expenses, in order to get the partner they needed. The risk was huge, but so might the payout be. And Rickey needed to resurface one of these days or the story would be over.

"Roger!" She stood up to greet the promoter as he walked into the pub. She'd looked him up online and had an investigator look into things before she'd set up the meeting, so she knew she was expecting this tall, red-haired, lean man with a beard and a friendly smile.

"Booker, nice to see you."

She settled at the bar beside Roger with a couple of pints in front of them, and the talks went so well that they soon progressed to a memorable, golden sample of fifty-year-old Scotch whisky, as they got ready to do the deal.

"What's the financing on this, Roger?" Booker asked.

Roger took an appreciative swallow of his drink. "I believe you know Henry Ryland?"

Ahh. "Yes, he's an old friend of Rickey's and a great friend to the Rickey T organization."

"Henry is in, but he wants to be a silent partner."

"Got it," Booker said. "So . . . Milan, Rome, Venice, Paris, London?"

"Yeah. Five dates only. Top-of-the-line venues, five-star all the way."

Booker was sure that Rickey would be onboard, and would be thrilled that she'd found a cleanup for the money disaster. And only five dates! For so much money! They'd come a long way since the days in the seventies, when they'd done tours with forty and fifty shows.

"Now, you're sure you can commit to the full schedule?" Roger said. "Rickey's solid?"

"He is, don't worry, Roger," Booker said. "You can tell

Henry I said so."

***

The fans had staked out every seat at the Royal Concert Hall. It was so easy for Booker to feel that success was something she could bank on when the smiles were this wide and the excitement palpable. Nights like this, Booker didn't feel as though they'd ever deceived anyone for so much as five minutes. Every one of these fans had had more than his or her money's worth, thanks to Rickey's music.

Booker wandered through the crowd outside the doors, as she had been doing for thirty years now. A small group of young women in their twenties blocked the entrance and Booker politely asked them to let her by.

"Oh, you can't go in there." The spokesperson for the group was about twenty, dressed like a truck driver and carrying an attitude about four sizes bigger than she was.

Booker pulled forward her lanyard and flashed her pass in the woman's face, immediately wishing she hadn't. Why did she still feel that she always had to establish her credentials and prove to somebody—anybody—that she had permission to be wherever?

When she got to Rickey's dressing room, she was shocked to see about twenty people hanging out. The door was open wide and people lined the corridor outside. She'd become used to Rickey's loner ways and she'd come to think of him as someone who didn't ever want other people around. She thought she knew him best of anyone but as time went on, she was realizing that while she might be responsible for his success and happiness, or perhaps once might have been, she was not the author of it. She'd like to be, but he made it damn hard to make him a continuing success, with the way he changed some things on her and wouldn't cooperate on others.

Booker pushed past some of the door-leaners and went across the room to Rickey. She hadn't seen him since he'd arrived from God-knows-where he'd been on his boat, and she'd been a bit concerned that he wouldn't be ready for this: too relaxed, too ordinary, perhaps. But he was ready, she could tell. The rock star attitude was all there, in the way he stood, the clothes he'd chosen to wear, and the look on his face.

He was getting older, though; they all were. Fifty this year—was that possible? Booker stared at Rickey's lightly lined face and his blond hair. They spent a lot of money every year on secret visits from the cosmetic surgeon, the hair stylist and the makeup artist, and they did it twice, making sure that Oliver and then Flinch had the same treatments. Rickey did his part, too, working out every day, stretching and taking care with his posture. Every once in a while, during rehearsal over the past few years, she'd seen him move a little stiffly or hunch over a bit, but he caught himself and corrected it immediately. It seemed inconsistent with his wish to get as far away from the rock star life as possible but on the other hand, it was consistent with his urge to control everything: he kept himself in shape so that if he wanted to, he could return at any time.

In this case, of course, it wasn't so much that he wanted to, as he had to. He hadn't dented the Billboard 100 in a long time and there was a danger that people would forget who he was. Oh, not the real fans, not the Rickets. But it was a big world out there, changing all the time.

"Hey, Rickey, how're things?" she greeted him. He waved back but didn't interrupt his conversation with Henry, who had flown in from California for the gig. A few minutes later, Henry shook his hand and turned to speak to someone else. Rickey slipped out of the crowd, appeared at Booker's side and took her elbow, to steer her out of the room.

Once out in the hallway, he headed toward a stairwell, leaving her to follow.

"Gotta get some space," he said. "Just for a few minutes before we start this sucker."

Booker closed the stairwell door behind them. "How are you, are you ready to go? Feeling okay?"

"Feeling like shit. I hate this, you know?"

He paced around in the tight space. Booker lowered herself down to sit on a step.

"I'm regretting my decision to do this show, I gotta tell you, Book."

"We had no choice, Rickey. We need the money."

"Yeah, yeah, I know. But I'm thinking, maybe we should go back to the system we had before."

"But you said, after Flinch got us in all that legal trouble, that you'd never hire another stand-in again."

"I know what I said. But I have some new information now, all right?"

She could tell that she'd irritated him, so she put a lid on all the things she might have said. For now.

"When I balance the risk of another stand-in doing something like what Flinch did against the cost of going back to work, I gotta think there really isn't much chance of picking a bad one," Rickey said." And the pain of having to go out on stage or do the videos and the interviews is constant."

"What are you saying, Rick?"

"I want you to hire another stand-in."

"Fake Number Four." Booker said.

Rickey sniggered, if fifty-year-old men could be said to snigger. "Yeah, four. Wow. But we've done it, haven't we? It worked."

"Except for getting our shorts sued off, thanks to Number Three."

Rickey waved it off. He was falling in love with the idea, she could tell. "Won't happen twice. Plus, we've learned some stuff, haven't we? How to watch, what to watch out for."

"We've got gigs coming up in a month, Rickey. Rome, Milan, Venice, London. And Paris!"

"Find a pro, get him motivated enough by the money,

and a month should be enough."

"What money?!"

"Okay, the promise of the money."

"Are you thinking this one will be expected to write new songs, too?" Booker hadn't often thought of the pleasure of a cigarette in all the years since she quit but this was definitely one of the times.

"He'll have to, Book," Rickey said. "I've dried up completely. It's like I had a box with a certain number of songs in it . . . or a voice that talked to me and now it's stopped talking. Maybe it was like a tap I could turn on and off, and one day I turned it and nothing came out. I've tried, believe me, I've tried. I've been trying to work the whole time I was on the boat but all I come up with is crap. I wish it was different but it's not. And I don't want to drive myself crazy trying to solve it, like some kind of problem, when I really don't care whether I write any more or not. Except, as you so regularly point out, that I need the money."

"Calm down, Rick," Booker said. She could see that he was ready to lose it. "I'll find somebody. Somebody who can look like fifty-year-old Rickey T, walk, sing, dance and talk like him, write songs, meet people. Do you plan to be the one in the recording studio?"

"Not if I don't have to."

His abdication was complete.

The show that night was adequate. No one would ever write that it was one of Rickey T's best and no one would go home to tell their friends, neighbors, children or grandchildren about the terrific concert they'd seen. Booker watched from backstage and while she did see that Rickey was giving it what he had to give, the thrill was definitely gone.

She chose London as the best place to look for his next replacement. It was close and she was in a hurry. One month to hire the guy and get him up to speed! As with the first three guys, she put out small, discreet ads for a singer-songwriter, thinking that it wouldn't be a good idea to ask around. Her circle in London was actually quite large but she couldn't risk her contacts starting to question why she was wanting to meet a singer who loved Rickey's songs and looked like him. They might get suspicious—she knew she would, if she were asked such a thing.

It only took one day for her email to blow up with messages from Duncan Donovan. When she first saw him waiting for her at The Ivy, she knew that her search, brief as it was, was over. He was a complete copy of Rickey Taggart, arms, legs, hands, face and hair. The eyes were quite different, a fact she didn't notice when he first walked in because he was wearing sunglasses. Sunglasses, at eleven a.m. Turned out it wasn't because they were bloodshot or that he was having trouble focusing. His eyes looked completely normal, just a dark shade of brown, a detail that could easily be fixed in an hour with contact lenses—just the way that the tattoos problem had had to be fixed for Oliver and for Flinch. Okay, maybe more than an hour and a little more pain. Booker wasn't familiar with the details and didn't want to be. She also noticed that two or three people seated at the tables they passed looked him over with that 'don't I know you from somewhere?' vibe. Maybe, though, she just imagined it.

"Do you need the glasses for some reason?" She asked, once they were settled in their high-backed wing chairs in front of the fireplace.

"Just like the look. Why, is it a problem?"

He's aggressive, she thought. "No, I'm just asking."

Duncan leaned forward in his chair, resting his forearms on his widespread knees. His jeans were faded, his shirt plaid, and there was no sign of a paunch anywhere. "Look, your ad had me sold in the first five words. 'Are you the ultimate Rickey T fan?' "

"Technically, that's six. If you count the T as a word." Why was she babbling? Maybe it was his take-charge manner, maybe the incredible resemblance to Rickey, maybe the testosterone, pure and simple.

His smile was tight. "Yeah. Look, I also liked the part about extensive travel. I have some reasons for wanting to shake London off for a while. What's the job? Session player? Bodyguard? Driver? But why would you be advertising for a singer, then?"

"What's your background in the music business, Mr. Donovan?"

"It's Duncan. I've been with a lot of bands, right back to the sixties. Almost perfect pitch, and any weak spots, I can distract 'em with the dancing, you know what I mean? I've been around, too."

"Any substance issues?"

"Not at all."

"In the past?"

"No, not in the past either. Dope and booze were never my thing . . . although I'm not a saint. Chicks were my thing. I slept with Janis . . . and a few others." Oh great, a bullshit artist. But the big smile he was showing beneath the shades would definitely be an asset, she could tell. "I knew them all, played with quite a few. Jimi, Ray Charles, Jim Morrison."

Name-dropping on people who were dead was a bit lazy, Booker thought. "Why do you want to get out of London?"

"Money problems, to tell you the truth. And it's bloody expensive to live here. That's the main reason I'd consider a job like this. What is the job, anyway?"

When she told Duncan the exact nature of the job, he just nodded as though he heard this sort of thing every day. Maybe he was just trying to appear to be as cool and sophisticated as he imagined a rock god would be. "I presume there'll be an NDA to sign. And that the money will be good."

"Very good. And yes, we'll expect complete secrecy and discretion on this. The money is tied to that, as much or more than to the quality of your performances and your songs."

He nodded. None of this seemed to bother him in the

least. "Of course. You can count on me. I know it must be a huge thing for Rickey, to let somebody into his world like this, and I won't let him, or you, down. When will I get to meet him?"

"Let's not get ahead of ourselves, all right? First thing is an audition and then more talk about the way it would work. With me," Booker said.

"Lead on, boss," Duncan agreed.

He showed up to the audition in a faded pair of jeans and a vintage Rolling Stone T with cut-off sleeves. It was just the two of them; if he worked out, Booker would ease him into the acting part of the job, the fooling of the session musicians, the journalists and the fans. She listened to him sing, nailing every phrase and every tone, and completely avoiding any trace of the Irish accent that was the foundation of his speaking voice. Booker knew she had her next Rickey double.

"How do you feel about tattoos?" she asked, motioning toward his white, blank-page biceps.

"Yeah, all right, I get it. If I'm in, and we do a contract, then yeah, I'll do that. Give me a list and I'll get 'em done."

"You have any already?"

He leered at her, but it was subtle. "Would you like to check them out?" Duncan waited only a few seconds before breaking the scene and returning to a businesslike manner. "Actually, I have none at all."

"That's good. We can set you up," Booker said.

A few days later, he told her he had it done. He was a Rickey copy right down to the ink on his skin. Booker gave Duncan some time to wrap up his affairs in London before joining the tour. She'd supplied him with DVDs of Rickey in every conceivable situation and made every speech she could think of, to indoctrinate the new stand-in with the idea that he couldn't breathe a word of this to anyone, without risking his payout and his future in the music business. She even hinted that it had to do with his life.

The next stop on this short European tour was Rome.

Booker had set up a week of rehearsals in each city before the shows and she'd hired local musicians to fill in. They'd brought along Bonaire from the U.S. to coach the two local girls they were to pick up in each place. It was a bit crazy—very crazy, Booker knew, but Rickey was convinced that it would keep everyone so busy they wouldn't have time or energy to notice anything 'off' about Rickey.

The Rome rehearsals were Booker's first clue that all might not go well with Fake Number Four. Duncan had a hard time showing up on time, right from the first day. Dammit. The musicians and the backup singers didn't appear to notice, and certainly no one was complaining. They thought they were working with the legendary Rickey T, after all. Didn't all rock stars show attitude?

Duncan made no attempt to get to know any of the musicians or the vocalists and that suited Booker just fine. All in all, it was quite a brisk, let's-get-down-to-business atmosphere, with a whole lotta music and not much talking. The language barrier added to the cocoon that Booker was able to create around Duncan.

She was hoping that a butterfly would emerge but the story wasn't even close. As Booker counted down the seven days to the concert, she had to start counting up the problems he was creating. By four-days-to-go, she was regretting her choice. By three-days-to-go, some of the players were asking her what was wrong with 'Rickey' and complaining that he was cutting the rehearsals very short ("maybe Rickey doesn't need the practice but these Italian guys don't know the songs that well and we gotta rehearse!"). By two-days-to-go (and after a profanity-laced scolding from Booker), Duncan was showing up on time and hanging in throughout rehearsal but she was getting calls from Jeannie the accountant about huge charges coming through on one of the tour credit cards. Booker confronted him about it and he promised to be good. With one-day-to-show time, she finally got the sense that all was under control.

And the show was good. After the second number, she could see the keyboard player, at his post on the piano bench, relax and start to smile. He turned toward her and gave her a thumbs-up and Booker let herself exhale.

The promoter phoned and said that he was happy. Roger had heard from Henry, too, and he was happy. The backup singers were happy, Rickey was happy.

Everyone but Duncan, apparently. He disappeared right after the show and when Booker asked the hotel manager, she was told that he'd already checked out.

It took eight phone calls and seven voicemail messages before she caught up with him.

"Where *are* you?"

"On my way to Milan. That's where you want me a week Friday, yeah?"

"I thought we'd all travel together. That's the usual way it's done. We have a seat for you on the plane."

"I wanted to try out one of those ultrafast trains they got here in Italy," Duncan said. "I'll see you in Milan—don't worry, I won't be late! I'll probably beat you there."

Booker didn't like it but there wasn't much she could do. "All right, I'll see you at the hotel. Don't forget we have rehearsal day after tomorrow."

"What for? These Italian guys are pros, right? We all know all the songs, Booker. It's not that hard."

Booker stood her ground. "We're expecting you at rehearsal day after tomorrow. Don't screw up."

"Well, that's bloody disrespectful."

"Come on, Duncan, I don't have the energy for this. Be a grownup, earn your money." After she hung up, she couldn't shake the bad feeling.

But even though she liked to pride herself on her instincts, it turned out she was wrong. Duncan was everything she'd hoped he could be the entire time they were in Milan, and later, in Venice.

At least, it seemed so at first. But, as it turned out, Booker wasn't the only one who thought so. Sophia, one of the backup singers, fell under his spell, and by the time they got ready to leave for Paris, she was into full-scale diva mode, demanding that she be allowed to continue on the tour, that he take her to America, buy her a house, a dog and a sports car.

Booker sat in the secret garden of the Palazzo Ferrante Grand Canal, nibbling at an antipasto and washing it down with a sublime glass of sangiovese. The hotel was one she would remember, long after all of the others, reliable, predictable and occasionally gorgeous, had vanished from her memory. Some people liked every hotel room to seem familiar, decorated in the same colors, with the same furniture and the same pictures on the walls. Booker had her phases like that, and she did appreciate that a certain standard was being maintained.

But every once in a while, she craved something she'd never seen before. This garden unfolded behind a door at the back of the restaurant. She'd walked past the indoor tables and then out to the patio, with its half a dozen tables and small stage for a string quartet. A waiter motioned toward the wall at the back of the restaurant, stepped forward to open the door for her, and she'd discovered this little garden with its boxwood and cypress clipped with complete precision and its jasmine, rosemary and lavender almost putting Booker into a swoon each time she took a deep breath.

He brought her a menu that looked like an encyclopedia, bound in leather. She asked him to choose for her, and he'd returned with a plate of meat, cheese, olives and anchovies.

Her telephone rang. *Shad Palmetto.*

"Hey Shad."

"Booker. Listen, we have a problem."

"When else do you ever call me?"

"Don't be a smartass. We're getting calls from someone named Sophia, demanding that we overnight ship her a credit card with her name on it, and put it on Rickey's tab.

Do you know anything about this?" Shad was breathing hard, as if he'd just run a few feet to the elevator.

"Yeah, I know Sophia. She's one of the backup vocalists we hired in Italy."

"Does Rickey want her to have a credit card?" Shad didn't stop to wait for Booker's answer. "Well, whether he does or he doesn't, it's not up to him, to put people on the expense account list. Tell him to use cash, like everybody else does when they're paying for a distraction!"

Booker almost reached for her glass of wine but stopped herself; she wouldn't allow this jerk to spoil anything so superb.

"Is that what everybody else does, Shad? Really." Booker looked around the garden, thinking *He's six thousand miles away, he's six thousand miles away.* "Yeah, well, I'll pass that along to Rickey, thanks for calling, oh, I'm getting some static now, I think we've lost our connection, bye!"

Booker felt so weary. She was just too old for all this crap. She hadn't expected that at age fifty, this Rickey-fake, this employee, would have the energy to cause so much trouble either. She would have to straighten all this out, with both of them.

Later that day, after a brief verbal tussle with Sophia, made even more difficult by Sophia's simple English and Booker's pretty much nonexistent Italian, she convinced the singer that she was thinking of leaving her entire life in Roma to follow a man who didn't seem that interested and who could get any woman he wanted, anywhere, and probably would. Booker was never quite sure whether she'd been able to dazzle Sophia with reason or whether it was the eighty thousand dollars she offered her, but that explosion quickly fizzled out.

From Venice, they moved on to Paris. Booker sat in the lobby bar of the Hôtel Colette, an exquisite glass of Grand cru Bordeaux on the tiny mahogany table in front of her. The walls were papered in green and gold velvet, interrupted every dozen feet or so with a painting that looked as if it belonged in a museum. Marble columns on either side of a fireplace added to the overall atmosphere of comfort and peace. Oh yeah, she could perch here for a while.

Booker was really looking forward to this stop. It was not that she expected to see much of it; there hadn't been much recreation time in any of these European cities on this tour. But it was the next to last stop and she was starting to feel that she had successfully managed Duncan Donovan through his first appearances as Rickey T. It was a relief and she was almost in a mood to celebrate. The first reports on the numbers were showing that they'd turned a corner on the financial troubles, too.

Her phone rang.

"You're giving them too much experimental shit." It was Roger. His voice was low and he sounded dangerous.

Booker held it away from her ear. "What experimental shit?"

"The songs! Nobody in Venice or Milano was recognizing the songs!"

"Well, there were a few that came from some of the more recent albums—"

"That! That's what I mean! They don't want to hear songs they don't know! They don't want to hear songs that were stolen from somebody else!"

Was he talking about *Island Afternoon?*

"They want to hear "Leaving Lorraine". And "Looking for Someone", those ones, the ones everybody knows. The ones they can sing along to because they know the sounds of the syllables even if they can't speak English. Come on, Booker, get him to change the set list for this last concert or we'll get ruined in the reviews! We won't be able to sell enough tickets anywhere else."

Even though, at this point, the only other 'anywhere else' was London, (and they were nearly sold out there), but she got Roger's point. Rickey, the real Rickey, was still in charge of the set list, even though he was thousands of miles away from the stage where the songs were being sung.

When Booker talked to him that night, she insisted that he had to change his choices for Paris, even though he protested that Roger was using him as nothing more than a jukebox. Booker tried to get him to see that Roger was just a channel for the fans, the European ones in this case, but Rickey wasn't buying it. He was pissed and he shut down the call in a royal snit.

Booker spent most of the Paris concert sitting backstage with her nose in her laptop computer, trying to come up with a plan. She did look up often enough to notice that Rickey had changed the set list to the 'greatest hits' show that Roger wanted, and that he insisted the fans wanted. Booker didn't really know what the fans wanted, and she didn't know whether Roger did either. Cosmo would know, but Rickey had given Cosmo his walking papers. They could sure use him now. What did they need to do to get the old-time fans coming back for more? And bring in a few new ones?

More than a few.

She needed a career strategy for the coming year. Not just Rickey's career—everybody's. Her own. How much more time off would Rickey take? Could they count on Duncan as their go-to? Should they invest this money they'd just made in more music and concert tours, keep the business going? Or was it time to shut down, figure out an annuity of some kind for Rickey, for herself, for anybody else they felt they owed, and just cash in their chips?

Booker got on the phone with Rickey the next day, while the others set out for the Paris sight-seeing tour. She crossed her fingers they'd leave the shopping streets off the itinerary; the credit cards were all nearly maxed out. The waiter stopped by her table and she could have sworn she saw him raise an eyebrow, then roll his eyes at her talking on her phone. In public, was that the problem? Too bad: she had business to do. She ordered a macaron and a glass of Chablis, then turned her attention to Rickey.

"Rickey, this has to be the end of it. I'm exhausted," Booker said.

"Exhausted why?"

"The touring, the running interference with the accountants, the dealing with the record label," she said. "But even more than that. Keeping Duncan in line and keeping 'our little secret'."

"Ha. You haven't called it that since about 1985," Rickey said. "All right, Book, I know. It gets harder as we get older."

"It's been hard since the beginning," Booker said. "And I've got Shad breathing down my neck again."

"What does he want this time?"

"He thinks you're having some kind of midlife crisis. Spending too much money. Being a juvenile delinquent with a pack of low-rent women. Phoning it in at the concerts instead of delivering your best."

"How can I be pulling all this shit when I'm not even there!"

Booker sighed. "Yeah, I know, it's Duncan Donovan he's reacting to. But he thinks it's you."

"And why would the money I spend be any of his business!"

"He's worried about finances constantly, and yours just got swept up in the general commotion. All the changes with the internet, with music sampling and all the downloading have him so spooked that he's convinced we'll all be broke in a year." Booker moved her chair a bit to get out of the direct airflow of the cigarette that had just been lit up at the table next to her. "I'm not sure he's that wrong, to tell you the truth, Rick. The way people listen to music these days, and the way they get it . . . I think it's going to mean that you'll have to bring in a lot more from the concerts. Get into bigger venues, maybe. Either that or start a perfume line or a clothing design business, like some of these other guys."

"I'm not going to make perfume, Booker, geez!" Rickey sounded like he was two inches away from the edge of a cliff. "I've never heard you so negative."

"Well, this guy, this Duncan, is just more work than any of the other three."

"Should we get rid of him?"

"No, I don't think that would solve anything. And I don't want to find and train anybody new. Assuming I'll have to do that? You aren't planning on coming back to work?"

His silence answered that question.

"Can we at least make an exit plan?" Booker asked. "Or do we keep doing this until we drop in our tracks?"

"A lot harder for you than for me, Book, I get that," Rickey said.

She was relieved—and quite surprised, actually, that he would admit that.

"How about this?" Rickey asked. "How about a farewell tour?"

Booker sat up so straight, so quickly, that the server thought it was a signal to him and came bustling over. She waved him away. "You'd do that?"

"Why not? Cher's done it, The Who, Kiss, Motley Crue, the Doobie Brothers."

"Interesting that all the acts you mention came back on the stage after the farewell show."

She could hear Rickey grinning. "There's always a loophole. But between you and me, Book, the idea is that this will be the farewell tour and it will mean the end to the shows. I'm the only one owns the legal right to the name. Our buddy Duncan there can't keep touring just cuz he wants to, and none of others will want to let go of their pay checks."

"How are we gonna keep on paying them if nobody works anymore?"

"We'll make so much on this farewell tour that we can set it up so that we pay them in perpetuity. We'll have royalties from the publishing, we'll have income from album sales. It'll all work out, Booker! Come on. I thought you'd be thrilled to hear this."

"There are some parts of it that appeal to me, I'll admit," Booker said.

"We have to crank it up higher than we've done lately. Five dates won't do it, we have to go big or go home. We need that fan club making lots of noise for us."

"The Rickets?"

"The Rickets. Making a racket. Ha! What's Cosmo doing these days?"

"Last I heard he was managing a hotel in Chicago."

"Let's get him on board."

"That might be hard to do, since the last time you saw him, you threw him under the bus."

"No harm in asking him. All he can do is say no."

***

You know that feeling you have when you do a jigsaw puzzle and you're down the last dozen pieces and you think you're getting there, to the final piece? You put the last one in, look over the thing . . . and there's one missing? That's what Rickey had going on this afternoon.

He sat on the deck of his latest sloop, the *Portofino Princess*, registered in Nassau and currently docked in Marseilles. He was close enough that he could have gone to Paris for the concert, if he felt like it, but he didn't. He didn't even let on to Booker that he was in France. He had felt completely disconnected from the Rickey T life, as if everything that happened was happening to someone else. Turned out they didn't need him at all, which suited him just fine. The Paris concert had gone very well, according to all reports.

He'd been hanging around the Cote d'Azur for a month now, using the boat as home. He hadn't gone anywhere and wasn't planning on going anywhere, but somehow it was comforting just to be on board, to know that if he really wanted to, he could pull up anchor and just frigging go.

Comforting was what he needed. He thought he'd had the whole puzzle done. He and Booker had figured out the money solution, he was convinced they could keep going with their long con for as long as they wanted, and needed to. But . . .

Rickey looked down at the piece of paper he'd been holding since the delivery guy had handed it over, after waiting for a signature.

I know the Rickey T on stage in Paris was a fraud and I know where you are. I'll be in touch again soon—and I'll be expecting a little something for my cooperation.

***

For the next few days, Booker and Rickey both held their breaths, waiting for some other communication from . . . whoever that was. Could it be one of the three previous Rickey fakes, Booker wondered? One of the session musicians they'd hired over the years? One of the fans?

Nothing else arrived, although that didn't soothe Booker's anxiety. It just left her with that awful feeling of waiting for the other shoe to drop. Rickey wasn't much help; he didn't seem nearly as tense about it as she was. She called Henry and he advised her to just ignore it, unless there was another note or a call. She called Cosmo, swore him to even more secrecy, and asked whether he had any thoughts. His suggestion was that it was just a fishing 'expedition'— somebody who really didn't have any information or know anything but who was casting a line out there, to see what might happen. Maybe it was even a prank, Cosmo thought.

He wanted to be back in their inner circle, Booker could tell, and she had no doubt that he'd kept the secret the entire time he'd been away. She decided to ask Rickey again, about letting Cosmo back in, after this particular bit of dust had settled.

Booker gave it a few more days of stewing, then just had to put it aside and get on to the next matter. Make that 'matters', plural. She had to settle the debts Duncan Donovan had run up on the credit card. Make that 'cards', plural. He'd maxed out the one she had given him for his own use and just this morning, Booker had discovered her own card missing. She'd managed to get it shut down right away and stop the bleeding, but she suspected Duncan and it just made her feel like punching him. She'd tried confronting him quite a few times and somehow, he managed to weasel out from under her questions, every time.

What was the matter with him? He was being given a ton of money, he had a gig most second-level singers would kill for, and yet he couldn't deliver what Booker was looking for: just a smooth ride, that's all, just for a little while.

She munched on her croissant and sipped her chocolate. This was her last breakfast at a sidewalk café. Tomorrow, they were taking off for London and after that, for the States. The bank accounts were healthy enough from this brief European tour that she could stop worrying about having to declare bankruptcy any time soon.

But it was only a temporary solution. They needed a much longer tour, new songs, and new fans. Old songs and nostalgic fans would help to do the trick, too. A farewell tour was the ideal solution, but Rickey was backing away from his promise to do one.

It was his idea in the first place, but now he was making noises about changing his mind. Booker was sure that a retirement tour would be the ideal hook to bring in ticket buyers and fill the seats in the big arenas once again. Nothing like thinking something will soon be gone to bring people to the table. She was pretty sure there was a famous, brilliant song about that.

But Rickey was now saying that he wasn't "ready" to retire.

Ha! Ironic, given that he had essentially retired in 1984, when he was only thirty years old.

CHAPTER TWENTY-THREE

2005

Chicago

A few months later, Booker was still working on the farewell tour idea. This year, Rickey would turn fifty-one, and for some reason, that age spooked him in a way no other had. Any mention of retiring, saying farewell, or slowing down in any way set off the rebel in him. Meanwhile, every day, she kept on working harder than ever to keep the secret that Rickey wanted kept.

The weather in Chicago was glorious that spring. During the weeks after the river had been turned green for St. Patrick's Day, the days were as warm as those coming in June. Booker met Cosmo for a pint of Guinness at a patio place on the Magnificent Mile and she had to smile as he came bouncing up to her table. Even in middle age, the guy still oozed enthusiasm.

Cosmo was delighted to be invited back in. He was a man who had no idea what a grudge was. Even if he were told that he was entitled to hold one, because of the way he'd been let go, he would have shaken his head and insisted that forgiving Booker and Rickey felt like a better idea. When Booker brought it up, he said that bygones were bygones. He felt eager to go, with the future a wide-open road ahead of them, instead of a narrow, potholed lane through a forest of nearly dead trees. Once Booker got her head cleared of the metaphors and images he was shoveling in front of her, she got to the point:

"Will you come back on board, Cosmo? Rickey thinks we really need you to finish up this story, bring it on home. And I really need someone who is halfway sane that I can talk to about this."

It took Cosmo all of two minutes to agree and Booker felt that relief that everyone feels when they get a new ally.

"Did you ever hear from whoever sent that threat note in Paris?" Cosmo asked.

Booker took a few seconds to inhale the delicious aroma of her deep-dish pizza before answering. "No, no more notes. But we've had a few strange calls at the office."

"Strange, how?"

"Silence. Nobody there at the other end of the line."

"Who do we think it might be? I think we can discount any possibility Rickey's in any danger of any kind. This person, whoever it is, probably just wants money. Or the glory of being on the 'inside', of letting Rickey T know he knows."

"Or maybe, she knows."

Cosmo looked impressed. "She. Hmm. Who do you think?"

"Nobody in particular, Cosmo. I just want to open up the thinking, to both genders."

"Got it. Any idea what they want?"

"None." Booker said. "We've got no clear information about what the person wants or how to get in touch with him. Or her."

"What about Sturgess Mesley?"

"I don't know, I just don't see that the guy could bring up that much initiative, not to mention planning or foresight," Booker said. "I mentioned his name to Rickey in Paris, but Rickey didn't think so, either." Booker could hear her own voice getting shrill with frustration. "I think we need another theory."

Cosmo got to his feet, pulling his jacket from the back of his chair. "I gotta go, Booker, but if I get a brainwave, I'll call you. I'm picking up the president of the Chicago branch of the Rickets. We're going to the concert tonight together tonight. Are we going to see a good show?"

Booker made a face. "Duncan is unpredictable, to say the least. He might be on his game, and we might see a shining example of Rickey T at his best. He could just as easily be in a mood to be a diva. But that might be entertaining, too. I don't know."

"What will he do, if the next tour is the farewell tour?"

"He'll be tough to handle, I know. May not need to think about that anyway. Rickey is starting to fuss about the idea. I don't know what he thinks we'll do—go on doing shows until we're sixty-five? Seventy?"

"Nobody wants to see a seventy-year-old rock star."

"Rickey thinks they do. Not every legend, just one or two, just the special ones. Like him."

Booker and Cosmo made eye contact and burst out, laughing. "You stop," she said, giving Cosmo a little push. "You're bringing out my disloyal side, and you know that makes me ve-e-ery uncomfortable."

Booker got up to walk out with him. "I'm glad we're back together, Cosmo. And that you've still got all your Fan Club contacts. Although I might have to go to the mat with the people in hotel world who want to keep their hooks in you."

Cosmo laughed. "I can do both, Booker, I can do both."

***

Once the dust settled and Booker had finished making what

she could of the goodwill and positive press that filtered out from the European gigs, she had twenty dates for them in a ribbon that stretched from Milwaukee, Wisconsin, west to Eugene, Oregon, south to El Paso, Texas and northeast to Portland, Maine. She was taking every booking that was offered. Rickey seemed to be preoccupied with something else. He had mentioned that he'd taken up painting and all he ever seemed to talk about was not missing the light. Sometimes he wrapped up a phone call in ninety seconds, because the light was suddenly right.

The upside was that he wasn't questioning the tour schedule very closely. He didn't seem to mind that they were booked into Fargo, North Dakota right in the middle of the blizzard of the century or Fayetteville, Arkansas during a plague of giant bugs, sweeping through.

Duncan minded, though, and after glowering for a few weeks, he stepped up his communications campaign. Ha! A better description was 'sabotage campaign'. In Boise, onstage, he pretended he couldn't hear the other musicians through his earpiece and screwed around with the band, starting into numbers then breaking off, eight bars in. In Savannah, he suddenly announced that he had a problem with his left leg and had to perch on a stool during most of the show. In Santa Fe, he launched into long, long guitar solos—one of them clocked in at fourteen minutes! Once they were back at the hotel, the local keyboard player they'd hired demanded a meeting of the three of them, then stormed around Booker's hotel room, raging that he just couldn't manage a show and a band full of players who barely knew each other under these conditions, Duncan just shrugged, in a very Rickey T way. Said he had such a sore throat he was in danger of losing his voice entirely and had to pace himself.

"Pace himself! He has to 'pace' himself." Booker could hear the piano player ranting all the way down the hall to his room.

"I saw that." Booker got herself up in Duncan's face.

"Saw what?" Duncan's tone was defiant.

"I saw that self-satisfied little smile, Duncan, you slug." It was riot-act time. "Look, these working conditions are challenging for everybody. Could you please suck it up and be a professional?"

"This is not what I signed on for," he said. "These are not Rickey T-level gigs. This is B-list and you know it."

Booker went to her hotel room door and held it open for him to leave. "Wait till you see the schedule for the next month. We're doing a corporate gig, then an anniversary party. And some IT company exec's 50th birthday party a few weeks after that."

"Rickey would never stand for that, if he had to play those places!"

"Rickey knows all about it and he's in favor of us doing anything that makes business sense."

Duncan took the hint and stormed off to his own room. One part of Booker really didn't give a shit what the egotistical jerk thought, but another part felt a little sympathy for him. He was right, this wasn't what he'd signed on for and it wasn't the picture she and Rickey had painted for him, at the beginning. But that's life, buddy, and nobody said it would be fair. Or predictable.

The next morning, Booker had an email from a promoter with an invitation that seemed to be saying that things would be improving. Las Vegas! They wanted Rickey T to do a concert.

She needed to do a little market research, though, and the best thing to do was get on the phone with Cosmo.

"The idea's great, Booker!"

"Really?"

"Really. That's what I think, anyway. But I can ask a few other people, long-time fans of Rickey T."

Whoa. Booker wasn't sure she wanted this potential news announcement, or the way they were strategizing it, to go outside their little circle. This gig, if it came up ever, might not happen for a couple of years.

It was as if Cosmo read her thoughts. 'Don't worry, I won't give anything away. I'll just ask how far they'd go to see a Rickey T concert, had they ever been to Las Vegas, that kind of thing."

"Who are they?"

"The ones I'm thinking of have taken committee jobs in the Rickets at various times. Don't worry, Book. Two of them are in the west and I can have some answers for you by this afternoon."

***

Cosmo was pleased to have a task to do for Booker. He knew that it was Rickey's call, to let him back in and 'un-fire' him, but he had to have Booker onside, too. It was a good thing this item was so easy. He knew thousands of Rickey T fans and getting an answer to his questions would be a piece of cake.

He called Bella in New York first. Bella had been a fan since the early eighties, throughout many moves from city to city, like Cosmo had. She was now a retired real estate agent and concert attendance was her favorite hobby. She said a concert in Las Vegas would be awesome, and no, she didn't think it signaled anything about Rickey's relevance. Anything Rickey did was all right with her. She was almost like a cult follower. He thought her reason for being a fan was that she had to believe in someone other than herself. The point was not whether Rickey was exactly Rickey or how cool he was, or was not, how trendy or how popular. It was what the songs said and how they made her feel.

Anne in Seattle was his next call. She worked with Cosmo at his first hotel in the Pacific Northwest and once upon a time, she was one of Linda's friends. She went with them to a few Rickey T concerts and she paid for so many years of annual dues for the Rickets that she got put into the lifetime membership section. Being a Rickey T fan was a major part of her self-image. She liked action/adventure movies, she read political thrillers, and she liked Rickey T's music.

She was also a Vegas kind of girl and she thought Cosmo's question about whether Rickey should play Vegas was dumb.

Ethan in L.A. was his third call. Ethan was as cynical as they get and if a Rickey T concert in Las Vegas was cheesey, he'd say so. His standards were high. Ethan thought that most of the music world was dark, self-centered and only after one thing—money. Would he go all the way to as Vegas for a Rickey T concert? First, he wanted to know what time of year they were talking about; then he wanted to know if the venue would be five-star. He dropped a hint about being paid to go but when Cosmo wouldn't pick it up, he returned to the main question. Yeah, he thought Las Vegas was a good place to go for a rock concert and no, he didn't think it was any kind of negative signal about Rickey T.

When Cosmo got back to Booker that afternoon, he proudly presented the results of his research but she barely seemed to hear him. Finally, he asked, "Is this not giving you some answers to your questions about sending Rickey to perform in Las Vegas? I thought that was what you wanted."

"Sorry, Cosmo, my mind is elsewhere."

"Duh."

The silence went on for a full minute, and Cosmo had to ask, "What is it?"

Heavy sigh. "It's Rickey. He's furious with Duncan and he's demanding I hire a new guy."

"Already? And aren't the numbers starting to be rather . . . large?"

"Exactly. I think the risk is too high, but Rickey says we can't tolerate a thief for even a few months."

"Duncan's a thief?"

"Well, he wouldn't call it that, but he has been helping himself to credit cards without getting authorization for expenses. Last week, he bought a cheetah."

"A cheetah!"

"Yeah, he says Rickey T has to be doing outrageous things, being wild, living on the edge, or lose the fans."

"I doubt it."

"Yeah, and you're the expert on the fans, you'd know! We'll use that ammo with Duncan but for right now, I have to get his mitts off the platinum card. And figure out a way to get the other employees to stop doing what he says without telling them he's not really him. If you know what I mean."

"Yeah, I get it. What did he do?"

"Told one of the roadies to go to his latest dolly, give her a plane ticket and tell her to get lost."

"Yuck."

"Yeah, well. Apparently, Duncan says, that's the way it's supposed to be done, by a "man in his position". And that's a quote."

"Asshole."

"Yeah. So, I agree with Rickey to a point, but I don't want to screw up the whole scene by firing him, if I can handle it some other way."

"I have total faith in you, Book, and I know that once Rickey gets done blowing off steam, he does, too. You can talk to Duncan, get him to see it your way, and you'll have him around for ages to come."

"I hope so. Because I'm getting bloody tired."

The next day, the Vegas offer blew up when the promoter decided to move an ice skating act to the top of his priority list and a rock 'n' roll legend concert to the bottom. He insisted to Booker that the only changing in their deal was the dates, and that he fully intended to put Rickey T on stage. Just not right away.

CHAPTER TWENTY-FOUR

2008

Las Vegas

Three years later

When they got to the resort for the Vegas show, Booker told Rickey on the phone that she was less than impressed. In fact, she was very disappointed. She said that Duncan would not be happy and that it wouldn't live up to his growing sense of his own importance.

The concert was going to be in the showroom of a legacy hotel downtown and they'd promoted it as more special than being on the Strip. Rickey looked it up online and told Booker that for once, his opinion was in sync with Duncan's: he didn't think the place looked grand enough for a Rickey T show. The show was part of a package deal and the ads clearly aimed the event at the gamblers, the cheap, unsuccessful ones. People paid a flat price, stayed at a hotel forty miles from the city. Rickey's name on the magazine ad was about the size of the health warning footnote at the bottom of a menu.

Rickey T and his band were feature performers as part of a "resort experience". Guests checked in, hung out in the room, played the slots and spent time at the blackjack tables. They had a DJ party when the weekend started, then the next day it was a long ride on a party bus to the Rickey T concert, into a "hospitality suite" for one drink, then herded up the stairs to seats at the back of the showroom. The next morning, the guests had to go to a pitch to buy a "rock-concert time-share" at an inflated price, on terrible terms.

As she'd predicted, once Duncan found out a bit more about the gig, he was as petulant as a spoiled brat who's been given ice cream when he thought he was promised a pony. She was sitting in front of a slot machine, staring at a bunch of different kinds of fruit, when her phone rang.

"Hey, Rickey. Yeah, he's pissed. He's making a lot of threatening noises about calling a halt to the arrangement."

"He doesn't fire us, we fire him!"

"Well, Rick, he doesn't see it that way." Booker pulled at the slot machine handle. Nothing. "What should we do? . . . Rick? . . . ?"

He was gone.

***

Rickey realized that it was time for him to get more directly involved. Geez, was this the kind of work that Booker thought they should be doing? It took him all of two minutes to make a decision. He'd have to pull in to shore, get his incognito trunk out of storage and plan for a few days of disguise. When an event like this Vegas gig felt like a sea change, something told you that you should be there.

He checked in at the Bellagio and no one gave him any attention, other than the courtesy they gave every guest. The costume was working. Longish dark hair, glasses, a little extra nose, and a business suit. It was the same one he'd worn in Dublin a few years back and he liked it.

Rickey was in a generally good mood; Vegas always put him there. Yeah, there was a bit of stormy weather but they'd get through it, like they'd sailed through everything. Booker had been crying the blues lately about the difficulty in getting gigs. She'd been beating the bushes, trying to build on the momentum from the Europe tour, and so far, all she'd been able to find was this Vegas show and an invitation to work at a resort in the Caribbean. But that one was quite a long time away, four years, and she was worried that Duncan wouldn't be happy that they were asking for a 'greatest hits' show. All oldies all the time.

Rickey told her to do what she had to do to keep Duncan in line. After the brief flurry of concern about that anonymous note a while ago, he had gone back to relying on his stand-in to do the work he didn't want to do. Duncan had to be available and Rickey counted on that, to manage his own stress. He wanted Booker to remind Duncan that he was an employee in a job that he was lucky to have. But, Rickey said, he had to agree, off the record, that being told to play an oldies show was his idea of a rotten time, too. It was perfectly fine for some guys, but not for him.

The show went as expected, pretty much as you'd expect all Vegas shows to go. The room was filled with people dressed in their idea of fancy, with their faces showing either high spirits or determination to have a good time, depending on whether they were near the beginning or end of their vacation and on how well their luck had run at the tables. Rickey sat alone right at the back, watching the fans come and go. Vegas, baby. It was actually kind of depressing.

Duncan put on a good performance, although he seemed to be moving a bit stiffly. Booker had mentioned that she thought he was aging, but when she'd brought it up with him, suggesting that he take up yoga or some other regular regime for stretching his joints and muscles, he blew up, accusing her of undermining his confidence.

Rickey wasn't surprised when Duncan didn't show up

as the band gathered in the hotel lobby to head out for some rest and relaxation after the concert. From the things that Booker had been telling him, Duncan wasn't in a good frame of mind. Also, it fit in with Rickey T's style over the years anyway; he rarely socialized with the roadies, the musicians, the suits—not with anybody, really.

Booker had told Rickey that the group had taken hold of an idea during rehearsal and that they'd like to try out a karaoke bar. He decided to stop by to watch the fun. The place was on a quiet side street, a long way from the neon, the noise and anything resembling sophistication. It was just the right place for professionals who don't want to be recognized to hang out. You might wonder why they'd bother, when they could (and did) sing and play for hours every day. You would think they had all the attention they could wish for, performing under spotlights on a stage in front of thousands of people.

Yet there they were, sitting around crummy little tables drinking cheap beer, pouring over laminated sheets of song lists and laughing about each other's choices.

Out on the dance floor, a couple cleared the space, as everyone stopped to watch them. She was in a short black dress, with a low-cut back and glittery slash lines on the bodice. Her heels were easily five inches, a great finish to legs that went on forever. Her partner was precisely the same height as she, slick and trim in black shirt and pants. The minute they started dancing, it was obvious that they had practiced. A lot. Professional training, probably. He held her firmly, occasionally tipping her backward over his arm and even pulling her up to straddle his hips on several of the fast numbers. Both of them had short silver hair, cut and combed in a very cool look. They were seventy-five years plus and they danced on and on, choosing their steps and style to match the karaoke songs the customers picked. You have to be impressed with people so confident and so sure they were meant to dominate a floor.

If it weren't for the dancing couple, Rickey might have stayed in his seat, quiet and invisible. But after half an hour or so, he had an itch to see them interpret one of his songs. None of his hired musicians was choosing a Rickey T song—they seemed to be in a country and western mood. Nobody else in the rest of the crowd stood up to sing anything Rickey had ever written or recorded, either. Maybe this was proof he was just as irrelevant as he feared.

Rickey sidled up behind Booker as she stood by the bar, waiting to pick up another beer. "Hey lady," he said.

She jumped about a mile. "R—! What the hell are you doing here?"

"Came over to watch the fun. Nobody knows it's me."

"Not even me! I noticed you a while ago but I just pegged you as some guy here for a convention who misplaced the Strip and got lost. Or maybe a taxi driver got a laugh out of dropping you off here 'by mistake'. Didn't recognize you at all."

Rickey was very pleased with himself. "Good. It works, and it'll keep on working. People don't see what they don't expect to see."

"What did you think of the show?"

Rickey shrugged. "Not much, one way or the other. But it pays, right?"

"Yeah, it does. It's nicer when you can throw the long bomb and get the points that way, but short yards works, too. I'm looking at a few other possibilities for this year. One at a casino resort spa in the Caribbean and one on a cruise ship."

"Aw, Booker, really? That's what we're doing?"

"That's what we're doing. As long as they have an audience and will pay an invoice, we can be there."

Full stop. She couldn't be more definite than if she were listing the oceans of the world or the colors in the rainbow.

"I gotta move around a bit, get some fresh air," Rickey said. "I'll leave you to your beer and your group."

"You're going?"

"Don't know yet. Maybe."

Rickey circled the room a couple of times, watched the vintage dancers, and then headed for a chair at one of the tables near the tiny stage. He picked up the laminated song list and glanced through it. Yeah, they did have "Looking for Someone Looking for Me". He signaled the server, put his five-dollar bill down on the table top and motioned for the microphone to be brought over to him.

The song was a good one, always had been, always would be. But Rickey could tell, as he sang along with the tinny, clunky background music, that no one in the place recognized it. No one looked at him while he sang.

Even the dancing couple took a break.

What was he doing all this for? What had any of it been for?

***

Rickey was not opposed to the idea of going to the Caribbean to supervise a show. It was just a matter of getting his boat into harbor in Nice, getting out to the airport, then sitting in a comfortable seat while he watched them close the door. A few rounds of drinks, a nice meal, a good night's sleep, and when they opened the door, he stepped down to a field surrounded by palm trees.

Dominican Republic

Rickey stood at the back of a room, watching his double do a show. How many times had he done this now? He was just bored enough to do the math and try to count them up. It had been over thirty years since the first time he'd hired a stand-in to perform in his place, but damned if he could remember how many times it was in each year that he'd had somebody going on for him. He'd have to look it up, he couldn't remember. Geez, he was over sixty now. He shouldn't be expected to remember anything.

He did recall that every one of these guys who impersonated him got a chance to live the rock star life, thanks to him, even if it was only for a little while. This one tonight had waited almost his entire adult life, as a low-grade, lounge-lizard type entertainer, before suddenly getting the chance to go on a big stage. The rush of doing a performance, the way that time stood still while you were in the zone, rocking that guitar and singing your heart out to tens of thousands of people—each one of his stand-ins had had that experience, without having to pay the price and face the nerves, the fear and the vomiting, as Rickey did. He didn't think they really appreciated that. But what could he expect? Those were his reactions, not theirs. He didn't think even Booker got it, sympathetic as she might be.

Rickey looked around the room. Not that big a stage, apparently. Where were they this time? Some island in the Caribbean. Booker must have negotiated some serious coin if they had agreed to bring Rickey T all the way to this remote place.

A young man stood in front of Rickey's table. "Is it all right if I join you?"

"Sure," Rickey said. "Let me buy you a drink."

The young man grinned. It was the standard joke at an all-inclusive resort, where the guests paid one, flat price and could drink 24/7 after that. "For free", some of them liked to think of it, forgetting they'd paid the three thousand dollars to be there in the first place.

"Where you from?" Rickey asked the young man, who put out his hand to shake.

"Solomon."

"Corey." Rickey used different names the way some men put on different jackets.

"Little village in the interior. About a five-hour bus ride from here. I go there on my days off, see the wife and kids. The rest of the week, I live in the dorm here with all the other staff."

"How do you like your job?"

"It's good. I'm paid to chat with people, take the solo ladies out to the dance floor, run the bingo games and activities by the pool during the day. A lot easier than roofing or gathering sargasso off the beach."

"You've done those jobs?"

"Done those jobs. And those are the jobs my cousins are still doing. I tell my kids 'learn to dance, learn to make conversation' or you'll be out in the hot sun till you're fifty."

"Or sixty, like I am," Rickey said, laughing.

"You, you're not doing manual labor, I can see that," Solomon said. "You couldn't afford to stay at a place like this for your vacation if you weren't rich."

Rickey took a few seconds and a gulp of his tropical drink to contemplate perspective: to him, this place was a comedown, so far down he felt like he was at the bottom of a chute. To Solomon, it was a place for unbelievably rich people.

Solomon wasn't done, chatting. "Some of us work as servers or tending bar, too."

"I've seen you guys on the beach," Rickey said. "Running back and forth, carrying trays of booze from ten a.m. on."

"We don't run far," Solomon said. "The bars are only about a hundred feet apart. I don't think that's for our convenience, though. I think the resorts are designed that way because they've figured out that's the way the tourists like them to look."

"I like to come to these places for the music," Rickey said. "How are the shows here?"

Solomon shrugged. "Depends what you like. They put on a lot of sixties and seventies oldies stuff. Each night of the week is a different theme. We got Broadway, we got *Grease*, we got Hollywood movie themes, you name it."

"Ever anything current?"

"Hardly ever."

"Always indoors?"

"The weather changes a lot. They don't want to risk

getting rained on or hit by lightning. And the humidity can be so high that the instruments go out of tune. That's a problem indoors, too, you know. That's why we use recorded music."

"Recorded music?" This was the first Rickey was hearing about this.

"Yeah, the singers sing along with an instrumental recording. Makes it easier with all their dancing, too, yeah? They get out of breath."

"Excuse me." And Rickey was up and out of his chair, on the phone to Booker.

"When do you get down here?"

"Late tonight, why?"

"We've got a few problems. They seem to think Rickey T sings along to recorded music."

"Like karaoke?"

He thought he heard Booker laughing. "Yeah, like karaoke. Come on, Booker! Weren't we going to hire local musicians when Duncan arrived here?"

"Duncan's gone, Rickey, remember? We let him go and we hired Sport Wellington."

"Does he know he's singing along to a tape?"

"Yes, of course. Everybody knows, Rickey. You knew it too, but you just forgot. Look, I gotta go. I've got a problem to take care of here if I'm going to make the plane this afternoon."

"Just tell them to wait for you for an hour or two."

"I don't do that anymore, Rickey, don't you remember that either? I'm flying commercial."

"What's your other problem?"

"I'm supposed to be meeting with a forensic musicologist this morning and he's half an hour late. Screws up the timing for my whole day."

"A forensic musicologist? What the hell is that?"

"Come on, Rickey, we talked about this. It's not enough anymore to be sure that every melody, every note and every line is unique. We also have to be sure the feeling of the song doesn't imitate any previous song."

"You're kidding."

"No, that's the way it's done. They have algorithms that can match up millions of songs and song fragments."

"Millions?"

"Billions! It's plagiarism checkers on the most incredible steroids ever invented. Intent means nothing, by the way. There's no such thing as a negligence or an accidental mistake defense when it comes to songwriting."

"You're really tense about this, Book."

"Don't you remember what happened to us when we got sued over Pretend Rickey Number Three copying that song? We lost so much money and so much face that it was the beginning of the slide."

"What slide? Again, come on, Book, you're overreacting." Rickey said. "Besides, that was a different situation. That guy actually knew he was copying somebody else's song and he went ahead and put his name on it anyway."

"Your name."

"Yeah, my name. So—he had to go."

"And I had a hell of a time, replacing him. Which reminds me—you giving any thought to returning to work permanently so that we don't have to walk this tightrope with replacements anymore?"

"Book, you've been asking me that every month since 1984."

'I should make it every week," she muttered. "Okay, look, this musicologist is walking in now. I'll see you later tonight."

"But what about the mess this concert is going to be?"

"I think it's a stretch to call it a concert, Rickey. Just go watch from the back, as usual, and be glad it's not you up there."

"But it's my name!" But he was wailing into a dead phone.

Since when did Booker end the telephone call?

Rickey scanned the room and saw that most of the seats were taken. People wearing tropical shirts, white pants or short dresses with a lot of flowers on them were wandering in from the lobby. There was no sign of a ticket window or anybody controlling access. Was Rickey T included as part of the all-inclusive?

The lights went down, some cheesey strobe light started raking the audience, and an announcer off-stage told them, in his best 'You'd better be impressed with this!' voice: "Ladies and Gentlemen, we are so pleased to welcome to our stage here at the Palm Fronds Resort, Mr. Rickey T!"

The latest substitute, Sport somebody, strode onstage and Rickey felt like turning around to shush all the drinkers and chatters around him. You'd think they'd realize they were out in public, not in their own living rooms He watched Sport struggle to get their attention, even with the first two numbers, two of Rickey's biggest hits.

Then, Rickey realized that something else was going on. Despite the help from the microphone, he could barely hear Sport's voice. After a few more bars, it was becoming very clear that the singer was losing it, croaking like an old frog, and stopping every few moments to rub his throat in pain. He gave the audience a few apologetic smiles but he wasn't getting much compassion. Without any backing vocalists or any other musicians on stage, Sport had no one to carry him for a while. He couldn't stop and drink some water or gargle with something. He stopped playing guitar and waved his hands toward the backstage area but the recorded music carried on. The guy in charge was probably out taking a smoke break—or turning up at one of his other jobs, calling bingo or teaching the salsa.

Rickey thought he heard a familiar voice and looked across the room. Was that Grant? Laughing? What was his brother doing in the Dominican Republic? He never left the States and certainly wouldn't leave home in the middle of NFL season. Sitting right beside him were Rickey's parents. They were laughing and pointing right along with Grant at

Rickey's pathetic performance onstage. Just like when he was a kid, Rickey wished the floor would open up and swallow him.

Or them.

"Mr. Rickey, Mr. Rickey!" A hand gripped his elbow and shook it.

It was Solomon, the staff guy he'd been talking and drinking with, earlier.

"Mr. Rickey, the manager would like to know if you would go on stage and sing with yourself."

"Why do you think I'm Rickey T? That's Rickey T, over there on that stage!"

"Whatever you say, sir. But will you go and sing? We all know it's you."

"No, I won't. This is bullshit."

"But you must, sir. There's a little problem with the bill and your credit card . . ."

***

Las Vegas

Rickey woke up to the red neon light wiggling its way into his room, between the blackout blinds he'd neglected to close completely. His cheeks, forehead and neck were sweaty and every one of his joints ached. He sat up in the hotel bed and tried to breathe as deeply as he could. Catching his breath wasn't easy—was he having a heart attack? His eyes focused on the stylized print of a slot machine that they'd used for room décor and he concentrated on calming himself down.

It was just a dream. There was no fifth Pretend Rickey named Sport, he wasn't being pushed to sing on an all-inclusive resort stage in the Caribbean, and he hadn't completely run out of money.

But was the dream just fear? Or was it prediction?

Rickey picked up his phone and speed-dialed. '1'. "Booker? We'll do the farewell tour. Set it up."

The Teens

CHAPTER TWENTY-FIVE

2014

New York

Six years later

It took five years to get Rickey T ready to say good-bye. Booker had gone to work on every person she'd met and every contact she'd made in thirty-five years, although the majority of them were retired now. Some had kids and grandkids running their businesses, though, or they had people they'd mentored to recommend to Booker. After a few sputters of the engines, it appeared she would be able to get *The Rickey T Leaving Lorraine for Good Tour* off the ground. Throughout the entire period, Booker sweated the possibility that Rickey would change his mind.

She'd had many sleepless nights in this office. It overlooked Central Park and the only reason she'd been able to get into it last year was that a friend of a friend had grandparents who leased it to people based on their own understanding of rental rates, an understanding that was formed sometime back when dinosaurs roamed the earth.

Booker had turned the two-bedroom apartment into a work-life space, like the ones on all the glossy websites nowadays, showing people how to adapt their lives to the gig economy. It was a new vocabulary for a new perspective on working and living. In Booker's opinion, it was the same as it had been back in the seventies: this was the living arrangement of the person who didn't have the scratch to rent an office.

But at least she was better off than she had been last year, when she was scouting coffee shops with reliable WIFI so that she could get her business done.

Rickey brewed a fresh cup of coffee, then sat down at her desk and pulled up the file for the Florida concerts. She had the Lakeland gig at Jenkins Arena pretty much settled and Miami wouldn't be far behind. She had meetings in the morning with Shad from the record company and a couple of publicity people from the upcoming shows. She had a lot of work to do before she saw them, and while a cup of strong coffee might seem dumb at two a.m., in fact, it was exactly what she needed.

Right after the Vegas show, Rickey took off and she didn't hear from him for almost a year. She juggled Duncan Donovan's calls as they beeped in about once a month—thank God for call display! He really didn't seem all that eager to get back to work, though. Each time, she told him they were working on booking a tour and that there wouldn't be any new material. Each time, he told her that he had new songs . . . well, actually, that he could have new songs very quickly, if they were going to go into studio to record . . . and each time she said "no thanks". She would let him know when there were details about the tour to pass along and she would give him plenty of notice when the kickoff date was firm.

Then, in 2010, two years after Vegas, Rickey resurfaced from somewhere near the Maldives and told her he was still going along with the idea of doing a Rickey T farewell tour. The commitment came with a lot of 'buts', though: "but I want to have at least five new songs ready to give them as a good-bye gift"; "but I don't want the concerts anywhere but in the U.S."; "but Duncan Doorknob has to promise to behave himself every step of the way"; and "but I want to give some careful thought to the timing". When Booker heard that last one, she told herself she could stand down. She went back to enjoying her New York City hobbies and she doubted that Rickey would ever be ready to say good-bye.

If there was any place it was good to be a sixty-year old single woman, it was New York City. Everyone she'd ever known came through town eventually, and she had many invitations to lunch, drinks or dinner on somebody's expense account tab.

The one who stood head and shoulders above all the others, and the one she dropped everything and all plans for on any kind of short notice, was Henry.

Whenever he wasn't around, she did not ever feel useless and irrelevant, as so many older people did. The streets of New York did more to make her feel alive and plugged-in than any golf course or lawn bowling club ever could. Booker did have occasional moments of self-study about her decisions to avoid marriage and children, but they were few and easily breezed through. She had never been one for trying to re-make decisions that had been made, and irrevocably made, long ago.

Cosmo had been popping up in Booker's email every few days ever since Vegas. At first, it was to ask what the tentative dates for the tour were. Then, as the months went by, it was to ask whether the tour was still on. Always, he offered to do whatever he could to help. The guy was a gem.

It turned out that she did have to take him up on his offer in 2011, when Duncan suddenly threatened to quit. The thought of hiring another Rickey stand-in just made her feel exhausted, and, as she explained to Rickey as vigorously as she could, the odds that she could find a fifty-seven-year old who could do a Rickey T show were dropping, while the risks that they'd be caught were rising. Booker wanted to smooth Duncan's feathers, whatever might be the reason for their ruffling, and with Rickey's reluctant agreement, she asked Cosmo to take on the job.

Cosmo returned from Duncan's hideout in New Mexico with the news that Duncan wanted to quit because he wanted to write a book. Dear God. Cosmo assured Booker that he'd been as persuasive as humanly possible and that he'd been able to get Duncan to see the downside for himself in writing a confessional. Apparently, Duncan had repeatedly insisted that it wasn't going to be a "confessional"; it was going to be a "how-to". *A how-to what??* How to play guitar, how to write a song, how to be a rock star, Duncan said. Cosmo said that it was going to take a personal intervention from Rickey to get Duncan to let go of the belief that expressing himself in print and online was what he needed to scratch whatever itch it was that he was feeling.

Booker had to put it into Rickey's hands and just let go, an experience that let her add two miles to her daily walk around the Park. He called back a day later and explained that what Duncan wanted was some attention and a feeling that the sun hadn't gone down on him yet. They made a plan for regular communication between Rickey and Duncan, no middle man. With frequent promises of the tour and more limelight time being just around the corner, Duncan was back on side. He stayed quiet and manageable through 2012 and 2013, and as New York mopped up from New Year's Eve, she started 2014 with *The Leaving Lorraine for Good Tour* well-slotted into her new project-management software program, with a tentative target launch date in 2019. Rickey had chosen the date, saying he liked the symmetry of forty-five years, but he still would not commit to a farewell tour.

Booker had her doubts that Duncan Donovan could be counted on for another five years.

***

New York

Booker scanned the large room on the 43rd floor of the Manhattan hotel. All of the seats at the tables were taken, and the dozens of reporters were impatient to get things rolling. Pretend Rickey, Shad, Sturgess and Mona Ray had seats at the table at the front of the room with Booker; real Rickey sat at the back, wearing a hoodie, a CNN T-shirt, jeans and a ball cap. After initial introductions, the first few questions had to do with logistics and then, almost right away, the skeptics took over, questioning Rickey's sincerity about this "so-called farewell tour".

Booker kept her cool, and assured the journalists repeatedly that this really would be Rickey's last public performances. The shows would start in Florida in less than a month. They were all sixty years old, after all—did they expect to carry on forever? And who would pay to come to see them, forever?

This year would be different, though, she rushed in to add, after catching sight of Shad's disapproving face. Last week at the meeting with Shad and Cosmo, they'd all agreed to treat this tour with just as much energy and attention, and just as little negativity, as if they were launching a career.

She glazed her gaze and scanned the room, zooming past Dwight Kettle and drifting over Duncan's sneer. She could practically read each of their minds: "I don't think this old guy will ever quit", from Dwight, and "Rickey T might be doing a farewell tour but I'll be in your face till you die", from Duncan.

Duncan had come to the press conference reluctantly. Despite all the extra attention from real Rickey over the past few years, delivered just as he'd demanded in the original job negotiation, he was quite unprofessional in his reactions to most of Booker's messages. Ever since Vegas, he'd been a king-sized pain in the ass—and he hadn't been a joy to work with before that, either. Booker did what she could, within the limits of her budget, Rickey's opinions, and her own resentments, to keep up with Duncan's expectations. It was practically a full-time job.

Of all of the questions asked at the press conference, she remembered only one. From Dwight Kettle—"So, Rickey . . . do you ever get tired of singing the same songs, over and over?"

***

Lakeland, FL

Duncan's room in the Ritz the night before the first stop of the tour was not a suite. It was a nice room, a large room, and right next door to Lulu's, but it was not a suite.

I don't know how Booker and Rickey expect me to do twenty shows in six months without making sure I'm happy every step of the way. I'll have to make it clear from tonight that I'm their golden goose. I'm not going to put up with any more of this low-rent shit. They might have forgotten some of that bullshit at that last resort, but I haven't. Nobody's going to tell me what I can and can't wear. Nobody's going to get away with tuning the wrong guitar or changing the key on me. Nobody's going to tell me how much we have to rehearse or how many times to run down each song.

And definitely, nobody's going to tell me who I can and can't sleep with!

Total crap, that night in Las Vegas, when they told me they were sending Tamara home. Then, they were lowering the ceiling on my credit card. Hell, it's like they don't know who I am.

***

The sound check went about as well as the previous afternoon's rehearsal (which meant not at all) but Booker told herself that that was a good omen for a good show. The musicians were all pros and very appreciative of the healthy fees they were being paid. None had ever worked with Rickey T before, none was under sixty-five, and none was a bitter sixties survivor. They'd just come to play the tunes and get the bread. Booker heard a bit of grumbling from the drummer, particularly when 'Rickey' would only play each song once, and in some cases, didn't even go all the way through. The temperatures went up even a little higher when 'Rickey' asked why the complaining, that Dylan did it that way. Booker came back with "So when are you getting your Nobel for Literature?", everybody laughed, and the moment passed.

It hadn't really passed for Duncan, Booker could tell, but he had learned years ago that in a showdown, she would try not to have to take sides and Rickey would look the other way, go dark and refuse to take Duncan's phone calls.

It was all quite annoying to Duncan but the money was so good he overlooked pretty much everything. Booker and Rickey had paid each of the fake Rickeys a percentage of the recording royalties, too. It had been a bit of a dance, keeping the details away from the attorneys and the accountants, but Booker made sure that none of the Rickey stand-ins' names appeared anywhere on any document except their personal-services contracts. None of the four of them knew about the other three.

When the concert started that night, Booker was in her usual place backstage. The band struck up the opening chords on "Leaving Lorraine" and the spotlight came up on Rickey's place on stage. That is, the place where Rickey was supposed to be. But somehow, he'd been delayed in the wings, and they could all hear him shrieking at the guitar tech. Bonaire turned her head slightly to take a look, staying in step with the other singers. Rickey was waving his arms around like a windmill in a Category Five storm.

"It is NOT tuned!"

Rickey stalked out onto the stage, clutching the guitar. "Get in line, you bitch," he hissed at Bonaire. Had he really said that? Booker put down her coffee and got ready—for what?

For whatever happened next.

***

Bonaire had known this job would be challenging as soon as she took it. Her reason was not that Rickey had turned into a grumpy old fart, big-time, or even that he'd crossed the disrespect line with her on the European tour ten years ago. It was the stage politics, here and now.

To her left, she could see Tamara Tides; it was well known that Rickey T had had a relationship with Tamara back in the day—and it was common knowledge that he and Lulu Sky, the singer to Bonaire's right, had a thing going on right now. Not that Bonaire was jealous; she'd never had any interest in the man. But whoa, couldn't you see this coming? Down the track at about ninety miles an hour? There would be a smashup, and truth be told, Bonaire would rather be at home, in Nowheresville, than on this stage in Lakeland, Florida, heading for bigtime Miami tomorrow night.

But the money was sensational, and so she planned to just keep her head down, her voice happening and her hand on her bag, while the rest of these babies thrashed it out.

They did not leave it back in the dressing room, like most professionals would do. All three of them were wearing gorgeous, long, slinky, glittery gowns, with white gloves to the elbow. As she stepped out in front, Bonaire saw Lulu step on Tamara's dress. It totally screwed up Tamara's slide to the side. Then one white arm-in-silk jabbed to the right, and Tamara's elbow connected with Lulu's ribs. Both women were just ready to lose their tempers in a manner that just might tear the roof off this old arena.

They lurched and stalled through the performance. Everyone was very relieved when the seventy minutes were finally over.

Afterward, Bonaire sat in her dressing room, looked in her mirror, and started to laugh.

Hey, I've been in other bands where the singers don't get along but never before when they let it show on stage. And never before when it was put in motion by the guy out front in the band! It was outrageous.

And this treatment from Rickey T has to stop. I mean, he's never been a gentleman, but this was over the top. He started in on us the minute we walked on stage. Bad enough, he ditched most of sound check, but he showed up near the end and just tore into people. Screaming, demanding. Everywhere else I've ever worked there at least was some recognition that we're all professionals, all in this together, you know? That if the music wasn't flowing right or even if there was a bit of pushing, you always felt like you weren't actually getting dissed, you know?

Not this time. He gets on stage late, takes it out on the guitar tech, knocks us all off balance with what he's doing to the songs, all the while making cow eyes at Tamara! And then five minutes later, staring at Lulu's ass!

I'll tell 'em after Miami tomorrow night. I'm goin' home.

***

Cosmo had come all the way from a gorgeous St. Thomas resort with a private pool attached to each suite for this concert. He'd left his to-do list for the Fan Convention only fifty percent done and he hadn't even finished unpacking before heading over to the show.

He was regretting it. There were the girl singers attacking each other, practically turning the concert into women's world wrestling, while Duncan Donovan was singing songs that the crowd could do better than he did. The drummer had decided that Rickey T was an asshole and he didn't care how much money he was risking—he wouldn't find the backbeat. And there was Booker—where *was* Booker?

Cosmo roamed around the concourse, looked into the upper rows behind the giant video screens, where Booker often liked to go to watch a concert, and then stuck his head into the green room. Nowhere.

He found his way to the steps to the stage, just at the moment when Duncan and the band were coming off. The sounds from the audience were less than enthusiastic, with the applause dying off after just ten seconds. No call for an encore, no stamping of feet, no whistling and definitely no smartphones lit and held up in appreciation. Duncan was angry; Cosmo could feel the waves of emotion just rolling from him. The three women singers carefully came down the steps, their six-inch heels preventing them from achieving quite the impressive stomping that Duncan was putting out. As soon as they reached the ground, they started shoving each other and if Bonaire hadn't intervened, he thought they would have seen full-on punching and hair-pulling.

Booker suddenly appeared and it was as if the whole place froze. Duncan glanced at her, straightened up and walked off toward the limo with an air of self-control. Bonaire lifted her chin, looked her two coworkers in the eyes, then led the way back toward their dressing rooms.

The four backing musicians came down the steps and Booker decided to feel glad that they had cleared the stage and didn't stay behind to light an amp on fire or something. They stopped in front of her.

"I quit!" The drummer was twirling his sticks between his fingers. It looked as though his next move would be to jump right out of his skin.

"And me," muttered one of the two guitarists. All the rest of the musicians chimed in.

"Hold on, hold on," Booker murmured, soothingly.

This would be interesting. Did she think she could turn this around with tone of voice alone?

Yes, tone of voice and a few thousand well-chosen words. Cosmo watched her listen to their threats to quit and their lengthy descriptions of what was so offensive about the whole experience. Then, she said, "Oh, I don't think you mean all that."

The musicians were cooling off already. "Well, it was just ridiculous," the drummer said. "You can't expect us to work under these conditions."

"And I don't." Booker said. "It will be very different tomorrow night in Miami. Just get a good night's rest, fly private with us tomorrow, and we'll do it all up first-class for the next show. Rickey will be in a much better mood, I promise you. He was just very nervous tonight. His first show in five years, what can we expect?"

"A frickin' grownup," the piano player supplied.

But it seemed their hearts weren't into revolt any more this evening and they headed off toward the dressing rooms. Cosmo just looked at Booker. They both exhaled.

***

Miami

Miami was as quirky and as dynamic as Cosmo remembered it. The resort was packed with a very large contingent of Rickets, plus vegans, artisans from hippie communities and grandparents. He would bet there were cribs in almost every room, judging by the number of high chairs in the restaurants. Grandparents were bringing kids and their babies to a Rickey T concert, then driving them up to the theme parks. Why not just the theme parks? Because older people wanted to go to concerts still. Gray hair, knees blown out, but they still wanted to see a concert. He figured he wouldn't be surprised next if the concerts were taking place at eleven in the morning!

All day, they'd listened to the lawn mowers and leaf blowers for so many hours that Duncan actually lost his mind. Cosmo could relate—the smell of gasoline, the noise like a dozen chain saws—anybody who was oriented toward audio and sounds in their dealings with the world would have to be seriously tested on a day like that. Duncan had said he was going to get a nap after the plane touched down and before showtime, but Cosmo doubted very much that anybody would have fallen asleep under these conditions.

He came roaring out of his room, and clearly, he'd lost it. He was screeching about the noise and his headache, and Bonaire said afterward that she wondered whether she should push him into the pool. Booker saved the day by throwing a blanket over his shoulders and guiding him back toward his room. Cosmo thought of James Brown.

A crescent moon decorated the dark sky above the stage on this warm evening, at the end of a hot day. The opening acts were a comedian (who gave an absolutely clean, profanity-free performance—where on earth did they find him?)—and a duo who did a vaguely urban-country set.

Cosmo listened to the buzz of conversation among the fans sitting nearby. A few seemed to think they were there to see a tribute band. A guy with an Australian accent (and a tone pretentious as hell) explained that the way you could tell was checking out whether there was wordplay in the name. Over the years, he'd seen Bjorn Again (a band doing ABBA music), Pink Fraud, the Pretend Pretenders, Mandonna, and Neil Zirconia. The consensus in the crowd was that this was no tribute band.

After the country singers Mandy and Donny Joe finished their three songs, the rent-a-player members of Rickey T's Florida band jogged onstage and launched into "Leaving Lorraine". No sign of Duncan, but it didn't matter. Everyone in the crowd knew the lyrics and they sang along with the band.

That was cool, that they'd do that for the first number but Cosmo knew it would be too much to expect that they could play it over and over for the rest of the show. At some point, the audience would expect Rickey T. Still no sign of him, and it was beginning to look as though the MC would have to make an announcement and risk the wrath of the crowd. What would they do? Throw their cups of tea and their canes at the stage?

The band struck up the opening chords on a tune from the nineties, "Dance Floor Dolly", and one spotlight came up, shoving Duncan into the audience's windshield like oncoming high beams on a monster truck. But wait … it was not Duncan actually, just the place where he was supposed to be. Cosmo felt his heart sink into his stomach, leaving it slightly sick, but after a few seconds of confusion Duncan came out onstage, waving his arms and shouting something. The audience cheered and clapped, but their rock idol wasn't paying them any mind. He grabbed the neck of the red guitar on the nearest stand, pulling it toward himself and then throwing it at the edge of the stage.

"Bloody tune the right one this time!"

Cosmo watched while a small man half-jogged, half-scrambled out from the wings, trying to be inconspicuous but finding it pretty damn hard since Duncan had turned the attention of the entire audience at him. He handed Duncan a teal blue guitar, the one he usually used later on in the show.

Everything was all screwed up.

Duncan looked at the instrument in his hand. "Not this one, you moron!"

Crap, could the audience hear and see all this?

Bonaire, Tamara and Lulu continued to step from side to side, gently dancing to the beat the rest of the band had set up while they waited for their cue. Man, did Duncan look old at this moment. Yeah, still cool, still lean, still charismatic, but up close every wrinkle, every patch of thinning hair, and every effort he made to hold himself upright while his shoulders fought to go the other way were showing.

Cosmo knew that Duncan was concerned about his age and his health, and over the years he'd seen the singer launch into about a dozen new diets, exercise regimes and unusual treatments. He'd also seen Duncan let things go from time to time. He did like his booze; there was one phase when the singer was downing four blueberry teas or margaritas before a concert began.

For tonight's show, Cosmo guessed that Duncan had

had at least one or two. Otherwise, how could anybody explain or justify his behavior?

His voice wasn't holding up, either. Cosmo heard him go off-key at least three times before he stopped counting, and on a few of the higher notes Duncan was definitely straining. Cosmo looked around at the customers he could see from his seat. Most seemed to be having a good time, enjoying their traveler mugs full of who knew what. A few were making faces of disapproval or even pain, but nobody seemed to be on the verge of walking out.

Then, Duncan called for an intermission. Cosmo was stunned—they never do that! It was once explained to him that the danger was that these old rockers would start into taking a nap or would sit down, let the joints stiffen up, and never come back after the break. Made sense.

But Duncan was on his way offstage.

***

Cosmo passed the twenty-minute break looking around at the audience and wondering what the hell was going on. People came back to their seats, complaining that very few of the food and beverage windows were open——probably because the venue management had no idea that people would be out of their seats for an intermission!

When Duncan came back, it was clear that the pause had done him some good. His voice was on key, his movements were smooth, and he seemed to be enjoying himself. The energy level was way up.

Cosmo squinted at the stage, then stared at the video screens for about ten minutes. That wasn't Duncan Donovan, it was the real Rickey! Small, subtle things, but Cosmo could tell it was really him. The posture, the exact placement of the wide-legged rock star stance, the movement of his head when he finished a song. God damn, that was Rickey T!

Nobody else seemed to have noticed anything—

nobody in the stands and nobody onstage. Cosmo watched Bonaire, Lulu and Tamara closely; if there were any disturbance coming, anybody ready to raise an alarm about this, it would start there. But they just kept on singing as usual. Everyone on stage looked more relaxed than they had been at any point in the past few days though. There were even a few smiles traded among the musicians when someone completed a particularly good lick.

Cosmo was just stunned. Where had Rickey come from? Had he been planning this all along? Did Booker know?

His phone buzzed with a text just as the second encore was finishing. *Meet us at Raise the Bar, half an hour.*

Cosmo muscled his way out of the row and toward the stairs, trying all the while to look up an address on the phone for this place. He bumped right into Sturgess Mesley before he saw him.

"Cosmo Lewis! Well, how about that! Small world!" Sturgess had himself planted squarely in front of Cosmo and there was no way past him.

"Sturgess! Nice to see you! Where you staying?"

"What? Oh, at the Doubletree, why?"

"I'll give you a call over there. Right now, I'm in a rush!" Cosmo said as he tried to smoothly side-step him.

"That's great! Meantime, let's walk together," and Sturgess inserted them both into the downward human traffic flow He was right behind Cosmo, the stairway was only two and a half feet across, and there was no escape.

"So, what do you hear from R and B?" he asked as they shuffled down the steps. Dear God, was he going to try to carry on a private conversation under these conditions? "Uhhh . . ."

"Because I came across a very interesting article recently that I think they should know about."

He was. "That's great! I'll let them know," Cosmo said, over his shoulder. "And what's new with you? How are things at Staten Island Records? Got any exciting projects underway?"

Sturgess seemed to have picked up a bit of the sarcasm and reticence in Cosmo's tone and he let the subject be switched. "I do have a very promising side hustle on the go right now. I am copyrighting the alphabet!"

It was so weird that Cosmo wouldn't have been surprised to see the long, gray-haired, pony-tailed biker walking in front of him turn around. But he didn't, and Sturgess went on.

"Now, not the whole alphabet, just the first seven letters. We're opening a club with those letters as its name, and when we trademark the brand, I'll do a copyright on the letters, too. I think there's a lot of spinoff potential here and I'm talking to Shad about the label opening a nightclub division."

Cosmo couldn't help himself—he was still trying to get his head around this idea. "What, so you think you'll own a copyright on A, B, C, D, E, F, G . . . . and then what? Nobody will be able to sing that part of the song without paying you a royalty?!"

"Sounds brilliant," said the vintage biker in front of Cosmo. He was about to say *Who asked you?* when he remembered that he was fifty, not twenty, and even though he could probably take him, he was too mature to resolve conflicts with strangers that way.

"You see?" Sturgess appreciated the vote, even from a stranger. "But that's not what we were talking about, Cosmo. I have to tell you about this article in *Big Pink Monthly*. The writer, Dwight Kettle—I know him, by the way—did a retrospective on Rickey T's career—it was the fortieth anniversary of something. Wrote that he was quoting a "confidential source" and made the comment that Rickey has "taken a lot of time off" over the years."

Crap, why did Cosmo have to glance over his shoulder just in time to see Sturgess making that "air quotes" motion? He hated that.

"No more than any other rock star." Biker Buddy was

in the conversation now.

"That's what I thought, too!" Sturgess said. "But this guy commented that the source seemed to have much more to say that he was holding back."

Cosmo couldn't restrain himself. "Wouldn't you think that would be the case with pretty much any confidential source?"

"Rickey's been traveling the world," our new friend tossed over his shoulder.

"And he might be writing new material," Sturgess said to him, over Cosmo's head.

"Do you know that for a fact?" Biker Buddy asked.

"Well, I *have* known him for a lot of years," Sturgess said.

"You know him? You're friends?" Biker Buddy seemed very excited by this. He poked the blonde woman in the tie-dyed dress in front of him. "Hey, this guy is a friend of Rickey T's!"

"No kidding!" The woman nudged the woman in front of her, and the news traveled all the way down the stairway. "And he says Rickey T is ready to bring out an album of new material!"

Cosmo's head hurt. He didn't say another word until they made it to the concourse level and then he split as fast as he could, leaving Sturgess surrounded by his new friends, telling them everything he knew about Rickey T and about his ownership position on the alphabet.

***

The Raise the Bar needed some. It was a dive about forty miles from the arena, which made Booker's "half an hour" instruction impossible to live up to. Cosmo walked in and saw them both huddled on the same side of a booth at the absolute back. Rickey was wearing a dark-haired wig, glasses, a beard, a moustache and a ball cap. He must be really freaked out.

Booker looked up as Cosmo slid in, across from them. "Hey, Cosmo. Glad you're here."

"Why?" Rickey demanded. "You don't think I can solve this?"

"Calm down. We need a third perspective, especially if we end up in a stalemate over what to do."

"You seem to think this is some kind of democracy," Rickey said, as he gave his beer ninety-nine percent of his attention.

Cosmo wanted to be anywhere else but here. Why had she summoned him?

"I think we have millions at stake and we have to work together," Booker said, taking a deep dive into her own beer.

"What's going on?" Cosmo asked.

"Well, Rickey took over the show after intermission," Booker said.

"Yeah, I got that," he said, waving my hand toward the bartender, who nodded back at him, thank God.

"You did? Do you think anybody else noticed?" Booker asked.

"No, I think it was only me," Cosmo said. "You're one of a kind, Rickey, but Duncan did do a very good imitation."

Cosmo could tell that Rickey appreciated the comment, but Booker was focused on dealing with the fallout she was sure was coming.

"Duncan might be a terrific impersonator, but he's a horrible human being!"

"Where is he now?"

"We locked him in his dressing room."

"Really? Literally?"

"Yeah." Booker couldn't help but crack a smile. "We told him we'd be back to get him in an hour."

"Was he ticked off?"

"He was so loaded that I have my doubts he'll even remember he didn't do a full show. But I plan to be there, in his face, as soon as he wakes up and I'll make sure he has nothing to say about it."

"You expect him to keep quiet through all the rest of the tour?"

"We were just talking about that," Booker said. "I think Rickey's landed on the answer."

"Meaning . . . " Cosmo looked back and forth between them and the light dawned on him. "Rickey is going to go back on the road? For the full tour?"

"Yes!"

"No!"

They spoke at the same time and Cosmo wasn't surprised at who said what.

"It's the best solution," Booker insisted.

Rickey didn't look so sure. They all took a break while the server brought Cosmo's beer, then Rickey took over. "I won't do it, Book. We've been over it and there's nothing left to say. I don't do this full-time, I haven't for decades and I won't start now."

"We've got contracts in eighteen more cities."

"Who set those up?"

"On your behalf! Rick, we have to do those shows! *You* have to do those shows!"

"No, I don't," Rickey said. "Hire another stand-in."

Booker sighed and slumped; Cosmo thought she suddenly looked like a much older woman.

"I can't go through that again, Rick," Booker said.

Rickey stared into her eyes and seemed to be really hearing what she was saying. He looked quite defeated himself and Cosmo had a sudden flash of two exhausted boxers circling one another in the tenth round, sweat pouring from their shoulders and blood from the cuts over their eyes, groping toward one another and then just hanging on. Was it up to him to be the referee?

"I know, Book, I'm sorry," Rickey said quietly. "I know it's been very hard on you. But what am I going to do if you quit on me now?"

They broke the eye contact and each seemed to retreat

into their own thoughts. Cosmo had a very strong feeling that neither one would be able to return to the ring.

***

Rickey stopped answering Booker's texts after that. He was just gone, and she didn't know where. In the past, they'd had stretches of a week or two when they weren't in touch, but she could always count on him replying, even with just a word or two. But this time, nothing. She texted him daily for a month, tried phoning Cosmo, then Henry, and finally, overcoming much ambivalence, she phoned Shad at the label. He had no idea where Rickey had gone, he said, but he was confident that Rickey would return in time to fulfill his contractual obligations. Wasn't she? One day, as she sat in her office facing a mountain of mail and phone messages, a text came in from Rickey.

> *Hey Book.*
> *Where are you??*
> *New Zealand.*

New Zealand! The other side of the world.

> *What for?*
> *On my boat.*
> *You just dumped me, Rick. What did I do wrong?*
> *It had nothing to do with you or anything you did. It was*

only about me. And . . . I met someone here.

> *When are you coming back?*

He didn't answer.

The weeks went by, then the months, and she didn't get a response from Rickey. She tried twice more—she even called Henry in Palm Springs to ask for help.

And then, she began to let go. He was not her responsibility any more, dammit—he was a grown man and she didn't want him at the center of her world now. "Rickey T, rock star", this project they'd both worked on, their baby, was done.

Booker would have to cancel the rest of the tour and they would take a huge financial hit, but so what? So, he could only sail as far as Hawaii next time? She didn't care. Her seat in the Rickey T emotional roller coaster was empty now, and available for somebody else. She was done.

Maybe Rickey could hire a double for her! Ha. Whatever he decided to do, she didn't care.

Her hurt lasted about a year and then, gradually, even that started to fade away. It was completely erased when a monumental check from Rickey arrived, enough to cover the losses from the farewell tour concerts that were cancelled and enough to get Staten Island Records and their law suit out of her hair. Where did he get so much money? She had to admit to some curiosity—but not enough to seek him out and ask him.

CHAPTER TWENTY-SIX

2019

Santa Capella

Four years later

The audience had inhaled and the room was as still as a racetrack on Derby Day in the seconds before they open the gate.

"Booker? Wherever you are? Would please come up here?" Rickey said.

Cosmo watched Booker weave her way through the tables at the awards dinner, heading for the stage. Most of the eyes in the room were on her and there really wasn't any need for anyone to say anything while they waited for her, but for some reason, Duncan thought there was.

At least, Cosmo thought it was Duncan. The guy was dressed like a hipster, looked about fifty plus and had a silver, goatee beard.

"You may be wondering what we're doing here. No, it's not a tribute band and it's not a practical joke on Rickey." He passed the microphone over to the Rickey at the far left.

"Jake? You're on."

This one was wearing an eighties-style suit. He stepped forward and struck the first chords of another one of Rickey's ballads, "Please Don't Go Tonight". It was such a familiar, infectious riff that within a dozen syllables most of the audience was singing along, their voices drowning out the tune he was playing on his acoustic guitar. By the time they got to the chorus almost everyone was in full voice and quite a few people had jumped to their feet to wave their arms in the air while they swayed back and forth. Oh, there was no limit to the emotions that a fifth of bourbon and a great rock & roll song can bring out!

Cosmo was one of the jumpers. How could he resist? Every time he heard that song it took him right back to ninth grade. A song can do that, bring back a memory as if it just happened. Barbara June let him slow-dance with her at Butler's party and this was the song. It was almost as good as "Hey Jude", which was excellent because it went on so long. This one had Rickey T's outstanding voice and lyrics that just seemed to make the little girls melt.

Jake took them to the end of the second chorus, then stopped the song and handed the guitar to the man to his left. "Thanks, Jake," the next singer said as he strapped on the instrument over his plaid-clad shoulder. "That's Jake Meisenstern, everybody. And no, he's not Rickey T. Am I? Am I Rickey T? Or is that Rickey T?" he asked, pointing to the man who had started the show, and who now stood off to the left of the stage, just watching it play out. "I'm Oliver Dash, ladies and gentlemen. Here's one that I think we all know by heart . . . "

Oliver signaled the drummer and mouthed the words "Cut and Run". The musician laid into the opening beats and the crowd roared while Oliver sang the first verse, then passed the microphone to the next singer, the one wearing Rickey T's seventies jeans and long hair. That was Flinch, Cosmo guessed. Flinch sang the second verse, note for note the way Rickey would do it and then, Duncan Donovan led the chorus. Everybody sang along.

Suddenly, the curtains behind the singers parted, and the audience could see a gospel choir, dressed in purple robes with gold-braid trim and singing as if they could be heard all the way to the River Jordan. A short, tubby man wearing a casual Hawaiian shirt and jeans walked out in front of them.

"Whose music are we doing?" he hollered into the cordless microphone he was carrying.

"Rickey's! Rickey T's!" all forty voices responded.

"How many albums did he make?" the man shouted.

"As many as he wanted to," the choir sang back.

"How many songs did he write?"

"Every one that was in his heart!"

As the call-and-response went on, Cosmo began to notice something very familiar about the choir leader. His posture, his hair, his glasses—it was Dwight Kettle, the *Coast to Coast* reporter.

"What year did he get his start?" Dwight roared at the choir.

"In 1974!"

"What anniversary is he celebrating?"

A 6-foot 5-inch man with a head of hair like a lion's stepped forward and began to sing, "It's the forty-fifth year since his first time on stage."

"He is celebrating forty-five years as a rock & roll legend!" Dwight yelled, then turned to the audience, raising his arms and hyping the crowd into cheering and applauding. "He is a Big Name and a Big Deal!"

"He started forty-five years ago but he started and he stopped," the big man sang back.

"Started and stopped?" Dwight shouted.

"Started and stopped?" The choir had its follow-up question.

"He shared his name, his writing and his work with all of us, and he shared his name, his writing and his work with these men." The big man turned toward Jake.

"Jake Meisenstern!" He sang the name and motioned with an authoritative manner; Jake stepped forward and the crowd applauded.

The choir soloist introduced each of the Pretend Rickeys and each came forward for his applause. Cosmo couldn't figure out whether this had been rehearsed or was as much of a surprise to all of them as it was to the audience.

"Is this a tribute band?" Dwight called to the choir.

"No, these are singers who played the part of Rickey T over the years," the choir sang back.

Cosmo realized that Rickey was turning himself in.

"Why are you revealing this now?" Dwight asked.

"Because I was being blackmailed and it was time to tell it all," the choir sang.

Dwight let two or three minutes of humming and 'hey yeah's' go by before he got to his next question. "Who was blackmailing you?"

The lead singer walked forward from his spot on the riser to the lip of the stage. He lifted a hand and pointed, "Her," he sang.

Cosmo stood up, along with everyone else in the audience, to look in the direction the lead singer signaled.

It was Adrian, the tattoo artist Cosmo had met at the Cannes concert party so long ago. Thirty-five years ago. The short skirt and giant bag of inks were gone but the tiny build and the dark hair were still there. She was sitting on a high stool at the left of the stage, just past Rickey. He smiled at her, she smiled back and then turned toward the audience, taking a bit of a bow. Obviously, all had been forgiven.

"But why did you let anyone else pretend to be you?" Dwight wanted to know.

"The life was killing me," the choir sang. "The stage fright, the loneliness, the travel, the pressure, the fame—they were killing me. I had to take breaks, I had to build walls, and soon, I had to stay away."

"Did anyone else know?" Dwight had picked up the rhythm of the show and the crowd; he delivered the first word, waited ten seconds and then finished the question.

The choir continued to hum a background sound while they turned to Booker. She was frozen at stage right and then she seemed to give herself a shake and start to laugh. She walked up the stairs, across the stage, and stopped to give Dwight a hug. Then she turned to the audience and took a deep bow.

"She is his manager, she is his friend," the choir sang.

"But who's idea was it?" Dwight wanted to know.

"Rickey's, all Rickey's," the choir responded.

Cosmo looked around the audience to try to gauge the reaction. They didn't seem too upset, and quite a few were laughing.

"Quite a show," Dwight commented, then he put his microphone on top of a speaker and walked off the stage.

"We got our money's worth," the well-drilled choir sang back, three or four times.

Cosmo knew it would be a while before they knew whether Rickey's effort to guide the reactions to his revelation was a success. He braced himself for a migration toward the exits, but it never came. No avalanche of "we want our money back—for this concert, for ALL concerts. What about our records? Is that Rickey T on there or somebody else?"

But it never came. The audience stayed put, probably thinking that there had been so many surprises this evening, they didn't want to head for the door in case they'd miss something.

The choir returned to the better-known lyrics of "Cut and Run" and finished their very soulful version. They stepped down from the risers, single file and then followed one another off the stage. Jake, Oliver, Flinch and Duncan took a few more bows, then left the stage to Rickey. He stepped up to the microphone.

"Thank you and good-bye," he said, before taking Booker's arm and escorting her off-stage.

Cosmo pushed his way out to the lobby, trying to rush

the people in front of him. He was eager to be backstage and get his own closure on what seemed to be the end of this relationship.

As he wiggled through the crowd near the coatroom he bumped into Ethan, Bella and Anne. Their expressions were unreadable, and he flirted with the idea of pretending not to see them. If they were angry about the deception, he really didn't want to hear it right now.

Just as he was about to stop to chat with them, Shad loomed up in his way, Sturgess and Mona Ray hovering behind him.

"Cosmo! What the hell?"

"Yeah, I know, right? Blows my mind," he said.

"Did you know about it?" Sturgess demanded.

"Didn't you?" Cosmo replied. "I sort of figured you did, being so close to Rickey and all."

"I did not!" Sturgess seemed indignant but Cosmo couldn't tell whether it was because he hadn't been in on the secret or because he thought the fraud itself was worth shouting about. "Some of the stuff going on with Rickey bugged me but I had no idea he was pulling a fast one on all of us!"

Ethan stepped forward. "I don't know, man, I don't think of it as a 'fast one'."

"You don't think he conned us?"

"The whole music business is a con, what's the big deal? I really don't care."

Cosmo saw his opportunity. "What about you, Bella? Do you agree?"

"I wasn't really surprised," Bella was just inches away from a yawn. "I mean, what the hell? It's a rock star, they all wear makeup, they all put on a performance, what's the difference? I really don't care."

In silence, Cosmo and Sturgess turned to Anne. "He didn't fool me," she said. "I had a feeling he came and went."

Cosmo grinned at the three other fans and they all

started to laugh. Sturgess didn't join in; he didn't know what they were laughing about.

Cosmo caught up with Booker and Rickey in the lobby just before they made their escape to their rooms. A tall, black-haired, expensively dressed woman stood beside him, holding his hand, and Cosmo caught sight of a wedding band and a massive diamond. Was this the 'someone he met'? The mystery woman from New Zealand that Rickey had hinted about? Maybe she was the source of the money that had bailed them all out?

"Cosmo! What's the fan reaction?" Rickey asked, as they all walked into the glass elevator.

"Nobody cares and nobody feels ripped off," Cosmo said. "What a show."

Rickey leaned back against the wall. He looked pretty pleased with himself.

"When did you decided to do all this?" Cosmo asked.

"Not long ago."

"Did Booker know?"

"Did she look like she knew?"

They both looked at Booker and she laughed.

Not all questions get an answer.

EPILOGUE

One year later

Rickey T: Last seen at the northern edge of the Bermuda Triangle.

Booker: Managing a new act—rappers from Vermont.

Cosmo: Living on a beach in the Caribbean, paying his bills by selling Rickey T memorabilia on eBay.

Shad Palmetto: Job-hunting after being fired by Staten Island Records for not catching Rickey in the act.

Sturgess: Raking in the big bucks in Rome with a trademark the Roman numerals.

Mona Ray: Running a seniors' dating website called "Monique's Antiques".

Fake Jake: Music director at the YWCA.

Oliver Dash: Wannabe busker in San Diego, applying for a new permit every year.

Flinch Warren: Holding his breath to see if his biography will be knocked off the National Book Prize List for plagiarism.

Duncan Donovan: Working off a six-figure debt by hauling equipment as a roadie with a Czechoslovakian heavy-metal band.

ABOUT THE AUTHOR

Gail Hulnick is from Canada and currently lives in Florida. In addition to the novels, she writes short stories and travel books.

If you enjoyed *Resorting to Fraud*, please keep in touch!

You can join our email group at www.gailhulnick.com

Find out more about our other books at www.windwordgroup.com

www.ingramcontent.com/pod-product-compliance
Lightning Source LLC
Chambersburg PA
CBHW010345170726
48284CB00009B/2791